KNIGHT
OF THE
SILVER CIRCLE

BOOKS BY DUNCAN M. HAMILTON

The First Blade of Ostia

THE WOLF OF THE NORTH
The Wolf of the North
Jorundyr's Path
The Blood Debt

SOCIETY OF THE SWORD
The Tattered Banner
The Huntsman's Amulet
The Telastrian Song

THE DRAGONSLAYER
Dragonslayer
Knight of the Silver Circle

KNIGHT
OF THE
SILVER CIRCLE

WITHDRAWN

DUNCAN M. HAMILTON

TOR

A TOM DOHERTY ASSOCIATES BOOK
NEW YORK

KNIGHT OF THE SILVER CIRCLE

Copyright © 2019 by Duncan M. Hamilton

A Tor Book
Published by Tom Doherty Associates
120 Broadway
New York, NY 10271

www.tor-forge.com

Tor® is a registered trademark of Macmillan Publishing Group, LLC.

The Library of Congress Cataloging-in-Publication Data is available upon request.

ISBN 978-1-250-30682-1 (trade paperback)
ISBN 978-1-250-30681-4 (hardcover)
ISBN 978-1-250-30680-7 (ebook)

Our books may be purchased in bulk for promotional, educational, or business use. Please contact your local bookseller or the Macmillan Corporate and Premium Sales Department at 1-800-221-7945, extension 5442, or by email at MacmillanSpecialMarkets@macmillan.com.

First Edition: November 2019

Printed in the United States of America

0 9 8 7 6 5 4 3 2 1

HUMBERLAND

SZAVARIA

Oudin

R. Vosge

MIRABAYA

Trel

Bastelle

Villerauv

Montpa

DARVARO

RA
2018

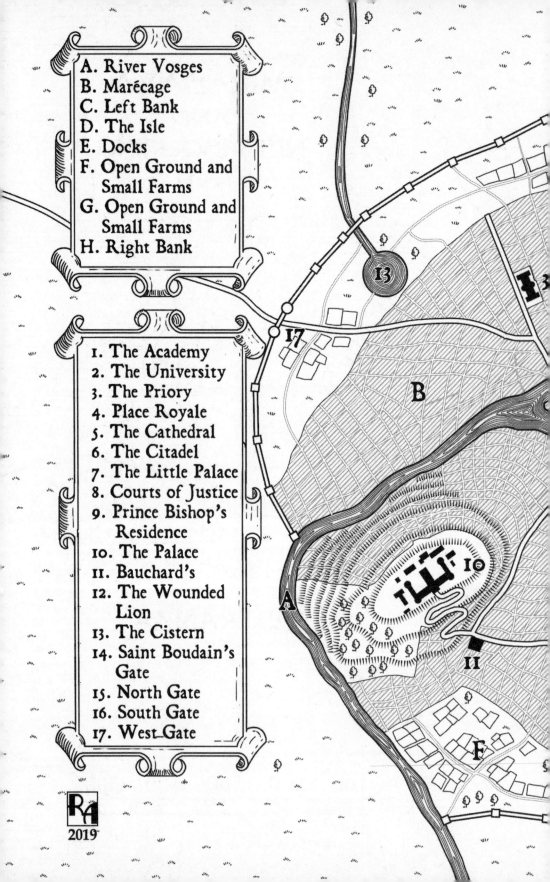

A. River Vosges
B. Marécage
C. Left Bank
D. The Isle
E. Docks
F. Open Ground and
    Small Farms
G. Open Ground and
    Small Farms
H. Right Bank

1. The Academy
2. The University
3. The Priory
4. Place Royale
5. The Cathedral
6. The Citadel
7. The Little Palace
8. Courts of Justice
9. Prince Bishop's
    Residence
10. The Palace
11. Bauchard's
12. The Wounded
    Lion
13. The Cistern
14. Saint Boudain's
    Gate
15. North Gate
16. South Gate
17. West Gate

RA
2019

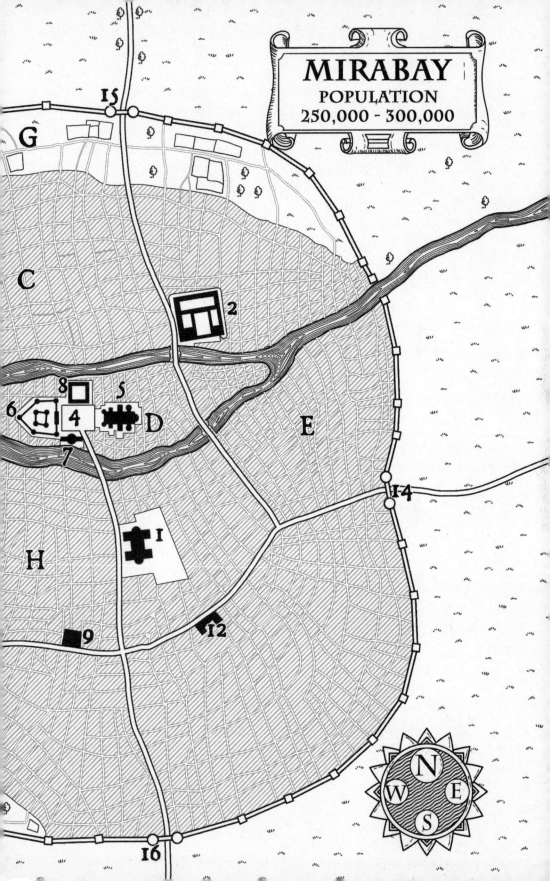

PART ONE

CHAPTER

1

Bernard pushed the wooden pin into place, securing the gate, and counted his herd again. He always counted twice, and had done ever since the hiding his father had given him when he was eleven, for coming home one short. After the beating, he had spent the whole night scouring the foothills looking for it, not returning home until dawn, when he had to break the news to his father that the wolves had gotten it. It had been a hard lesson, and not one he had forgotten. To leave one of the cattle out in the pastures at night was to condemn it to the wolves. Usually you could hear them start howling as soon as the sun went down, but they were silent tonight. Bernard didn't know whether to be glad or to worry more. Wolves were wily beasts. At least when they were howling, he knew where they were.

Satisfied that every cow was accounted for, he gave the pin one last check and one final tug on the gate before heading for the farmhouse. He always worried his way through the summer. There was no getting around taking the cattle up to the high pastures every day if he wanted them at their best come market time in autumn. It was why he loved the winter—his herd were tucked up in the barn, safe from wolves, bears, and belek. He had never had much trouble from the latter two—perhaps the idiot noblemen of the county had hunted them to extinction—but the wolves were an ever-present threat.

There wasn't much waiting for him at home—just a pot of broth heating on the fire, stale bread, and cheese. He had some wine, but he had to make that last until he went into town at the end of the month. Like as not, he wouldn't see another soul until then. It was a lonely existence, and as he was rapidly approaching thirty, long past time he started trying to find himself a wife. He had no desire to end up like one of the crazy old herdsmen in the mountains, driven mad by the hardship and solitude.

He thought of Martina, who worked at the post office in Venne. She had danced with him at the spring fair, and he wondered if it was worth asking her to step out with him. He didn't have much to offer her, although his house wasn't bad—well built by his father and well cared for by his mother. He'd done his best to maintain the place since they'd both passed, and he didn't think he'd done a bad job. It was pretty up the valley, and he thought Martina might like it here. *Only one way to find out,* he thought. He wondered if he should make his monthly trip to Venne a little earlier than usual. Tomorrow perhaps? He scratched the thick brown stubble on his chin, and realised he'd need to tidy himself up a bit before he went. A lot, if he had any hope of Martina stepping out with him.

Inside, Bernard took off his cloak, sat on his chair by the fire, and reached for the pot of broth. It had been a long day, and he was hungry. There was too much to be done around the farm for one person—a wife and family would certainly help with that. And with the loneliness.

Bernard woke with a start, and the half-eaten bowl of broth on his lap clattered to the floor, splattering its contents as it fell. He had no idea how long he had been asleep. There was no light coming through the cracks in his window shutters, so it could not have been overlong. The time would better have been spent in bed, however. He kneaded his stiff neck as he surveyed the mess made by the broth, and debated with himself over whether he should clean it now, or wait until the morning. Sleeping in the chair never did much to rejuvenate him, and he couldn't think of anything he wanted more than his bed at that moment. However, dry broth would be harder to clean. It was only then he wondered at what had woken him.

He stood and stretched his back. As the confusion of sleep cleared from his head, he realised there was noise coming from outside—from the cattle pen. Wolves. He knew it. When his gut told him something was amiss, he was always right. Bernard went to the trunk by the door and opened it, pushing aside the various things that had accumulated atop the object he sought—his father's old crossbow.

It had been a long time since the bow had been out of the trunk, but everything seemed in working order to Bernard's inexpert eye. He wound the string and pulled the trigger to test it. Satisfied that it was firing properly, he grabbed a lantern and a handful of bolts from the quiver in the trunk, and set off to shoot some wolves.

As soon as he stepped outside, the magnitude of his task made itself known. It was a moonless night and he could barely see his nose in front of his face. How could he hope to shoot something he couldn't see? He swore, stuffed the quarrels into his pocket, slung the bow over his shoulder, and worked his flint to light the lantern's wick. Once its warm orange light began to grow, he lowered its glass cover and picked up the pitchfork he had left leaning against the wall by the door. It might come in handy if a wolf attacked him.

The commotion from the cattle pen was far louder now—the rough stone walls of his house did a very good job of keeping the noise out. It sounded as though the herd had clustered at the far end of the pen, but there was noise at the near end also—the sound of beasts feeding.

Bernard had raised each and every cow in the pen from the moment its mother had birthed it, often with his help. That one of them had been savagely killed and was being devoured enraged him. He let out an angry shout, knowing it was unlikely to scare off the wolves but needing to give voice to his frustration.

"Go on! Clear off, you filthy bastards!" He shook his pitchfork in as threatening a fashion as he could muster.

Though he neared the pen, he could still see nothing; the lantern's light did not reach far into the gloom. But he could hear: the tearing of sinew, the cracking of bones, the grinding of teeth. Why hadn't the beasts reacted to his challenge? He had expected a growl at least, if not more. Then it occurred to him that the feeding didn't sound like wolves. It sounded like something larger. A bear? A wave of panic swept through him. A belek?

Bringing his pitchfork to guard, Bernard backed away a pace. If it was a belek, it was welcome to the cow. That didn't make sense, though. Belek loved the cold, and it was summer. Even in the winter, it was rare that one of the enormous, cat-like creatures would come down into the valleys—only in the very coldest of years. Belek were said to love the hunt, too, and slaughtering captive livestock wouldn't be of much interest to them. They were vicious beasts, as big as a bear, and he had heard it said one night in the tavern in Venne that they had the intelligence of a man. Now Bernard half smiled at the memory of the joke he had told, that beleks couldn't be all that smart, going by most of the men he knew, but the memory couldn't extinguish the fear the thought of the beast instilled in him.

The air was filled with the hideous, sickening noise of a carcass being torn apart—a sound that every living thing would instinctively flee from. Why was he fool enough to challenge it, to draw whatever lurked out there in the dark to him?

If he didn't, who would look after his cows? Everything he knew spoke against it being a belek. If it was a bear, his best chance was to frighten it off.

"Go on!" he shouted. "Off with you!" He let out a roar, a brave challenge that went against everything he felt. Perhaps the lantern's light would keep whatever it was away? He wanted to run back to the house, shut the door behind him, bar it, and hide there until daybreak.

"Off with you!" he shouted again. He shook his pitchfork once more.

The sound of feeding stopped. If anything, the silence was more terrifying than the noise. A small tendril of flame appeared in the darkness, casting a pool of light. Two great yellow orbs became visible, staring at him, their oval irises as black as the night. The ovals narrowed until they were barely more than slits. Slits that were locked on him. Bernard dropped his lantern, which spluttered out, leaving him in darkness. He clutched the pitchfork with both hands as though his life depended on it.

The beast's eyes sat above and to the sides of a long snout containing the most wicked-looking set of teeth he had ever seen. The flame, almost hypnotising as it danced, cast a buttery sheen on the edges of the scales that covered all that he could see of the beast.

He knew what it was. He had heard rumours of one having

appeared several villages over, but like everything that was said to have happened several villages over, he thought the stories were most likely to be untrue. He knew what it was, but he could not bring himself to say the name, even in the quiet of his own head. He felt warmth run down the inside of his legs, but ignored it. His eyes were fixed on those yellow orbs that seemed to study him so intently. He knew what it was. Something from legend, from a time when the tales of men merged with fantasy.

Dragon.

The flame disappeared and the night was plunged into darkness once more. He heard nothing. Had he frightened it off? He thought of Martina, probably tucked up in bed only a few miles away. If he looked to his right, he could probably see the village's lights, but he couldn't tear his gaze away from the inky black where the dragon had been moments before.

A thought came to him—if he couldn't see it, perhaps it couldn't see him. He took a step back, as quietly as he could, tensing every muscle to react if he stood on a twig or anything else that would reveal his location.

The flame at the end of the beast's snout returned, larger now, casting a greater pool of light. The sight of two more creatures behind the first one filled Bernard with a sense of utter despair. They had killed a cow each—despite the danger he was in, he could only think of how he recognised the markings on one, and could remember the day he pulled her out of her mother by the hooves during a difficult birth.

The other beasts ignored him, but the first, the one with the gentle stream of flame coming from its nostrils, kept its eyes locked on him. Bernard thought of shouting again, of shaking his pitchfork at them, but something told him it would make no difference. Something told him nothing would make any difference. Tears streamed down his face; he wished that he'd asked Martina to step out with him at the spring dance. When the jet of flame hit him, he wondered who was going to look after his cows. He felt growing heat for a moment, then nothing.

Covered in gore, sore in every place that had feeling, Guillot hadn't felt much like conversation on the way back to Trelain. Solène seemed equally exhausted, so their moods complemented each other as they both spent the last of their energy to get back to a hot meal and a warm bed. Guillot's horse trundled along at a pace barely faster than a man would walk, towing behind it a makeshift litter bearing a large burden covered with a blood-soaked blanket.

Guillot well remembered the stories of how valuable dragon ephemera had been in the old days. The scales had a variety of uses, from armour—extremely expensive armour—to potions and elixirs. The bones had less value, but the carcass would be a treat for the multitude of wild animals that lived in the valley.

If he'd been able to return with the entirety of the dragon's remains, he would have become a wealthy man. However, he had given in to the pain in every limb and the exhaustion that made him wish for sleep above all else. He primarily needed a trophy, something to show everyone that the beast was indeed dead, that they no longer had to live in fear. The head was the only option, so that was what his tired horse now obediently dragged behind her.

Even in death, the dragon's head—with its curved, needle-pointed horns, shiny scales, and wicked teeth—filled him with primordial fear. Being terrified of these creatures seemed like a sensible thing. The dragon had nearly killed him, despite his magical advantages.

He glanced at Solène, whose posture suggested she might be asleep, upright and on her horse. The last few days had been nearly impossibly difficult for them; it was no surprise that she was no longer able to fight off exhaustion. A few strands of her copper hair escaped the cover of her cloak's hood, but he could see nothing of her face. It struck him as ironic that he had saved her from an execution pyre and she had then been instrumental in keeping him alive. Perhaps the gods had not forsaken him after all.

Another glance back confirmed his cargo was still secure on a litter of roughly tied branches. He had killed a dragon—and he was the only person alive who could make such a claim. Everyone had said winning the Competition was a lifetime achievement that could not be topped, but this? It was beyond consideration. He still had difficulty believing what had happened. He had done what the heroes of his childhood had done. It filled him with a burgeoning sense of pride that made him uneasy.

He had lost everything he had valued because of pride and arrogance. He'd believed that he was strong enough, skilled enough, smart enough to do as he chose without even thinking about consequences. He had drunk and caroused with the idiots he had once called brothers and friends, and not spent his time where it truly mattered. What would he give for one more moment with Auroré? Yet he would give up even that if it meant she and their child might live. There was a bitter taste in his mouth and he sneered at how wonderful hindsight was, how easy it was to be foolish in your youth. Why did self-awareness come only when it was too late?

He wondered if slaying a dragon redeemed him. Did he deserve to be redeemed? Was he being too hard on himself? He had not done anything intentionally wrong or particularly bad, he had simply been young, stupid, and drunk too often. He had been following the example of his brother Chevaliers. All the wonderful things he had thought he was achieving were working toward his undoing. At least Guillot's father hadn't lived to see his fall. Wife, unborn child, career, position at court; a lifetime's work all gone in a matter of days. Then he'd squandered what little he had left, neglecting his estate and his people. Now they had been taken from him too.

All he had to show for it was the snarling, disembodied head tied to his litter. What a success he was.

When Trelain's walls loomed up from the horizon, Guillot felt a flutter of nerves stir in his gut. He had not given much thought to their return to the city beyond his desire for food and sleep. When they had left, Trelain had been on the verge of panic at the prospect of a dragon attack. Those who had the means to leave were packing up and going, and Guillot had seen more than one or two characters who looked as though they were waiting for the right moment to start looting. There might not even be anyone still there. Would that be better than a city full of people, and their reaction to the news that their homes and families weren't about to be burned and devoured by a dragon?

There was a time when Guillot had loved being the centre of attention. When you were as good with a sword as he had been, in a society where that skill could bring limitless advancement, you grew accustomed to fame at a young age—and quickly came to expect it. Now? The thought terrified him. He had spent the better part of half a decade wanting nothing more than to be left alone; to be forgotten. There was no chance of that happening now. He was the first person in nearly a thousand years to kill a dragon, to restore the countryside to safety. What chance did he have of being left alone now?

Even more worrying was the fact that part of him was excited by the prospect of adulation, as though some facet of his personality that had been pushed into a dark recess saw the opportunity to come forward. He didn't know if he wanted to allow it out again. No, he knew he didn't. His fingers tightened painfully on the reins.

Perhaps he should find a ditch and dump the head. Eventually someone would find the head or the body and proclaim the terror ended. Perhaps they would claim the kill as their own, letting Guillot off the hook entirely. Part of him was drawn to the notion, and part of him was horrified. He had been brought up with a sword in hand; it was his duty and purpose to do things like he had just done.

And yet . . . the fame and adulation that winning the Competition had brought him was false. He had revelled in it, but it was an illusion built on illusions. None of the accolades had any real meaning. This would be no different.

The wars he had fought in had been vehicles for rich and powerful men to protect or increase their wealth. Which side of a border they lived on made little difference to ordinary people. Watching their homes looted and burned did. Watching their fathers, sons, and husbands conscripted to fight battles that had nothing to do with them, never to return, did.

Killing the dragon was the first truly useful thing Guillot had done in his life, and he was frightened by the reaction it would create. All that was worthwhile was done, all that was to come was devoid of value. The trophy was needed to prove to people that they were safe. That was important. His discomfort was not, and he abandoned the idea of cutting the litter loose.

There was also Amaury—the Prince Bishop—to consider. Gill was less concerned about him. He fully expected that Amaury would try again to have him killed, but facing men with swords and bad intentions had never bothered Gill. For a time, he would be too great a hero for Amaury to touch, but Guillot knew better than most how quickly fame fades, and he was certain Amaury would be carefully watching for that moment. Assuming Guillot let him live that long. Amaury had already tried to have him killed, and there was still something in Gill that wouldn't let him forget that.

Amaury had racked up enough transgressions against him to be called out on the duelling field were Amaury an ordinary man. His position as Prince Bishop meant he was not an ordinary man, however, and killing him would be far more complicated. Guillot wondered if it was even worth the effort. He was tired, and worried, and he just wanted to go home. His heart grew heavy as he was reminded he didn't have a home anymore.

▲▲▲▲▲▲

There was a single, nervous-looking guard on duty at the Trelain city gate. Usually there would be three or four—even more in a time of danger. He barely acknowledged Guillot and Solène; his gaze roamed the horizon and the sky, searching for danger from above. That the guard was there at all was testament to his bravery, sense of duty, or perhaps stupidity.

The streets were all but deserted. Gill could see some signs of looting—broken windows, boards ripped away from where they had been nailed across doors. It was amazing how much the character of a town could change in only a few days. Even when they passed someone, that person would pay them little attention, and Guillot felt his hopes rise that he could get to the Black Drake, get fed, and perhaps even steal a few hours of sleep before having to deal with the fuss the news he brought would cause.

"Streets are quiet," Solène said, rousing from her doze or stupor at last.

"People were getting ready to leave when we rode out," Guillot said. "Looks like they made good on that. Can't say I blame them, all things considered."

"Good for us," Solène said. "There'll be less attention. Means we might get some rest." Her voice was heavy with fatigue.

Gill nodded, feeling much as she sounded, although there was something in her voice that wasn't entirely fatigue. The tone reminded him of something, but he couldn't be sure exactly what.

CHAPTER
3

Amaury, Prince Bishop of the United Church and First Minister of Mirabaya, looked out of his office window into the garden below. The king dallied there, in flagrante delicto with his latest flavour of the month, a young country noblewoman who still bore the innocence of a life spent far from court, an innocence that would wither and die after a few months in Mirabay. By then, King Boudain would have long finished with her. The king needed to marry soon, to create a political alliance that would increase his power, and provide him with an heir. It was time he set aside the frivolity of youth.

Amaury sighed. Not long ago, the king's affairs had amused him no end. Now, levity was something he was finding increasingly difficult to come by. He had just received word that the people he had sent to Trelain to finish off dal Villerauvais and retrieve the Amatus Cup—some of the best members of his Order of the Golden Spur—had been found dead on the side of the road. Details were sketchy, and it sounded as though there had been little left of them by the time the remains were found. They should have been difficult to kill, so Amaury wondered who might be responsible for their deaths. It was worrying on a number of levels, and something he'd have to get to the bottom of, but later. For now it was simply another problem on a long, ever-growing list.

He had sent for Commander Leverre, but the man was conspicuously missing. Amaury had even sent a pigeon to Trelain, to see if Nicholas dal Sason could shed any light on the matter. He was in the dark on many things, and that was not a circumstance he appreciated.

He wondered if Guillot was dead, but suspected he was not. Dal

Sason would have notified him if the job was done. If dal Sason had failed, it was likely he was dead. The Prince Bishop was beginning to feel quite careless in his application of manpower. In the past few weeks, the Order had suffered more casualties than in its previous entire existence. What was worse was that those killed had been the best available, meaning the talent he had so carefully gathered and nurtured was being diluted. If things continued like that, the Order would be wiped out before long, and with it, Amaury's hope for the future. He would need to bolster its ranks with mercenaries, and make new officer appointments. Another set of problems for his list.

Amaury returned his attention to the king's indiscreet behaviour in the garden below. Boudain was indolent, often idle, and were it not for his arrogance and stubbornness, the young king would have made an ideal figurehead, concealing someone more suited to ruling but happier in the shadows, where real power dwelled. As it was, he was proving trickier to manage than Amaury would have liked, at a time when his attention was needed elsewhere.

Perhaps he had been wrong to have the old king killed. Well, it was too late to regret that.

The Cup remained a tantalising solution to Amaury's problems. That Gill appeared to have it was frustrating. Amaury had been right to counsel the old king to punish Gill harshly. He had it coming. Guillot's supposedly careless sword stroke during the Competition had robbed Amaury of his dreams when they were little more than boys. He didn't believe for a second that the blow had been an accident. Amaury had often considered settling the score once and for all, but he was always so busy. Then he'd had the king strike him down, and ever since, the Prince Bishop had comforted himself with the knowledge that Gill was rotting in obscurity.

It seemed, however, that the man was destined to be a thorn in Amaury's side. It was long past time to pull it and destroy it. He was determined now that Gill would not see out the year.

Amaury knew it was foolish to view the Cup as the answer to all of his problems, but if it did what it was said to, it might very well be just that. He neither understood how the Cup worked, nor cared. All that mattered was that every scrap of information he had found about it unanimously agreed: it conferred on the person who drank from it a level of magical ability similar to that which they could have hoped for if they had trained from youth.

To think that the old Chevaliers of the Silver Circle had managed to lose the thing when transporting their treasury to a new headquarters somewhere in the southwest of the country was sobering. Dragons attacked and carried the gold away, along with the Cup, and it was all downhill for the Chevaliers after that.

From what Leverre had said, Guillot had stumbled on the Cup during an attempt to kill the dragon. Gill's dumb luck again—why couldn't Leverre or dal Sason have picked it up?

Amaury quelled his frustration. Perhaps dal Sason had killed Gill and the Cup was on its way to Mirabay at that very moment. He doubted it, somehow. He swore and turned from the window, tired of watching the king groping his new paramour like a sex-starved rabbit. Returning to his desk, the Prince Bishop considered practising shaping magic, but knew he was far too preoccupied to find the necessary clarity of thought.

He picked up a book he had taken from the secret archive on his last visit, in hope of finding distraction. Like everything else in the archive, the volume was extremely old; the thrill of discovering something long forgotten in its pages made Amaury's skin tingle. He had first learned of the Cup in a similar book. This book dealt with dragons, which he had hitherto paid little attention to; now that they had encountered one, it had become a necessity. The presence of the creature made his need for the Cup all the more pressing, both for the power it could give him, and the fact that he could use it to create his own cabal of dragonslayers within the Order. If more of the beasts crawled out of the mountains, he would be ready to deal with them, and the Order would reap a huge amount of glory and adulation.

Amaury started to read, allowing the fascination of ancient secrets to embrace him and push his problems into the shade.

Gustav Vachon had never been one of those soldiers who hungered after fame for fame's sake. Quite the opposite. Fame brought other fame-hungry bastards out of the woodwork, looking to kill you. Better off with a solid, reliable reputation, which brought plenty of work, without too many eyes watching. When you didn't have a big public persona, you inevitably ended up doing the jobs the fellows with a big reputation couldn't, but Vachon didn't mind. They paid well, and he didn't have much of a conscience to trouble him when he was trying to sleep.

The people of Grenaux did not share his sentiments when it came to fame. It was unusual for a village of peasants to have a reputation, but these had. The beef cattle of Grenaux and its surrounding farms had been called the "finest in Mirabay" at some point in the past by whoever had been king at that time. He had refused to eat any other. That meant the aristocracy did likewise. As demand increased, so too did price, which meant Grenaux had become a wealthy little commune that some bright spark had seen the sense in taking measures to protect. They dictated what could and could not be sold as Grenaux beef. They dictated the price, and until recently, had always offered up a dozen head of cattle each year to the king. An annual thank-you for the good fortune his ancestor had bestowed upon them. Therein lay the problem, and reason for Vachon's current employment.

Vachon surveyed the village, wondering what the beef tasted like. He'd never been able to afford any. It was said there was a secret method to the raising of a Grenaux cow. Some said they were fed beer. Others said it was chestnuts, while others still whispered that it was magic. Vachon suspected it was simply the fact that the region around the village bore the lushest green grass he had seen in over two decades of campaigning around the world, and the cows were allowed to wander about, feeding as they saw fit. Whatever it was, a single Grenaux cow could fetch ten times the price of a beast only one valley over.

This year, someone in Grenaux had decided that the king ought to pay for his twelve head of Grenaux beef. That didn't go down well at court. What fool ever expected a king to pay his way? Vachon had met that type before—he was the response to such folly. He admired the village's fine stone buildings, testimony to the great wealth the cattle had brought them. The town's grandeur was disturbed now by shouts and crashes and commotion.

His men were rounding up the villagers. Vachon hadn't decided what to do with them yet—his instructions had been somewhat vague, as they often were. He knew what his lord and master *wanted,* and that he would never explicitly state it. Funny how the men ordering killing were often the most squeamish about discussing it.

He rode into the village's centre. His job was primarily to collect the king's tribute and to deliver a message. There was a delicate balance to the latter. The good people of Grenaux needed to learn that withholding the king's tribute was no different than stealing from him. The lesson needed to hurt, so that they would remember it, and fear being taught it a second time. However, it had to be done without impacting the supply of beef, for that would inconvenience both the king's dining table and his tax revenues.

His men had herded the villagers into a tight group, allowing Vachon enough space to ride around them at a slow pace, giving them plenty of time to consider the error of their ways. Once he had completed his loop, he stopped and spoke.

"By order of His Highness King Boudain the Tenth, I am commanded to collect the tribute owing to him, twelve head of finest Grenaux cattle. I am also instructed to impose fines for the withholding of said tribute." He studied the people staring back at him, seeing a mix of fear and defiance on their faces. "The fine is money or goods equal in value to the tribute owing. Who is the mayor of this village?"

No one stepped forward. Vachon nodded to one of his men, who pulled a townsman at random from the crowd and punched him hard in the stomach. The man crumpled to his knees.

"The mayor of this village. To encourage him to step forward, the next one gets a blade, not a fist."

A man pushed his way through the press of bodies.

"I'm the mayor."

"No longer."

Another of Vachon's men seized him.

"Let this be a lesson," Vachon said. "Disobeying the king is treason." He pointed to a building that overlooked the square, separated a bit from the buildings on either side. One of his men got to work with a torch and tinder. The flame lit, he went inside. He emerged a moment later, followed by thick black smoke. Destroying the village was counterproductive. The king wanted his beef and his taxes. Razing Grenaux to the ground would get him neither. One building, though? A disobedient mayor?

Vachon nodded to the soldier who held the former mayor, who then bundled the man into the burning house. Two others closed the door and set to nailing it shut. A few of the defiant ones in the crowd surged forward, but some rough handling from his men ensured they quickly learned the error of their ways. Screams started from the building a moment later. Vachon's men were alert and ready. This was the tipping point. If the villagers were going to turn on them, it would happen when they thought their mayor could still be saved. He sat atop his horse, hand on the hilt of his sword, and watched them with cold, remorseless eyes until the screaming stopped.

"We will wait outside the village for you to bring the cattle. Do not delay and force us to return."

CHAPTER
4

Gill and Solène left their horses with the puzzled stable boy at the Black Drake, giving the lad no explanation of what lurked beneath the tarpaulin on the litter. Gill had thought about telling the boy not to peek under the tarpaulin, but realised that doing so would guarantee the boy would look. The last time he'd been in that stable yard, Guillot had fought dal Sason to the death. He felt neither grief nor triumph—dying by the sword was the risk they had both accepted on becoming bannerets.

The innkeeper's face lit up when he saw Guillot. He had stayed at the inn enough times to be recognised as a good customer, the duel to the death in the stable yard notwithstanding. Such things were commonplace when dealing with the nobility, so the innkeeper was probably used to it.

"Your usual room is available, my Lord," the innkeeper said. "You can go straight up. I'll have any luggage sent up directly."

"We'll need two rooms," Gill said, quickly correcting the innkeeper's assumption.

"Of course, my Lord." He rang a bell on his desk and a porter appeared. "The porter will show you to your rooms."

Gill and Solène parted company at doors on opposite sides of the hallway. Guillot had many battle-acquired injuries to deal with, but happily none that some rest, good food, and time wouldn't cure. He considered pulling off his boots once he closed the door, then thought better of it and flopped forward onto the bed. No sooner had he settled into the soft comfort than he heard a scream from outside. He groaned and pushed himself up.

Glad that he'd left his boots on, he went downstairs. By the time he got down, several staff had gathered at the door to see what was going on, although Guillot had a fairly good idea of what had caused the commotion. Sure enough, the stable boy was pressing himself against the wall on the far side of the yard, and the tarpaulin on the litter was partially pulled back, revealing shiny black scales and enough razor-sharp teeth to make even the hardiest flinch. One of the inn's staff let out a gasp.

"Is that . . . ?"

"The terror of the land?" Guillot said, as nonchalantly as his rumbling stomach would allow him. "It is. Dead."

"You killed it?" the other man said, his tone switching from fear to awe.

"I did." Guillot made no attempt at modesty. How could one hope to be modest after slaying a dragon?

"How?"

"I won't lie to you. It wasn't easy. It's no danger now, however. You're all perfectly safe. All the same, I'd appreciate it if you keep it covered up." Gill took a penny from his purse and tossed it to the stable boy—the lad snatched it from the air with more dexterity than Gill would have given him credit for.

"Perhaps you'd keep an eye on it for me. Keep the souvenir hunters away." Gill gave the gathering a nod and went back inside.

"I'll see to it, my Lord," the lad called after him.

Gill went to the lounge instead of returning to his room, feeling the continued rumbles of hunger in his belly. He considered asking Solène to join him, but thought she needed the rest more, so ordered food only for himself. When his meal arrived, he ate ravenously, even though the food wasn't quite as good as it had been during his last stay. The bread was at least a day old and the vegetables were not as fresh as he would have expected from the Black Drake. He supposed it was a sign of the times. Food shortages always followed a panic. Then the violence started. In Guillot's experience, the aftermath of a panic was far worse than whatever had caused the panic to begin with. That was the threat the kingdom was facing now. He wondered what the Prince Bishop had in mind to deal with it.

Gill wondered if Amaury had finally overstepped. Announcing the dragon's existence was a calculated risk, and Gill wasn't sure the Prince Bishop would be able to spread news of the slaying in time to stop the worst of the public reaction that was sure to come. One way or the other, it wasn't his problem. He ate until he could eat no more, then clumped up the stairs to his room. When he lay down again, sleep came quickly.

▴▴▴▴▴▴

Guillot woke with a jolt. It took him a moment to remember where he was and why he was there. He looked out the window—the sun was shining high in the sky, and filled the room with light when he pulled back the curtain. Noise from below drew his attention to the courtyard.

A number of people had gathered there. Frowning, Gill left his room, feeling a sense of obligation to check on his trophy. The inn-keeper was standing at his desk in the otherwise empty inn. Usually the place would be abuzz with staff and guests, but it seemed that everyone was elsewhere.

"I'll take breakfast shortly," Guillot said.

"Very good, my Lord."

"Those people in the stable yard?"

"Ah, yes," the concierge said. "I think word has gotten out about what you brought back with you."

Guillot grunted with displeasure. The last thing he wanted was people helping themselves to bits of his dragon. He went outside to clear them away and discovered that the reason they were congregated in a huddle was because the stable boy was keeping them away from the tarpaulin-covered trophy with a pitchfork. The lad couldn't have been much more than fifteen, and was as much dirt as boy, but clearly he had more mettle than many who would consider themselves his better.

"What do you want?" Guillot said to the group in as imperious a tone as he could muster. He already knew the answer, but wanted to get their attention. He rested his hand on the pommel of his sword the way bannerets often did when trying to affect a casual air.

"Came to see the beast's head, Lord," one of the townspeople said. "To see if it's really dead."

The bunch had a rough look about them, and Guillot had to admire the boy's courage in standing up to them. There was nothing to be gained in trying to shoo them off—they'd only come back as soon as Gill left.

"Pay the lad a penny each and you can have a look. If anyone tries to touch it, I'll make sure their head lies next to the dragon's."

The men reached for their coin purses with far more enthusiasm than Guillot had expected. Then again, seeing a dragon's head was a story they'd be telling for the rest of their lives. The fact that it had tried to kill him twice meant the novelty had lost most of its lustre for Gill. Until that moment, it hadn't occurred to him that there was income to be made from it.

"The money's all yours," Gill said to the stable boy before going inside for breakfast.

With the inn all but empty, Guillot had his pick of tables in the lounge. He was curious to see how people reacted to the grotesque sight beneath the tarpaulin, so chose one by a window with an oblique view of the stable yard, including the large pile of manure therein. Even had the dining room been full, he suspected this table would have been vacant because of that. The view was a little more interesting today, however.

Over the course of his meal, more and more people arrived at the yard; apparently word was spreading among those who remained in Trelain. He reckoned that the stable boy would earn enough to retire on by the end of the week if things continued like that. Unfortunately, the dragon's head, though recently slaughtered, was unlikely to cooperate for much longer without the assistance of a taxidermist. While Guillot had long since put his pretensions of glory behind him, a dragon's head was too impressive a trophy to allow to rot into oblivion. Hopefully there was a taxidermist still in town, or the proof of Gill's deed would be little more than a bleached skull in a few weeks.

He wiped his mouth on the napkin, and with one more amused glance at the stable boy's efforts to adapt to his new role as curator, tour guide, and guardian, Guillot headed for Solène's room. He had no idea how long it was possible for someone to sleep, but he couldn't leave her there forever.

He knocked, and she bade him enter. She was sitting up and had opened the curtains, but didn't look as though the rest had refreshed her much.

"I was beginning to think you'd never wake up," Guillot said.

She smiled, but it looked forced.

"How late is it?"

"Nearly midday."

"What's all the commotion outside?"

"Word's gotten out about the dragon," Guillot said. "Everyone wants to take a look."

"You should charge them," she said.

Guillot blushed and shrugged. "Is there anything I can get you?"

"If you could send up something to eat? I'm starving. I don't really feel up to going to the dining room."

"I'll send down to the kitchen. Anything in particular?"

"Hot and lots of it."

Guillot laughed.

"Have you heard anything from Mirabay?"

"No. Word of what we did will get there soon enough. It always does."

"What do you think he's going to do?"

There was only one person she could be talking about. "Who knows? Maybe he'll try to kill me again. I knew he hated me, but I didn't realise he'd kept that flame burning for so long. Maybe he'll forget about me again when something more interesting comes along."

"What is there between you two?"

Gill rubbed his face with a mixture of jadedness and frustration. "It's ancient history. He blames me for ending his career as a swordsman. It was his own fault, though. He got injured while trying to do something he shouldn't have. All things considered, I'd have been within my rights to cut him down for it. I was willing to let it lie. He should have, too. Once word of the dragon's death gets out, I don't think he'll be able to touch me. Not for a while, at least, and that'll be long enough to disappear."

"Are you going to go after him for trying to kill you?"

Gill shrugged. "I thought I would, but now? I don't see much point in it. I'll likely only get myself killed in the process, and for what?"

"You don't think what he's trying to do with magic is dangerous?"

Gill let out a sigh. "Yes and no. If the people keeping an eye on things are like you, I'm a lot less worried. It seems like magic is coming back one way or the other. The tyrant of Ostia was said to be using it. I've heard rumours that it's being used in the south. It's best that the power is controlled and that the right people do that."

"You think the Prince Bishop is the right person?"

"Maybe. Maybe not," he said with a shrug. "Who am I to say? In any event, it's not my fight. I dealt with the dragon. I've done my part. Other fights are for other people. I'm tired."

They sat in silence for a moment, and Gill was about to get up and fetch her some food when she spoke again.

"Tell me how it felt. The fire."

Gill thought for a moment. "Like nothing more than a blast of warm air. It was the strangest thing. Magic." He shrugged again. "I have to admit I thought I was done for. I think the dragon did too. There was more to it, though I might just be imagining some of it.

"One I'm pretty sure of—when we rode into the valley, I could *feel* the dragon. It was like something was tugging on me, on the very fibre of my being, showing me what direction to go in to find it."

"That makes sense," she said. "Maybe that's how the old Chevaliers tracked the dragons down."

"That's what I thought too," Gill said. "Anyhow, I know you're hungry. I'll go and get you something to eat."

▲▲▲▲▲▲

Music floated through the salons and lounges of the opulent townhouse in an upmarket part of Lanham, the capital of Humberland. Katherine dal Drenham navigated from room to room, making polite small talk with the good and great of society who had been lucky enough to warrant an invite. Hers had come because of the never explicitly stated, but very much implied, untruth that she was the new mistress of the Prince of Humberland. It was a convenient falsehood. One of many, such as her name, and everything else about her.

Katherine's employer, the Duke of Bowingdon, had started the rumours, and a young, newly arrived nobody had suddenly become someone important enough to earn an invite to the autumn ball of Grand Burgess Whitly. When she stopped to chat, she carefully gave only hints as to who she was and where she came from. She was beautiful enough to be forgiven her obliqueness, and obviously intelligent enough to create an aura of mystery. For those harder to influence, she had other talents, ones that could see her burned at the stake, and on one occasion very nearly did.

In Mirabaya, the burgesses—some of them wealthy beyond belief, even richer than some of the aristocracy—knew their place. They were commoners—rich commoners perhaps, but commoners nonetheless. In Humberland, it was very different, and it was something Katherine—or Ysabeau dal Fleurat, as she was more properly called—struggled to come to terms with. To see a grand burgess play host to people whose ancestors had been ennobled by an emperor, to treat them as his equals, was jarring. For a duke to need her services to get an edge on a commoner was astonishing. Nonetheless, that was the way they did things in Humberland, and it meant she was able to make a good living while in her self-imposed exile.

The ball was a lavish affair. Grand Burgess Whitly was doing his best to impress, and to make it seem effortless and perfectly normal. If he was as wealthy as rumoured, perhaps it was. He held the monopoly on the trade in tea with Jahar. It wasn't a drink Ysabeau had managed to acquire a taste for, but the Humberlanders couldn't get enough of it and the monopoly was worth a fortune. Unfortunately for Whitly, her employer had set his heart on controlling the tea trade, and in Humberland, as in Mirabaya, it was rare for a nobleman of Bowingdon's influence not to get his way. He was also not one to negotiate a deal on the matter—he took the things he wanted.

Ysabeau watched the guests doing what guests at such parties always did—trying to be seen, to appear wealthier and more sophisticated than they were, to make connections with those more influential than themselves. There was hardly anyone present who didn't have an agenda, and Ysabeau was no different. She built a mental map of the house as she moved about under the guise of social grace, identifying where she could get out should things go wrong, and trying to locate the grand burgess's study.

Somewhere within the house—most likely in the study, she reckoned—there was a ledger book that outlined the dealings between Grand Burgess Whitly and a Mirabayan merchant of note. It was more than a simple ledger, however. It was the history—in numbers and lists of items—of how Grand Burgess Whitly became one of the wealthiest men in the kingdom. In a mercantile nation like Humberland, enterprise such as Whitly's was lauded. But not when someone's chief trading partner was a land with which the kingdom was at war. That was very different. That was why the ledger book was kept at the house, rather than in Whitly's offices, overlooking the quays from which his merchant ships departed. During this evening's festivities, Ysabeau had to discover where the book was kept, obtain it, and bring it to the duke, who would use it to pick over Whitly's empire, seizing the juiciest portions for himself.

Ysabeau smiled sweetly at a uniformed gallant, then returned the jealous, frosty stares of several young women who viewed her as competition, though they knew they could never gain the attention of the heir to the throne. She didn't care. In a couple of days, Katherine dal Drenham would cease to exist. Her hair, currently the colour of spun gold, would be black once more, and dal Drenham's magnificent powder-blue skirts would be replaced by Ysabeau's riding britches—so much more practical in her line of work. The accent was the thing she most looked forward to being rid of. Her magical gifts allowed her to ape the Humberland twang perfectly, but the tones of Mirabay were the ones she longed to hear. It was rapidly approaching a year since she had fled Mirabaya, but already it felt like a lifetime. She had seen half a dozen countries, and crossed the Middle Sea more times than she cared for. She wanted to go home.

Before she could, she had a job to finish.

Amaury sat in his carriage, the message he had received by pigeon shortly before leaving the palace crumpled in his hand. He was torn between a great, sweeping wave of relief, and one of fury. In the morning he would be able to tell the king that the great threat to the kingdom had been destroyed. However, he would not be able to claim the credit for his Spurriers. According to the message, a man had brought a dragon's head to Trelain. *Guillot dal Villerauvais, Banneret of the White, Chevalier of the Silver Circle.* The message had come from one of the spies Amaury employed in the town. Of dal Sason, there was still no word, and Amaury was coming to accept the idea that he was dead.

It was hard to view the Order's performance as anything other than a failure—the brothers and sisters he had sent with Gill to kill the dragon were dead. Perhaps he had been expecting too much of them? Perhaps they had simply been unlucky? Perhaps he had underestimated Guillot—that option created a bitter taste in his mouth. How could half a decade of idleness and drinking not have dulled the man's edge to the point of uselessness?

Tapping a knuckle against his forehead, he wondered how events might be spun to his favour. The dragon had only ever been a bump on the road to his true goal, and while it had represented an attractive short-term opportunity, it was irrelevant in the greater scheme of things. He took solace in that, and in reminding himself what he was truly after. The Cup, which would grant him nearly unlimited power. All he had to do was get it from Guillot.

He took a deep breath to still himself. The Cup, then, was his immediate priority. His homegrown talent, both those with magical ability and those without, had been unable to deal with Guillot. As disappointing as that was, Amaury had to accept that Guillot's skill remained finely honed. To best him meant bringing in outside help. He had some contacts who would undoubtedly be able to point him in the right direction, but his first choice—Ysabeau—might prove impossible to find. And, as much as he wanted to settle things with Gill once and for all, the Cup had to come first. Everything else could wait, no matter how frustrating that was—killing two birds with one stone had simply not worked. His course decided upon, there was no point in delaying. He leaned forward and hit the roof of the carriage three times.

"Three Trees Tavern," he shouted.

After a muffled response from the driver, the Prince Bishop relaxed back into his cushioned seat. It was unseemly, going to a well-known mercenary hangout, but he knew his mind wouldn't rest until he had set something in motion. The Three Trees was his best chance of finding what he needed; it was where the best fixer in the city— Luther—spent his days. If Luther couldn't find the person Amaury needed, they weren't to be found.

The carriage jolted to a halt. Amaury stepped out before the driver had the chance to open the door for him. He drew his cloak tightly around him, pulling the collar close, glad he had chosen to wear something a little less ostentatious than his pale blue robes of office. It was always better to be unrecognised in such places, save by those with whom you were dealing.

He had visited the tavern on a few occasions over the years, most memorably when he was still training to be a banneret and was curious to see what type of life might await on the other side. Back then, he had thought there was something compelling about the life of men who earned their living with their swords—freedom, excitement, mystery. Now he knew most of them had barely two coins to scrape together. If you were seriously wounded, as he had been, your career was over and you were out on the street. It wasn't the career for a man with sense, or any other choice.

The Three Trees was much as he remembered it. Its patrons weren't men who cared much about the upkeep of their drinking establishment. So long as the ale was fresh and reasonably priced, Amaury reckoned the walls could be daubed with cow dung, and no one would care. He kept his head down as he headed toward the snug in the back where Luther held court. He was hailed before he was halfway there.

"Monsieur Grachon, what brings you to the Three Trees?"

Amaury turned, recognising the false name he had used the last time he had hired men there—to disappear the man he suspected of sleeping with his mistress.

"Luther, just the man I was looking for," Amaury said, relieved that it was Luther, and not someone else, who had recognised him.

"The lovely lady straying again?"

Amaury smiled to conceal a flash of anger. He hated it when people were overly familiar with him. "No, I cut her loose some time ago. I've something different in mind."

"Always a pleasure. The snug is empty, if you'd like to talk with a little more privacy."

"That would be perfect," Amaury said, his smile genuine this time. Luther might be overly familiar, but he knew his business, and how to ensure his clients returned every time they had a problem. Luther led him back into a small seating area surrounded by well-worn, decorated mahogany partitions set with panels of frosted glass. A small door gave access to the side of the bar, making the placing and delivery of orders more convenient.

They sat, and Luther wasted no time in getting to business. "What do you need, my Lord? There are a few fine blades looking for work at the moment, so I'm sure we can find someone who fits your needs."

"I'm not in need of a blade this time," Amaury said. "There's an item I would like to obtain, and the owner is proving rather . . . truculent in handing it over."

"Smash and grab? Cut and run?"

"I was thinking 'light fingers,'" Amaury said.

Luther sat back and stroked his chin. After a moment, he nodded. "I can think of a man who might fit the bill. But, truculent, you say?"

"Truculent."

"Is he handy? Alert?"

"I think it safe to answer in the affirmative to both."

Luther resumed stroking his chin. "And he's keeping a close eye on this object?"

"I expect so, although he's prone to certain lapses of self-control," Amaury said, nodding toward the bar.

"That could certainly make life easier, but I'll be honest with you, if he's handy and keen to keep hold of whatever it is you want, I'm thinking it's two men you want, not one. Someone to do the lift, and muscle to back him up if things go wrong."

Amaury frowned, thinking. As with all matters, the fewer people who knew what he was about, the better. He had no doubts regarding Luther's ability to keep his mouth shut—men in his line of business who couldn't never had long careers, and Luther had been in the game since Amaury had first wandered into the Three Trees in his youth. Luther knew damn well who "Monsieur Grachon" really was, but never showed even a hint of amusement at the subterfuge. Reflecting that trust, Amaury couldn't resist asking the question that had been in the back of his mind since he had decided to visit this tavern.

"Have you had any word from . . . *her*?"

Luther shook his head. "Not since I gave her safe passage out of the city. I gave her contacts in four cities. She could be in any one of them. Or, by now, somewhere else entirely. She might even be dead. Hers is not the safest of careers."

Amaury felt disappointed, then concerned. He assured himself that she was a master of her trade, making it unlikely she'd be killed doing it. Sending her out of the country after she'd killed the old king had made the assassination a more costly venture than expected—and personally disappointing as well. He missed her. Not an emotion he was familiar with. Could he have protected her if she had stayed and the job had gone wrong? Probably not. Making her leave was the right choice. The only one. Thankfully, there had never been any suspicion that the old king died of anything other than natural causes. She had done her job perfectly, and could safely return to the city whenever she wished, if only he could get word to her. That was a problem for another time, however.

"Two, then," Amaury said. "The thief needs to be discreet and competent. The muscle needs to be as good a blade as you can find."

Amaury had thought of requesting one of the big-name bravos, a man with a reputation that turned bowels to water, who had a list of kills longer than the six-volume *Decline and Fall of the Saludorian Empire*. However, that might draw attention. The big names were best used when you wanted to make a statement, and that was surplus to requirement. He just needed the Cup. For now.

"Just how handy is this fella?" Luther said.

"Very, but all a bravo needs to do is give the light fingers time to lift the object and get away."

Luther grimaced. "There'll be a premium if there's a chance of serious injury."

Amaury cast him a sharp look. "I wasn't aware you were in the habit of engaging delicate flowers these days, Luther."

Luther shrugged. "It's a different world we live in now. Lots of wars, lots of work. Lads can pick and choose."

"Fine, but if they make a mess of it, no premium will cover what I will do to them."

"I'll need to know who you want to rob—eh, *relieve* of the item."

Amaury supposed he was going to have to reveal it eventually, so why not now. He was committed to this plan. "Guillot dal Villerauvais."

Luther stared into the distance and chewed his lip.

"You've heard of him, then," Amaury said.

"You were right in saying he's handy. Just wondering what the best approach is."

"It's something of a pressing matter."

"I'll have something for you tomorrow."

Amaury stood. "I'll call on you here at eleven bells."

"Eleven bells," Luther said.

⸎

Pharadon's eyes blinked open with the urgency of a great shock. His huge heart gave a thump, then another, and another, the time between beats shortening until it achieved a regular rhythm. He took a long breath and let it out. His body was cold and stiff, and he knew he had slept for a long time. He had always been prone to long slumbers, but this one was different. The air sizzled with magic, and it had been an age since he had last felt that. It would have taken many years—centuries even—for the power to have returned to such strength. The thought of having slept for so long didn't bother him—enlightened dragons often hibernated to speed their passage through the years, heading toward whatever it was that awaited all living things at the end of days.

He stood up, his legs shaky at first. His body was covered with dirt and grime. Bats had taken up residence in his cave at some point since he'd fallen asleep; the smell of them was all too evident. Still, it was nothing that couldn't be solved by a quick dunk in a lake and a jet or two of purifying flame. He walked to his cave's entrance and looked out. The inner lid of his eye snapped shut to protect him from the bright sunlight, the muscles protesting at abrupt action after long disuse. The beauty before him was a feast for his eyes: snowcapped mountains, lush forested valleys, rivers, lakes, evidence of abundant game. Then he remembered the wars and his mood soured.

Pharadon had come to this remote peak to distance himself from the conflict. He had found a mountain that no man could reach, and left his foolish brethren and the upstart bipeds to their squabbles. He had lived among mankind for a time, and it saddened him that war had come. There was decency in them, and it disappointed him that his kind couldn't find common ground with them. Humans had some problem individuals, just as his own kind did. Such was the way of free will. Perhaps if dragonkind had made more of an effort to control the unenlightened, rather than leaving them to their chaotic ways, conflict could have been avoided. Humankind were quick to blame all for the actions of the few, a precarious thing to do considering the actions of members of their own race.

Still, regret was a waste of time. Nothing could be done about the mistakes of the past. There was more than enough world for all living things, and to his mind, there was no patch of ground worth killing for. It was an irony that he had always thought that way, given that he had been considered one of the finest fighters of his kind. Perhaps that was the reason. When you genuinely knew there were few, if any, who could best you, the need to constantly prove it seemed inane. As he looked out across a world he had not laid eyes upon in centuries, he hoped all of that was long forgotten. Hope and joy rose in him at the thought of exploring it all once more.

He looked about for a lake that would be large enough to bathe in, then tested his wings with a stretch. The first flight after a hibernation was always a dangerous thing, a mix of the joy of soaring through the air and terror at the possibility of plunging to the ground and a very messy death. It would be a ridiculous way for an enlightened to die, although he had seen it happen to one or two of his base brethren. There was only one way to find out if everything still worked—a leap of faith. He took a deep breath, allowed himself an ironic smile, and plunged from the side of the mountain.

CHAPTER
6

As the evening wore on and the wine continued to flow, it wasn't difficult for Ysabeau to slip away unnoticed. The main staircase to the house's upper levels was impossible to ascend without being spotted, but she managed to find a servants' stairwell hidden behind a panel door. She watched the progress of servants in and out, making regular trips back to the kitchens and cellars, and timed her move perfectly, disappearing from the crowded lounge under a blur of magic, heading up the stairs while the servants were all elsewhere.

She reached the first floor and opened the door a crack. It was likewise concealed in the panel walls—good servants were ever-present but rarely noticed—and checked to make sure there was no one about. The hall she looked out onto was deserted, quiet and dark, though she could dimly see and hear the light and noise drifting up the main stairway from the party below. The dark suited Ysabeau. In it, she could be almost invisible, while her magic would allow her to see perfectly. She shut her eyes and focussed her thoughts, and when she lifted her lids, the corridor was bathed in pale blue light that flickered over every surface.

She moved from door to door, first listening, then opening them to see what was inside, all the while keeping an eye out for any patrolling guards. The final door before she reached the top of the main staircase was locked. She furrowed her brow as she focussed on crafting a more complicated, powerful piece of magic. She struggled to ignore her sense of satisfaction and maintain her concentration when she heard the lock's tumblers turn and click into place. Opening the door, Ysabeau smiled—this was the room she was looking for. Lined with bookshelves, with an ornate wooden desk dominating the room's centre, it looked every inch the grand burgess's office. She stepped in and closed the door behind her. As she moved deeper into the room, several expensive magelamps illuminated, filling the space with warm light.

When she was tasked with the job, her initial thought was that the grand burgess had probably destroyed the ledger, but the duke's informants had indicated there were still monies outstanding from the deal the book documented. The grand burgess needed to keep the ledger to ensure he was paid what he was owed, so greed would prove to be his making and his undoing.

She made a quick circuit of the office, careful not to disturb anything or make any noise. There was nothing obvious to lead her to her goal, but then again, there never was. Ysabeau expected that a document as important, and potentially damning, as the ledger would be in a safe, or perhaps a hidden compartment.

A touch of magic showed her what she could not see with her eyes—the Fount lined the surfaces of the room's interior spaces, revealing one large enough to contain a safe. She opened the darkly stained oak panel to expose a thick-walled, metal safe concealed within. She took a deep breath and relaxed. She was already feeling the side effects of opening the door lock, and this would be more complicated and more draining. The more energy she used now, the less she would be able to draw on for emergencies during her escape.

Completing the process, she turned the safe's handle and opened the door. The hinges were well greased, moving without a sound. Inside were the things she expected to find: small ingots of gold; leather purses containing coin; some items of jewellery, which she pocketed; and a stack of papers and notebooks. She pulled them out, and started to go through them. While she was being paid only for the ledger, Ysabeau wasn't averse to making a little extra coin, so she kept her eyes open for anything else that might have value.

Ysabeau worked as quickly as she could; she wasn't fool enough to think Whitly would allow his house to fill with strangers while leaving his belongings—especially such dangerous ones—unprotected. They might have been invisible amongst the partygoers, many of whom were bannerets and military men, but she knew the burgess's men were also present, watching. She was confident she had gotten this far unseen, but that didn't mean trouble wasn't nearby.

She flipped through the notebooks, scanning them for what she was looking for—anything that mentioned trade with Mirabaya. If she couldn't find exact mention of the trades in question, she would take everything relevant and allow the duke to determine what was of most use. She made a pile of documents that seemed to have value, along with the ledgers that mentioned Mirabaya, then stuffed the rest back into the safe. It didn't matter if Whitly soon discovered the theft—the duke would be contacting him with his blackmail offer as soon as the incriminating evidence was in his hands.

Recalling the dates in question, Ysabeau decided she wasn't satisfied she had the right ledgers. Of course, any thief was always going to go straight for the safe. Where would a wily merchant like Whitly hide information that could ruin him? She reached out for the Fount, willing herself to see it again, studying how it covered the surfaces. She held it longer, juggling the need for concentration with surveying the shelves and cupboards for a void that might be a secret compartment.

There—a row of books that seemed to have an empty space behind them. If anything in here was likely to be booby-trapped, it was a secret compartment, so she inspected it further for any sign of danger, but could see nothing untoward. It seemed to be safe. She released the Fount, and found that the perfectly normal-looking spines of six leather-and-gilt books covered the open space. They were the six volumes of *The Decline and Fall of the Saludorian Empire*, a popular collection for those who wished to appear more clever and cultured than they actually were, but she thought it oddly fitting.

A little pressure on the spines, which were one solid façade, and, with a click, the panel swung open from one end. Inside was a single ledger, bound in black card and red cloth. She lifted it and leafed through, quickly confirming it was what she sought, then slipped it into the pouch that had been specially installed into her gown for this purpose.

"Don't think you're supposed to be in here, miss," a man's voice said.

Ysabeau froze on the spot. She hadn't heard anyone come in. He was as quiet as she was.

"Haven't you ever wanted to explore somewhere you shouldn't be?" she said, turning to face him.

"Sure," he said, in the strong accent of a northern Humberlander. "But I've always resisted the temptation to thieve."

Tall and well-muscled, though slender, the guard—for such he had to be—leaned against the doorframe, one hand resting on the pommel of his sword. It was a pose that was equally dashing and threatening. Ysabeau wondered if he knew the importance of what was in that room, or if he thought her to be little more than an opportunistic burglar.

"I'm going to need you to come with me, miss," he said. "Don't make a scene. I'm not above thrashing you if I have to."

She smiled sweetly as she pulled a dagger from her skirts and launched it at him in one smooth move. Spying and thieving weren't her only talents, and the dagger struck true, embedding itself up to the hilt in his throat. His eyes widened with shock and his hands reached for the offending weapon as he struggled to breathe. Ysabeau moved quickly, grabbing the dagger's handle and pulling it across his throat and free. Blood splattered, but a sidestep kept her free of an incriminating splash.

She spun the dying man about, grabbed him under the armpits, and dragged him into the office. Gasping and spluttering, he clutched at his neck in hope of keeping the blood in. His weight increased as the fight went out of him. Once he was clear of the door, she dropped him to the floor and finished him with a stab to the heart.

After wiping her dagger clean on his britches, Ysabeau returned it to its hidden sheath, then made sure the ledger was still in the pouch. She eased the office door open and looked left and right—the hallway was empty. Ysabeau slipped out of the room, closing the door quietly behind her. The man she had killed was unlikely to be the only guard on duty, so she knew she couldn't get complacent. She needed to get out of the house, and fast.

She had scouted several options, but using the front door like any ordinary guest was her preference—the longer she could maintain the illusion of normality, the better. She returned to the servants' stairs, opened the door, and listened. Behind her, she could hear people coming up the main staircase, but the servants' passages were quiet. She went in, but no sooner had she started down than she heard movement below her. It could be a servant, whom she could bluster past, or it could be another guard, who might have her at a disadvantage. Either way, it would raise the alarm.

Cursing at her lack of options, she went up. This was the only eventuality she had not planned for, and she had no idea where the stairwell would take her. Every moment she spent in the house brought her closer to the discovery of the dead man and the burglary, at which point life would become far more difficult.

She continued up the stairs, trying to remember how many floors the house had. At the fifth, the stairway ended, and she found herself in an undecorated, shabby passageway—the servants' quarters. She hurried along the corridor, trying to determine where to go next. At the end of the hall was a window with a rough curtain pulled partly across it. Ysabeau looked out. It gave a fine view of the city at night, magelamps glittering in its older parts, but she had no time to admire it. Almost as she reached it, the first shout of alarm reached her ears. She saw a narrow walkway running along the roof, between the balustrade and the slate-covered slope.

Ysabeau unlatched the window, hopped out, and looked over the balustrade. There was nothing but a long drop to the street below, and the buildings on the other side were too far away to reach.

Glancing back, Ysabeau saw two men advancing down the corridor, swords drawn. They had reacted far faster than she would have liked, but she supposed Whitly had hired the best men money could buy. She bunched up her skirts, freeing her legs and revealing the flat shoes she wore, rather than ones with a fashionable heel. She ran along the walkway, angry shouts following her as she did.

The far end of the building offered greater hope—there was a gap of only a metre or two between her and the next house. She looked back to see someone clambering out of the window. She didn't have much time to find another opportunity, and might not be able to get back to this one. She climbed up onto the balustrade and looked about for anything she might grab on the way down if she didn't make it to the next roof. There were some decorative features that would provide a handhold, assuming they were solidly attached. Where she would go from there was a problem she would deal with if it arose.

Another backwards glance had Ysabeau dismissing the notion of fighting her way out. She was great with a dagger and good with a sword, but Whitly's men would be better, and even with magic to aid her, there was no way she'd get past all of them.

She took a deep breath and jumped. The world seemed to slow as she flew through the air. She realised her survival instincts were drawing on the Fount to see her through. This was something she had done all her life, since long before she even knew what magic was. When it was added to what she had already used, there would be a price to pay, however.

She reached for the opposite balustrade, stretching for all she was worth. It seemed so far away that she wondered how she could have thought it was possible to reach it. Her hands slapped onto the balustrade and her fingers found purchase. Her body slammed into the wall, jarring one hand free. She dangled for a terrifying moment— long enough to get a good look at how far below the ground was. She contorted hard and managed to get her free hand back on the balustrade, then scrambled up and over, to safety. Only then did she allow herself a sigh of relief.

Still catching her breath, she looked back at Whitly's house. A moustached bravo stood on the roof, staring at her, sword in hand. His expression said there was no way he was following her. It wouldn't take him long to figure out his next step—to race downstairs and catch her leaving this building. She gave him a cheeky smile and a mock banneret's salute, then bolted, heading for the street.

Guillot sat in the Black Drake's lounge, turning an empty coffee cup on the table. Solène was sleeping again. The past days had taken their toll on her, but Gill wasn't convinced it was exhaustion keeping her to her room. He had seen it before: sometimes, when someone killed for the first time, a spark in them was extinguished. Solène had taken killing as hard as any he had seen, and he was worried. He had no idea how to help her. On campaign, people either got over it or it broke them and they went home, in shame, usually accused of cowardice.

What could he say that would help? That after she'd killed a dozen times, she wouldn't be able to remember the individual faces anymore? He shook his head; that was unkind. An unknown voice distracted him.

"My Lord dal Villerauvais?"

It occurred to Guillot that he might need to change his name now that Villerauvais was nothing but a pile of ash, rubble, and charred bones.

"The same," he said.

"I wanted to offer my congratulations at your great feat in slaying the beast," the man said.

"You're too kind," Guillot said. He couldn't deny that he was flattered, that he delighted in the recognition, and it shamed him. He had been a prancing show pony in his youth, and it had brought him nothing but ruin and regret. That he was still drawn to it brought bile to his throat. "I'm afraid you have the advantage of me."

"My apologies. I'm Edouard Renart, mayor of Trelain."

"Pleased to make your acquaintance," Guillot said. "I hope life in town returns to normal now that the threat has passed."

"I do also," Renart said. "Word has been sent out. I understand the bells in Mirabay rang all day to celebrate the news. I'd have seen to it that the same happened here, but sadly the Bishop and his entourage are . . . out of the town at the moment."

Guillot smiled. "Like a great many others, unlike your good self."

Renart blushed. "I've received word from His Grace, the Duke. He's rushing here and is very much looking forward to meeting you."

"My celebrity seems to grow by the hour," Guillot said, wondering if he should go out to the stables, saddle a horse, and ride until no one had heard of him or dragons.

"Not at all surprising considering what you've achieved. I'm sure you'll be on your way to Mirabay for an audience with the king before long. We'll have to make the best of you while we have you."

Guillot felt his stomach twist. "Perhaps a parade," Guillot said. "We could rig up a cart and I could stand on the dragon's head, waving to people as we pass."

Renart nodded eagerly, missing the irony in Gill's voice. "Not a bad idea at all. It will take a little organising, but leave it with me."

Dismayed by the man's reaction, Guillot quickly said, "I was joking. To be quite frank, Mayor, I'd appreciate as much privacy as I can get. I understand that will be difficult, but nonetheless."

"Oh, of course. I'll do my best, but all things considered, I don't know what will happen. You're a hero. You've delivered people from their worst nightmare, and that's not going to go unremarked."

Escape on horseback seemed like a better and better idea. He wondered how long it would be before Solène was ready to go.

The mayor picked up on Guillot's intentional silence. "Well, I'll do my best, out of gratitude for you saving the town, but I'm afraid my counsel counts for little with the duke."

"I appreciate your efforts, Mayor," Guillot said. "I'll deal with His Grace when the time comes."

"Until then, I wonder if you'd considered organising viewings for the beast's h—"

"Good day, Mayor," Gill said.

Renart nodded apologetically. "I wish you good day, then, and my most heartfelt thanks."

Guillot felt churlish, and touched his fingers to his forehead in salute, but knew he was in danger of being dragged down a road he had no desire to walk again. No sooner had Renart left than Gill's attention was drawn to a scruffy group of people who had arrived at the door.

Staff had started trickling back to the inn over the course of the day, coming out of whatever cellar they had been hiding in. The innkeeper approached the new arrivals with the demeanour of a man who didn't even want to breathe the same air as them. A quiet but heated discussion ensued, with several nods in Guillot's direction. He knew that he would be surrounded by powerful nobles whom he could not say no to soon enough. These people, however, he could choose to see.

"Let them in, if they wish to speak to me," Guillot said.

The innkeeper cast a look back, then gave Gill a forced smile and nod before stepping aside.

The lead member of the party approached Guillot, while her comrades remained by the door, taking in the luxury of their surroundings with open mouths.

"My Lord," the woman said. "My name is Edine. I'm the mayor of a village called Venne."

It seemed he was popular with mayors this morning. Guillot searched his memory, and vaguely recalled a village by that name a few valleys over from Villerauvais.

"Guillot dal Villerauvais at your service. What brings you to Trelain, Mayor?"

She looked about nervously. "Dragons, my Lord."

"I can assure you, it's dead," Guillot said, turning to gesture to the stable yard where the head resided.

"No, my Lord. *Dragons.*"

The polite smile on Guillot's face fell away as her words sank in. He took a long inhale, composing himself, before speaking.

"Dragons, you say? As in, more than one?"

She nodded. "Yes, my Lord. I've seen three of them at the same time. They've attacked every night for a week. Cattle, sheep. People."

Guillot's stomach turned over. He knew why she was bringing this news to him, and the memory of how one dragon very nearly killed him was still fresh in his mind.

"I don't suppose there's any chance they're *small* dragons?"

She nodded, and Gill felt a wave of relief.

"They were small at first, my Lord, no bigger than a horse. But they've been growing fast. They're bigger every time they're seen. They attack, they feed, they get bigger. Much bigger."

The relief washed away as quickly as it had come. He waved for the waiter.

"I'm sure you and your people have had a long journey," Guillot said to Edine. "You must be thirsty? Hungry?"

"I wouldn't say no to something, my Lord. My friends the same."

"Bring these people something to eat and drink," Guillot said, turning to the waiter. "Whatever they want."

The waiter hesitated for a moment.

"It's all on the Prince Bishop's account," Guillot said. "You can bring me a glass of Lower Loiron."

"Right away, my Lord."

Gill grimaced. A little stressful news, and his instinct was to reach for the bottle. He took a deep breath. "Actually, forget the wine."

He wanted to tell this woman that the dragons were not his problem, that the king, the Prince Bishop, the duke, would protect them, but he knew they would not. If he sent Edine to any of those men, all it would do was delay the matter. They would end up knocking on his door, wherever that turned out to be. He wondered if this was his lot now, to be a dragonslayer. It did not fill him with enthusiasm.

When he looked across the small table at Edine, he could see Jeanne's earnest eyes looking back at him. The tavern keeper in Villerauvais was now no more than dust, a fate he had not been able to stop. If there was even a chance he could prevent the same from happening to Edine and her people, there was no question of refusing to help her. Shame had followed him long enough.

He leaned back in his chair and steepled his hands. "It's my help you want?"

She nodded.

"It must have taken you a day or two to get here. How did you find out about my slaying the other dragon so soon?"

"We came seeking the duke's help. We heard what you'd done when we got here, and reckoned you were the man to see."

He thought it over for a moment. He knew how to use the Cup now, knew the benefits it brought him. He also had the experience of dealing with a dragon behind him. Men had made their living as dragonslayers in the past—he could see no reason why he might not do the same. A few more months of regular practice and some active living and he'd be able to call himself in good shape.

Also, it wasn't as if he was going into this alone. For one, he'd need Solène's help, both in conducting the Cup ritual and in fixing his broken bits after the fact. Surely others would happily accept the risks and add their swords to his.

Who, though? His mind flicked back to dal Sason's deceit, and Gill found himself wishing for some of his men from the old days— Mauvin, Barnot, Vincin, among others. Some of them had tried to contact him over the years, but he was too shamed by his disgrace to respond. He never thought he'd come to regret that, but he had no idea where any of them were now, or if they even still lived. Finding new men, competent men, and learning to trust them would be a challenge.

Guillot realised that Edine was staring at him intently.

"I should add," she said, "that there are no villages between Venne and Trelain. When they are done with us, they'll come here."

Three of them unleashed on Trelain was a terrifying prospect. Stopping them then would be impossible without causing death and destruction on a major scale. There was no way he could refuse her request, so he nodded.

"I can't promise you anything, other than that I'll do my best. If that's good enough for you, then I'll help."

She broke into a relieved smile. "Thank you, my Lord. Thank you. We'll be in your debt."

She stood, but he gestured for her to sit again. "Please, wait for your food. It will take me a little time to get my affairs in order." He wondered how long Solène would need. "I should be ready to leave the day after tomorrow. Do you and your people have somewhere to stay for the night?"

"I'm sure we can find somewhere," she said. "A stable, or barn, or some such."

Guillot smiled. "I don't think there'll be any need for that." He knew for a fact there were only one or two other guests at the inn, and he had few pleasures in life more enjoyable than running up a bill at the Prince Bishop's expense. Though he tried to make the most of the contented feeling that brought, his good humour soured. He wondered how Solène would take the news.

CHAPTER
8

Luther was at the bar in the Three Trees when Amaury returned, watching, as always, for clients old and new, and anyone worth putting on his roster of sell-swords. He nodded as Amaury approached, and without a word, both men headed into the snug, where they could talk without fear of being overheard.

"I have to admit I was a little worried when you first gave me the name," Luther said. "I made a few inquiries though—"

Amaury's face darkened, and Luther held up a hand.

"All discreet. Nothing that can be traced back. You don't get to where I am by making mistakes."

Amaury nodded.

"Anyhow, it gave me enough to put a plan together," Luther said. "He's spent years at the bottom of a bottle—"

"You'd be a fool to underestimate him."

Luther held up his hands again. "I don't underestimate anyone, but I know men like him. He's been surviving on the memory of better times, and we can use that.

"I've found a fellow who will be able to get close enough to dal Villerauvais to get the job done." Luther waved to a man at the bar—one of his heavies. A moment later, the man returned, ushering another into the snug.

Amaury gave the newcomer a second look, and frowned. Something about him was familiar. "I know you," he said.

The man nodded. "Sergeant Barnot, as was," he said.

Of course, Amaury thought. Thinner, a bit older, and clearly not enjoying a prosperous retirement from military service, but it was indeed Barnot, Guillot's former sergeant and one of his right-hand men. Amaury gave Luther a crooked look.

"You know who I am?"

"I do, your Grace," Barnot said.

"There's nothing to worry about. Sergeant Barnot's fallen on hard times, and I said we could help him out, if he was willing to help us."

Barnot looked up at Amaury with the eagerness of a puppy hoping for affirmation from its master. Amaury noticed the pallor of his skin, the drooping bags under his eyes, and a few other signs of long-term dream-seed addiction. It was common in old soldiers—that and the bottle. Once, Barnot had been Guillot's fiercely loyal retainer. Now? Now Amaury had leverage.

"I've told Sergeant Barnot that we need something he's in the unique position to obtain for us," Luther said as Barnot sat down.

"Have you told him from whom?"

Luther shook his head. Amaury glowered at him. He'd expected all his dirty work to be done, given what he was paying Luther. He let out a breath. "Guillot dal Villerauvais has something that the king needs. I suspect Luther has contacted you because he reckons you're the only man who'll be able to get close enough to dal Villerauvais to get it. I think he's probably correct."

He studied Barnot, whose once-solid face now looked wilted, for a reaction. The more time he had to consider it, the more Amaury realised that Luther had happened upon a plan that might very well succeed. Guillot had always been a trusting fool, and Barnot had been one of his most loyal men. He wouldn't be able to imagine Barnot be-traying him. Whether they could get Barnot to do that was an entirely different matter.

"You will be well paid for your time and effort," Amaury said. "Doing the king this service will put you in his favour, and I can speak from personal experience in saying that is a transformative thing. There won't be many opportunities for you to pull yourself out of the rut you're in," he said, an edge to his voice. "This could likely be the last chance you get to turn things around. The item in question is inconsequential in the grand scheme of things. The details are unim-portant. Suffice to say, Guillot will barely notice it's missing. Keeping hold of it is a matter of stubborn pride for him. In reality, it's doing nothing but hurting himself, the king, and Mirabaya."

Amaury didn't want to lay it on too thick, but men who had spent their lives soldiering under the king's banner had deeply ingrained notions of honour and duty. Even one fallen so low as Barnot. Barnot might not be willing to act to help himself, but the thought of having value, of being able to serve his king again, might stir him to action.

"What do you want taken from him?" Barnot said. "You have to tell me that much, at least."

Amaury pretended to think for a moment. He had constructed the lie while giving Barnot time to consider things.

"It's a small cup made of Telastrian steel. Other than the value of the metal itself, its worth is entirely sentimental. It was stolen from an individual at court—not by Guillot, I hasten to add. I'm not sure how it came to be in Guillot's possession."

Barnot smiled.

"In any event, Guillot has it, the king needs it, and we think you are the man best positioned to get it for us. Will you help us? Will you answer your king's call one more time?" Amaury glanced at Luther, wondering if he had overdone it, but Luther showed no reaction.

"I just need to take this cup from him? Nothing else?"

"Absolutely nothing else," Amaury said. "We'll even have a courier waiting for you to hand it over to."

Barnot nodded slowly. "I can do that. I'll do it."

Amaury smiled, and looked over at Luther, who leaned back in his chair with the confident expression of a man who had once again de-livered a suitable candidate for a tricky job. There was something else playing on Amaury's mind, however. What provided leverage could easily become a major problem. Relying on a dream-seed addict to deliver for you was foolish. The healers in the Order could deal with that. He cleared his throat as he tried to choose the right words.

"I can't help but notice your . . . problem. I think I can be of help with that."

CHAPTER
9

Guillot dined alone, not wanting to have to make small talk with the villagers, and ruminated over how he was going to break the news of his decision to help the villagers to Solène. His meal finished, he trudged up the stairs to her room, still with no clue as to how to broach the matter. After talking with Edine, Gill had written an advert that would be put in Trelain's morning news sheet, seeking candidates to join his nascent dragon-slaying company, and thus committing himself to this course of action. He hoped a few suitable candidates would present themselves over the course of the following day. As he thought it over, it was difficult not to start having second thoughts. The first dragon had nearly killed him, and that had been only one. How he could hope to face three?

"You're looking better," he said as he entered her room, mustering as much cheer as he could. He still had no idea how receptive she would be to the plans he had made for her, without her consultation. Anything seemed better than trying to console her. He hoped she would help him. The focus on something else might help her push her feelings over killing out of her mind. If not, perhaps doing some good might help her come to terms with it. If they turned their backs on this request, others would suffer. Burden though it might be, there was never a choice but to do what needed to be done, or to at least try. Not if you wanted to be able to live with yourself afterward, that was.

"I'm feeling much better," she said. "I need to get up and about."

"Speaking of that," Gill said, sitting on the chair by the door. "Something's come up."

She narrowed her eyes.

"Word of what we did has gotten out, and it seems the dragon we killed isn't the only one."

The newly returned colour drained from her face. "What do you mean?"

He took a deep breath. "There's a village called Venne. It's being attacked by dragons."

"Dragons?" Her eyes widened.

"Three," Guillot said, matter-of-factly. "From the sounds of it, they aren't fully grown. Although that seems to be changing pretty fast. Some of the townsfolk are here and have asked me to help. I said I would."

"You really want to do all of that again? Three more times?"

He shrugged. "No, but what choice do I have? I'm the only man alive who's killed a dragon. I'll need your help, though."

"What can I do?" she said. "*You* killed the last one, all by yourself."

"That ceremony with the Cup—it needs to be carried out every time, doesn't it?"

She nodded. "I think so. But I can't help you, Guillot. I wish I could, but really, I can't. There are things I have to do. Things that can't be put off. That's clear to me now. It's why I'm feeling a bit better."

This wasn't the response Gill had been expecting. He knew it was unlikely she'd take it well, but what was this?

"I can think of a lot of things I'd rather do," he said, "but if I don't help, a lot of people will die. Just like at Villerauvais."

She gave him a sad smile. "If I go, I'll probably die."

"It'll be dangerous, for sure," Gill said, "but nothing we can't handle. I've been thinking we could recruit—"

"No, you don't understand," she said. "It's not the danger of the dragons. It's the danger I am to myself. And to others."

Gill frowned. "What do you mean?"

"My time with the Order has made my magic stronger, but I haven't learned to control it. That's why I've been so tired. It's magical burnout, and if I allowed it to go much farther, it would kill me. I can't tell when I'm using too much and I can't control how much I'm using. I have to learn, and I have to do that *now*. I've pushed my luck too far already. If I try to take on these dragons with you, I'm going to end up killing myself. If I knew more, I'd have been able to disable those people temporarily. Not . . ." She let out a sob.

He did his best to hide his disappointment, knowing he had to put his feelings to one side. He crossed the room and sat on the edge of her bed. After a moment's awkward hesitation, he laid what he hoped was a reassuring hand on her shoulder.

"You can't beat yourself up about this. If you hadn't done what you did, they'd have killed you." He grimaced at his lack of success as she continued to sob. She stopped a moment later and took a deep breath.

"I know, but there was a better way. I don't want that to happen again. I won't let it. I have to learn more, and I can't do that on my own."

"I understand," he said. "But where can you go?"

"Back to the Priory."

"The Priory? Amaury will have you thrown in the dungeons the moment you set foot back in the city."

"I don't think he knows I was involved in any of it. Leverre said he left a note explaining what he intended to do, and putting all the blame on him. I can come up with a reason for my absence easily enough. There's someone there I know will help me. I don't think there's anywhere else I can learn what I need to learn."

"Are you sure?"

"There's only one way to find out." She smiled wryly. "I don't have many options. There's the Priory. There's a library in the city—an old, secret one, a bit like the vault you found under your house. Even if the people at the Order can't help me, I'm sure there's something in there that will.

"If I try to work it out completely on my own, I'm likely to kill myself. Controlling the use of magic is the one thing the Order has a good grasp of. With their limited power, they've had to learn."

"You're right, of course," Gill said, wondering if there was anything else in his vault he might find useful. Did he have the time to make the diversion on the chance there was? How many lives might that cost?

"You have to put your well-being first," he said. "If you learn to control your magic, who knows the good you'll be able to do with it."

"I'm glad you understand," she said. "I think there's a way you can keep using the Cup, though."

Gill perked up at this. He knew he had no chance of surviving three dragons, no matter how young they were, without the Cup.

"All the magic used in the ceremony comes from the Cup. You don't need any extra power. The words spoken simply channel it. I think the reason there were mages in the old ceremony the statues showed was because they wanted to keep control of the magic. There's no reason I can't teach you how to carry out the ceremony on yourself, or on someone else."

He nodded slowly. "That could work. If I can use the Cup, that should be enough to see me through. Particularly if I can recruit some help, which I'm hoping to do. There's bound to be a few decent blades kicking around, looking for work."

"When will you go?" she said.

He shrugged. "There's not much time to waste. The dragons have been attacking for a week now. Coming closer to the village every time, and getting bigger. I'll put the word out, see what comes of it, and try to set off tomorrow if I can. The day after at the latest. You?"

"The same. There's nothing to be gained by my staying here any longer. The sooner I get going, the sooner I can take control of my life. Who knows, I might even be done in time to come and help you."

He laughed. "If it takes that long, I suspect I'll be beyond help." He paused, feeling he should say something more, but couldn't work out what. He took a deep breath and returned to practical matters. "So, about the Cup?"

"May I see it?" she said.

Guillot took the little vessel from the pouch on his belt and handed it to Solène. There was something comforting in touching its smooth steel sides, akin to the primal sense of ease that he felt sitting next to a crackling fire on a dark night.

"First things first," Solène said. "I doubt the quality of the water used is really going to have any impact. The magic in the Cup is too strong for that to matter. As long as it's not going to poison you, I expect it'll be fine." She turned the rimmed bowl over in her hands. "The amount administered might be a different matter, so I'd stick to what the carvings said—one droplet and no more. It's all about transferring magical energy and focussing that energy to a particular end. Transferring too much could have all sorts of unintended consequences, and those aren't things to play around with. The old mages decided one drop was enough to achieve the desired result, and we—you—should stick to that."

Gill nodded intently. Magic terrified him, as it did most people, and being turned inside out or incinerated by magical flame—the first unintended consequences that popped into his mind—was not how he wanted to meet his end. He'd have preferred having nothing to do with magic at all, but he could speak firsthand to the Cup's benefits, from healing to flame resistance.

"I can write the words down for you. The original is in old Imperial, but it's not the words themselves that shape the magic. I'll translate them as accurately as I can for you, which should work perfectly well."

Gill forced a smile. He wasn't sure, but she seemed confident, and she was the expert.

"It's important to concentrate on the words and their meaning when you're saying them. Their power is in focussing thought, and it's the focussed thought that shapes the magical energy. It doesn't matter if there are slight differences between the original and the translation as long as the meaning is the same. If you're thinking about . . . I don't know, a field of ponies when you're saying the words, they won't work. It might even turn you into a pony."

"Definitely not what I want," Gill said, worried now that he wouldn't be able to think of anything but a field of ponies when he was saying whatever Solène wrote down for him. He tried to gauge if she was joking, but her face gave nothing away.

"That's one of the hardest parts of shaping magic—holding that focus and concentrating on a single, pure thought. You won't have to worry about any of the other stuff—the Cup will take care of the magical energy."

"How long will the effects last?" Gill said, trying to determine if he felt any different from the way he had after Solène had first carried out the ceremony on him. He couldn't tell and had no intention of sticking his hand into the fire in the lounge downstairs to find out.

"You'll have to work that out for yourself. It could be hours, days, or even weeks. I really can't tell. I'm not even sure how much magical energy is being used for the spell. The old Chevaliers seemed to go through the ceremony every time they went out to face a dragon, so I reckon it's best to do the same.

"I wouldn't do it any more frequently than that, though. Unintended consequences . . . If you figure out its duration, go with that. Otherwise, only use it when you need to."

He nodded, wondering if he should start taking notes. She got out of bed stiffly, and walked toward the writing desk by the window. He stood to offer help, but she held up her hand to stop him. She wobbled a little on the first step, but quickly found her balance and made the brief journey unscathed. Once secure in the chair, she took a piece of paper, dipped the pen in the inkpot, and started to write. Done, she scanned the page and smiled.

"That's it," she said. "I can still see the carvings as if they were in front of me now." She handed the page to Gill and leaned back in her chair. "Repeat after me . . ."

CHAPTER
10

The cathedral bells started to ring when Amaury's carriage was about halfway to the palace. Moments later, the bells of other churches rang out as well and the Prince Bishop knew something was up—and suspected what that something was.

He had his driver stop the carriage.

"What's all the fuss about?" he asked of a passer-by.

The man shrugged, then, when he realised who he was talking to, said, "Don't know, your Grace. Sorry."

The next person he asked gave the same response.

Then someone shouted, "The dragon's been slain!"

So word had reached the city. Amaury's first reaction was anger—at himself. Information was valuable only when you were the sole person to possess it. He hadn't moved quickly enough, and now that word was out, what Amaury knew was all but worthless. He sat back in the carriage and thumped the roof for the journey to continue. The news being out meant he was running out of time to execute his plan to bring the Order out into the open. He was behind the curve already, which meant he had to work quickly and precisely.

When Amaury reached the palace, he asked his aide for the specifics of the news. The only thing anyone knew was that the dragon was dead. There was no word about who had killed it, which gave the Prince Bishop the space he needed. He sent people out into the city to gather up every bit of information being bandied about and cultivated the hope that there was still time to shape the story to his advantage.

He stared into the empty garden below his office window, stroking his chin, thinking furiously. All was not lost—if he could find a way to twist things to his benefit. The dragon had been slain by a great hero of Mirabay, but that didn't mean Amaury could not claim the credit. After all, he had tasked Gill with the mission. The Order had been equally involved. If he acted fast, he could shape the story to his liking. Even if doubt was cast on it later, who would they believe? Surely no one would question the word of the Prince Bishop of Mirabay, Arch Prelate of the Unified Church, First Minister to the King.

Turning to his desk, Amaury quickly jotted down an announcement. He sprinkled the still-damp ink with pounce to dry it, blew the powder clear, and surveyed his words. His skill in rhetoric had improved over the years, but he would never go down in history as a man who could win hearts and sway minds with words. In this instance, he didn't need to. He scratched out a few words here and there, added a sentence, removed one, then wrote the altered statement on a fresh sheet. Once it was blotted, he called for his secretary.

"Distribute copies of this statement to the news sheets, the city criers, and the bill posters. Make it clear that further details will be made known in due course. Also, send for Seneschal dal Drezony to attend on me at once."

<hr />

Dal Drezony wasn't one to play power games, so Amaury knew she would be there as soon as was possible. Waiting had never been his strong suit, however. Up until recently, he had filled those spare moments with quick exercises to improve his magical skills, but considering all that he had learned about the Cup, that was now a waste of time. In a few days, the Cup would be in his possession, and he would wield a magical power the like of which had not been seen in a millennium.

Instead, he ruminated on the other plan he had set in motion that night. Guillot had trusted Barnot without question for years, and there was no reason for that to change now. Amaury, on the other hand, found trusting Barnot a far more difficult proposition. Asking a man to go against notions of honour and brotherhood born of battle was like asking him to cut off one of his hands, even if he was a ruined old dream-seed addict. When the moment came, Amaury needed to be certain that Barnot would do what was expected of him.

Conveniently, Barnot came with his own leash, and Amaury was in the singular position of being able to exploit it even more effectively than a dream-seed dealer. However, to do that, he needed dal Drezony's help, and he suspected the seneschal would have objections. People with strong principles had their uses, but they had no understanding of the compromises necessary to run a kingdom and keep it safe.

Every time he needed her to do something she thought was morally questionable, such as rapidly advancing Solène's training, they had an argument. It had been the same with his daughter. Amaury usually won, but arguing was tedious, the concessions he had to make were not completely satisfying, and now the time for keeping his underlings happy had passed. This was a crucial moment, when things needed to be done quickly and effectively, without consideration of anyone's interests but his. He knew what was best for the kingdom.

After knocking, his secretary showed dal Drezony in; she looked resplendent in the Order's cream-and-gold robes. When he had first encountered the woman, Amaury had developed a brief romantic interest in her, but attractive though she was, he had quickly realised that their personalities and outlooks diverged in too many fundamental ways. Had she not been such a brilliant fit for her role in the Order, he would never have considered working with her in the long term.

"Good evening, Kayte," he said. "Thank you for coming at such short notice." She nodded respectfully and he flicked his gaze to his secretary. "Coffee, I think."

His aide nodded and disappeared silently, leaving Amaury and dal Drezony alone. He gestured for her to sit in one of the comfortable armchairs by the coffee table, then took the seat opposite.

"There's something I need you to do. It relates to extremely important state business that has fallen to me to address." He could see he had her full attention, so continued. "There's a man we need to undertake a mission. He's uniquely suited to carrying it out, but is possessed of a minor problem. He's a dream-seed addict. I want you to cure him."

Dal Drezony visibly relaxed. "I'd be delighted to. Dealing with addiction in the population is one of the roles I see the Order taking on once we come fully out into the open. I have to admit, I thought you were going to ask for something far worse." She smiled and leaned back in her chair.

"Unfortunately, I suspect I am. We need to keep control of this man. I don't want you to cure him completely, just enough that he's clearheaded and able-bodied. Competent to do what he needs to do. I need the addiction itself to remain, so that he'll do what he's told."

The colour drained from her face and all levity in her expression was extinguished. "You want me to maintain his addiction, but free him from the symptoms?"

"Precisely," Amaury said.

"I . . . Even if I would agree to do something like that, I wouldn't have the first idea of how to go about it."

"I suggest you work it out," Amaury said.

"I said *if* I agreed to. There's no way I can agree to do something like that. It's wrong on every level."

Amaury gave a wry smile, angry with himself. Because of his past compromises, dal Drezony felt she was entitled to make autonomous decisions.

"You misunderstand me," he said. "I'm not asking for your opinion. I'm giving you an order. People with a greater appreciation of what needs to be done have made the determination that this needs to be done. You, as an agent of the Crown, will do as you are instructed."

Dal Drezony let out an incredulous laugh. "I'm not going to do this. Your Grace."

The confidence in her voice bordered on arrogance. Amaury felt his temper flare.

"If you are unable to continue in your position as Seneschal of the Order of the Golden Spur, I will, with regret, accept your resignation," he said sharply. "Before I do, I would point out that in the eyes of many—indeed, most—you are a witch. Within the Order, you are protected from the consequences that status would bring in open society. Outside it, you will be exposed to those consequences.

"Let me assure you of one other thing. Your father does not have the influence to protect you from the Intelligenciers." He paused.

"I wonder, when was the last time you saw a sorcerer burned at the stake?"

She glared at him, hatred in her eyes. In that moment, he knew he would have to start looking for her replacement, but for the time being, she was the only member of the Order with the magical finesse to do what was needed without killing Barnot. Solène might have the power—were she not missing—but from what he had seen thus far, she was all power, no control. He couldn't risk using her on something like this, nor did he wish to turn her against him as he just had Kayte dal Drezony. Dal Drezony would never have the power to be a real threat to him, but Solène most certainly did. He needed to treat her with more care.

"Well?" he said. "When?"

"Not for years," she said, from gritted teeth.

"And why do you think that is?"

"The Order."

"Precisely. For many years now, I've gotten to promising young mages before the Intelligenciers, and hidden them behind the protective walls of the Priory. I'm sure I've missed a few here and there out in the provinces, but there hasn't been a single burning in Mirabay in five years. It would break my heart for you to be the one to end that streak."

She fell silent, frowning, and Amaury revelled in her discomfort. He had won. Like as not she would try to draw some small illusion of victory from the defeat, but so long as that didn't stand in the way of what he wanted, he would give it gladly.

"On one condition," she said. "Once this person has finished whatever it is he's doing for you, I can cure him completely."

"I have no problem with that," Amaury said.

"Fine," she said. "I'll do what you command."

"Excellent," Amaury said. "He's waiting in the next room. You can attend to it immediately."

The hatred with which she had looked at him was a clear message. If he didn't get rid of her, she would become a problem.

"All right," she said, a smile spreading across her face, "but before

I do, you should read this." She threw a letter onto the table between them. "It's from Leverre. It was found in his rooms at the Priory. I don't think you'll like what it says. Now, where is this man I need to treat?"

▲▲▲▲▲▲

Betrayal.

Amaury crumpled the note and let it drop from his fingers. Betrayal was a new experience for him—at least, being on the receiving end was. Leverre had always had a troubling stubborn streak and a warped sense of honour. If he hadn't been so good at his job, Amaury would have cut him loose a long time ago.

When Amaury had selected the first recruits to the Order, ability and a sympathetic attitude to what he was trying to create had been his only criteria. The difficulties that arose from conflicts of personality had been the least of his concerns at the time. Now that had come to bite him in the backside.

With Leverre gone, the matter of replacements was pressing, and needed to be prioritised. He briefly considered asking Luther for recommendations, but hated the idea of making rushed appointments. Then he realised he didn't need to look so far afield—there were perfectly suitable men closer to home, already on the royal payroll. They might not have magical talent, but for now, muscle would do. He could replenish the ranks of magisters at a later time.

Amaury knew of a royal requisition official with a creative flair in sourcing what he needed. He'd first come to the Prince Bishop's attention when Amaury was trying to clear out the rot in the Crown's administration service. His initial impulse had been to have the man—Gassot, Amaury thought his name was—beheaded, but something else had come up, and fate had earned the man a reprieve. Now, it seemed, fate would bring him a substantial promotion, if he had the sense to play along. That would be the chancellor taken care of.

For the blood-and-guts work, one name sprang to mind. Amaury knew of at least one village Vachon had put to the sword in order to make a point, and that was the kind of mettle that Amaury reckoned the Order would need in its marshall. He rang the small bell on his desk, summoning his secretary.

"Send for the Clerk of Requisitions, Gassot I think he's called. Also Captain Gustav Vachon. I believe he's in the city at present. I want them both to attend on me as soon as possible."

The secretary nodded and disappeared. Amaury looked to the crumpled ball of paper on his floor and grimaced. If Leverre—whom he had thought of as little more than one of his faithful hunting hounds—could betray him, whom could he trust?

CHAPTER
11

Bravos tended to flock to where the action was, and Gill knew that from the moment word of the initial dragon attacks spread, men of arms would head for the region. As a result, he hoped there would be more fighters in Trelain than might ordinarily be found there. Guillot wanted to head for Venne as soon as possible, so he could not afford to be choosy, but all he really needed was one or two good swordsmen. The rest could be cut loose when better options were available.

The first interested party turned up not long after breakfast, and his initial appearance was enough to get Gill's hopes up from near desperation to the thought that his plan might not be a *complete* disaster.

He was the type of man that could be instantly identifiable as a jobbing banneret—athletic, confident, hungry. In such a man, the first thing Gill always checked was his sword. The leather scabbard was scuffed and worn, but looked like it had been oiled recently, and the hilt of his sword, though elegant in the swirling shape of the complex guard, was of plain, unadorned steel, with a wire grip. It was the weapon of a man interested mainly in function, and such men were always the ones Gill thought most likely to be of value.

The man stopped in the foyer and looked about. Gill raised an expectant hand, ready to hear the bravo's pitch. The man nodded and made his way over.

"My Lord," he said.

"Sit, please," Guillot said.

"I'd prefer not to, if it's all the same. I'd rather wait by the door until you're ready to leave."

Gill frowned, and the man looked puzzled.

"Lord Relau?"

"Ah," Guillot said. "I think you've got the wrong man."

"My apologies. Good day to you, sir."

"And you," Guillot said. "I don't suppose you've any interest in dragon slaying?" he added as an afterthought.

The man let out a laugh, but cut it short when he realised that Guillot was being serious. "Gods, no," he said. "There's plenty of well-paid work to be had that doesn't come with the choice of being well-done or extra crispy." He frowned when he saw Guillot's reaction. "I apologise again—you're that fellow, aren't you? Villerauvais? Congratulations." He clicked his heels and gave a curt nod, the traditional salute bannerets gave to acknowledge a colleague's success. "I can't say I envy you the job, but you seem to have come through it in good trim. I'm afraid I must be going; I've a client to find."

He gave Guillot another nod, and wandered deeper into the inn, leaving Guillot feeling foolish and wondering how much attention killing the dragon was actually going to bring. Had he overestimated? Might the thirst for fame that young swordsmen had once possessed diminished?

Then another man walked into the inn, and Gill let out an audible groan. The newcomer looked equally the type—athletic, tanned skin, confidence bordering on arrogance. He was well dressed, his black hair was pulled back into a ponytail, and he had a finely waxed black moustache. He stood with his thumbs hooked in his sword belt, adopting the casual slouch of a man so confident that he's relaxed to the point of passing out. Guillot's eyes drifted to his sword. The scabbard looked like it was fresh from the tanner's shop, the hilt was filigreed with gold wire, and the pommel contained a large jewel. "Peacock" was the word most often reserved for a man like that. Guillot wondered, if he kept his head down, might the man leave without bothering him?

The fellow looked around, spotted Gill, gave him a nod, and strode over.

"Banneret Didier dal Beausoleil, at your service," he said. "Very pleased to make the acquaintance of the only living dragonslayer."

Guillot forced a smile and gestured to the chair opposite him. Beausoleil smiled and sat.

"What brings you to my table, Banneret Beausoleil?" Gill said.

"I read in the news sheet that you're looking for men to help you deal with some more dragons. Is that correct?"

Gill considered lying for a moment, but couldn't see anything to gain by doing so. "It is. And you're interested in the job?"

"I very much am," Beausoleil said.

Guillot nodded. "Why don't you give me an idea of your background and experience?"

"I'm twelve years out of the Academy. I spent the first three of those on the duelling circuit."

Guillot did his best to look interested. The duelling career went some way to explaining the sword. Professional duellists were all about the image and the show. That didn't mean there weren't some superb swordsmen on the circuit—some of the world's very best made their livings duelling in the arena. It was a place with defined rules, however, and in Guillot's experience, duellists tended to be less prepared to deal with the unexpected, to improvise when things went to crap in the blink of an eye, as was so often the case on the battlefield.

"After that, I spent a few years in private service—first in the retinues of a couple of burgesses in Mirabay and Tarbeaux, then with the Company of the Silver Arrow until it disbanded a few months back. Since then, I've been odd-jobbing here and there. Body-guarding mainly."

He had more varied experience than Guillot had expected. "I've not heard of the Silver Arrow. Who was the principal?"

"Banneret-Captain Garonne de la Maison Noir."

Guillot did his best to stifle a laugh at the ridiculously ostentatious name. It didn't bode well, however. Men who hid behind a fancy, self-appointed name tended to have only that name to trade on, rather than a respected reputation.

"See any action with them?"

"The usual," Beausoleil said.

Guillot remained silent and smiled with expectation.

"Oh, you know, we'd get hired, be seen about the place by the enemy, then terms would be agreed. We'd get paid and move on to the next job. The usual."

Guillot wanted to tell him to take his fancy peacock sword and piss off, but the line of eager volunteers he had expected to form by the door was conspicuously absent. Perhaps adding a few names to his roster would get some momentum going. If nothing else, Beausoleil could distract the beasts while Guillot got down to the real work of killing them.

"Well," Guillot said reluctantly, "I can't offer anything in the way of payment, but the reputation and fame you'll get from this will be priceless."

"That works for me," Beausoleil said.

I reckoned it would, Guillot thought. "It will be dangerous, and no amount of potential glamour or fame can take away from the fact that there are three dragons that need to be dealt with. The last one killed several people who were as well prepared to face it as could be. I know a little more of what to expect now, but the danger will never be diminished."

Beausoleil shrugged with the sangfroid of a man genuinely un-afraid—or very good at appearing so. "To tell the truth, I've felt my blade was a little underutilised the past few years."

It was as good an answer as could be hoped for. "That brings up another problem. Your blade. A regular steel rapier blade won't be of much use against a dragon. Telastrian steel is effective, but I wouldn't expect anyone to have a Telastrian blade."

Beausoleil held up his hands and shook his head.

"A heavy field blade might serve, but I think lances and spears are a better bet. You're comfortable with those?"

"Of course. Four years at the Academy teaches a lot more than just the sword."

The banneret raised his eyebrows in a suggestive way that made Guillot think they might not be referring to the same type of lance. He tried to think of any other questions. He knew everything worth asking about. The things that really mattered could be learned only out on the field.

"Do you have any questions?"

"Of course," Beausoleil said. "How did you do it? The first man in a thousand years to kill a dragon! That really is something."

"Luck, mainly."

Beausoleil laughed. "I'm sure there was far more to it than that."

"There always is, but that's the big part."

"So you'll have me, then?" Beausoleil said.

The man wasn't what he was looking for, but Guillot couldn't think of a single valid reason to refuse.

"Why not? I've no contracts of engagement to be signed. Truth be told, this approach is a new idea. For the time being, a banneret's oath will have to be enough."

"It's always been enough for me in the past."

"Well then," Guillot said. "I hope the gods smile on our ventures together."

▲▲▲▲▲▲

Guillot followed Solène out to the stable yard. He didn't like letting her ride off to Mirabay on her own when she was still so upset, all the more so when she had no idea what awaited her there. She seemed confident that her absence could be easily explained away and that there was nothing to connect her to the fight she and Leverre had with the other Spurriers on the road to Trelain. He did his best to take solace in that, but he knew Amaury—the man had eyes and ears everywhere, and as Gill knew only too well, he never forgave when someone crossed him.

Her horse was saddled and waiting for her, and she accepted a boost into the saddle without complaint.

"You're sure you'll be all right?" Guillot said.

Solène chuckled. "You're starting to sound like an old woman."

He blushed. "It's just that . . . Well, I've lost too many people who were important to me. I don't want to lose another."

She blushed now. "I'll be fine. I promise. At the first hint of trouble, I'll run."

"And come and find me."

She chuckled again. "And I'll come and find you."

"You never know, it might be me needing your help. I'm still not convinced I can do that spell properly."

"We spent half the night going over it. You know the words. You know the intended meaning. It will all work as it's supposed to."

"When I'm done with the dragons, I'll come to Mirabay and find you. If that's all right."

She smiled. "I'd be hurt if you did anything else. You look after yourself, Guillot dal Villerauvais. You're too good a man to die."

There was a moment of silence, then she urged her horse on, and was gone.

He stared after her, and his gaze unfocussed. There was more he should have done. Should have said. They both knew the chances of seeing one another again. Within a few days, it was likely either one or both of them would be dead. It was one of those moments where the welcoming embrace of the bottle called to him like the song of angels. If ever there was a time, surely he could justify it at that moment?

"She's a fine-looking woman. You're together?"

Guillot looked over as Beausoleil walked out of the inn and into the stable yard. "No," he said. "Friends."

Beausoleil nodded. "Never much liked Trelain," he said. "Very much looking forward to getting on our way."

"I suspect most able-bodied swordsmen with a death wish will bypass Trelain and head straight for Venne, now that word of the attacks is out," Guillot said. "If we need to, I'm sure we can find more men on the road."

"Whatever you think, Captain."

Gill fixed him with an ironic stare. It had been a long time since anyone had called him captain, and he wasn't sure how he felt about it. He couldn't help but feel something of a fraud, considering how few volunteers he'd managed to attract. He looked up at the sun; the day had gotten away from him, and there seemed little point in setting off now—they'd make most of the journey in darkness. Leaving in the morning would change nothing.

"Let's aim to set off before dawn. If we press hard, we should make Venne by nightfall."

"I'll be ready."

Beausoleil headed back into the inn, leaving Gill standing alone, considering the magnitude of what lay ahead.

"The taxidermist collected it."

Shaking the funk from his head, Guillot turned to see the stable boy standing next to a pile of hay, pitchfork in his hands. "Pardon me?"

"The head. The taxidermist collected it. I sent for him as you asked."

Gill looked at where the head had been, only now noticing its absence. "Of course. Thank you." He reached to his purse for a coin.

"I'd rather a favour than a coin," the lad said.

Guillot raised an eyebrow and shrugged. He must have made a fortune, charging a penny per person for a look at the dragon's head. "Name it."

"You're going with those peasants to kill their dragons?"

"It would seem so."

"Take me with you."

Guillot barked out a laugh. "Come again?"

"Take me with you. As your squire."

"You've lost your wits, lad," Guillot said. "You saw the beast's head. You know what we're up against. It's not all Andalon, Valdamar, shining armour, and heroic deeds. I can think of a lot of things I'd rather do."

The boy nodded to a pile of manure in the corner of the yard. "You can shovel that lot, if you like. Soon as I'm done with the hay, I have to. And tomorrow, after I wake up, I'll shovel more hay, then more manure. Then one day, I won't wake up. Just like my da. I'd rather see a real live dragon, and take my chances. If I can live through that, maybe the Academy will take me on."

"You're better off here, lad. I promise you."

"You've not got the first clue what it's like here. I can decide for myself where I'm better off. That's anywhere but here."

Gill studied the boy's face, his resolute look of determination and hope. He thought about how the lad had kept the crowds away from the dragon's head.

"I've enough coin saved from work and showing people the head to buy travelling provisions and a pony. I won't be a burden on your purse. All I ask is you show me a few things, and if we get through it all, you write me a letter for the Academy."

In the darkest recess of his mind, Guillot could still hear the bottle calling to him. He shut it out. "We leave before dawn. If you're not here and ready, we go without you."

The boy was out of the yard before his pitchfork had hit the ground.

CHAPTER
12

S olène had been alone for much of the last ten years, but when she rode out of the Black Drake's stable yard, she felt painfully lonely. Since being forced to flee her home and her family, she hadn't relied on anyone, nor cared about anyone. It was obvious to her that this had changed without her awareness. The thought that she was abandoning Gill to his death sent such a chill through her that she considered turning her horse around.

The truth of it was that she knew that facing three dragons would push her body too far, and kill her. That worry was secondary to her fear of killing someone else, however. It seemed the choices in her life were always tough. Run away from everything she knew and loved, or face the execution pyre as a witch. Abandon the first decent person she had met since leaving home, or risk killing herself and others around her. She knew Guillot could take care of himself, and in teaching him how to use the Cup, she had given him most of the tools she would have brought with her. Still, she could not shake the feeling that she had let him down.

She urged the horse to a brisk pace. The roads of Mirabaya were not safe for a single rider more than a few hours beyond the larger towns, and all the more so for a woman travelling alone. There would be a terrible irony in burning herself out—unintentionally draining her entire internal reservoir of magical energy—fighting off highwaymen on the way to learning how to rein in her power.

She was certain there were magical ways she could speed her journey, or shroud her passing, but since she didn't know how to create either of those effects, the danger of creating something far less desirable was ever-present.

Assuming they hadn't connected her disappearance to Leverre's, she would have to explain her absence from Mirabay. Hopefully he'd done as he'd promised and left a note behind, explaining his actions and taking all responsibility on himself.

Solène concentrated on creating a story to excuse her actions. Returning home because of a family bereavement seemed like the easiest excuse, but she wasn't sure it was plausible. How would she have heard the news? By design, no one from Bastelle knew where she was. Considering why she had left, it didn't seem likely that going back, no matter what the reason, would ever be a good idea. No, that wouldn't pass scrutiny. Both the Prince Bishop and the officers at the Priory knew too much about her background to believe such a tale.

Still, try as she might, she couldn't come up with anything better. There was simply no reason for her to leave the city. She had no friends, no family, no responsibilities. Bastelle was her only connection to the outside world. Solène chewed the idea over as she rode. There was little in the way of interesting scenery to distract her. The countryside was mainly forest, grassland, or farms. The road was good for the most part, as the weather had been dry, so the horse was able to take care of the navigation with only the most minor involvement on her part.

It occurred to her that she might not need a *good* reason to go back to Bastelle. A childhood home—and a family—that she'd run away from for fear of being burned at the stake was always going to provoke illogical, emotional responses. Bastelle was only a day or two east from where the dragon Guillot had killed had been attacking. She could claim she needed to see the place, the people, to confirm to herself that they were alive and well. Of course, there was the possibility that the town *had* been destroyed during the dragon's rampage. That seemed unlikely—word of it would surely have gotten as far as Trelain—but the possibility couldn't be dismissed. She supposed she could claim the destruction had happened after her visit, and call on her dramatic skills in a showy display of grief to hide her lie, and potentially save her life.

How much simpler it would all have been if Arnoul had left her alone, and she had been able to stay at the bakery in Trelain. There was a time, back in Bastelle, when she had fed her imagination with the books from the village's church library. Back then, the idea of a simple life—the only life that everyone around her seemed to be able to comprehend—had filled her with dread. The books had told tales of cities filled with great lords and ladies, universities and libraries larger than the village, places where people from all over the world met, mixed, and exchanged news and ideas from places she had never even heard of. She had been to those cities and libraries now, but wished for that naive enthusiasm again, when she had thought of the world as a place of wonder and excitement.

A visit back to her hometown it was, then. While the story had flaws, most of them could be explained away. She continued to mull it over as she rode, growing comfortable with the tale, making it part of herself, almost coming to believe it.

▲▲▲▲▲

"I'd say it could eat you whole," Beausoleil said.

"Leave him alone," Guillot said. They trotted along the road in silence for a moment before he felt the urge to justify himself. "I tried to talk him out of it. He wanted to come anyway. Takes more guts than most have."

"Or a measure less common sense," Beausoleil said. "What's his name, anyway?"

Guillot realised he didn't know. "Lad" had served well enough up to that point. He looked at the youth, who, true to his word, had bought a pony and travelling kit, and managed to wash off some of the dirt and smell of the stable, which was a welcome change.

"Val," the youngster said.

"Like Valentin?" Beausoleil said.

"No," the boy said sullenly.

Beausoleil had been teasing Guillot's new "squire" since they'd left Trelain, and it was starting to get on Gill's nerves. It was the type of banter and ribaldry that Academy students typically indulged in, particularly those who felt they had something to prove. Some never quite grew out of the behaviour, and it seemed Beausoleil was one of those. For someone unaccustomed to it, like the stable boy, Gill could see how the treatment might feel grating.

"What, then?" Guillot said, curious now himself.

"Valdamar."

Beausoleil let out a guffaw, and Guillot cringed.

"Valdamar?" Beausoleil said. "Big shoes to fill, those."

"Not so big as you might think," Guillot said. The boot plates from Valdamar's armour were in his saddlebags, and they fit him almost perfectly.

Beausoleil gave him a curious look.

"Never mind," Guillot said.

"It strikes me that we're travelling a little light," Beausoleil said, switching his attention from the former stable boy to the leader of their little expedition.

"We'll have lances and spears made in Venne. Any carpenter or pole turner will be able to make up what we need. No point in carrying them all the way there. I have Telastrian spearpoints to fit on them so they'll be effective against the dragons."

"Telastrian spearpoints?" Beausoleil said.

Gill shrugged. He had taken them from the chamber under his ruined manor before killing the first dragon, but there was no reason to reveal that. "The Chevaliers had some old dragon-hunting equipment left. I took what I thought might be useful."

Beausoleil nodded, looking impressed. "I've always wanted a Telastrian blade. To think someone wasted the steel on spearheads."

"Necessity, I imagine," Gill said. "They proved handy last time. It wouldn't hurt to have some more hands to put them in, though."

"You think we'll be able to find more men there?"

"I think so," Guillot said. They had seen a number of riders on the road who were making all speed in the direction of Venne. Only one type of man rode toward danger, so Gill reckoned there would be at least a few bannerets there interested in joining him.

"I'd be happier if we had some backup people," Beausoleil said.

"There are only so many lances young Valdamar here will be able to carry." He gave a mischievous smile. "I'm sure the name is burden enough already. But enough of that. I've been wondering, how does one actually go about killing a dragon? Charge in, lance leading the way, close your eyes and pray it strikes true?"

Guillot shrugged. "Didn't get to try that, as far as I can recall. Admittedly, the memory is a bit hazy. Got my bell rung a couple of times that day. Telastrian steel will get through its hide. Can't say the same for regular steel. Might work, but I didn't have any luck. Anyway, if we're there to protect the town, the least they can do is lend us a hand with the details. To answer your question: bait them out, then kill them as fast as we can, however we can."

He thought it judicious to keep the fact that he might be able to track them by unconventional means to himself for the time being. "My Telastrian blade and the spearheads are the best assets we have, but against a younger dragon, regular steel might work too. There's only one way we'll find that out." Gill chewed his lip as he wondered how much to reveal. As if it knew his thoughts, he became aware of the weight of the Cup in the purse on his hip.

Beausoleil nodded thoughtfully, as though he had enough information on the matter to properly consider it.

"There're other things, too," Guillot said, "but we can discuss them later. We need to push on. I want to get to Venne before dark."

CHAPTER
13

The sun had dipped below the horizon by the time they reached Venne, but there was still enough dusky light to take the village in. It looked much like any other village in the rural provinces of Mirabaya—a small number of buildings clustered around a church steeple. It was larger than Villerauvais had been, but was still a long way from being called a town. The countryside surrounding it was lush green pasture, with hills rolling gently toward the mountains that dominated the horizon to the south.

As he stared at the countless peaks where dragons came from, Guillot wondered if this was the new normal, if the time of dragons had returned, if life in these parts would always be lived in the shadow of the beasts. Was this how he was to spend the rest of his life? Hunting and killing them, until one day—perhaps sooner than he might like—when he was a little too careless, or a little too slow, one of them killed him?

"Not much to look at, is it?" Beausoleil said.

"What were you expecting?" Guillot said.

Beausoleil shook his head. "Never been in this part of the country before. Wasn't sure. It's very green here. Beausoleil's not a whole lot farther south. Doesn't look anything like this, though."

"Fields of sun-drenched vines and lavender stretching down to an azure sea?"

"Pretty much."

"It rains a lot here. Something to do with the mountains, I expect. Good land for cattle, though. And game."

"Plenty of food for a hungry dragon. Makes you wonder why they bother with people."

"Maybe they like the taste?" Val said.

Gill cast him a look and shivered. He preferred to think of the dragons doing what they did because they were mindless beasts that acted on instinct. That they might actively seek out human flesh was a chilling thought.

"Perhaps they don't see us any differently to cattle," Gill said, realising he didn't like that idea any more than Val's.

"I suppose it doesn't matter," Beausoleil said. "It's simply a bigger and more dangerous type of beast that needs killing. And we're the men to do it, eh?" He reached out and gave Val a slap on the back, eliciting an uncomfortable smile from the lad.

"Let's get into town and see about some supper," Guillot said. "My backside's killing me and if I get any hungrier, it'll be me eating the dragons."

Towns like Venne tended to be sleepy places. Most of the villagers would spend the day working in the fields; the markets and taverns came alive only later, when the toil on the land was finished. Visitors were infrequent, and tended to be welcomed with a mixture of curiosity and suspicion. This far from centres of power, bandits were common, and a new arrival was as likely a man intent on theft as an honest traveller with news from other parts.

It came as a surprise, then, to find that Venne was a bustling hive of activity. The men they had seen on the road were only the tip of the blade. Every swordsman in the south of Mirabaya must have been there. Before she left Trelain, Edine, the village's mayor, had given Gill the name and location of the tavern where their arrival would be expected. Seeing how busy the village was, he hoped that there would still be rooms held for them. Otherwise they'd be relying on campaign tents and bedrolls—not so great an inconvenience so long as the weather held, but they were moving into the autumn now. Guillot and the others dismounted and led their horses along the narrow lanes into the town, at times having to push past groups of men who gave them the inquiring looks of those measuring their competition.

The tavern was easy to find, occupying one side of the small village square. There was no attached stable yard, nor anyone to take their horses. With no alternative, and feeling somewhat guilty, he shrugged and handed his reins to Val. Beausoleil followed suit.

"Watch the horses until we find out what's what," Guillot said.

The lad took the reins with eagerness. Gill had expected to be greeted with sullen disappointment at being left out of things, but the boy's desire to please, to act as Guillot's squire, made Gill feel doubly guilty.

"Shall we?" he said to Beausoleil.

Beausoleil nodded. He seemed to have regained some of the swagger he had displayed earlier, before the sight of Venne and the significance of the gathering of fighting men had silenced him for a time. Inside, they were greeted by even more curious looks. The taproom was small, but filled to capacity. If even one of the men there was a local, Gill would have been surprised. He wondered how the villagers were responding to the glut of arrivals, and how long it would be before saviours came to be regarded as an unwelcome inconvenience.

They forced their way through to the bar, where a delighted-looking keeper was filling an ale mug from a tapped barrel with one hand, while pouring a cup of wine with the other. Gill cleared his throat to gain attention, then realised that even he hadn't been able to hear it over the noise of boisterous conversation. The room was filled with men trying to convince one another of how brave they were, and that was never done in hushed tones.

"Barkeep!" Gill said. He had to repeat himself before getting a response. As soon as two more cups and one more mug were filled, delivered, and paid for, the barkeeper made his way over.

"The food is finished, but we've ale and wine enough to keep you happy," he said.

"When did all this lot get here?" Guillot said.

"Started arriving before dawn. Been coming in all day. Word is out. We've dragons here, as I'm sure you know. Everyone wants to claim one, just like Guillot the Dragonslayer."

Guillot's stomach turned over at the moniker, but he supposed it was only to be expected. At least it rolled off the tongue a little easier than Lord Villerauvais the Dragonslayer.

"Where have you come from?" the barkeeper said.

"I'm looking for Edine," Guillot said, choosing to ignore the question. "Do you know where I can find her?"

"Across the square, in the mayor's house. She's a mite busy, mind. Trying to organise all this lot. Find out who everyone is, what they can do. What they'll want in return. She's told me to direct you all to her, but last time I checked the queue, you'd be as well off staying here awhile." He waved a wine bottle before Guillot. "What can I get you?"

"A room," Guillot said, finding the noise and the crowd increasingly oppressive.

The barkeeper barked out a laugh, but Guillot cut him short.

"I think Edine asked you to hold rooms for us," he said. "I'm Gill . . . the, um, well, she asked me to come to help with the dragon."

The barkeeper's eyes widened. "You should let her know you're here right away. I have two rooms for you. They're not much, my Lord. They're usually storerooms, but that's all that's left."

"I'm sure they'll serve admirably," Guillot said, trying his best to put the man at ease, and get out of the taproom as quickly as possible.

It was already too late. One or two of the swordsmen closest to Gill had obviously been eavesdropping. A wave of silence, followed by murmuring, spread through the gathering as everyone strained to get a view of the heroic dragonslayer. Beausoleil lapped up the attention. Every jobbing banneret wonders, at some point, what it would be like to be a famed warrior. Pretty much every swordsman who steps into the duelling arena dreams of it. Even for Gill, the appeal of recognition from one's peers, particularly after so long in the doldrums, was hard to deny.

"I've left my squire outside with the horses and baggage," Guillot said. "Perhaps you could help him have them all squared away, and I'll pay a call on Edine. Right across the square, you say?"

The barkeeper was still staring at him wide-eyed. "Straight out the door and keep going. Can't miss it."

Guillot gave him a nod of thanks. Assuming that Beausoleil had been paying attention, Gill made for the door, shouldering his way through the crowd until he was back out in the evening air. He took a deep breath and let out a sigh. True to the barkeep's word, there was a queue of men outside the building opposite, leaning casually on the pommels of the swords at their waists in the almost weightless fashion that all Academy students manage to perfect no later than their second term. Guillot tipped the brim of his hat as he passed; the stares he earned held more outrage than curiosity. Some had clearly been waiting far longer than they thought their reputations deserved, and he wondered if he would make it into the mayor's house without being challenged for queue jumping.

Happily, it seemed that no one wanted to blot their reputation before even catching sight of a dragon, and all swords remained sheathed. The queue continued inside, stopping at an old wooden table, behind which Edine—who, along with her party, had left Trelain well before Gill had—sat, marking a ledger with a wooden-handled copper-nib pen. He suspected he wasn't the only potential dragonslayer she had called on when in Trelain, and he couldn't deny that that bruised his ego.

This time, clearing his throat had the desired effect. Edine looked up and smiled.

"Bannerets," she said, "if you wouldn't mind waiting on me a moment in the square outside, I've some urgent business to deal with."

He waited until the small, whitewashed room cleared before speaking. "I wasn't expecting to see so many people."

"Neither was I," she said, "but it seems everyone wants to slay a dragon. You're still the only man to prove he can actually do it, though."

She seemed different here. While in Trelain she had come seeking aid, now she seemed calm and in control, mistress of her domain.

"Any idea of how many there are?"

"Forty-seven so far, and that's just today."

"How will you feed them all?"

"Hopefully they won't need to be here too long. Hopefully they keep paying while they are. I've heard stories of how soldiers behave when they're broke and hungry. We've never had to deal with anything like that here, and I have to admit I'm worried. Gaufre at the tavern thinks it's wonderful, as does everyone else who can make a few pennies from it, but so many armed men? How would we stop them taking what they want? It might not be dragons I need you to protect us from after all."

"Are they looking for payment?"

"No, the promise of glory seems to be enough for them, but if they're to be given food and drink while they're here, I've made it clear they all have to sign the ledger. If there's trouble, I can see the duke's steward gets the names. I'm not sure if it will mean anything, but it's all I can do."

"I'd try not to worry about it," Guillot said. "Most of these men are bannerets. We're not pure as the driven snow—far from it—but most of us hold our personal honour high and won't do anything to jeopardise it. They'll keep the ones who don't in line."

"I hope so. Them being here might make your job a little easier, though."

Or harder, Guillot thought. "Perhaps. If I see one or two that look useful, I might ask if they want to sign on with me. A few more blades couldn't hurt. Have they given you any idea of what they have planned?"

"I think just getting here was as much thought as any of them have given it."

They're not the only ones, Guillot thought. "I suppose it's new to us all. Have there been any more attacks since we last spoke?"

She nodded. "One more, shortly after we left for Trelain. Only cattle, but the farmer got the fright of his life."

Gill nodded. Seeing her keeping notes had made him curious, so he asked, "Is there a school here?"

"No," Edine said, shaking her head. "I'm not from Venne originally. The duke sends administrators to all his towns and villages to make sure things run smoothly. It takes the pressure off him and allows him to spend his time in Mirabay. The lords and seigneurs aren't always happy about it, but they learn to live with it. Everyone does better when things are run properly."

"That's enlightened of him. I didn't think he had much interest in anything outside the ballrooms and cardrooms of Mirabay."

She smiled. "A well-run duchy means more tax revenue for the duke. Which means he can stay in Mirabay, and spend it."

"Ah, yes, that makes sense," Guillot said. "It's too late for there to be any use in riding out for a look around this evening, but I wonder if someone could show us where the attacks happened, first thing in the morning?"

"Of course. I'll have someone meet you at the tavern at dawn. Once you're done with that, I was hoping you'd pay a visit to the seigneur at his manor house. It's not far. He isn't much involved in what goes on in the village, and hasn't shown any sign of doing anything about our problem, but it's best to let him know what's happening."

"After I get a look at the area," Guillot said firmly. If he was going to hunt dragons, he wanted to have a good sense of the lay of the land.

"We've been caught behind the news once already, your Highness," Amaury said. "I think I managed to get on top of it, but we can't expect to get that lucky every time. We need to announce the Order now, before any more news arrives, and we lose the ability to turn events to our benefit, and keep public opinion on our side."

The king looked pensive and scratched his beard in that faux-thoughtful fashion that was coming to irritate Amaury so much he had to fight the temptation to walk across the office and slap the king across the face.

"No," Boudain finally said. "The time's not right. We've yet to adequately deal with the Intelligenciers."

"I've been clipping their wings for months now," Amaury said, his irritation piqued once more. "They are not an issue. Their ranks are depleted and they're under-resourced. Even with the losses the Order has suffered, the Intelligenciers no longer pose any real threat."

"You forget the international nature of the Intelligenciers, your Grace," the king said. "They can call on their brethren the world over, and under the threat of magic, I believe national rivalry will be set aside, and they will answer."

How dare you try to school me, you arrogant little shit. Amaury smiled. "Ostia, Estranza, my spies tell me the King of Humberland has people experimenting with magic in secret. The Intelligenciers the world over have their own problems to deal with. By the time they turn their attention here, in the unlikely event they ever do, there won't be anything they can do to stop us. In any event, I have something in place to deal with them when the time co—"

"The Intelligenciers are reliable servants of the Crown, even if they claim to answer to a higher calling. I won't have them killed in the streets."

"A rabid dog might once have been your most faithful hunting hound. That doesn't mean it's not necessary to put it down."

The king frowned. "You have my answer. There are bigger concerns than just public opinion in Mirabay. A crusade against Mirabay is the last thing we need."

"That's a fantastical notion, your—"

"You. Have. My. Answer." The king's expression softened. "In principle I agree with you, but one must be cautious in overturning a thousand years of law and tradition. The time is near, but not quite at hand. You went ahead without notifying me this time. Do not do so again. I want to know before you do anything. Using the privy is the only decision you are to make without notifying me in advance. Understood?"

Amaury smiled, quelling the urge to do murder.

CHAPTER

14

Guillot could remember being brought out to the site of a recent battle in the entourage of a general when he was still a fresh adjutant. The man had surveyed the field, ravaged in the way only violence can, and littered with bodies. The general had maintained an expression of distant interest, taking in all that he was being told, and all that he could see. At the time, nothing had struck Guillot as unusual about the scene. The man was simply another general who held the lives of his men cheaply.

Later that night, while enjoying a few bottles of wine in the camp with some of the other junior officers, Guillot learned that the reason the general had asked to see the field—the site of a battle he had not commanded—was because three of his sons had been in one of the infantry regiments that had been cut to pieces. All three of them had been lying dead on the ground that afternoon as the general surveyed the devastation, no doubt flicking his gaze from body to body, both hoping to see, and terrified of seeing, a familiar face.

The other officer had continued, saying that the general had returned to his tent and wept as he wrote a letter to the boys' mother, telling her that he would not be bringing any of their sons home with him. It was grit, and knowing the full story, Gill had remained moved by it for the rest of his life.

As one of the farmhands led Guillot, Beausoleil, and Val from site to site, clearly terrified to be visiting the locations of the recent dragon attacks, Gill did his best to maintain the general's sangfroid. From time to time, he would jump down from his horse and inspect the scorch marks on the ground, or kneel next to a talon print and prod it with a twig as though it was revealing something important to him. It was all for show, but he knew that giving people confidence was as much a part of his job as killing the dragons. Even if the people were killed, there was nothing worse than living out your last days in terror. At least if he did his best, he could give them hope.

There were titbits to be gleaned from what was left behind. The prints on the ground definitely indicated that these beasts were smaller than the one he had already dealt with, but not by much. They grew fast. At the location of the most recent attack, they found some remains of the dragons' last meal. They were so mangled, and there was so little left, Gill couldn't tell if they were human or animal. Either way, he didn't think anyone would be eager to come out and collect them for burial.

"Whose farm is this?" Gill asked their guide.

"Louis's. He came down to the village when the attacks started. That isn't him."

"That's something, at least," Gill said. He didn't know what fate awaited Louis now that his entire herd had been slaughtered. For a peasant farmer, loss of their herd might be as bad an injury as death.

"What do you think?" Beausoleil said, speaking for the first time that morning.

Gill gave him a solemn look. "I think there was a dragon here a while ago."

Val let out a laugh, and Beausoleil cast him a filthy look.

"What I think," Gill said, "is that whichever dragon left this print is smaller than the last one I fought, and that's a good thing. That there are two more of about the same size, and that they seem to enjoy each other's company, is a very bad thing."

"You think we'll be able to manage?" Beausoleil asked.

Gill shrugged. "I don't see why not. Particularly if we're able to pick up another blade or two from the assemblage in the village. If we can separate the beasts, I'd rate our chances as pretty good. I think we should head back and set the village carpenter and smith to work. I have to ride out with Edine to speak with the local seigneur, so I'll leave that to you."

He had taken the precaution of using the Cup that morning, before leaving his room at the tavern. He wasn't ready to reveal it yet, and eased a guilty conscience that he was protecting himself and not them with the thought that if they were attacked, he could hold the beast off while they retreated back to the village. He hadn't had any sense that there was a dragon close by, but he knew that didn't necessarily mean there wasn't one—he still wasn't fully sure of everything the Cup did, what was real, and what he'd imagined. He looked toward the mountains, seeing mist starting to descend from them. Such fogs had been common in Villerauvais at the same time of year. Anyone who got caught in it would be wet, cold, and miserable in a few minutes.

The fire in the tavern's taproom was a very welcoming prospect by comparison, and he needed some time to consider the task they had ahead of them. He turned to their farmhand guide. "I think we've seen enough. We can return now."

▲▲▲▲▲▲

The city looked much as it had when she left. Though a lot had changed for her, a great city was almost timeless in the way it slowly evolved, oblivious of the toils of those who lived within its walls. Centred on an island in the middle of the River Vosges, it spilled over the isle's confines and spread out over both the north and south banks. Mirabay was a splendour of white limestone and slate roofs, all observed silently by the palace with its cone-topped towers and streaming banners, on the high ground of the south bank.

Solène nervously approached the gate, wondering if the guards would be looking for her. A stream of people were passing in and out, as they had been the first time she came to the city. There was no sign of the panic Guillot had feared would spread with word of the dragon.

She urged her horse on. As she grew closer, Solène wondered if she'd overestimated her importance, and if all her concerns were nothing more than narcissistic paranoia. The guards made no attempt to stop her—they barely even gave her a second glance.

The next test would be at the Priory. If they knew she had been with Leverre and taken part in the killing of other members of the Order, they would hardly expect her to return. They would recognise her on sight, though, and things could go badly wrong if they tried to arrest her. Did she have it in her to defend herself if she had to? She couldn't answer that. She thought about hiding somewhere and sending word to Seneschal dal Drezony, who she felt certain would help her.

She shook her head. She had no reason to doubt that Leverre had left a letter behind. The story of her journey home was plausible enough, especially if dressed up in sentiment and irrational emotion.

The Priory was in the city's northern ward, which meant having to pass the whole way through, crossing the bridges that linked the isle with the two banks. There were few other points at which to get over to the north bank, one of the reasons Mirabay was situated where it was. Solène took her time, trying to behave as just another citizen going about the day's business. A bill posted on a wall caught her attention when she neared one of the bridges to the island. In bold lettering were the words DRAGON SLAIN.

She went over and scanned the short notice, which stated that the beast had been killed by a team sent on the king's behalf. It assured the people that the land was safe and that there would be a more detailed announcement from the palace in due course. There were no details, no mention of anything that was actually of interest to Solène. She wondered how much the king and Prince Bishop actually knew.

With nothing further to be gleaned from the notice, she continued on her way, more relaxed now that she'd spent some time in the city without any problems. It didn't take her long to pass through the heart of the city to the north bank. From there, the building density decreased until she reached the walled compound occupied by the Order. Once she went inside, there was no turning back. She took a deep breath and rang the bell to notify the gatehouse.

It took a moment for the door to open, revealing a young novice. Solène drew back her travelling cloak to reveal her initiate's robe, and he stepped back to let her in. She headed straight for dal Drezony's office. Despite her misgivings as to what the Prince Bishop really intended for the Order, Solène liked the Priory. In bustling, hectic Mirabay, it was a serene place where calm and contemplation ruled, barring the occasional explosion when magical experimentation went too far.

Committed to her path, she knocked on dal Drezony's door.

The seneschal opened it a moment later, not looking at all well. Solène frowned. "Is everything all right?"

"Solène?" dal Drezony said, ignoring her question. "I was worried. Where have you been?"

Solène shrugged. "It's a long story. I went back to Bastelle. It's near the dragon attacks. I had to see for myself if everyone was all right."

Dal Drezony frowned for a moment, then relaxed. "Come in, come in. You know how dangerous that was, don't you?"

"Yes. No one saw me. I didn't go close enough. Just to a nearby hill where I could get a good look. I don't know why. I felt like I needed to, is all."

"It's normal to still feel a tie to the place. Maybe one day, you'll be able to go back in safety. Attitudes might be different in the future."

Solène let out a sad laugh that she did not have to feign. "In a place like Bastelle? It takes centuries for them to change their outlooks."

"I suppose so."

"I wanted to come and apologise for not letting you know I was going. It was a last-minute thing. I was already on the road before I realised what I was doing."

"I would have appreciated it," dal Drezony said. "But that can't be helped now. All sorts of things have happened while you were gone. I was beginning to think you might have been caught up in them."

Solène gave her as curious a look as she could muster. "Really? What?"

Dal Drezony studied her for a moment. "It seems Commander Leverre had something of a crisis of conscience and refused the Prince Bishop's orders. There was a fight between him and some other members of the Order. He didn't survive."

Solène let her mouth drop open. "I'm sorry to hear that. I didn't know him well, but he seemed like a principled man."

"He was. Rough around the edges, but he knew right from wrong. The Order will feel his loss badly. His replacement is far from ideal." She let out a long, tired sigh. "As I said, things have been . . . difficult here over the past few days. If there's nothing else?"

"Actually, there is," Solène said. "I had to use some magic on the road. A highwayman. It nearly killed me."

Dal Drezony nodded slowly.

Fearing she had raised dal Drezony's suspicions, Solène continued quickly, drawing on her experiences when travelling with Gill and dal Sason. "His name was Captain Fernand. Have you heard of him?"

Dal Drezony frowned. "Should I have?"

Solène let out a nervous laugh. "He seemed to think he was famous. It doesn't matter. All that matters is I still can't control my magic. I didn't mean to kill him. It was horrible. I feel like I have access to so much raw power, but no way to restrict its flow. Whenever I use it, it's like opening a flood barrier. All or nothing."

"That's what always worried me, but the Prince Bishop wasn't interested in my concerns. Your affinity to the Fount is so strong, the levels of control you need are far beyond anything we've had to develop here. The things we can teach you simply aren't strong enough."

"What am I going to do?"

"We'll work together on it. Until we have this problem solved, I'm not going to allow the Prince Bishop to use you for anything else."

"About the Prince Bishop. Is he going to be angry with me for disappearing like that?"

"He's been so busy, I suspect he's barely noticed. But your story is a good one," dal Drezony said with a knowing look. "If we stick to that, everything should be all right."

Solène squirmed in her seat, but dal Drezony went on.

"I'm sure you must be tired from your journey. Eat, rest, and we'll start first thing in the morning."

CHAPTER
15

The archive beneath the cathedral had become something of a sanctuary for Amaury. There was a time when he had been able to find peace staring out of his office window into the tranquil garden beneath, but that had quickly become a tool to spy on aristocratic misbehaviour. Now the ancient library was his preferred place to find peace. The king's behaviour had so incensed him that Amaury had decided to give himself some extra time in the archive, as both a treat and an opportunity to clear his head and consider his plans.

His long disappearances undoubtedly added to his ephemeral mystery, and by corollary, to the fear he could elicit. If people didn't know where he was or what he was doing, that might mean *he* was watching *them,* that he knew what they were doing.

It was only down in that cool, dry cavern of a room that he felt at ease. Truly alone, with no one watching him. Not only was he away from prying, plotting eyes, he was surrounded by a wealth of knowledge. Gleaning that knowledge could be tedious, however. His comprehension of old Imperial was ever-improving, but to complicate matters, the old mages often wrote in codes. His basic magical skill helped a little there, but it was no more than a droplet of oil on a rusty gear. One book could take him days, sometimes weeks, to decipher.

He had hoped Solène would be able to speed things up in that regard, but she seemed to have disappeared. He knew dal Drezony was deliberately keeping her away from him, and probably all the more so after what he had forced dal Drezony to do to Barnot. There could be no doubt in dal Drezony's mind now that everybody was a means to an end for the Prince Bishop.

With the Cup so close to being in his grasp, Amaury was determined to find out anything he could about how best to use it. Dal Drezony was trying to protect Solène for a reason—magic could be incredibly dangerous for the user. After all his efforts to get the Cup, the last thing he wanted was to kill himself the first time he tried using it.

He had discovered the Cup through reading about the first mage, Amatus, so that was where he now turned his attention once more.

He had long thought of himself as similar to Amatus. They both sought to bring refined, controlled magic into a world that knew little of it. There were lessons to be learned from a man who had achieved so much; and irony in the fact that if Amaury was successful, both men would have created their legacy by using the same ancient little object.

It was rare to find a book devoted to Amatus. He disappeared from the historical record late in the reign of the first emperor, before the College of Mages had grown large enough to devote armies of scribes to coding and recording everything of importance. Even the book Amaury held had likely been created decades or centuries after the first mage had disappeared, and likely was only a slightly less polished version of the myth than those which followed it.

Every story of Amatus spent a great deal of time talking about his humble origins and how his natural intelligence set him apart from others, but Amaury wasn't interested in any of that. At some point in his youth, Amatus set off to learn more of the world. When he returned, he could wield incredible magical power. He used his abilities to help build an empire that consisted of all the nations around the Middle Sea. Despite that, he had never taken power for himself. At first Amaury had struggled to understand that, but now realised that Amatus, like Amaury himself, must have chosen to exercise his power from the shadows.

Amatus's travels were what interested Amaury—the period during which he had encountered the Cup. Where had Amatus found it? How had he learned to use it? That was the knowledge Amaury hungered for. He'd never found more than tantalising hints.

He skimmed through the pages, pausing every so often to decipher a few lines to gauge where he was in the story. He started to grow frustrated. It seemed the writer was interested only in the years Amatus spent scratching in the dirt in the fishing village that would later become half of the great Imperial capital of Vellin-Ilora. He flipped pages with increasing speed and diminishing patience until a word caught his eye.

Mira.

He went back a few lines and started to read more carefully. The text said that Amatus travelled west across the sea to the land of Mira, where he spent time studying with a group called the "enlightened" at their ancient temple. Amaury's skin tingled with excitement. Mirabaya had been known as "Mirabensis" when it was an Imperial province. Might it have been known as "Mira" before that? There was nowhere else he knew of with so similar a name, and it lay in the right direction from Vellin-Ilora. This was purely speculation on his part, but it was hard not to get excited by the thought that magic had started in this very land, perhaps not far from where he now sat. What if it was *exactly* where he now sat, and that was why the College of Mages chose that site for their library in Mirabensis?

He was fit to burst when he read the next few lines:

"Sadly, no trace of the Temple of the Enlightened was found when the Empire laid claim to this ancient land and named it the Province of Mirabensis."

His mind raced with possibility. The irony of the Cup being found here, taken across the sea, then brought "home" only to be lost struck him hard. That the discovery of magic had been here in Mirabay sent his head into such a spin that it took him several moments to compose himself.

He knew he had too little to go on, so he took a deep breath and continued to read. There wasn't much left in the book, and Amaury feared that this hint about the "enlightened" would be all he got. Did they still exist? Might he be able to learn from them? Or would they be a threat?

His heart sank as he read. The writer clearly didn't know much of what went on, other than that Amatus gained his power at the temple and became a powerful mage, possessing a cup that allowed him to guide others to the same level of magical potency. On the final page, almost as a postscript, there was one more morsel that served only to whet Amaury's appetite, rather than satiate it.

"Later in his life, Amatus returned to the temple in the land of Mira to take his place among the enlightened. He was never seen again, but his legacy endures."

He had something new to search for—the Temple of the Enlightened. It might lead him to other fragments of knowledge, that would allow him to put the entire picture back together. He sighed. How would he find it? Where would he start?

The world represented a great dichotomy, Pharadon thought, as he allowed warm updrafts to lift him in a long, lazy glide. In one respect, it was timeless—mountains, oceans, forests, and lakes. Changing, but remaining the same. In another, it had altered beyond all recognition. None of the marks of man nor dragon that he had expected to see were present. Everything was different. Even to his old soul, witness to so much, this was unsettling.

He could smell all sorts of things on the air, and knew that among his kind, he was not alone. The scents were unfamiliar, fresh and youthful, and he was certain they represented dragons he did not know. While that was something he would investigate soon, there was a stronger smell that he could not ignore—a familiar one that filled his heart with a mixture of joy and concern. It was the scent of his old rival, and older friend. Alpheratz.

He followed his nose, the route as clear to him as a forest game trail. The direction in which it led surprised him—toward humankind. Alpheratz had never been humanity's greatest fan. He had always refused to take on human form, and Pharadon thought it unlikely he'd have changed his mind about that—an old dragon tends to be quite set in its ways. He took another great breath and wondered what had drawn him to a place filled with creatures he held in utter contempt.

Pharadon could not smell any other dragons he knew, nor had he seen a trace of any of them in the short time he had been awake. While the wars had distressed him to the point of self-imposed exile, he had enjoyed the company of many humans over the years, and had travelled extensively through their realm. Music, art, literature, architecture—they excelled at all, and had they confined themselves to these things, how much better a place the world might be. They had been a young race, however, and like dragonkind in its own youth, they were ruled by their baser instincts—avarice, jealousy, violence. By the absence of compassion. He couldn't be too critical, though. The unenlightened amongst dragonkind were no different.

He'd fed on a small herd of deer, sating the hunger he had woken with. He could smell clusters of humans beneath him, and occasionally see the lights and fires they lit at night. There were far more of them than when Pharadon had gone to sleep, and they had spread. Even in the dark he could see the way they had changed the land around them. Forests were gone and rivers diverted; roads etched their way across the land like old battle scars. Places he remembered as being occupied by humans were larger, and they lived in more towns than before. They had thrived, while dragonkind apparently had not.

When he located the source of Alpheratz's scent, Pharadon stopped and hovered awhile, deep in thought. The smell came from the centre of a large town. Could Alpheratz actually have chosen to live amongst them in human form? It seemed hard to believe. Had humans won the wars with dragonkind and enslaved them? Or had a way been found to live together in harmony? He liked that idea, but there was only one way to find out.

He fell into a long, spiralling descent that ended when his talons bit into the ground. Then Pharadon did something he had not done in a very long time. He reached deep within his soul, to the dense concentration of the Fount located at its core, and bade it change him. He felt his muscles heat and tingle. It was not painful—more like a deep, uncomfortable ache in every fibre of his being, one he willed to soon be over. When it was done, he remembered that in human terms, he was naked. It had been so long since he had taken on human form that some of the details had escaped him. It would have been far easier to obtain clothes from one of the hanging lines humans used while he could still fly. The benefits of hindsight.

The only thing he had to cover his nakedness was the darkness, and there was not much of that left. It would be hours before he had absorbed enough of the Fount to replenish what he had used and be able to create clothes—he was still very out of practice. It would be longer still before he had enough to transform back to his natural state. The switch between human and dragon form was one of those strange magics that was entirely reliant on one's internal reservoir of magical energy, making it dangerous to the caster but incredibly potent. The transformation required the expanded capacity enjoyed by the enlightened, and even then could be performed only after much practice. Their base brethren could not do it.

He wondered what to do next. His nakedness would mark him out among other humans, and that was never a good thing, even had he genuinely been one of them. Also, he couldn't ignore the possibility that his transformation was not perfect, that he had not left a telltale patch of scale on his back, or some such. His first priority had to be to find something to cover himself with, so he struck off into the darkness to accomplish just that.

▲▲▲▲▲

The garments were dirty, and smelled as though someone might have used them to wipe their backside. There were holes and tears, and they didn't fit properly. All that could be said for them was that they covered Pharadon from neck to ankle, and for his purposes, that was good enough. It was with some trepidation that he approached the town's gates, which had opened shortly after dawn. There was a steady trickle of people in and out, including one or two who looked just as dishevelled as Pharadon.

In his experience, humans treated the indigent in one of two ways: either they ignored them completely, or they behaved as if they were vermin. Pharadon hoped for the former; his unpleasant smell might convince others to give him a wide berth. You could never tell with humans, however, and he wondered if he should smear some horse dung on the cloth to make his odour more potent. Realising he was in view of the guards, he decided it would look odd and would guarantee unwanted attention, so elected not to.

He shambled along, mimicking the air of defeat and lack of purpose exuded by others of a similar appearance, locking his gaze on the ground before him. Being accosted by the guards would not be an enjoyable experience. While in human guise, he was unremarkable in all respects. He could fight well enough, and his body was strong, fit, and healthy, but none of that could stop several guards from beating him senseless. He'd experienced that once, and had no desire to do so again.

These guards didn't prove to be a problem; they let him pass without interruption. Pharadon maintained his defeated gait until he had put some distance between himself and the gate, then eased into a more comfortable stride. It didn't take him long to get to the source of the smell, a small building with letters painted along the lintel. Many years ago, Pharadon had made an unenthusiastic attempt to learn to read the human language, but he'd never mastered it. He squinted at the letters, and despite a strenuous effort at recollection, he couldn't make out the words. He considered applying some magic to the problem, but was still tired from his transformation and didn't care all that much what they said. A window of small glass lozenges held together by lead cames afforded a distorted view of what was inside, but Pharadon could not work out if the figure moving about inside might be Alpheratz in human form.

The building looked like a business of some kind, so Pharadon let himself in. The man inside was facing away, working at a large object on a bench that was covered with a sheet of linen cloth. Pharadon cleared his throat. The man turned, and frowned.

"No vagrants here," he said. "Be gone, or I'll call the Watch."

That was the type of trouble that Pharadon was trying to avoid, but perhaps Alpheratz had sunk so far into his new form that he behaved like the humans too. The scent was certainly coming from in front of him.

"Alpheratz?" Pharadon said, hesitantly.

There was no sign of recognition in the man's eyes. "I've no idea what you're talking about. Please leave. Now."

He took a step forward, revealing what had hitherto been obscured by his body. Pharadon's eyes widened in horror. He couldn't see much, but it was enough. Alpheratz. Still very much in dragon form, with a great glass ball staring at him from where Alpheratz's eye should have been. It took Pharadon a moment to realise that the man was still talking. He made out the word "Watch" again, so he nodded and stumbled backwards, out onto the street. The shopkeeper followed and slammed the door in his face, leaving Pharadon to absorb the shock of seeing the head of his equal parts friend and enemy of countless years, disembodied in a human workshop. What had happened to him? How had it come to this? He had to find out. Dumbfounded, Pharadon walked straight out of the town.

PART TWO

CHAPTER
17

A campsite had sprung up overnight next to Venne, and it looked very much like a royal regiment was being billeted there, though this camp lacked both a chain of command, and discipline. As confident as Gill was in what he had told Edine about bannerets, he was certain that plenty of other men—former enlisted soldiers, bandits, confidence men—bolstered the numbers. Of them, he had a far lower opinion. Without the threat of flogging or hanging, that camp would soon become a hive of vice.

Where large numbers of single men went, others followed. Hawkers, prostitutes, thieves—it was only a matter of time before they saw opportunity, and the quiet, picturesque little village of Venne turned into an open sewer. It was up to him to make sure there was no reason for them to stay long enough for any of that to happen. He wondered where the real danger lay—the three dragons, feeding indiscriminately on people and livestock, or this accumulation of armed men and all they brought with them.

He gave Beausoleil a list of tasks and sent the man to find the smith and carpenter, then headed for the mayor's house. There was still a line of men outside, but it was shorter than it had been the previous evening. He cast an eye over them as he passed, trying to see if any of them looked the type he wanted in his little company of dragonslayers, but no one stood out. Edine was ensconced behind her desk, diligently writing down the answers to the questions she asked each banneret.

"I've looked over the attack sites," Guillot said. "We've some preparations to make, but I expect we'll be ready to go hunting in short order."

One of the men in the line, sandy-haired with a ruddy complexion, gave Guillot an intense look.

"You're Banneret of the White dal Villerauvais, aren't you?"

His accent was unmistakably Humberlander, from a country Guillot had fought two wars against. He hesitated—it was difficult to tell, but the man looked just about young enough to be the son of someone Gill had killed in the first war. With no alternative, he gave a curt banneret's salute—a click of the heels and a nod of the head.

The Humberlander responded in kind. "Banneret of the Red William Cabham, at your service."

"A pleasure," Guillot said, before turning to Edine. "I'm ready to leave for the manor whenever you are." He gave her an apologetic smile as he ducked out the door.

▴▴▴▴▴▴

A short while later, Edine found Gill hiding in a corner of the inn's taproom, hoping he wasn't going to have to deal with a mob of angry, fatherless sons. With Val tagging along behind, Edine led the way up to the seigneur's manor house, which sat on the higher ground behind the village.

"Lord Venne doesn't come down to the village much," Edine said. "He's never been interested in anything that isn't hawking or hunting. When the duke sent me to the village, Lord Venne took it personally, and has almost nothing to do with the place now."

"Sounds like a nice fellow," Gill said. At least *he* had resided in his village, and not out at the manor. Not that it had done much good. "Does he have family?"

"A wife. Two sons away at the Academy. Some staff: steward, huntsman, cooks, butlers, maids, stablehands. He entertains quite a bit, holds hunts at least once a month. There's good hunting around here. Belek too, if you go looking for them. There's a constant stream of the well-to-do passing through the village. Brings in quite a bit of income."

"He wasn't interested in helping deal with the dragon?"

Edine let out a snort. "No, he prefers hunting smaller beasts. Particularly those who can't hunt him back. He wasn't even willing to go looking for help. Too busy, apparently."

"I've encountered a few like him," Guillot said with a sigh. Even at his lowest and most neglectful, he'd been willing to ride to Mirabay for help.

Gill felt a strange sensation pass over him. It was fleeting, and he wondered for a moment if he'd imagined it. The last time he had felt that way was when he'd ridden into the valley where he killed the first dragon. It was part of the Cup's effect—a way of detecting dragons.

"Everybody stop," he said, in barely more than a whisper. They did, and he tried to concentrate on the sensation. It was far weaker than it had been on the previous occasion, so weak he had barely noticed it. It was confirmation, though, that with the Cup he could indeed sense when dragons were near.

"What's wrong?" Edine said.

"How far are we from the manor house?"

"It's just over the next rise. A few minutes at most. Why?"

"It might be nothing. I'm not sure." He concentrated for a moment longer, but the sensation had passed. "I think it's safe to continue."

"Can you tell when a dragon is close?"

He didn't want to tell anyone about the Cup, so he said, "No, nothing like that. Just instinct."

She nodded, and he smiled inwardly at having added to his warrior mystique. They continued on, slower now, as he kept every sense alert for a dragon. The mist that he had seen from afar earlier now swirled around them. It wasn't thick enough to make him worry they might lose their way, but there was enough to allow something unpleasant to lurk in the gloom. As he had suspected, the fog was cold and damp, and the sooner they reached the house, the better.

It was always important to show due respect to the local lord. It would be rude not to, and it could cause problems farther down the road. Best to pay lip service to formality, and then get on with what needed to be done.

The manor house loomed out of the mist, and Gill could immediately tell that there was something wrong. As they grew closer, the damage became visible, and Gill realised that some of what he had taken to be mist was actually smoke.

"Gods alive," Edine said.

Gill drew his sword, more out of habit than from fear of an immediate threat. The place had the still, dead atmosphere of a location where things had already occurred; the world had already moved on.

"Wait here," he said. He urged his horse on toward the house. Scorch marks on the walls made it clear what had happened. Gill rode slowly around the building, watching the drifting clouds of mist and tendrils of smoke for anything they might be concealing. When he had completed his circuit, he sheathed his sword.

"I can't see any signs of life," he said. "You're sure all those people were still here?"

"They'd have had to pass through the village to leave the area. No one saw them do that, so they must still be here. You think a dragon attacked the house?"

"It looks that way. I'll go inside and take a look around," Gill said. "Wait here and keep your eyes open. It might still be in the area."

Gill dismounted and walked to the front door. It swung open to the touch, and his heart sank. The inside of the building had been smashed apart, as though the dragon had burned and broken through the roof, then forced its way down, tearing through the floors and any walls that weren't built of solid stone. The remains of a person—a man, to judge by the clothing—lay on the hall floor, the legs and a significant portion of his torso missing. Gill stepped carefully around the remains and the slick of blood as he moved deeper into the manor.

Wood panelling had been torn from the walls and scattered about in chunks and splinters. There were scorch marks everywhere, but it was a raking claw mark in the plaster finish on one of the remaining walls that confirmed to Gill what had done this. The only light in the gloomy interior came from smouldering heaps of ash and glowing embers, or from rents in the exterior walls that let in the fading, misty daylight. He pushed past a door that was hanging from its hinges and was greeted by the smell of charred flesh. He could make out three bodies in this room, burned beyond any hope of recognition.

This was what had happened at Villerauvais. What had happened to his home, his people. The thought made him want to throw up. He covered his mouth and nose with his hand and backed out.

Edine and Val were waiting for him outside, concerned looks on their faces.

"Is anyone left alive?" Edine said.

"Not as far as I can tell. The house has been destroyed and everyone in it killed. We should get back to the village. The bodies can be collected and given a proper burial later."

▲▲▲▲▲▲

"Banneret dal Villerauvais, I was hoping I might have a word with you?"

The Humberlander. He had approached Gill the moment they'd gotten back to the village. Guillot stopped, turned, and forced a smile, his hand resting on the pommel of his sword. It may have looked a casual pose to the uninformed observer, but the movement served to push the handle forward, making it quicker to reach.

"Certainly," Guillot said, studying the face to see if it bore any similarity to one in his mental catalogue of men he had killed. It was a fruitless exercise—there were many that he'd faced in the heat of battle, or covered by armour, whom he hadn't gotten a memorable look at.

The Humberlander approached at a half jog. "As I said, my name's William Cabham. I think you knew my father."

Guillot tensed.

"It was at the Battle of Carling Bridge."

Gill killed so many that day that he had never been able to put a number on it. He spread his hands in a conciliatory gesture. "I'm sorry, but it was war."

Cabham laughed. "Oh, it wasn't that. You duelled my father outside the Humberland camp. Beat him, but spared his life. Banneret of the Red Alfred Cabham."

Brow furrowed, Gill dug back into the murk. He remembered a single combat with a blond Humberlander officer, after they'd fought their way across the bridge. He'd been good, but not good enough to match Gill in his prime. He'd spared the man, because the battle had been won at that point. There was no need for any more killing.

"I think I recall," Gill said. "I'm not sure if I ever knew his name, though."

"He knew yours. Said you were the most honourable man he'd ever met. The bravest and the best too. He reckoned we'd have won Carling Bridge if it wasn't for you."

He wasn't the only one, Gill thought, but kept it to himself, not sure whether to feel proud or uncomfortable. "How is your father?"

Cabham gave a wry smile and shook his head. "He was killed fighting the Ventish a few years back."

Gill shrugged. "Soldiering. I'm sorry for your loss."

"Soldiering," Cabham said, nodding in agreement. "I suppose we're both here for the same purpose, and I wanted to say that I'd consider it an honour if you let me ride with you."

"I'm flattered," Gill said, put on the back foot now that what he was looking for had come to him, "but you have to understand how sensitive a time it is to be partnering with unknown talent."

"I'd never have thought the contrary," Cabham said. "I'd be happy to give you a list of my experience. While I realise time is too pressing to allow for references to be checked, there are one or two fellows I've served with in the past here at the moment who can vouch for me."

Gill shrugged. He supposed it didn't hurt hearing the young man out. "Please, go ahead."

"I served in the King's Fourth Infantry Regiment in Humberland for three years after graduating from the Academy. After that, I spent a year as aide de camp to the prince regent, mainly taking care of his hunting requirements, so I have experience tracking and killing dangerous game, including belek. I wanted to see a little more of the world, so I signed on with the Red Company. With them I saw service in Estranza and Auracia. That brings me up to the present. I was in Tarbeaux, on my way home, when I heard about dragons. Hard to walk away from something like that!"

"You've a solid list of credentials," Guillot said, meaning it sincerely. Cabham had certainly packed a lot into his time since leaving the Academy. He needed to take someone on, and here was a young man with a solid career and the right types of experience. "There's no pay and a high risk. All that you'll get out of it is a little fame."

Cabham raised his eyebrows. "A little? This is the type of opportunity that makes a career. A few coins will last a matter of months. A solid reputation? That'll feed you for a lifetime."

Guillot smiled. "Well said. I'm happy to give it a try if you are."

"More than happy," Cabham said.

"Welcome to the Company of . . . Dragonslayers," Guillot said, and saluted him. "It's early days yet, so there's not much to tell you. I've one other banneret with me, and a lad who fancies himself a squire, but he's new to it and still finding his way. We'll all be finding our way, to a degree. This is new for everyone, myself included."

"I'll help however I can," Cabham said. "What's first?"

"I'm having some lances made up. I want to ride out in the morning, even if it means the smiths working through the night. The sooner we get to business, the less this village loses."

"I'm sure they'll be glad to be rid of this crowd, too," Cabham said.

Guillot gave him a knowing look. "They're putting us up at the inn, two rooms between the three of us—four now, so find a comfortable spot and make it yours. The other two are Banneret Didier dal Beausoleil, and my squire of sorts is Val. They're feeding us too, so we'll eat together this evening, and talk through everything that needs to be done."

Cabham nodded. "Until then."

Guillot walked a little way out of the village to be alone with his thoughts. He reckoned he had enough men for the job, and if Cabham didn't work out, he could be replaced easily enough. The same went for Beausoleil. With Val, he had a slightly higher duty of care, but squiring could be just as dangerous as being a banneret. Best he learned what he was getting himself in for early. Gill walked along a hedgerow, sheltered from above by the trees dotted along its length, enjoying the serenity of the countryside, thinking about the Cup.

There seemed to be many reasons to keep it to himself, but the idea made him feel like a gluttonous child hoarding sweets. He knew there was danger, however. No matter how well he had rehearsed the words with Solène, there was the very real possibility that he would make a mess of them. Who knew what damage that could cause? If he tried to carry out the ceremony on one of them, he could easily kill them. Or himself. Or both.

He knew he could minimise the risk by practising and being very careful. However, that left the question of how Cabham, Beausoleil, and Val would react to having magic used on them. That could just as easily result in someone's death at the end of a blade.

Finally, there was the more nebulous problem. The Cup was ancient, and had powers far beyond his comprehension. It occurred to him that it was something that might be better kept a secret, particularly from men about whom he knew very little. Something about it made him nervous, but he couldn't put his finger on it. He had always believed his instincts to be good, and exercised caution any time they told him something was wrong. There being sense in his keeping the Cup to himself did nothing to alleviate his feeling of deceit. How could he ask men to ride into a battle such as this without giving them every advantage, without giving them the same chance of survival that he had? It was a callous, selfish thing to contemplate, and it shamed him. Was he simply being greedy, or might his concerns be valid?

He knew how he would feel if one of them died, if having the boon offered by the Cup might have allowed them to survive. A risky choice it might be, but it seemed like the only one he could make. His fears were based in speculation, while the chance they would be killed without it was a very real thing. He stopped for a moment to enjoy the feel of the cool, fresh country air in his lungs, free from thought or worry or stress, then turned back to the village, his decision made.

CHAPTER
18

Amaury was tempted to stop at his house and call an end to his long day rather than heading for the palace. He had spent far longer in the archive than he had intended, as he always did when he found something new and alluring. It was late, and he was tired. But there was still paperwork that needed to be completed for the following day. Not for the first time, he wondered if his position as first minister was worth all the hassle. Once the Order was out in the open and had taken its proper place in the affairs of state, perhaps he could hand off the ministry to an underling, and merely oversee matters as Master of the Order of the Golden Spur.

Despite his exhaustion, his mind still buzzed with possibilities. As always, his time in the archive had raised as many questions as it had answers. If the Cup could give such great power, what must enlightenment offer? Might the latter be the result of the former? Whatever it was, if this temple of enlightenment still existed, he needed to control it too.

As the carriage passed his townhouse, Amaury closed his eyes and tried to quiet his mind. He would make time for further investigation, but until he did, his mental resources were needed elsewhere. The carriage stopped, and he swept through the darkened palace, his robes flaring out around him as he walked. Although the main halls were quiet, he knew in some of the parlours and salons, activity would continue until the participants were too exhausted, too drunk, or had lost all of their money. In some rooms, his agents watched, looking for something the Prince Bishop could use as leverage, but until one of those juicy morsels cropped up, what went on behind the palace's closed doors was of little interest to him.

His secretary had gone home for the day, leaving Amaury's office suite subdued and peaceful. It seemed like a very different place absent the usual hustle and bustle of the day. Amaury closed his office door and briefly contemplated trying to light the office with magic, then let the idea go. He could create light, or work, but not both. Seating himself at his desk, he lit a magelamp with the touch of his fingers.

"I hear you've been looking for me."

The voice came from an armchair in the corner, beyond the reach of the meagre desk lamp. Amaury was startled, but did his best not to show it. He'd recognised the voice instantly.

"I wasn't aware you had come back to the city."

Ysabeau dal Fleurat stood and walked from the shadows. Dark hair cascaded over her shoulders, framing a face of fair skin, luscious red lips, and smouldering eyes. She was wearing a dress that would turn heads in envy and admiration, even at a centre of fashion like the palace.

"Just arrived."

"I expect so," Amaury said. "I'd ask how you got in, but looking at you, I think I can tell."

She shrugged, then sat in one of the chairs facing his desk. "I fit my clothes to the occasion."

"It's good of you to make the effort. You certainly look . . . prosperous."

"The contacts your friend set me up with paid well."

"What brings you back, then?" Amaury said.

"Homesick."

He raised an eyebrow and she laughed.

"One job too many," she said. "You know how it is. That's why you made me leave in the first place."

"It seemed like the sensible thing to do, although I'll admit it was probably unnecessary."

"So everyone thinks old Boudain really did choke on that fish bone?" She laughed. "It was nice to see a bit of the world. Most girls who grow up in the Marécage rarely get a glimpse outside the city walls."

Amaury wasn't sure if the mention of the Marécage was a slight against him. It was a downstream district that was mainly reclaimed swamp, mostly inhabited by cutpurses, whores, and the dregs of society. It was where she had spent the part of her life before he knew of her existence.

"How did you know I'd be here?" he said, changing the subject.

"You've always been one to burn the midnight oil. I'd no reason to believe you'd changed. Although I have to admit, I've been waiting awhile, and was beginning to wonder."

"You know me too well," Amaury said. "Are you . . . planning on staying in Mirabay for a while?"

She shrugged. "If there's work. I hear that there might be."

He was hurt that she had called on Luther before him, but refused to show it on his face. He wondered if he could still trust her, but had no reason to believe not.

"I'm confident I can find some tasks for you." He leaned back in his chair and steepled his fingers before his face. "In fact, I can think of something that needs attending to right now."

"Excellent," she said.

Her smile could melt the coldest of hearts. It could also lull a man into walking onto her dagger. It was the smile that had almost led her to being burned for witchcraft. That, and the fact that she was more than a little skilled in shaping the Fount.

"You'll need a more suitable outfit," he said.

"I'm sure I can rustle up something."

▲▲▲▲▲

When Ysabeau left, Amaury turned to his last remaining task for the day. Word had filtered back to the city that the dragon had been slain by Guillot dal Villerauvais. To most, the name meant nothing, but soon enough someone would connect it to a hero of Mirabaya, a former bodyguard to the king. It would be a name that belonged to a Chevalier of the Silver Circle, rather than a member of the Order of the Golden Spur. Amaury's plan to own the news was simple—claim Guillot for the Order. Say he had been inducted, providing a continuity between the Silver Circle and the Golden Spur. Explain that he was able to do what he did because of the powers that joining the Order had given him.

The time had come to announce that magic was back. It was a moment he had been waiting for, one he had worked long and hard to bring about—but now that he was teetering on its edge, he found himself paralysed with fear. Taking this step meant going directly against the king. This was no act of omission. It was disobedience.

Pen in hand, Amaury stared at a blank piece of paper. He felt the way he had right before his first competitive duel—as if a kaleidoscope of butterflies were trying to beat their way out of his stomach. He could not write a single word.

Back then, all that had been at stake was pride. What he now sought to do could lead to him being burned at the stake. The thought was too terrifying to bear. Nonetheless, his entire life had brought him to this moment, and he knew he couldn't back away now. To do so would be to admit that at the moment of reckoning, he had been found wanting. That he had failed. He dipped his pen in the ink and started to write.

When he was done, he pulled on the tasselled rope that snaked unseen through the palace to his secretary's apartment, where it was connected to a large bell. He then turned the egg timer on his desk. His secretary had never once failed to arrive before the last grain of sand dropped. It was why he had lasted so long in the job. Not wanting to waste a moment, Amaury returned his attention to the rest of his correspondence.

He also wrote a note to dal Drezony. He had yet to induct his new appointments, so she remained the Order's senior officer. It was only right that he notify her that in the morning, the Spurriers' true purpose would be public knowledge.

By the time he finished crafting the announcement and making a clean copy for the printers, it was late, and he had not yet decided how to deal with the king. The king's final command had been to do nothing without notifying him first. Getting permission was implied but had not been explicitly ordered. The young king had yet to learn how important precision was, when it came to matters of state. He sent off the paperwork that needed to go out, once his sleepy-looking secretary arrived, and then turned his mind back to the plan at hand.

Amaury quickly penned another clean copy for the king, and headed for the royal bedchamber, for surely Boudain had gone to bed hours earlier. The king's steward resided in a small antechamber, seemingly always awake in the event that his master needed anything. The Prince Bishop knocked, and when the faithful lapdog opened the door, greeted him with a warm smile. "I wonder if His Majesty is still up?"

"I'm sorry, your Grace, he's retired for the night."

"Ah, that's unfortunate, but can't be helped, I suppose."

"If it's important, I can wake him, your Grace."

It was nice to know he still warranted waking the king. "No, no, it's nothing that can't keep until morning. He simply asked me to notify him of something." He handed the folded copy of his proclamation to the steward. "I wonder if you might see to it that this is included in His Majesty's morning papers?"

The steward took the parchment and nodded. Amaury smiled to himself.

The king had been notified. The letter of his command had been followed.

CHAPTER
19

Guillot asked Gaufre, the innkeeper, to serve their supper in one of their bedrooms. He needed privacy to say what he needed to say, and that wasn't to be found in the taproom, where Gaufre was making more money in a single night than he usually did in months. Turning away from Gaufre, Gill spotted Cabham leaning against the bar when he looked about the taproom, and gestured for him to follow.

The room Val and Beausoleil were sharing was small—and smaller still with a table and chairs added.

"Banneret Cabham, this is Banneret Didier—" Gill faltered and was surprised when Cabham continued smoothly.

"Dal Beausoleil, and young Val. Banneret William Cabham, at your service." Smiling, Cabham gave them both a banneret's salute, then turned to Gill, his smile turned apologetic. "I tend to remember anything I hear. Used to drive my parents crazy when I was a child. Not to mention my friends. . . ."

Gill returned the smile and gestured for them all to sit. They huddled around the small table with barely enough room to push their stools out before hitting the wall. Guillot was nervous. He had chosen the stool by the door, so if they reacted badly, escape wouldn't be completely impossible.

He waited until they'd finished eating. He reckoned full bellies would make for a more receptive audience, and if worst came to worst, they would slow them down in the event of swordplay. Meanwhile, they made awkward conversation of the kind that always took place when professional swordsmen tried to gauge one another's ability. Beausoleil and Cabham posed veiled questions as they tried to determine the pecking order. Having tenure, no matter how brief, Beausoleil clearly believed he was the senior, but they were both about the same age, with similar levels of experience. The true test would have to wait until they encountered a dragon.

Val had remained quiet throughout the meal, focussing his full attention on the food, as though it was his last meal. If they encountered a dragon the next day, it might very well be. Gill waited until Gaufre's new hire—a young woman named Martina, who had been recruited to help deal with the extra business—finished clearing the table and left the room before turning to business.

"Tell me," he asked Beausoleil, "did you have success with the carpenter and smith?"

"Yes, Captain," the younger man replied. "They'll have a half-dozen spears ready by morning, with Telastrian heads affixed. Additional replacement shafts will be finished by the time we're home in the evening."

Gill nodded and did his best to smile. He took a deep breath. "You all know of the Chevaliers of the Silver Circle?" he said.

Beausoleil and Val both nodded. Cabham only shrugged. With a sigh, Gill explained.

"The Silver Circle were founded to combat dragons in the dying days of the Empire," Gill said. "Then their skills were forgotten as the need for them abated." He drew the Cup from his purse, regarded it for a moment, then placed it on the table in front of him. "This cup is responsible for some of their success." He paused, allowing the statement to sink in. It would take them a moment to make the connection, but he preferred it if they came to the notion of magic by themselves, so when he had to use the word it would come as less of a shock.

Val was the first to react. "Is it . . . magic?"

Beausoleil frowned, then gasped with indignation. The idea that the old swordsmen would have relied on magic was an insult to their modern descendants and his was an understandable reaction. Cabham, whatever he felt on the matter, revealed nothing.

"It is, and it helped give them an edge in a fight they would otherwise have perished in." Val was hanging on every word, Cabham remained unreadable, but Beausoleil was having none of it. Guillot continued. "I've seen brave men and women, skilled and determined, die painful deaths fighting these things. I barely escaped my first encounter with my life. I would not have prevailed in the second without this cup's help."

"What does it do?" Cabham said.

"It seems to protect you from fire, and also give you a sense for where the beasts are. I think that can be developed to track them."

"So you'll be casting a spell on us?" Beausoleil said.

Gill couldn't work out if his tone conveyed anger or fear. "Not in the way you might think. 'Medicine' might be a better way to put it. We take a drop of water from the Cup, say some words, and that's it."

"That's it?" Beausoleil said.

"All I can tell you is this. I found it, discovered how to make it work, tested it, and found that it does. I won't force any of you to take a drop from it, but I can guarantee you a much better chance of living through a fight with a dragon if you do. Although I'd like to get the process out of the way this evening, it doesn't take long, so I can wait until morning for your answers."

There was no immediate response, which Guillot had realised was too much to hope for. All in all, it had gone well. He waited a moment longer before speaking again. "I'll give you your leave to consider it, gentlemen."

Gill got up and left without a further word.

"Isn't it cheating?" Val said, having followed him out.

"Pardon me?"

"Using magic. Isn't it cheating?"

Gill shrugged. "When the game you're playing requires one participant to die for the other to win, the only rule is do everything you can to make sure you survive. In any event, dragons are creatures of magic. Using magic to combat them levels the scales."

Their conversation was interrupted by a scream from outside.

The taproom had emptied by the time Gill got there The crowd had spilled out into the square, where the darkness was illuminated by jets of flame and patches of fire. Cabham and Beausoleil were only a few steps behind him.

"Gods alive," Cabham said, drawing his sword.

"What do we do?" Beausoleil said.

Gill had no idea. Perhaps with an arbalest or something similar, they could shoot one of the creatures from the sky, although they moved so fast he didn't have any great hope of managing that even if they had one.

"Try not to get killed?" he said.

There were villagers running about the place: men, women, and children, all of whom he had been brought to Venne to protect. They were panicking and each bright jet of flame that illuminated the sky brought a fresh batch of screams. Even the bannerets and other swordsmen were rushing about without direction. Guillot had to do something, the only question was what. Without the Cup's boon, he would be as vulnerable to the dragons' flames as a rick of dry hay. Unless he could convince one to land so he could try to finish it with his sword, he didn't see what he could do. He looked about frantically. All the houses were brick-and-timber-frame constructions with wooden shingles tiling their roofs. They were as susceptible to fire as any of the buildings in Villerauvais, and he could remember only too bitterly how that had turned out.

"The church," he said to himself. He looked about for a local, and when he spotted a man without a sword at his hip, Gill grabbed him. Terrified, the man struggled to free himself from Gill's grip.

"The church," Gill said, "it's roofed with slate, isn't it?" He had given the building only the most cursory of glances when he had arrived at the town.

"It is. Let me go!"

Shouting, "Get to the church. It's the safest place," Gill released the villager, but he wasn't sure if the man understood as he raced away.

Guillot turned to Val, Beausoleil, and Cabham. "Get as many people into the church as you can. The stone walls and slate roofs will give the best protection against the flames. Go!"

He began to follow his own orders, seeking out clumps of people. "The church," he shouted. "Get to the church!"

Two dragons circled above the town square, illuminated from below by the fires they had created. For a moment Gill stood transfixed, watching them in all their magnificent, destructive brilliance. It was the type of sight a man experienced only once in his life, and as terrible as it was, it was captivating. The heat was intense, but now that the initial surprise of the attack had passed, he wasn't afraid or confused. Only angry. This was what had happened to Villerauvais, only there hadn't been anyone to stop it. He was here now, and he had to make a difference. But how?

The others were hurriedly urging everyone they could see to the church. That was all well and good, but unless he made some effort to stop the beasts, Gill knew he would be considered a fraud, assuming anyone survived the night.

He had nothing to knock them from the sky with, nor did he think he would be able to correctly recite the Cup's words with all the havoc going on around him. The only thing that occurred to him was to try to lure the creatures away from the village.

Spotting Edine outside the mayor's house, he shouted at her to make for the church, but she didn't seem to hear him. A memory popped into his head, of Solène saying that dragons were attracted to gold. Then he recalled the pile of fused coins in the first dragon's cave. He ran toward Edine.

"The town treasury—is there any gold in it?"

She frowned at him, clearly suspicious.

"Why?"

"Dragons are attracted to gold. I've a few coins in my purse, but I doubt it's enough. Do you have any more?"

She looked confused, trying to process his request against the backdrop of fire and chaos. "It's mostly silver, but there's some gold."

"Bag every bit you have and bring it to me as fast as you can."

She nodded and went back inside. Gill spotted Val herding people toward the church. A burning wooden beam exploded in a shower of sparks across the square, sending them scattering.

"Val!"

The boy met Gill's gaze.

"Saddle my horse and bring it around. Fast as you can."

Val nodded and charged off. Gill looked around; the square was deserted and it seemed almost everyone was in the church. He prayed to the gods that it would keep them safe.

"Here it is!" Edine reappeared and handed him a plump leather bag, bulging with coins. It wasn't as large as he'd hoped, but it would have to do. He took the bag just as Val returned with Gill's spooked horse. Gill mounted quickly.

"Get into the church. Wait for me to give the all-clear." With that, he galloped off, his horse's hooves clattering on the cobbles above the sound of roaring flame. He nestled the coin bag between his legs and the saddle's pommel, with the top open. He had no idea how sensitive the beasts were to gold—if they could smell it or if they needed to see it. He hoped it was the former, but took a handful of coins out, and when one of the dragons passed over him, he flung them in the air.

Once out of the village, he cast a glance back and saw a great dark shape in the air turning to follow him. He let out a laugh of satisfaction, which momentarily displaced the terror in his gut. There hadn't been time for the Cup. A jet of flame sizzled past to his left, his only saving grace being that the young dragon's aim wasn't good. He hoped the second dragon was on the scent too, and wondered briefly where the third one reported was—hopefully not somewhere down the road waiting for him.

He swerved off the road and into a grassy pasture. Although the night was clear, it would be easy for him to miss a rabbit hole that could be the end of him and his horse. He felt the animal start to labour as a fireball erupted ahead. The horse needed barely any guidance from him to avoid it, but Gill knew he couldn't push his mount much longer. He took the bag of coins and slung it as far into the night as he could, then wheeled the horse around and started back toward the village, where he could see flames burning bright.

"Just a little farther," he said to the mare, hoping she could understand him. He had no idea if his plan would draw the beasts away from the village, or for how long. He could only hope that the gold would provide enough of a distraction to leave the town in peace for the rest of the night. In the morning, he could get started making sure it didn't happen again.

CHAPTER
20

Amaury sometimes wondered if killing the last king had been a good idea. While the old man had grown increasingly belligerent and obstinate, aging had robbed him of some of the faculties that had made the earlier part of his reign such a success. The last several years, when Amaury encountered the king's opposition, it would have been easier trying to knock down the city walls with his head than win an argument. So he had removed the obstacle, in the hope that the king's young, bon-vivant son would continue in the ways of his youth and busy himself with the pleasures of his kingdom, rather than the running of it.

That had proved to be a miscalculation. While the young king's capacity for excess remained unchecked, he still somehow found his way to his desk well before noon each day and went through all his paperwork by the time he rose for supper. Then he spent most evenings entertaining himself before collapsing into bed, often with company.

That morning, by the time the monarch had finished his morning toilet, the citizens of Mirabay had been listening to the town criers for some time; those who were literate had learned more from reading the bills posted on walls and notice boards across the city. The king had saved them from the ravages of a dragon by training an order of warrior mages. Magic was back, a necessary evil in the face of the great dangers threatening the good people of Mirabaya. They had new heroes, new protectors, and they could sleep soundly at night, knowing that these brave men and women were defending them from things that came out only in the dark.

Amaury felt that it was one of his finer pieces of rhetoric, but he knew that wouldn't make any difference when Boudain discovered what had been done in his name. The summons had come before lunch; Amaury made his way through the palace as slowly as he could, not wanting to make it appear the king could make him rush. He could hear shouting from the king's office as soon as he entered the corridor that led to it. Whether the monarch's anger was genuine or for effect, Amaury could not tell—and it might not make a difference. With the king's name attached to the proclamation, he was as likely to feel the flames reserved for sorcerers as Amaury was.

The Prince Bishop had known he was risking all when he penned the announcement the previous night, but it seemed the gods had smiled on him, for he had received good news before dawn.

One of the king's attendants waited outside the office door; he showed Amaury straight in. The king sat at his desk, with his steward standing at his shoulder. Opposite the king sat Chancellor Renaud, Commander Canet of the City Watch, and one of the king's generals, whose name escaped Amaury—all stone-faced.

"What's the meaning of this?" King Boudain demanded, holding up a copy of the proclamation.

From the look of the paper, it had been torn from a wall. Amaury briefly wondered what had happened to the handwritten copy he'd given to the steward the night before, then focussed on the tasks before him—soothing the king and protecting the Order.

"It's the announcement proclaiming the Order of the Golden Spur as the new champion of the people. A politic way to place them, I thought," Amaury said, as casually as he could. "We had discussed this, and I felt that with rumours spreading through the city, I needed to move quickly. The opportunity was there. It needed to be seized. I did send word . . ."

"You are the First Minister of Mirabaya," the king said, his voice rising with anger. "You do not so much as sneeze without my permission."

"If I sought out permission for every decision I make as first minister, very little would get done. Rubbish collectors would not get paid. The City Watch," he said, gesturing to the commander of the City Watch, who sat silently, watching his ruler and the head of the church duelling with each other, "would not get paid. The army would not get paid. Management of a kingdom requires delegation, Highness, and I am here to see that you are not troubled by the minor things that need to be dealt with as they arise."

"Announcing that the Crown has embraced the use of magic is not the same as signing off on the weekly payrolls," Boudain said. His voice wavered and the vein in his temple pulsed with anger.

Amaury looked pointedly at the steward. "I called at the king's apartments last evening, when the issue first became pressing, did I not?"

The steward hesitated for a moment, then nodded. Amaury turned back to the king.

"You requested I notify you. I did exactly that. The information was in your possession. The matter was time-sensitive, as I warned you it would become."

"Do you think you fool me, your Grace, by paying lip service to my commands? Would it have been so difficult to wait an hour or two?" Boudain said, his voice full of fury.

"I believe it would, Majesty," Amaury said. "You know how quickly people react to rumour in this city. By breakfast, the opportunity would have passed. Credit for your great victory would have passed to someone else, and the chance to announce your order of warrior mages might never come again."

"It's the wrong time, Highness," the chancellor said.

Many of Amaury's responsibilities had been usurped from the chancellor's office during his predecessor's term, and Renaud hated Amaury for it. Their relationship was a constant war of competing authority. To date, Amaury had won all the battles, but the chancellor was a tenacious and proud man. He might have to be dealt with once Amaury had the Cup.

"Pray tell, why?" Amaury said.

"The people are still reeling from the terror of a creature out of horror tales returning to ravage the land. No sooner has that threat been extinguished, than they are told an ever-present fear has raised its head, with the help of none other than their own king. You'll see us all on the pyre, Amaury. This was an act of madness."

The use of his given name sent a flash of anger through Amaury's body. He took a moment to still himself. Anger would get him nowhere just now. He suddenly realised that he was still standing, while all the others were seated. Worse, he had not been invited to sit, and in the king's presence, such permission was required. Alone with the king, Amaury might have chosen to ignore protocol, but with an audience, and given the tension in the room, he knew that would be a mistake.

This was a demonstration of power; he was the naughty schoolboy being judged by his masters. The realisation that they thought this little mind game might cow him made him want to burst into laughter, but he knew it was not the right moment for that. He focussed his thoughts, but was interrupted before he could launch an attack.

"He's right, your Grace," the king said, using Amaury's ecclesiastical title rather than his royal appointment. "It was the wrong time. The people are too unsettled. This could push them over the edge. After a period of calm, we could have announced the Order as a new safeguard against any future threat. We were ably positioned to claim credit for dal Villerauvais, and to use him to highlight the need for a new body of warriors to deal with dangers such as this."

Amaury bit the inside of his lip. Boudain was no fool and his point was well made. It was as valid a course as the one he had set them on—indeed, more valid, if one were to take into account only the king's plans for a stable kingdom. Amaury realised he had perhaps been hasty, but the fact remained, there would be few chances to do what needed to be done. Amaury couldn't imagine a better one coming along, timing be damned.

"I saw the opportunity, Highness. I took it, in the belief that it was the best thing for the kingdom. I stand firm in that belief."

"I don't doubt your earnestness, your Grace," Boudain said. "But you've overreached."

Amaury glanced at the chancellor, who was doing his best to contain a smile. Had he in fact pushed too far?

The king leaned back in his chair and drummed his fingers on the table. "I think the time has come for a change."

There was a knock on the door; the steward moved to answer. The king paused, staying Amaury's sentence for a moment longer. There were some muted whispers before the steward shut the door and hurried back to the king. He spoke quietly into the king's ear; Boudain's eyes widened and the colour left his face. After a moment of silence, he spoke.

"Word has reached the city that three more dragons have been sighted in the southeast. They've already attacked a village there."

There were murmurs of disbelief and outrage from the men sitting, while Amaury did his best not to smile.

"It is moments like this," King Boudain said, "that I thank the gods that I am blessed by a man with the foresight of His Grace, the First Minister of Mirabaya. A great terror has been delivered upon my people, but thanks to him, we already have the solution. It seems I was wrong, your Grace, and must be grateful for your steadfast duty to the state, irrespective of the personal cost it might exact." He drew a breath.

"I wish to speak further with the Prince Bishop. The rest of you may leave."

Amaury could feel tension fill the room as it emptied of bodies. The king was gripping the edge of his desk with white knuckles by the time the door closed behind his ministers.

"We'll need to deal with the Intelligenciers," the king said.

"We will, your Highness," Amaury said firmly.

"You've forced my hand on this, and if you think I have a short memory, you're sadly mistaken. Keep in mind, the Intelligenciers aren't the only hunting dog in my pack, and now that I've got a taste for putting one down, I won't hesitate to do so again if I'm disobeyed. Do I make myself clear?"

"Perfectly, your Highness."

CHAPTER
21

Solène stared out through the window of the coffeehouse as dal Drezony spoke. Since before dawn, it had seemed to Solène that all dal Drezony wanted to do was talk. They had spent hours discussing magic, and thought processes, but most of the conversation had focussed on other things—Solène's childhood, the years she had spent on the run, her thoughts about her future. She quickly grew impatient: she wanted to learn what she needed to learn and get on with her life, away from Mirabay. There was no doubt in her mind that the Prince Bishop had some grand plan in motion, and she had no desire to be caught up in it.

The two women had taken a long stroll through the city and spent hours in coffeehouses, discussing what seemed like irrelevant rubbish from the life Solène had left behind. She tried to have faith in the idea that dal Drezony was going somewhere with it all, but it was a struggle.

There was, however, one benefit to being back with the Order. Solène had never been wealthy enough to enjoy the finer things in life, like expensive coffee and the sweet cakes served with them. She had first eaten chocolate only the day before, and it was as though a whole new aspect of life had been laid before her. The rich coffee and cakes made the tedium of having to review her life in detail with dal Drezony easier to bear. At one coffeehouse, the chef had created a pastry that included chocolate, spice, and sour cherries, and now that she had tasted it, life would have less meaning if she could never have it again.

Despite all this, something had been bothering Solène all day—the nature of the conversation they were having. On the noisy, busy streets, discussing magic hadn't seemed like a problem, but in a coffeehouse?

"Is this really the type of thing we should be talking about in public?" Solène said.

Dal Drezony laughed. "Worry not! What we say, and what those around us hear, are very different. It's a bit of magic I learned a while ago. Surprisingly easy once you've done it a few times. No one will hear anything that will get us in trouble.

"Tell me," dal Drezony continued, "have you given any thought to why I'm asking you all these questions?"

Solène shrugged, toying with her fork and eyeing the final piece of cake. "I must admit that I have, but I haven't been able to come up with a reason yet."

"What we do requires incredible control over our minds. In order to control our minds, we have to understand why we think the way we do. That's shaped by the life we've led, the things we've experienced. Deep-rooted fears can shake our concentration. So can temptations, or feelings of duty, attachment, or obligation. You need to pull all those things out of the dark corners of your memory and understand them, so you can take control over them. Does this make sense?"

Solène applied that reasoning to her current situation. Part of her wanted to give due consideration to what dal Drezony had said, and part of her was absorbed by the last piece of cake on the plate. Did dal Drezony want it? Would it be rude if Solène took it? She snapped her mind back to her teacher's question.

"Yes," she said. "Now that I think about it, it makes perfect sense."

Dal Drezony gave a satisfied smile and said, "Take it. I've had enough."

Solène didn't need to be told twice, and devoured the delicious morsel, pleasantly surprised to find it contained a large chunk of moist cherry. As she chewed, out of the corner of her eye she saw someone staring at them. It was not unusual for them to draw curious looks when out in the city. At first, she had thought it odd that they would wear their robes outside the Priory, but dal Drezony had pointed out that there were several monasteries and convents in and around the city. She had said that it was part of the Prince Bishop's plan—if the people were familiar with the Order's cream robes, then when their true nature came out, they would be comfortable with the sight of them. They would realise that in all the years they had seen the Spurriers around the city, the Order had posed no threat. Still, this man was giving them more attention than usual, and it was making her uncomfortable.

"I think we should get back to the Priory," she said quietly.

Dal Drezony frowned. "Why?"

"A man over there's been staring at us for a while now. I don't like it."

Though dal Drezony restrained herself from looking, Solène could see her grow tense. "We're finished here, so there's no reason to linger. Shall we?"

Solène nodded eagerly, but as she stood, so did the man who had been watching them. "He's coming over," she said as he stepped toward the two women.

Dal Drezony turned to face him. "Can I help you?" she said.

"You're them, aren't you?" he said.

"I'm not sure I know what you mean?" the seneschal said.

"*Them*. The king's new order. Them that killed the dragon. I saw the sigil on your robes—a golden spur. That's the king's new order, isn't it?"

Solène could tell that dal Drezony's confusion was not feigned. The man pointed through the window. Across the small square, a town crier stood on a dais with a small crowd gathered around him.

"It's all they're talking about," the man said. "Is it true? That you use magic?"

If dal Drezony was shocked by the question, she didn't show it. Solène did her best to hide her surprise.

"I'm sure I don't have the first idea what you're talking about," dal Drezony said, casting Solène a glance that said it was time to get going. "Good day to you, sir."

They had gone some distance at a quick pace before either of them spoke.

"How did he know?" Solène said.

Dal Drezony pulled a letter out of her cloak, broke the seal, and opened it. She stopped to read, then sighed.

"This arrived during the night. I'd like to say I forgot about it, but the truth is I've been ignoring the Prince Bishop as best I can lately. Stupid, juvenile behaviour, but . . . He's worrying me. More than I'd like." Solène was surprised to see fear on dal Drezony's face. "Don't trust him, Solène. Never trust him, and always be careful dealing with him. He's a dangerous man."

She looked down at the paper again.

"Anyway, it seems he revealed the Order to the people this morning. Let's go over there," dal Drezony said, gesturing to a town crier farther down the street. "I want to hear what he's saying."

The tension on the streets was palpable. It reminded Solène of Trelain when news of the dragon had first spread and people tried to determine if they were in imminent danger. It was a perilous time, as emotions were high and precariously balanced, teetering in the direction of panic and violence. The women listened in silence, part of a transfixed crowd. The town crier sounded hoarse, no doubt from repeating the news over and over since it had reached him.

The report started well. The dragon had been slain. A great hero was named—Guillot dal Villerauvais, Chevalier of the Order of the Golden Spur. Knowing the situation, Solène was surprised to hear Gill being given credit. All became clear when it was said he was a member of the Order, thus allowing the Prince Bishop to claim the plaudits for himself. She wondered if Guillot was aware that he was now a Spurrier. She herself was not mentioned, to her relief.

With the details of the slaying dealt with, more unsettling news was delivered. The people had been saved by the Order of the Golden Spur. The king had deemed it necessary to permit them to use magic to carry out the difficult and dangerous missions he tasked them with. There were gasps from the crowd at mention of this, then silence as disbelief took hold. Solène looked about as surreptitiously as she could, wondering what would happen next, how the people would react.

The jeers started with one, unconfident voice that would have been drowned out were it not for the silence. Others joined it, until no individual could be distinguished any longer, and the volume was deafening. As if of a single mind, Solène and dal Drezony moved away. It looked as though it might be some time before she got to enjoy her new favourite chocolate cake again.

⁂

"That didn't look good," Solène said, as they hurried away.

"It wasn't," dal Drezony said. "And these things only get worse. What was he thinking?"

Solène presumed the question was rhetorical, so didn't answer.

"We're simply not ready for this. There could be an angry mob forming outside the Priory right now. We need to get back there and see what's happening. Let the others know if they don't already."

They hurried through the streets, robes bundled up in their arms, not making eye contact with anyone. Though their clothes were unmarked, tunics and britches were unusual outfits for women, so they drew more inquiring glances than Solène liked. She was terrified. All it took was for one person to denounce them as sorcerers, and mob rule would prevail. She shuddered to think of the consequences if she was forced to defend herself. She still couldn't control her magic. If she had to use it, she would prove people were correct to fear mages.

The sight of the Priory's walls came as an overwhelming relief, so great that she almost burst into tears. Thankfully, there was no angry crowd gathered outside. Perhaps people hadn't made the connection between the Priory and the Order. However, it wasn't until they were safely past the gates, with them securely bolted, that Solène was able to properly relax.

"That was a very unpleasant ending to the day," dal Drezony said. "I have to call in the officers and get everyone prepared for the possibility of an attack. We can talk later."

Solène nodded, and was about to take her leave when the Prince Bishop appeared, accompanied by a number of men she hadn't seen before.

"Seneschal dal Drezony, I've been looking for—" His eyes widened when he saw Solène. "Nice to see you. I've been wondering where the seneschal was hiding you."

"We've been busy with my training," Solène said with a glance at dal Drezony.

"Well, I hope you've been making good progress," he said.

Her voice dripping with sarcasm, dal Drezony said, "Thank you for consulting with me before making the announcement."

Without a pause, the Prince Bishop replied, "Things moved at a rather quicker pace than I was expecting. I had to react quickly."

Dal Drezony let out an incredulous laugh. "Try telling that to an angry mob coming to burn you at the stake." She frowned, and cocked her head, fixing her gaze on the men with the Prince Bishop. "Why are they wearing Order robes?" she said.

It was only then that Solène noticed that all the men wore the Order's cream garb beneath their riding cloaks.

"With the losses we've sustained over the past few weeks, I thought it prudent to draft some additional manpower. They don't have any *talent,* of course, but that's not what they're here for. Think of them as bodyguards, just as the old bannerets were to the Imperial mages."

"They're here to protect us from the citizens of Mirabay? From the mess you've made."

"Tread carefully, Kayte," the Prince Bishop said. "If you give me the chance to fully apprise you of the situation, you'll understand."

"I find that very hard to believe," dal Drezony said.

"Dragons," the Prince Bishop said. "We've just received word that three more have been sighted. The people need the Order now, more than ever. Once the news spreads, which you can be assured is happening as we speak, they will embrace the Order with all their hearts."

Solène had to stifle a laugh. She'd known about the other dragons since before leaving Trelain. She'd thought a man as well informed as the Prince Bishop would have also. She liked the feeling of knowing something he did not. Moreover, it gave her hope that he wouldn't find out what she had truly been up to. It seemed he didn't have eyes in quite as many places as he'd like people to think.

"If the people are about to fall in love with us, why the hired muscle?" dal Drezony asked.

"We're going dragon hunting, so we need the extra manpower. We've also lost most of our military command: Leverre, Gamet,

Dreue. Soon the Order will ride out in full array, and I want a few men filling out the ranks who look the part. We need some battle-hardened veterans, which these men most certainly are. I've appointed Banneret Gassot here as acting chancellor, and Banneret Vachon as acting marshall."

They each gave dal Drezony a nod. She responded with only a curt smile.

"I need you to make a list of the most competent mages we have left, and any others who might be useful in a support role," the Prince Bishop said.

"I think we really need to sit down and talk, your Grace," dal Drezony said.

"Indeed, but at the moment, there isn't time. There's an expedition to prepare. I expect that in a few days the dragons will move on from the area they're in, so there's no time to waste."

"You do remember what happened the last time we sent people after a dragon? It's the reason you've had to hire Bannerets Gassot and Vachon."

"Unfortunate, but a valuable learning experience thanks to Leverre's reports. This time will be different. We know far more now, and these dragons are smaller—juveniles, by the sounds of it. The perfect proving ground for the Order, and excellent experience, should dragons become a recurring problem. Anyway. Vachon is up to speed, so he can brief you on my instructions." He turned his attention to Solène. "I need you to stay here," he said. "I've an important job for you."

Dal Drezony frowned.

"Don't worry, Kayte," the Prince Bishop said. "I simply need her to help me find something."

CHAPTER

22

When Guillot went into the taproom early the next morning, Beausoleil, Cabham, and Val were waiting for him, swords sheathed and expectant looks on their faces. They were wearing armour—plate cuirasses, pauldrons, and vambraces, with articulated lamellar tassets that extended to the knee, allowing freedom of movement while supplying good protection to the upper leg. There wasn't too much decoration, and their harnesses looked well maintained, things that gave Guillot confidence.

Val wore an old chain-mail hauberk that he must have picked up during his rushed preparations in Trelain. It was ancient, but looked like it had been reasonably well maintained, and was serviceable. The boy had the earnest look of one who was willing to do whatever was expected of him, while Beausoleil and Cabham both looked more serious. They knew the reality of what was to come. Gill gave them a nod, and gestured for them to follow him to his room. He grabbed a fresh pitcher of water and a fork from the bar as he passed, and waited for them to join him.

"What happens now?" Beausoleil said.

"I'll administer it to myself first, so you can see what is involved, then to any of you who still want to go ahead with it." Taking their silence as agreement, Guillot filled the Cup with water. Holding the Cup in one hand and a fork in the other, he reviewed the words in his mind, then started to speak. The others watched in silence and Gill did his best to ignore their presence. The words said, he dipped one of the fork's tines into the water, then let a single droplet fall on his tongue. He swallowed and smiled to show that he was all right.

He didn't feel any different, but he couldn't recall noticing anything in particular after the last time. So long as he didn't die in magically induced agony, he was content.

"Who's first?" he asked, keeping his voice steady.

"Me," Beausoleil said.

Gill suppressed a smile as he saw the curl of frustration on Cabham's mouth. Neither wanted to go first, but neither wanted the other to go ahead of them. Gill could see a look of trepidation on Beausoleil's face as he approached. If the man was having second thoughts, now was not the time to express them—the loss of face would be too much for any self-respecting banneret to bear.

Beausoleil presented his tongue like a child about to be given a dose of bad-tasting medicine. Gill recited the words and placed a drop of water from the Cup on the younger man's tongue. He shut his mouth, and Gill could tell he was holding his breath. He let it out a moment later, doing his best, but failing, to hide his relief.

"That was hardly anything," he said.

"There's not much to it," Gill said. "The old Chevaliers had this administered to them every time they went out on a hunt. Now, who's next?"

Gill repeated the process with Cabham, and finally Val.

"I don't feel anything," Cabham said, when it was done.

"I think that's the point," Gill said. "Particularly when you're having fire breathed on you."

"There's not supposed to be any . . . sensation?" Beausoleil said.

"No. You'll probably feel something when we get closer to the dragons. Almost like a tug, but that's it. If you're unlucky enough to get hit by flame, you should be impervious. That's all there is to it, so unless you want some more breakfast, we should be on our way."

▲▲▲▲▲▲

They rode out of Venne minutes later, under the curious gazes of the soot-stained villagers. There were casualties. Gill's insistence on getting people into the church had saved many lives, but until the village was rid of the dragons, he couldn't waste any time congratulating himself.

The village was a hive of activity; the other adventurers were preparing to head out themselves, while the townspeople were making efforts to assess and repair the damage the dragons had caused. Buildings, or what remained of them, still smouldered, and Gill wondered how many concealed charred bodies. The fight against the flames had gone on much of the night, but Gill and the others had slipped away early, to get some rest for what they had to do.

His trick of the night before seemed to have worked. He struggled to contain a smile as he imagined the dragons scrabbling around in the dark trying to pick up the coins with their talons. He expected Edine would have a difficult time explaining the missing tax revenue to the duke's steward, but considering everything that had happened, he reckoned the excuse would be acceptable.

Guillot had hired an extra horse to carry the spare lances, but he thought it best if they were ready to fight the moment they left the village. The lances seemed well turned and true and the Telastrian tips were securely fitted. Though he did his best not to look around as they rode out of Venne, it was impossible not to think of Villerauvais. He didn't just want to slaughter the dragons. Before they died, he wanted them to know how foolish they had been to meddle with humanity.

He studied his companions. Val had gone the colour of milk and Gill suspected it was everything the lad could do to hold down his breakfast. Gill wondered if he still thought being a squire and working toward being a banneret was a good idea. Probably not. In that moment, shovelling horse dung didn't seem like such a bad career choice, even to Gill. Beausoleil and Cabham both had the set jaws of men who were afraid, but had faced that fear before and survived it. They weren't boasting that morning, which was something—Gill always appreciated the small mercies. He realised his concern for the others was nothing more than his own coping mechanism for the fear that was gnawing away at his gut. It frustrated him—he wanted his anger to outweigh his terror, but it had not.

No amount of anger could shake his deep-rooted horror at the prospect of riding out to once again face a creature out of nightmare. He couldn't help but recall the heat and choking smoke of the cavern the first time they had encountered the dragon, of being unable to see the deaths of the men with him, but hearing it in excruciating detail. Of Sergeant Doyenne draining the life from herself to give her surviving comrades the chance to escape. The memories were seared into his mind.

They had not gone far before he noticed the first sensation. It was similar to the feeling he'd had the last time, but it seemed to be stronger now. Perhaps that was due to the repetition of the ritual?

He tried to focus on the sensation, but it felt as though it was pulling him in several directions at once. It took him a moment to conclude that the feeling indicated each dragon individually, but that concept was quickly scotched when he felt a fourth tug, coming from Venne. Might there be more than three dragons? If there were three, he supposed there could be four, perhaps more. If that was the case, it was time to ride back to Mirabay to tell the king to reestablish the Silver Circle, and fast.

They followed a herdsman's trail into the foothills until midmorning, with Gill trying to fine-tune his sense of where the beasts might be. The others were silent, perhaps concentrating on their own sensations, perhaps simply trying to appear unafraid. Either way, they were all lost in their thoughts. The directional sensations remained confused, although they seemed to be growing stronger.

He decided that if they hadn't found something to go on—a carcass or tracks—by noon, he would find an animal to kill and use as bait. There was no more gold to be had in Venne, but the scent of blood should attract the beasts. He would feel a fool if some of the other adventurers beat them to the kill, but the goal was to save the village, not win more fame by adding to his tally of slain dragons.

Stopping his horse, Guillot took a moment to survey the countryside they had been riding through. It was a beautiful landscape; green and fertile, laced with rivers and dotted with forests. He imagined it burning, strewn with the half-devoured carcasses of people and animals. As he urged his horse on, Gill tried to push the thought from his head. A wave of nervous energy coursed through him, so strong that he thought he would vomit. If that wasn't a warning, what was?

CHAPTER

23

G et ready," Gill shouted.

"For what?" Beausoleil said.

"It's coming."

The other three wheeled their horses around, searching the sky for their quarry, but there was nothing to be seen. Gill looked about frantically, his helmet narrowing his field of vision, even with the visor up. Nothing. Was the tugging feeling simply a side effect of the Cup? Had he gotten the ritual wrong? His question was answered by the sound of crunching from ahead of them. There was an escarpment a little farther up the trail. A head appeared from behind it, similar to the first dragon's, though this one was smaller and a deep bottle green, rather than black. The creature fixed its gaze on the hunting party.

"Gods alive," Beausoleil said. "It's big."

It was. Smaller than the first, for sure, but far bigger than Gill had hoped. He did his best to be positive. "It could be much bigger," he said.

The creature continued to stare at them. It seemed to lack the chilling intelligence and expressiveness the other one had possessed.

"Spread out and be ready to charge it," Gill said. "Wait for my word."

Their position on the trail was far from ideal for a charge on horseback, but if they surrounded the beast, they could advance slowly, trap it against the escarpment, and slay it.

"What should I do?" Val said.

There was more grit in his voice than Gill had expected, and certainly more than he felt himself. "Stay behind me. Keep me between you and the dragon."

The dragon remained still, flicking its gaze from one to the other as they moved to surround it. If it was in any way concerned, it didn't show it. He tried to see if its scales were any less armour-like than its predecessor's, but it was impossible to tell, and he had no great enthusiasm for the idea of trying to get a closer look.

"Steady now," he said. "We want to corner it against the rock. Don't do anything to spook it."

One of the horses scuffed a rock with its hoof. The dragon's head snapped to the sound and it let out a hiss. Gill winced in anticipation, but there was no flame. In another few seconds, they'd have it surrounded. Despite his helm, he could hear Val struggling to control his horse. He dared not look back to see what was happening. The horse let out a whinny and Gill could hear it rear and scrabble back. Val grunted and Gill cursed between gritted teeth. He hoped the lad had spent as much time riding horses as he had clearing up after them—he hadn't thought to ask. He and the others all rode warhorses, trained to cope with noise and the chaos of battle. He hadn't asked where Val had acquired—

The dragon moved before Gill had time to finish the thought. It burst into motion with speed that would shame a thousand-crown horse. Gill was unseated and lying on his back on the ground before his brain had fully registered the movement—it was even faster than the one Gill had killed. The wind had been knocked from his lungs, and he gasped, trying to breathe and stand up at the same time.

A tail swipe as soon as he got to his feet sent him flailing through the air long enough to feel victimised by the fact that out of three armoured targets, he was the only one to have been hit, and had been so twice. He hit the ground again with a crunch of armour, but was unhurt.

Gill looked back in the direction he'd come from. The dragon was approaching Val slowly, like a cat stalking its prey.

"To me, lad! To me!" Guillot shouted as he scrambled to his feet.

Val had managed to still his horse—either that or it was so terrified that it was unable to move. Everyone seemed frozen in place. Gill could see Beausoleil and Cabham staring with a mixture of horror and fascination as the beast approached Val. Looking around frantically,

Gill spotted his horse, along with his lance, too far away to be of any help. He drew his sword and started to run, but as the dragon paced ever closer, he knew he would be too late.

Cabham was the only one close enough to Val to be of use.

"Cabham!" Gill shouted. "Protect Val!"

If Cabham could get between Val and the dragon, he could keep the beast engaged while Beausoleil charged it from the side and give Gill time to get into a useful position. Even if Beausoleil's lance couldn't get past the scales, Gill would be able to strike with his Telastrian sword and they could all go home healthy and better for the experience.

There could be no doubt that Cabham had heard Gill—their eyes met. *Don't freeze,* Gill thought. But instead of charging into the dragon's path, he backed his horse away, then turned and galloped in the other direction. Val was locked in place, his gaze fixed on the dragon, apparently mesmerised by the creature.

Gill ran toward them for all he was worth. He had never been the fastest, and despite his recent exertions, was still very much out of training. It felt as though the world was slowing as the dragon began its death strike. Gill roared, hoping to distract the dragon for just one more moment, but he might as well not have existed. It moved forward explosively, fore talons and fangs leading the way.

At the moment Gill expected the fatal blow to land, Beausoleil somehow occupied the rapidly shrinking space between Val and the dragon. He struck with his lance, letting out a great shout of raging defiance that was punctuated by a splintering crack as his lance gave way under the force of his thrust. The banneret drew his sword, but as he brought it to bear, the dragon reached him, its wicked talons puncturing his armour as though it was paper. Beausoleil let out another great shout, but not of defiance. The dragon tossed him from his saddle, swiped the horse out of its way as effortlessly as a person might shoo a kitten, and bared its razor teeth at Val, who had at last started to back away.

Holding his sword like a dagger in both hands, Gill raised the weapon above his head. He knew he would likely have only one opportunity. Damn Cabham for his cowardice. The dragon screeched and twisted, turning away from Val and Gill, who plunged his sword into the beast's neck. The Telastrian steel cut the dragon's flesh like a hot knife through butter. He wrenched the blade up as the dragon's body continued to roll toward him, trying to cause as much damage as he could—to make that one blow a fatal one.

The dragon hissed and gave one last thrash before its roll stopped with it lying on its side. The tension spilled out of its muscles. Gill gave the body a kick. He looked at Val, who seemed to be fine, his expression of terror aside.

"My kill," Cabham said.

Gill looked up. Cabham had returned. He was seated on his horse, sword in hand. There was a lance sticking out of the dragon's flank, buried between two thick, bony scales that didn't look as though they were yet fully developed. Gill said nothing, still labouring to draw breath.

"My strike was the first. It's my kill," Cabham said.

Beausoleil had not moved from where the dragon had tossed him. Without giving Cabham a word or another look, Guillot walked to the younger man's prone form, knelt beside him, and rolled him over. Beausoleil's eyes were glassy and his lips were splattered with blood. There were a half-dozen rents in his breastplate, gleaming with blood. Gill closed Beausoleil's eyes and stood, the bitter taste of anger flooding his mouth.

"One down, two to go," Cabham said, a broad smile on his face.

"I told you to move in front of it," Gill said, from between gritted teeth.

"Then it would be me lying there."

"You had time for a proper strike. It would have given the rest of us the time we needed. All Beausoleil could do was get in its way."

Cabham shrugged. "It's dead. I'm sorry Beausoleil is also, but dragon slaying is a dangerous business."

"You're an expert now?"

"To the best of my knowledge, there are only two men alive who've killed a dragon, and I'm one of them."

"This isn't your kill," Guillot said. "It's Beausoleil's, you selfish, arrogant bastard."

"No need to be like that," Cabham said, his voice taking on an edge. "But this is my kill, and I'm going to claim my trophy."

Gill realised his sword was still stuck in the dragon's neck, while Cabham's was in his hand. All Gill had was the dagger on his belt.

"Lay a hand on that beast," Gill said, "and I'll have your arm off at the shoulder."

Gill could see Cabham weighing his options. Gill was defence-less, but right now Cabham could claim to have helped slay a dragon, with the unfortunate loss of one of their men. Cut down Guillot, and he would be a murderer. The only question was if he cared, or if he thought he could get away with it.

Cabham forced a smile and tipped his fingers to the open visor of his helmet in salute. "This marks the end of our association, sir. Good day." He turned his horse back in the direction of Venne, guiding it as it stepped gingerly over the dragon's neck, then rode away at a brisk trot.

Gill watched him go, angry at Cabham, angry at himself. Angry at the world. Beausoleil had been the man he was most concerned about, and he was shamed to have questioned the man's honour. When his test had come, he had been found anything but wanting. His cour-age had gotten him killed, but Guillot was damned if it meant he was forgotten. Cabham could claim what he liked when he got back to Venne, but Gill was the one with the reputation. He realised that Val had dismounted and come up beside him.

"It's my fault, isn't it?" Val said.

Gill shook his head. "No. If it's anyone's, it's mine. I didn't pre-pare you all properly. No one really knows how to prepare, but I could have done more. Should have. We'll see to that when we get back to Venne." He tousled Val's hair. "You're as much a part of killing this thing as anyone. You're a dragonslayer now."

The boy smiled uncertainly.

"See about getting my horse, will you? I'll get the spearheads and put Beausoleil up onto the pony so we can take him back to town."

"What about that?" Val said, nodding at the dead dragon.

"Let it rot."

It was early evening by the time they got back to Venne. Gill was starting to hurt from being knocked about by the dragon and his mood remained foul. The village was less crowded than it had been in the morning and people were busy, clearing the wreckage left from the previous night. Gill suspected many of the adventurers were still traipsing about the countryside, looking for a dragon. Gill could sense the beasts—three of those strange pulling sensations on him now—so assuming his theory about the feeling was correct, no one else had managed to kill one. The errant sensation seemed to be coming from the north. He was convinced now that there was a fourth dragon. Still, that was a problem for another day.

As Guillot and Val rode into the village, the people they passed stopped what they were doing to look at them, their eyes filled with the same question. Gill knew he had to let Edine know one of the beasts was dead. His gaze fell on the small church that had provided succour for the villagers during the attack. At least there was someone to look after Beausoleil and carry out the proper rites. Then he remembered his promise to Val. The living were more important than the dead.

"Go see the smith again," he said. "Get him to make you a short sword, no longer than your forearm from elbow to fingertips. Sharp on both sides, with a pointed tip good for use against plate armour. It won't be a rapier, but it'll be better for learning on the job. Off you go."

Val departed with surprising eagerness, leaving Gill alone to wonder if he should hire more men, or if that was simply inviting disaster, inviting another Cabham. One way or the other, he didn't need to decide right away, so he slipped down from his horse, hitched it and the pony, and headed to the mayor's house.

Just as he reached the door, Edine exited the building, closely followed by Cabham. She smiled broadly at Gill.

"An excellent start," she said. "Well done."

Guillot nodded, unsure he wanted to dampen her enthusiasm, but clueless as to how he could respond and not do so.

"We killed one of the dragons, which is a positive start, but it cost us a good man—Banneret Didier dal Beausoleil." He stared at Cabham, but decided there was nothing to be gained by bringing up what had happened. When the Humberlander realised that Gill wasn't going to say anything, he relaxed. Still, there was something in Cabham's eyes that told Gill that he didn't consider the matter dealt with, which was fine with Gill.

"I'd ask that your village chaplain carry out the necessaries for Beausoleil."

"I'll see to it," Edine said.

Her eyes narrowed and Gill could tell that she detected something was up. Rather than explain, he doffed his hat and headed for the tavern.

CHAPTER
24

Auroré walked through the grassy field, holding a young boy's hand. Gill knew the child was his, and knew that he was dreaming, but that didn't make it feel any less real. His wife had died in childbirth and their son had taken only a handful of breaths before he had followed her to the afterlife. He hadn't dreamed of them in a long time—the bottle had helped him escape that spectre. The dream was ever the perfect moment, which made it so much harder when the inevitable came, and he woke up to discover that it was not his life. He prayed for the dream to last, for the gods to give him a few more moments of the joy that could never truly be his. He remained deathly still, barely daring even to breathe as he watched his family walking in the warm summer sunshine. Happy.

He was so transfixed by the scene that he didn't notice the shadow that glided across the field. A jet of flame roared through the air, shattering the serene silence that had been punctuated only by the laughter of mother and child. Guillot looked up and saw a great black dragon swooping down on them, the flame jetting from its nostrils leaving a great charred streak on the ground. As Gill tried to shout a warning, he realised he hadn't been still and silent out of fear of waking from the dream, but because he could neither move nor make a sound. He had to stand where he was, his heart being ripped asunder, as he watched them laughing and talking, while flames tore toward them. Auroré looked back at him and smiled. His heart broke.

Guillot's room at the back of Gaufre's inn was pitch black when he woke with a jolt, Auroré's smiling face burned into his mind. His sheets were soaked with sweat and his heart was racing. His lingering sense of personal failure wouldn't go away, because it was warranted. He had lost a man and had trusted another whom he should not have. He tried to think of what more he could have done, or of any situation that required armed men where no casualties could be guaranteed. That was impossible, but he couldn't shake the feeling.

Now, down two men, he still had to deal with two more dragons. What was he to do? Take on more men? Keep throwing them at the problem until it was dealt with? That would leave a pile of bodies on his conscience so big that he wouldn't be able to recall any of their individual faces. He could try to slay them by himself—perhaps not depending on or looking out for anyone else was the safer option. If fate had chosen him to slay dragons, chosen that moment to bring them back, when he was the only remaining member of the Silver Circle, who was he to argue?

Then again, fate or the gods had taken Auroré and their son from him, so why should he do anything that fate mandated? Part of him wanted to turn his back on the whole thing, return to Villerauvais and sink into a bottle of wine. But there was no Villerauvais anymore, and there wouldn't be a Venne either, unless he did something about it.

He rubbed his face roughly, as though the sensation would pull his mind out of the hole it was in. When he was younger, decisions had come so easily. Life had been a great adventure with everything to gain and nothing to lose, and consequences had been distant things he couldn't imagine ever brushing against. Now, consequences were all there was.

▲▲▲▲▲▲

Gill met Val in the square not long before dawn. After the Cup ritual, Gill checked over their saddles and equipment, wondering if, in his fatigue after a night of interrupted sleep, he had said the words properly.

"Do we have to do it every day?" Val said, as he tended to the packhorse carrying the extra lances.

Gill shrugged. "To be honest, I don't know how long it lasts for, but I'd rather not find out the hard way." Gill rummaged about in his head for an innocuous word, lest there be someone listening. "If we administer it every day, we know we're covered."

"Makes sense," Val said, then after a moment, added, "It won't harm us, will it?"

"No. I've no reason to think so. The old Chevaliers used this, and some of them are said to have lived into ripe old age. The ones the dragons didn't kill, that is."

Val laughed, just as the sound of clattering hooves filled the square—Cabham at the head of a group of five horsemen, all armoured and ready for a fight. Cabham touched his helmet's visor as he rode past, puffed up and proud at the head of his little band. Gill had to admit they very much looked the part. For a moment he felt like a fraud, wearing the original Valdamar's armour, but then he recalled that Cabham was even less entitled to his newfound status than Gill felt he was.

"Peacock," Val muttered under his breath.

"Ignore him," Guillot said. "We have our own work to be about. Speaking of which, let me take a look at that sword."

Val drew it from its scabbard—a roughly shaped and stitched piece of leather that Gill reckoned Val had made himself. Judging by the expression on his face, the blade was his pride and joy. Gill wasn't expecting to be impressed—so long as the weapon was sturdy and sharp, it would do. He was pleasantly surprised. The sword was of a style frequently used by infantry sergeants, halfway between a long dagger and a rapier, with a simple hilt and a broad blade. These weapons could be brutally effective, and their compact size meant they could be used in a crowd or by someone who did not have a great deal of skill. The balance wasn't bad, the steel looked good, and the edges were keen. He suspected it wasn't the first such sword the smith had made.

"A good blade," he said, flipping it in an overly flashy manner before offering it back to Val, hilt first.

The lad beamed a smile and sheathed it.

"We can go through some cavalry cuts while we're riding out," Gill said. "If we've found nothing by lunchtime, I'll show you the first five positions."

Val furrowed his brow.

"The positions. They start off as fun, but once you've done them a thousand times, you'll dread even mention of the word. They're the basic guards and attacks of swordsmanship. You practise the movements over and over until they come more naturally than scratching your arse. If you get to the Academy, every day will start with an hour of work on the positions."

Gill hauled himself into the saddle and centred his mind on the sensations that indicated dragons were near. He could feel the tug, could tell that the source wasn't far off. It looked like they might not get to the positions that day, after all. "Let's get going," he said.

"What's it like there?" Val asked as they rode out of town.

"Where?"

"The Academy."

"It's fine. Tough, and competitive, but fair. Anyone who works hard will be respected, regardless of their skill or position at birth. The talented tend to get away with a lot, but that's the same everywhere. Most work hard there, but some think the most difficult part is getting in. They learn how wrong they are pretty fast. Any that don't are gone by the end of the first term. I liked it there. You always had purpose, something to do. Life isn't complicated there."

"How hard is it to get in?"

"I won't lie to you. It isn't easy. Plenty who started training for it far younger than you don't make the grade." By the look on Val's face, if he'd punched the boy in the stomach, he couldn't have knocked the wind out of his sails so well. "That's not to say you won't succeed. And you'll need a patron to pay for it, since you're not wealthy. It'll all be hard, have no doubt of that. But with a lot of work, and a little talent, it's achievable." Val stared dead ahead with the expression of one whose dreams had just been shattered.

"I'll make sure you're as well prepared as you can be," Gill said. "I promise. There was a time when people considered me to be rather good."

"I know how to work hard," Val said. "And I know what's waiting for me if I don't. It's not a mansion and a farm and a title."

"We'll get you there," Gill said. "After all, how many applicants can write down on their admission form that they've slain a dragon?" That finally elicited a smile.

"That's another thing you'll have to show me," Val said.

"What?"

"How to write."

▲▲▲▲▲▲

Guillot spent the greater part of the morning's ride trying to come up with a name for the ability the Cup gave him to sense the presence of dragons. He had already come to think of the general benefits the ritual conferred to be the "boon," but he felt that he needed another word for the power to tell when he was in proximity to dragons. It felt as though someone took hold of his insides and then pulled on them, as if his entire body was being urged in a specific direction. Unless, of course, he sensed more than one dragon, in which case the feeling was more of a confusing tussle. For want of anything better, the "pull" seemed to be the term he was settling on.

He could feel three distinct pulls that morning; one strong, the other two much weaker. The weaker ones were enough to muddy the water, so he had only the most superficial belief that he and Val were riding in the correct direction. He wondered if, with time, he would indeed be able to refine this ability into a useful tool, though he very much hoped that wouldn't be necessary. Still, it occurred to him that two drops from the Cup, rather than one, might help. It also occurred to him that that was a slippery slope, and most likely the reason the Imperial mages had never trusted full possession of the Cup to the Silver Circle.

He pushed the thought from his head, and tried to concentrate on the strongest sensation. It was growing more forceful, bolstering his confidence that they were headed toward it. One of the other pulls was confusing, though. If he hadn't known better, he would have said it was following them, but the sky was clear, and there was nothing to be seen—no dragon swooping down on them from behind. He focussed ahead, wishing the countryside they rode through was open pastureland, rather than a landscape pocked with intermittent forests and escarpments. It was the type of place that could hide an army of ten thousand men, lulling an enemy into thinking they were in peaceful, safe countryside.

A single dragon was a lot more easily concealed than an army, and Guillot couldn't tell when he was growing close, only when he was about to trip over the thing. He realised in that moment he hated this job. He was tense and his heart was racing. He had been like that ever since leaving Venne, and it was a puzzle to him why anyone would have willingly signed up for this back in the early days. Even a real battle had been easier to deal with. War was terrifying, yes, but you were facing other men, something you'd trained for and were prepared to deal with. Now, the unknowns gnawed at his confidence like hungry rats, giving fright to the butterflies that were scrambling the insides of his stomach.

He had no idea how big or fast this dragon would be, how aggressive, what it looked like, if it would breathe fire. The one they had just killed had not.

That question seemed to answer itself. A mile or so up the valley, on the far side of a stand of trees that concealed what was actually happening, a dark tendril of smoke crawled skyward.

25

The use of magic in this land goes back far longer than the Empire's control of it," the Prince Bishop said.

Solène tried to stay calm and appear unworried, all the while fearing he was lulling her into a false sense of security before having her flung into the dungeons.

"I've found some tantalising clues as to where it might have all begun—where Amatus discovered the spark of magical enlightenment and brought it back for the benefit of all humankind. I believe it was somewhere in Mirabay. I need your help to find it."

"Why me? Surely you've got enough people with the talent to seek out what you need?"

Amaury wasn't going to tell her the real reason—that she was the only person he knew who didn't need the power the temple might offer, who wouldn't be tempted to take it for themselves. "The fewer people who know about it, the better. It's a tense time. Something as potentially powerful as this will tempt some with more ambition than sense, and that's a situation that's easier to avoid than to clean up."

"You trust me?" Solène said.

The Prince Bishop laughed. "Of course not, but you have the magical talent to do the work of dozens of Order initiates. You can bring me what I need quickly, with only one person knowing about it."

She did her best not to swallow hard. The threat was unmistakable—if she turned on him, she would be easier to kill than an entire faction of the Order.

"What am I looking for?" she said.

"Once there was a temple or shrine, somewhere in Mirabaya, used

by a people called 'the enlightened.' This was apparently where Amatus learned to use magic. I believe it's where he found the Cup you
mentioned to me a while back. I think it was key to his gaining so
much skill and power. I want you to find out who these people—these
'enlightened'—were, and where their temple was. Along with whatever you can find out about the Cup. What it is, how it's used. I believe
the Cup and the temple to be intrinsically linked."

It was the first time he had said anything about the Cup to her, so
she waited, hoping he would say more. He merely looked at her intently, and there was only so long she could bear the silence.

"You think the answer is in the archive?" she said.

"Perhaps. That's where I found first mention of the enlightened,
but perhaps not. I expect we'll have to get out into the country and
search for it. Still, your ability to comb through the material is far
greater than mine, so I'm hopeful you'll be able to turn up something
where I could not. Sift it for whatever information you can find, and
we'll go from there."

"I understand. I'll do my best."

"This needs to stay between us," the Prince Bishop said. "If anyone
asks what I have you doing, make something up. Tell them I have you
coaching me in magic if you like. Anything but the truth. This stays between us."

▲▲▲▲▲

"What does he want you to do?" dal Drezony said, pushing her way
into Solène's apartment.

Solène hadn't been back long, and was tired. When the Prince
Bishop made a request, he expected it to be acted on immediately, and
she had spent an unfruitful day in his secret archive as a result.

"Just to do some research for him," she said. "He seems to think that
only someone with my magical power will understand some old documents he turned up. I don't think he's right, but I can hardly say no."

Dal Drezony scrutinised her. "That's all?"

She considered telling dal Drezony everything, but for some reason wasn't certain it was the right time. "Yes. Why?"

"He's been making some pretty unreasonable demands of the Order recently. He was always overly ambitious and impatient, but I believed the core of what he was trying to achieve was good. Now I don't know. The men he's bringing into the Order—they represent the opposite of everything we stand for. I'm frightened, Solène."

"I haven't seen any trouble on the streets," Solène said. "I'm sure we'll be safe in the Priory. The new soldiers the Prince Bishop hired will be able to defend the walls, at least."

"That's not what I'm talking about. Promise that if he asks you to do something you're not comfortable with, you'll tell me."

Solène nodded.

"Above all, don't do anything that will put you in danger. He's going to call on you to use your power, and sooner rather than later. We need to make sure that when he does, you're ready. You can't afford to spend all of your time doing whatever he tells you."

"What option do I have?"

Dal Drezony sighed and thought for a moment. "Once you've found whatever it is you're looking for, he'll want you on the dragon-hunting expedition. I've tried to slow preparations down as much as I can—I won't be complicit in the deaths of any more of my brothers and sisters because they were sent into danger underprepared. Our new comrades are making that difficult. Say what you like about the Prince Bishop, one thing he's good at is picking talent. Vachon and Gassot know what they're doing, and if it were up to them, the expedition would be equipped and ready to go." She let out a chuckle. "I've insisted that they interview pretty much everyone in the Order before selecting the hunting party. They wanted me to pick the best and most experienced, but I said they should make that decision for themselves. They didn't like it, but deep down I think the idea of relying on anyone else's selection was something they liked even less."

The thought of dealing with another dragon sent a shiver down Solène's spine, and for a moment she was tempted to tell dal Drezony about the Cup, the ritual, and how they had helped Gill. If there were more dragons, no one could expect Gill to deal with them all. Perhaps the Prince Bishop was right wanting to bring the Cup back to the Order, so they would have a proper chance of facing the beasts, and surviving. She didn't like the Prince Bishop, didn't trust him, but he was the man in power. There was the king, of course, but as best she could tell, his interest in running the kingdom was limited to delegating everything to men like the Prince Bishop.

Could she live with herself if she let the men and women of the Spurriers march against the dragons, and probably to their deaths, if she knew a way to give them a chance? She couldn't. In addition, it would take the pressure off Gill. She knew that at some point the Prince Bishop would try again to kill Gill. If the Prince Bishop had the Cup, and whatever power this temple might bring him, he would certainly succeed.

She couldn't stand by and allow that to happen. There had to be another way, one that wouldn't give the Prince Bishop insurmountable power to do as he chose.

She decided against telling him what she knew about the Cup, at least for the time being.

"Solène? Solène, did you hear what I said?"

Solène smiled. "I'm sorry, Seneschal. I was lost in my thoughts."

"I said, we'll need to make use of every spare moment to squeeze in your training. You might not get much sleep over the next few days, but the Order's physicians will be able to help you with that in the short term. We'll do whatever it takes to make sure you can keep yourself safe. Increasing our ability to draw on the Fount is what takes most of the effort for us normal souls. Once you're in control of your mind, you're in control of your magic.

"Now that you know how to go about that, it's simply a case of developing the confidence to be able to do it consistently. You could reach that point by tomorrow, or never. That's a destination you will have to reach on your own."

Solène nodded. Her frustration was growing as people tried to pull her in different directions. At least dal Drezony seemed well intentioned. Solène thought fondly of what it was like to be another invisible face in a city where no one cared enough to bother you, where her only worry was getting to the bakery in time to light the ovens. It felt as though the thing she had so long thought of as a curse, then so briefly thought of as a great gift that could change her life for the better, was very much a curse once again.

Dal Drezony smiled. "Don't look so daunted. Nearly everyone manages it. I'm sure you can too."

CHAPTER
26

Guillot spurred his horse to the gallop. There was nothing else out here that could cause a spontaneous fire, if the pull wasn't already proof enough. The only question in his mind was what the dragon was burning. Val followed close behind. Gill untethered the lance he had kept on his horse and tried to calm his mind.

"Stay well back again, Val," Gill shouted over the thunder of his horse's hooves. "I'll come back to you for another lance if I need one."

They reached the stand of trees, and started to skirt its edge. Gill was pushing his horse hard, harder than he needed to, he realised. There was no one from Venne out this far. The dragon was most likely eating a stray farm animal or a chamois come down from the mountains, not a person. He was halfway around the trees when he heard someone shouting in the distance. Wrong again, Gill thought, urging more speed from the horse.

Both man and beast were breathing hard by the time they cleared the trees. Guillot's gaze was immediately drawn to the black, hulking mass that was liberally spraying fire about itself. Gill was immediately taken back to the cave where he had first seen a dragon, a great, malevolent collection of sinew, fangs, and aggression. A shiver ran over his skin. This one was bigger than the last, much bigger, nearly the size of the first dragon he had killed.

Cabham, mounted, was circling the creature at a distance, the visor on his helmet up, lance in hand. He seemed to be trying to direct two armoured men who were not on horseback. It looked to Guillot very much like Cabham was trying to use them as bait. Piles of charred remains were, Gill assumed, all that remained of the other two men who had ridden out of Venne with Cabham that morning. It seemed that Cabham had learned that there was more to dragons than claws and fangs. Like all lessons relating to dragons, it was a hard one. Harder for his men than him, however.

Gill brought his horse to a stop and waited. He had no desire to get himself killed digging Cabham out of a hole. Val appeared at his side.

"It's bigger," he said.

The lad was perceptive, at least. That might benefit him when it came to swordplay, Gill supposed.

The men before him dashed left and right while Cabham tried to keep his horse calm. Gill assumed he was searching for a chink in the beast's more developed scale plating. With the thing belching flame with every breath, Cabham would get only one chance, if that. Gill suspected the Humberlander was wondering if his fire protection from the previous day would still be effective. Gill wondered that too, and was glad he wasn't the one testing it.

One of Cabham's men changed direction a second too late. His scream would have been unlike anything Gill had ever heard were it not for the fact that he had been in that cave with the first dragon. The man was cooked in his armour like a chicken in a cook pot, roasting and boiling in his own fluids at the same time. It took a distressingly long time for the screaming to stop.

Cabham didn't seem to be in any hurry to put himself in danger. Still, the beast needed to be killed, and if he wasn't going to make the most of the poor unfortunate still dodging jets of flame on foot, Gill would. He spurred his horse to a gallop and levelled his lance. He glimpsed Cabham's look of astonishment but gave it no further thought, focussing on his task.

The dragon turned its attention to Guillot and, with a screeching roar, unleashed a jet of flame. The air sizzled, but the blast felt like nothing more than a warm breeze to Gill. His horse reacted, shying away, but the fire had struck only Gill's head and shoulders, passing over the horse. He had just decided to carry out the ritual on his horse in future when his lance tip connected with the dragon and his ears were filled with the sound of splintering wood.

The lance would have had more effect had he charged a castle wall.

The shaft must have contained a knot, and had shattered, though the initial impact was still strong enough to drive Gill from the saddle. As he hit the ground, unseated for the second time in as many days, it occurred to him that perhaps going against a dragon on horseback wasn't the best idea. He rolled to his feet, his well-fitting armour barely impeding his movement, and turned to face the dragon, sword drawn. It sprayed him with flame again, its eyes filled with fury. Gill braced against the barrage of hot air. When it stopped, the dragon had turned its attention to the last of Cabham's men and finished him in the blink of an eye, perhaps assuming that Gill, like its other victims, was dead.

Guillot charged, leading with his broad-bladed Telastrian sword in an underhand grip that would allow him to drive it deep and true. He could almost feel its tip touch a scale when a talon swipe sent him to the ground again. He allowed the momentum to tumble him back to his feet but was struck again, on the back this time. Gill stumbled forward, doing his best to stay upright. The ancient Telastrian armour he wore absorbed most of the blow, but it still felt as though he had been hit by a battering ram. He wasn't sure even a suit of Jauré's finest tournament armour would have withstood the impact, and thanked the gods that he had measurements similar to the original owner, Valdamar.

He swiped behind himself with his sword, a blind strike born more of frustration than any hope of scoring a hit, but felt the blade connect and heard the beast screech. Turning, he was satisfied to see the dragon holding one of its talons against its body. He faced it and took his guard out of instinct, feeling foolish, knowing how little good it would do him in fending off an attack. The beast looked hesitant—it had clearly never before encountered anything that could hurt it. As satisfying as that was to Guillot, it was a lucky shot, and not one that would do any lasting damage. The killing stroke would be far more difficult to land. He thought of calling to Cabham for assistance, but a quick glance over his shoulder showed that this challenge was a little too rich for the Humberlander's taste. He was gone.

Gill backed away slowly, his eyes locked on the dragon's as they both tried to work out what to do next. It belched out another jet of flame, but it was a less determined attack. When the flame and smoke cleared, and Gill stood unharmed on a patch of baked soil, the dragon pounced. Gill dived to his left, doing his best to roll out of the way. He remembered to watch out for the beast's tail the instant before it struck him—not soon enough to get out of the way.

One of the barbs found its way to the unprotected spot at his left armpit, and he roared as he felt it punch into him. He instinctively pulled away, then struggled to his feet and staggered backwards. There was no pain. At first he thought that a plate had blocked all but the blunt force of the impact. The blood flowing down his vambrace and cuirass dispossessed him of that idea, however.

He had been injured before, and not felt the pain right away. The shock of the moment, he reckoned, though that didn't last long. When the shock faded, he would be in trouble. He needed to get his business finished, and fast.

The dragon turned, and knew it had done damage, for its eyes went straight to Gill's wounded left shoulder. It moved around to Gill's left, trying to position itself on his weak side.

He tracked it, keeping his sword out in front of him for the ever-diminishing sense of security it gave him. The dragon rasped out a threatening hiss, baring its fangs. Gill held his ground. He reckoned his best hope was to allow it to come at him, try to dodge, and strike, hoping he'd find a way through its hide to something vital. It held its place, seeming a little more circumspect now that it had realised he was able to hurt it and that its main weapon had no effect on him.

"Come on then!" Gill said. There was no reaction other than a low, throaty grumble. Although he still didn't feel any pain, Gill was losing blood; he realised the dragon was waiting for him to weaken. Shouting, he threw himself forward. He sliced at the dragon's face as soon as it was within range, but the beast moved it out of the way with time to spare.

His blade swished through the air. Off balance because of his injury, Gill staggered a few paces, and was then helped along by a swat of the dragon's talon, which launched him into the air. He did his best not to land on his wounded shoulder, but the impact rattled him nonetheless. He expected a sharp pain, but instead felt a dull, nausea-inducing sensation that made him realise he'd been hurt badly.

He was slow and awkward in getting up, hanging on to his sword with his one good arm. A shadow stretched over him, and he felt the hairs on the back of his neck stand up. The air was filled with the smell of charred flesh.

A roar broke the moment, one that vacillated between the shout of a man and that of a boy. Gill looked up to see Val charging the dragon with one of the spare lances. The lance shattered, and Val was thrown through the air. Gill knew he was unlikely to get another opportunity as good as this. He scrambled along, ignoring the discomfort that seared through his chest from his shoulder, and hurled himself forward, sword first.

He drove with his feet, slipping to his knees, then trying again. He continued until the blade was buried deep, then wrenched at the hilt for all he was worth, pulling it in every direction, trying to cut up as much of the dragon's innards as he could. The dragon's thunderous roar pounded in Gill's head, sounding angry and hurt. Gill pulled his sword free and scrabbled away on his hands and knees. Only when he was clear of the beast's shadow did he turn to look.

The dragon was still on its feet, its head lolling gently from side to side. It let out a short puff of flame, then turned toward Gill and let out more fire, although the jet fell far short. A final act of defiance. With that, the dragon toppled over and didn't move again.

This just does not get any easier, Gill thought. He prodded the beast with his sword, stabbed it a couple of times to make sure it was dead, then rushed to where Val was lying. His heart was in his throat when he rolled the lad onto his back. If it was anyone's turn to die, it was Gill's. Val was little more than a boy, with so much of life left to see.

"Did we get it?" Val said groggily.

Gill let out a laugh of relief. "We got it."

Val tried to get up on his elbows, but Gill held him in place. "Rest easy a moment. We can wait for as long as you need."

He slumped down beside Val and took a breath. A dead dragon lying nearby was becoming a familiar sight for Gill. That wasn't something he thought he'd ever find himself thinking. He realised he had forgotten about his shoulder—the intense pain had yet to arrive. He unbuckled his left pauldron and gently removed it, then did his best to loosen his cuirass and pull it off. His quilted under-jacket was dark with blood, but the wave of pain that he had expected remained conspicuously absent. He took his dagger and cut the quilting, enlarging the hole left by the dragon's tail barb, then used a piece of the cloth to wipe away some of the blood. That he was no longer bleeding heavily was a relief, but it didn't change the fact that he had already lost quite a bit of blood and was utterly exhausted.

Despite being accustomed to gore, he steeled himself for what he was about to reveal before lifting the cloth away—seeing a bad wound on yourself was always far harder than looking at one on someone else. To his surprise, he found only an angry red welt, seeping fluid and blood—a superficial injury. It looked like the barb had grazed him rather than penetrated, but he distinctly remembered the sensation of it striking bone. He probed the area gently, but there was no sign of a deeper wound.

Had he thought it was worse in the heat of the moment? No, he knew what he had felt, and he remembered not being able to lift his arm. Now he could do so with no difficulty, except for a little tightness where the injury was. Had it been the Cup? Both the Order's healers and Solène had been able to speed healing and remove fatigue—might that be another of the Cup's offerings?

He allowed himself to relax for a moment, to let the chaos of the past few minutes wash away as the normal sounds of the countryside started to return. Then his heart raced in panic before his mind had time to catch up.

The pull, as strong as he had ever felt it. He grabbed his sword and jumped to his feet with as much energy as he could muster. The other dragon must have been nearby and come to see what was going on. He scanned the sky but saw nothing. Disbelieving, he looked again, but the sky remained clear. He spun on his heels, fearing that it might be lurking in the trees, but something that large would have trouble moving about in a forest, and would make a lot of noise. His eyes were tired—baked dry from the heat, and clogged with smoke. He blinked repeatedly to keep them clear and in focus, but he saw nothing close enough to—

Then he saw Cabham. Sitting on his horse a safe distance away, watching. No doubt he had waited to see if Gill managed to kill the dragon and now would ride back to Venne as fast as he could to claim it. Gill blinked again and focussed, and realised this man wasn't wearing armour. It wasn't Cabham. His hair was brown, his complexion darker, and he looked more Mirabayan than Humberlander. Gill couldn't make out many details from that distance, but there was nothing about him that was familiar. What was he doing there? Why did he simply sit on his horse and watch?

Perhaps the man realised that Gill had seen him, for he gave a wave, and then, in no great hurry, rode away. Gill watched him for a moment. Val groaned behind him, reminding Guillot that he needed to get the horses and get himself and the boy back to Venne for some hot food and badly needed rest. Overall, the day could have gone far worse.

▲▲▲▲▲▲

Pharadon was ambivalent at having witnessed the slaying of a dragon. There were many moments when he had been tempted to intervene, but he'd resisted.

The dragon had been a large, but not quite fully grown, blackscale. It was difficult to say how old it was—depending on how much food and Fount was available, a dragon could reach its full size in anything from a couple of weeks to several months. Both were more plentiful than Pharadon had ever known, so he guessed this dragon had hatched very recently.

That raised another issue—and an alarming one. This dragon had advanced to a level of maturity beyond which enlightenment was no longer possible. That was why he had allowed the human to slay it. If the man had not, Pharadon would have been forced to do it himself. Base dragons, never brought to enlightenment, were a scourge— violent, aggressive creatures driven by instinct. He had hoped to bring these young dragons to enlightenment, but both this one and the greenscale were too mature. He could sense only one more, and worried now that he was too late. Beyond this last creature, he detected no more of his kind.

All dragons were born base and would remain so if an enlightened dragon did not intervene and lift them from their wretched fate. That was a normal thing for a dragon hatched of enlightened parents. Within days of their breaking out of their eggs, their parents would ensure that the ceremony was carried out and they would join their enlightened brethren.

On a rare occasion, something went wrong and the offspring of an enlightened would not be raised in time. The window of opportunity was short—juvenile dragons grew fast even at the worst of times. When that happened, it was a tragic thing, the kind of devastating event that a parent rarely recovered from—to see their child descend into darkness.

All dragons had been base once. At some point, long before even Pharadon had drawn his first breath, the spark of enlightenment had taken hold in a goldscale and it had been able to share that spark with others. That had created the divide between enlightened and base. The first enlightenment seemed to have been a matter of luck, if the old stories were to be believed—simply a case of being in the right place at the right time.

Those who were not elevated had to suffer on as they were. There were those amongst the enlightened who tried to set that wrong to right; they had spent their lives seeking out base juveniles and enlightening them. It was a difficult, overwhelming task, and often dangerous—base dragons were hostile to everything they did not understand.

Those who were missed—those base beasts that grew to adulthood— caused problems for all the rest. They sought out territory and would fight to the death to possess it. The enlightened were eventually forced to keep them under control, and so, for a time, Pharadon had found himself killing troublesome base dragons.

The large blackscale the knight had killed had already marked out a wide-ranging territory and would soon have come into conflict with the greenscale, which had done likewise. Pharadon had found several places where their scents had overlapped. The valley was not large enough for both of them, and certainly not with a third in the area. They had probably been brood mates; that was something that Pharadon had never understood about the base. They shared blood, something of supreme importance to the enlightened, but to the base, it meant nothing. They would have killed one another without hesitation, just to protect their chosen scraps of territory, in a time when it seemed that the world was all but emptied of dragonkind. However, there was one more out there, and if he was lucky, it might not yet have matured beyond his reach.

Seeing the battle, Pharadon had learned something else of interest. Something as disturbing as having seen Alpheratz's head on the table in that small human shop. The Silver Circle still existed. That would make his quest more difficult. A slayer couldn't be ignored or run from—they were relentless. This one would have to be dealt with. Bringing a base dragon to enlightenment was a dangerous process. If one of the Silver Circle turned up during this time, the consequences would be disastrous for both Pharadon and the base dragon. He would check on the dragon first, and then, all being well, he would kill the knight.

CHAPTER
27

By the time Gill and Val got back to Venne, Gill's left shoulder felt no different than the rest of him. On the way, he had done his best to surreptitiously rinse some of the blood from his armour with his water skin so he wouldn't have to explain away the evidence of a wound he didn't have. Val had not been too shaken by the results of his reckless act of bravery, and Gill was satisfied that things had gone as well as he could have hoped. There was only one dragon left, and he was beginning to believe they could successfully kill all three.

In the village, they headed straight for the tavern, eager for something to wash the tang of smoke and charred flesh from their throats, and for a hot meal to help them recover from the strains of the day. As they approached the building, Gill thought he felt the pull and quickly turned his attention to the sky, a flash of panic sweeping through him. There was nothing up there. He was exhausted; his body was sending him all sorts of unusual signals and sensations, none of them welcome.

"Is something wrong, my Lord?" Val said.

Gill scanned the sky a moment longer, but it was clear. Perhaps the feeling was a sign the Cup's effects were wearing off. Perhaps he was just so tired he was imagining the sensation. In any event, he couldn't really tell where it was coming from.

"Nothing," Gill said. "Let's get inside." He was surprised to see that the taproom was empty save for one man sitting at the bar, hunched over a mug of ale.

"Where is everyone?" Gill asked when Gaufre appeared.

"A few were killed yesterday," Gaufre said, his voice mournful. "A few more today."

Gill couldn't work out if the tavern keeper was lamenting the men's untimely deaths or the fact that they could no longer patronise his tavern. Either way, it was bad luck they had met with the dragons before Gill had gotten there.

"Some have gone home," Gaufre continued with a shrug. "Too dangerous for them. Others are still out in the field. I expect it will get busy later."

"I expect it will," Gill said, feeling his second question had been answered without his having to ask it. "We'll take some hot food and water as fast as you can rustle it up."

They took a table near the fire. Guillot had always preferred empty taverns, where there was less to distract him from his drinking and his self-loathing. As the warmth from the fire soaked into his stiff muscles, Gill tried to get his head around the idea that he had to go out first thing in the morning and do it all again. He wondered how many times he could go dragon hunting before his luck ran out.

He stretched out his shoulder, allowing the heat to do its work. As Gaufre brought the food, the door opened, and a man wrapped in a cloak, topped with a wide-brimmed hat, walked in. Judging by the firelight reflecting on the beads of water covering his cloak like tiny red jewels, it was drizzling outside. The man looked about the place, his gaze stopping on Gill.

"Captain?"

Gill frowned.

The man removed his hat and pushed back his cloak. He was thinner than Gill remembered, and a bit older, but there was no mistaking him.

"Barnot? Sergeant Barnot?"

"As I live and breathe. What brings you to this armpit of nowhere, Captain?"

Gaufre shot Barnot an unappreciative look. Gill had no doubt he was calculating how much money the new arrival might have, and if he could make up for the day's loss of custom. If the coin was good enough, anything could be forgiven.

"The same thing I expect brought you here," Gill said, his pleasure at encountering a friendly face filling his voice. "Come, sit with us. Gaufre! Bring another plate! A mug of ale too."

Barnot sat with a nod of thanks.

"How long has it been, Barnot?" Gill said, delighted to see a man he knew he could rely on.

Barnot raised his hands. "Just before you left the city. The duel. I tried to get in touch after, but . . ."

"It took me some time," Gill said. "To, you know. I wasn't very good company. But tell me, what have you been doing? Still soldiering?"

"Not for a time now. I'd saved a bit, so I opened a tavern. Not much bigger than this. In a village called Nordonne."

Gill frowned. "What happened? Couldn't leave the life of adventure behind?"

"More like it wouldn't leave me behind," Barnot said. "Wasn't suited to the tavern keeping business. Neither was Missus Barnot. She ran off with the baker, and the bailiffs took the tavern."

"I'm sorry to hear that," Gill said.

Barnot shrugged. "That's the way of these things. I've much to be grateful for. I've already lived far longer than I deserve. I've enough left in me for one more adventure, at least."

Gaufre arrived with another plate of food and a mug of ale.

Barnot lifted the mug. "Ale and good company. What more could an old soldier want?"

Gill lifted his cup of water, to Barnot's mug of ale. The old soldier gave him a crooked look.

"You know it's bad luck to toast with water, don't you, Captain?"

Gill shrugged. "I try to stick to water these days."

The door opened again before Barnot had a chance to comment. Gill looked up to see Cabham walk in with two men behind him. The Humberlander shut the door and bolted it behind him. That told Gill all he needed to know about what was to come. When Cabham spotted Gill, he started over, then hesitated at the sight of another man at Gill's table. A moment later he stepped closer, his two new associates in tow.

"What can I help you with, William?" Gill said. There was no way he was going to afford Cabham any of the usual courtesies bannerets reserved for one another. Not after their short, shared history.

"I'm going to need that cup thing you have."

Gill laughed out loud, although he had a sick feeling in his stomach. Revealing the Cup to Cabham and Beausoleil had been a bad decision. "That's not going to happen," he said.

"If it sounded like I was asking, that was just me being polite. I'm telling you to hand it over."

Gill flicked his eyes to Barnot, who raised an eyebrow.

"I see you've made some new friends," Gill said. "Have you told them what happened to your old ones?"

"Hunting dragons is a dangerous business," Cabham said. "People get killed."

"You certainly know more about that than I do."

"I didn't come here for a chat. Either hand over the cup or there'll be trouble."

"Trouble?" Gill said. "Go home before your luck runs out, Cabham."

"There's three of us. Only two of you."

Gill looked over to Val. "Three of us. Or can we add counting to the list of things you're not very good at?"

"Leave the lad out of it," Cabham said. "You'll only end up getting him killed like you did Beausoleil."

"Beausoleil was killed because *you* were more interested in personal glory than getting the job done properly."

"Enough," Cabham said. "Hand it over and we'll be on our way."

Gill shrugged. "Even if you have the Cup, you need the words. I seem to have forgotten them."

Cabham smiled and started to recite them, perfectly. Gill's heart sank.

"I heard them four times. I'm pretty sure I had them all after the second time. Like I said before, I tend to remember things."

"I'm not giving you the Cup," Gill said. "So either you draw steel or you piss off."

Blades were out before he'd even finished the sentence. Gill jumped up from his chair and drew. Barnot didn't need an invitation; he stood at Gill's side, sword at the ready.

"Don't know you, friend," Cabham said to Barnot, "but feel free to leave."

Barnot's response was a lunge at the man to Cabham's left. Cabham went straight for Gill, thrusting across the table, but Gill was able to parry with ease. He cast a concerned glance at Val, hoping the boy had the sense to stay out of the way. Like as not they'd kill him anyway if they got past Gill and Barnot, but he'd be committing suicide if he tried to take on a banneret. Gill kicked the table to one side—it was heavier than he had expected, and the blow hurt his foot, but he ignored the pain and feinted at Cabham. He'd never seen the Humberlander's swordplay, but there was no reason to believe he wasn't a decent swordsman. He might have had many flaws, but he might still have been useful with a blade.

Not taking the bait, Cabham waited to see what Gill meant to do. Gill feinted again, then changed the line of his attack and tried an opportunistic cut at one of Cabham's companions. The man jumped out of the way and Gill moved to close the space between them. He could see Barnot and Cabham's other man having at one another.

The man Gill had cut at came at him, with Cabham alongside, pressing Gill. For a moment he found himself enjoying it. There had been a time when he had thrived on such challenges, and as he slipped into a flowing rhythm of parrying and riposting between the two, he could almost see himself back in those days. Almost.

The taproom was filled with the sound of clashing steel, shouts, and the stamping of feet. Gill's shoulder started to ache and he had to grit his teeth and force it to keep moving. He was tired. Too tired. As wonderful as the Cup was, it seemed there was a personal cost to using it. Cabham sensed that Gill was slowing and pressed his attack. His comrade did the same, and Gill knew that he was fighting against time. He started looking for a way to make his life easier.

Switching from speed to force, he knocked Cabham's sword off to the side in the hope of opening some space. As he tried to bring his blade back to defend himself against Cabham's comrade, he realised that he had underestimated the other man's speed. The banneret's blade caught Gill in the same shoulder that had been injured earlier that day. As pain seared through him, he wondered how much of the

Cup's healing effect was still in operation. Judging by the pain—so intense it made him struggle for breath—it was definitely running out.

Cabham pounced. Gill pulled himself off the blade in his shoulder and parried. Suddenly the heat from the fire, which moments before had been welcoming, felt oppressive. Sweat beaded on his brow, but he managed to parry Cabham's attack with the fatalistic satisfaction of one who knew he wouldn't be able to pull that move off again. The second man's attack was thrown off when he was struck on the side of the head by a barstool. Cabham's head twitched in distraction. Not one to pass up an opportunity, even without time to reset and execute a tidy thrust, Gill cut to the right with all the force he could muster. He felt the blade make contact. Cabham let out a grunt, but Gill didn't have time to rest on his laurels.

He pulled his blade clear, then thrust it into the second man's throat. A vicious flick of his wrist was enough to ensure that the man wouldn't trouble Gill again, leaving him free to make sure that he had finished the job with Cabham.

Cabham was sitting on the tavern's floor, doing his best to hold his guts in his belly. He was dead, but his dying would be long and painful yet. Gill dispatched him with a precise thrust to the heart. Barnot was finishing with his foe, leaving Guillot time to catch his breath and press a finger against his new wound. He looked about the taproom to find the source of the stool—and received a nod from the man who had been sitting at the bar when he and Val came in.

Barnot let out a shout as he executed the killing cut, then a laugh as he sucked in lungfuls of air.

"Just like the old days, Captain!" Barnot said.

"It felt easier in the old days," Gill said. He looked around and saw Val standing in the corner, his sword clutched in a white-knuckled grip. "You need to hold it softly, lad, like something fragile. You can put it away for now, though."

The stranger was now leaning against the bar, his stool lying on the floor next to a corpse. Gill returned his nod and walked over.

"I owe you my thanks," he said. "You didn't have to do that."

"It didn't look like a fair fight," the man said.

"I'm in your debt. Guillot dal Villerauvais is my name."

"I'm Phar . . . ançois."

Barnot made his way over, followed by Val.

"Honoured to make your acquaintance, François. This is Sergeant Barnot, and my squire, Valdamar."

Gill saw François's eyes narrow at Val's name, and laughed. "A little ostentatious I'll grant you, but he's a good lad. Gaufre!"

It took some time for Gaufre to appear from a back room. He grimaced at the sight of the mess, and Gill felt a pang of guilt at the damage they'd done. Still, it wasn't their fault.

"A bottle of brandy," Gill said.

"That's more like it," Barnot said.

"Don't get too excited. It's for my shoulder," Gill said.

Gaufre brought a bottle and four glasses.

"A cloth too," Gill said.

Gaufre nodded, still not having uttered a sound since leaving his hiding place. He set a rag on the bar in front of Gill. It didn't look too dirty, so Gill took it, doused it liberally in brandy, and pressed it to his wound.

Barnot studied the bottle and gave an approving grunt. "Can't let a decent bottle like this go to waste," he said, then filled a glass and slid it over to François. "The least we can do is stand you a drink, friend." He filled another and gave it to Val. "It'll put hairs on your chest. Take your time with it, mind." He then filled one more glass and gave Gill an inquiring look. "Sure I can't tempt you? A man needs something a bit stronger than water after a fight like that."

Gill looked at the glass. His shoulder burned like the fires of hell. If nothing else, the brandy would ease the pain a little. One drink couldn't hurt. He'd killed two dragons and as many men in the last two days. He'd stop after the first. He took a deep breath and let it whistle out between his teeth. Then he nodded. Barnot smiled and slid the glass over to him, then filled the final one for himself.

"Old friends, and new," Barnot said. "And bad fights well won."

They all took a drink, with Val spluttering most of his across the bar. Gill felt the welcome heat of the brandy flood down his throat into his gut, then spread through his body. He closed his eyes and revelled in the feeling. It was like welcoming home an old friend that he had not seen in far too long. It was odd—for a moment he thought he could feel the pull, but the brandy drowned it, and all the other aches, out.

"Tell me, François," Barnot said, as Gaufre started to clean up the mess in the taproom. "Where are you from?"

The newcomer shrugged. "Here and there. Came to see a dragon with my own eyes."

"Not to kill one and make a name for yourself?" Gill said.

François laughed. "No. Seeing one in the flesh's enough for me."

Gill looked down and saw that Barnot had topped up his glass. His shoulder still ached. He'd finish what was there, then refuse any more.

CHAPTER
28

The entire village was gone," Gill said, with the determined precision of a man who was trying to prove he could speak without slurring. "Everything. Everyone. Ash. Nothing more."

François nodded gravely. "I'm sorry to hear that."

Gaufre had cleared the bodies and done his best to mop up the blood, in the hope of putting the place to rights before other customers arrived. A few people had poked their heads in after Gaufre unbolted the door, but, greeted with chaos and carnage, had elected to spend their evening elsewhere. The news must have spread, for no one came near the place for the remainder of the night. Eventually Gaufre damned them all to hell and went to bed.

Barnot did his drunken best to show the equally inebriated Val some basic cuts and guards, using some long pieces of kindling he'd taken from the log bucket by the fire. He wasn't doing a very good job, but Val was enjoying himself, and the lad deserved a bit of fun.

Gill filled his glass again. They'd finished the brandy. He was drinking wine. It wasn't very good wine, but he was long past caring. He knocked it back and filled the glass again. The thought of Villerauvais and all the people who had died there created a pain within him that felt worse than the wound to his shoulder. He drank again. It seemed no amount of booze would ease the hurt of the memory of Villerauvais.

"I'm sorry too," Gill said, not trying to hide the slurring anymore. "I should have done more. If I'd gotten to that bastard beast a day or two sooner. They'd all still live.

"Men, women, children. People just trying to scratch a living out of the soil. All dead. For no good reason."

"Is there ever a good reason?" François said.

Gill shrugged. Maybe. There were people out there who deserved to die. Evil bastards who wanted to shape the world in line with their own twisted ideas. Amaury, for instance. His eyelids were heavy. Too heavy. He let them rest for a moment. His head lolled forward and sleep took him.

▲▲▲▲▲▲

Barnot had been drinking water for hours. The young lad had passed out early enough, but the captain seemed to have hollow legs. He pretended to be asleep on the bar as Gill grew drunker, and his words lazier, until at last his head had thudded onto the table. Their new friend, François, had chuckled, moved Gill into a more comfortable position, then left the tavern.

Barnot had waited a while longer, until he was sure he was the only man awake. He stepped over Val, who was lying on the floor, then tiptoed over to Gill, although he reckoned a bull could have stampeded through the taproom and not woken someone who had put away as much as Gill had. He had hesitated then. It had felt good to be back with the captain, fighting at his side. It reminded him of who he used to be. Before he had turned to the seed to drown out all the screams. Seeing that much killing robbed a man of his soul. You had to fill the emptiness with something. Dream-seed smoke had seemed like the thing—just the odd time at first, when the screams in the night were bad.

He didn't know when "the odd time" became every day. Then the tavern was gone. His wife was gone. His life was gone. For a moment this evening, he'd had it all back, and it had felt better than the freshest seed. Now what was he to do? The king had called on him, given him a chance at living again. The Prince Bishop's healer had taken all the rot out of his body—but the captain was his friend, had saved his life half a hundred times, as he had done for Gill. Betray his friend and do his duty, or betray his king? The answer was simple for an old soldier. It was the same one he had given with blood, sweat, and tears, every time it had been asked of him.

Barnot patted Gill down and quickly found the object the king needed, an odd-looking little cup. He studied it in his hand a moment, and wondered how so small a thing could be so important to such powerful men. Barnot knew there was bad blood between Gill and the king, even though it had been the king's father who'd done Gill the wrong. Still, Gill lived by the same rules as Barnot, and you never turned your back when the king called on you. As bad as he felt doing what he was doing, Barnot could take some solace in the fact that Gill had made the wrong choice.

He put his cloak on, gave his sleeping friend a salute, and went outside. He had been told that there would be a courier waiting to take the Cup back to Mirabay, but did not know who that would be.

No sooner had he stepped outside of the tavern than a voice whispered from the shadows.

"Do you have it?"

The voice was harsh and strange-sounding. A woman's? That he had not noticed anyone watching him was alarming to a man who had spent much of his life in the lands of men who wanted to kill him.

Barnot felt like an idiot for what he was about to say, but sometimes such things were necessary. "The swallows flew south early this year."

"A sure sign of autumn snow," the voice replied.

"Yes," Barnot said. "I have it."

It saddened him that the stories of Gill's alcoholism were true. He had been as fine a captain as a soldier could ask for. Competent, and never careless with his men's lives. Although Barnot told himself he had reason for what he was doing—the good of the nation, the will of the king, always a good soldier's priority—he wasn't able to shake the filthy feeling it left him with. He had betrayed one of the few men still alive he could count on, and for what? A purse of gold, the king's favour, and freedom from the seed?

His bargain was struck, and there was no turning back now.

A figure emerged from the shadows. A woman, as he'd thought.

"The Prince Bishop sent you?"

"No more talk," she said. "Give me the item and I'll be on my way."

Barnot nodded and took the odd little cup out of his tunic. He had never held Telastrian steel before. It was pretty to look at and pleasant to the touch, and he knew it was worth a fortune, but it seemed like a lot of fuss over something so small. Still, it was never a soldier's place to ask questions, and he supposed this was as close as he had come to being a soldier for a very long time.

The woman took the little bowl and dropped it into a leather bag, which she then tucked into her cloak.

"I was instructed to convey our employer's gratitude for your assistance," she said.

By the gods, he thought, *she's fast.* The blade was in and out of his chest before he had even realised she had one in her hand. She was good too. A killing strike so swiftly executed, and in the dark. What kind of king had a loyal, faithful servant killed for carrying out his orders? He should never have betrayed Gill. The gods were punishing him for his lack of fidelity to a friend. No soldier should let his mates down. It was a bitter thought to die with.

CHAPTER
29

Solène felt trepidatious going into the archive once again. She had spent the previous night working with dal Drezony, disciplining her thoughts by applying all she had learned about herself. With her fears and insecurities drawn into the open and their origins understood, it was much easier to stop them from intruding when she was trying to maintain focus. Whether that would still be the case when she was under extreme stress, she didn't know. Nonetheless, it felt like she had passed over a threshold and taken hold of a set of controls that she hadn't even known had existed before. There was still much she needed to learn and practise, but thanks to her new awareness, she was no longer so afraid of the power that resided within her.

Her biggest trouble that morning was staying awake. She'd been using modest amounts of magic all night and had not slept. A quick refresh from one of the Order's physicians had helped for a time, but it had worn off. Doing something that required physical activity would have been easier—using magic just whittled away at what little energy she had left.

While her previous search of the archive had been aided by magic, it had been a simple matter of discovery, with little expected of her. This one was not. She needed to refine her search methods, and quickly. If nothing else, this would be a useful test of her new approach to magic, safe in the confines of the subterranean archive with its limited Fount and no one trying to kill her.

The Prince Bishop had left some notes for her, but there was little that he had not already told her—an ancient temple hidden somewhere in Mirabaya, visited by Amatus around the time he gained the magical power that would change the world. The Cup came from there. The temple might guide them in its use; it might unlock secrets they could not even imagine. It seemed to Solène that the Prince Bishop was grasping at whatever new magical trinket came across his path. She realised how much pressure he must be under, and how appealing anything that could relieve that might be. That didn't change the fact that she didn't trust him.

Despite its best efforts, the Empire had never discovered this temple. Why the Prince Bishop thought that she could manage it, with her limited magical talent and resources, was beyond her. Nonetheless, it was in her best interest to be seen to be doing everything she could, so that was what she would do.

She leaned back in her chair, closed her eyes, and took a deep breath. Dal Drezony had told her she was free of the shackles life had placed on her mind. Her thoughts were hers, and hers alone, to control. Nothing outside existed. And there it was. Clarity. Focus. It was such a pure moment, she felt giddy.

As quickly as it had come, as perfectly controlled as it had felt, it disappeared. Her excitement at having achieved it had destroyed it. That didn't worry her, however. The novelty would wear off quickly. Eventually she might even be able to do it when surrounded by distraction.

She tried again, and this time held that single focussed thought: the enlightened. She waited, the concept hovering in her mind's eye like a hummingbird. But nothing happened. Realising she had been holding her breath, she let it out with a sigh, losing the pure thought. It was the most precise piece of magic she had ever shaped, but nothing had come of it. She wished dal Drezony had been there to see it.

Solène couldn't help but feel that her lack of results meant there was nothing to find. The first time, she had located what she was looking for with far clumsier magic. Perhaps her shaping had not been as precise as she had thought? No, it couldn't have been that—she could tell she'd achieved everything she had been trying to do. Yet no book had fallen from the shelf. No sensation was drawing her toward a section of the archive. Either she had failed, or there was nothing to be found.

She tried again, holding the thought, and allowing her body to continue breathing. She applied more of herself, desiring the enlight-ened with the force of someone dying of thirst and yearning for one last drink of water. Still nothing. Exasperated, she let out another sharp breath.

A wave of dizziness swept over her. Once it had subsided, Solène considered other searches, such as material on Amatus. That seemed unhelpful: in an Imperial archive as large as this one, there would likely be countless mentions of him. How to refine the search? The only thing she could think of was holding two ideas together, some-thing she hadn't even come close to trying yet. Perhaps if she could blend them somehow?

Her first effort lasted less than the blink of an eye. Her second was not much better. She tried again and again, until she was finally able to hold a merged thought in her mind long enough to shape magic with it.

At last she stopped, exhausted. There was no way to tell what time it was in the archive, deep below Mirabay's cathedral, but she knew she'd been down there for hours. Her tiredness was nothing that a good night of sleep wouldn't fix—she knew what it felt like when she was on the verge of burning out, and this wasn't it.

She stood and took a look around, wandering up and down the rows of shelves, listening to her footfalls on the stone flags echo and hoping that she might have moved something without noticing. How-ever, she was disappointed. Nothing appeared to be out of place; all the dust remained undisturbed. It was time to call it a day.

⸎

Banneret-Commander Yves Dorant moved through the city like a spectre. People got out of his way. They all knew what his black robes meant—Intelligencier. Most had nothing to fear from him, for the number of people who fell afoul of him and his was small, yet it was enough to perpetuate their legend.

There was an air of tension in Mirabay unlike anything Dorant had felt in all his years in the city. First dragons, now sorcerers. Be-nevolent mages, if the Prince Bishop was to be believed. Dorant had never come across benevolent magic, not once in his career as a mage hunter. The concept that the Prince Bishop was peddling was preposterous. The man had always been arrogant and ambitious, but this time he had seriously overreached himself. Nonetheless, Dorant was genuinely worried. If the Prince Bishop had the king's support on this, there could be very big problems ahead. How could any civilised monarch consider such a thing?

As soon as he had caught wind of the Prince Bishop's announcement, he had sent word across the country, calling back all his men. His senior officers were in the city, so he had ordered them to the commandery for a meeting. This was the greatest threat he had ever faced, the crisis that would likely define his career. It might also become a battle for survival, and try as he might, Dorant struggled to find any enthusiasm for that prospect.

The Intelligenciers were not a democratic organisation. They were a rigid hierarchy with a dual leadership—the ruler of the land in which they were based, and the Grand Commander, elected from one of the national commanders. In Mirabaya, the king commanded in all things of national concern, while in matters relating to magic, the Grand Commander—currently a Ventishman living in Voorn, far to the north—held sway. There was rarely a conflict between the two, as magic was ordinarily a minor headache that the Intelligenciers policed in addition to the clandestine duties they carried out for their state. It was a strange dichotomy, left over from the time of their founding, before the Imperial provinces broke into independent states. On the rare occasion when there was a conflict, the national commander was to be guided by his conscience in determining how to best carry out his duty. That was what Dorant was trying to do.

They gathered in the great hall of the commandery building, an austere structure tucked away in an unremarkable street behind Mirabay's cathedral. The room was illuminated by the coloured light coming through the stained-glass windows that lined the space. Dorant's senior officers were dressed in their uniform black, punctuated with the silver sigil that struck fear into the hearts of all who saw it—the staff, skull, and sword. They all knew why they were here. They had all seen or heard the Prince Bishop's proclamation. They all knew that for the first time in a millennium, the threat for which they had been established had come to pass.

"Gentlemen," Dorant said, when they were all seated. It was unusual for them to all be in the same room at the same time, but none seemed inclined to take the opportunity to renew professional friendships or make pointless conversation, so they came to order quickly. "I realise some of our brethren haven't yet been able to get here, but all things considered, I feel we must move ahead. In light of recent events, I am invoking our founding oath, that our duty lies first and foremost in preventing the scourge of sorcery from rearing its head once more. It appears our king is in league with sorcerers, and this has absolved us of our oath to him. We must do whatever it takes to ensure his plans for magic proceed no farther."

He waited a moment to see how they reacted to his invoking the oath, but none showed any sign of surprise. They must all have known it was coming.

"It will take time for word to reach the Grand Commander and for his orders to reach us," Dorant said. "That is time I fear we don't have. If we don't act now, we may be too late. As this is an unprecedented act, I ask for your agreement in invoking the oath, and your support in the orders I shall have to give until we hear from the Grand Commander."

Murmurs of assent rose from all. He expected that would be the case, but it had to be properly done all the same. It was not just a question of duty—there was also an element of fear. Intelligenciers had persecuted would-be sorcerers for a thousand years. If those with magical abilities were given free rein, it would not be long before they came looking to settle the score. Every man in that room knew they would be marked for death if that came to pass.

"Suggestions, gentlemen," Dorant said. "How should we go about stopping this madness?"

One of his lieutenants cleared his throat. "Civil unrest, Commander."

Dorant smiled for the first time since reading the proclamation. It was a solid start. When there were no more suggestions, he frowned.

"Take the rest of the day to give the matter some thought. We'll reconvene after supper to discuss our options and choose our plan. Consider this matter secret. Word cannot get out. This is the greatest challenge any of us are ever likely to face and it cannot be treated lightly. As soon as they are secure, the Prince Bishop's new Order will come for us. They might not even wait that long. We must not be caught unprepared."

He looked around the gathering, making eye contact with each of them, attempting to drive home how serious things were. That done, he pushed back his chair and stood.

"Until this evening, then."

CHAPTER

30

*S*o this is what I missed out on when my military career was taken from me, Amaury thought, as he watched the hive of activity that filled the Priory's courtyard. A line of wagons were being filled with victuals, weapons, and anything else that might be useful on a dragon-hunting expedition. It was exciting to see people moving about, filled with a sense of purpose and adventure. The thought of the life he might have had reminded him of his injury, and of the dull ache that was starting to return. The treatments didn't seem to last as long as they once had, although that might be due to the fact that the Order's best healers had died in recent weeks. Soon enough he would have others who were far better, but he didn't expect he'd need them by then.

Vachon was striding across the square toward Amaury, barking orders to his men as he came. Though his role was still new to him, it looked like he had things well in hand. Dal Drezony was nowhere to be seen, likely off sulking somewhere at the changed character of the Order since the arrival of Amaury's new hires. Too bad, but the days of quiet academic study were over. If they were to take their place in the world and carry out the role Amaury had in mind for them, they needed people with steel in them, who were willing to dirty their hands to get things done.

"How are preparations going?" Amaury said as Vachon neared.

"Well," the burly man said, moderating his tone only slightly now that he was speaking to his commander. "We're all but ready to depart. All I need is your order."

"There are some matters yet to resolve," Amaury said. "I'm not sending you out until I have all the information we need to slay this beast." In truth, the Cup was the only thing he was waiting on, and a pigeon had informed him that morning that it was on its way. He tried not to dwell on that for too long—he had been disappointed before. Better to wait until it was in his hands.

"Remain in a state of readiness. This expedition is as much an exercise in winning the hearts of the people as it is in slaying a dragon. For that, timing plays a bigger part."

"Can't put the entire city to the sword, I suppose," Vachon said.

Amaury let out a chuckle, but wasn't at all sure Vachon had been joking.

"When I give the order," Amaury said, "you'll need to be able to march within the hour. Will you be able to do that?"

"We'll be ready. We'll march out of the city looking every bit the glorious heroes you need us to be."

▲▲▲▲▲▲

Guillot's face was stuck to the table when he woke. His eyes were dry, and the lids protested as he tried to draw them open. The light seared through his head, setting off a bell clapper inside his skull. His mouth was as dry as his eyes, and it took a moment to separate his tongue from the inside of his cheek. He sat in a half stupor for a moment, then vomited. He managed to turn his head so that the liquid contents of his stomach splattered onto the bloodstained floor. He spat sour bile, then sat up and tried to take stock.

The first thing to work out was where he was. He pushed through the cloud shrouding his memory until he could recall Cabham coming into the tavern. The tavern in Venne. He remembered what happened next, which explained the blood. His heart sank when he remembered what happened after that, which explained the vomit. And the empty bottles covering the table. And the thundering headache. Gill took a deep breath and let it out with a sigh. What had he been thinking? As his anger with himself increased, so too did the violence with which the clapper in his head bounced off the sides of his skull.

He looked around, turning his head slowly so as to avoid the worst of the clapper's wrath. There was no one else around. He vaguely re-called Val and Barnot fencing with sticks, up and down the length of the bar, but wasn't sure if he had imagined it. If his present state wasn't reason enough to give up drinking for good, he didn't know what was. There were many good reasons to stop. They were the reasons he *had* stopped. Why had he allowed himself to start again? He felt like crying in frustration.

He stood up as gently as he could and walked to the bar to see if there was any water to be had. His hand brushed against his hip, and something felt odd. His head was so muddled that he had to concentrate on the feeling—the sense that he had forgotten something, or that something was missing. He concentrated on it as best he could, feeling like his thought channels were clogged with wool and that there was something trying to smash its way out of his head.

He closed his eyes and did his best not to panic when he realised that the Cup was gone. He found a pitcher of water and took a long drink, then vomited most of it back up. He was going to have to give Gaufre quite a bit of coin to make up for the mess they'd caused. Assuming he still had his purse. He checked, and it was there, the momentary relief quashed by the knowledge that he would have far preferred for it to be gone, rather than the Cup. He sipped more water and struggled to remember. There had been someone else with them. A strange fellow. Oddly wise, like a professor at the Academy, but built like one of the masters of swords. François. There was no sign of him, nor of Barnot or Val, for that matter. They might have been sleeping it off somewhere, but he needed to find them. He was clinging to the thin hope that one of them might have the Cup.

Val was snoring contentedly on his straw mattress in the room that he had once shared with Beausoleil and Cabham, but that was now all his. A trail of dribble extended from the corner of his mouth, and Gill suspected that Val would feel even worse than he did when he woke.

Walking back down the stairs, Guillot made for the front door. The dim light in the taproom had hurt his head. The full light of day made him want to crawl into a dark corner and die. He stood in the doorway for what seemed like an age, waiting for his eyes to adjust. The village was quiet. He thought it probably looked much like it must have before the dragons drew in all the hopeful swordsmen from the surrounding regions.

When he felt as though his head could take it, he ventured out. He took a few steps, walked a little, trying to find some refreshment in the cool morning air. There was a horse trough filled with water next to the inn, and Gill strongly considered dunking his head, but prioritised his search for Barnot. He only had to reach the side alley to find him. The old soldier lay in the small lane to the side of the inn, a maroon stain of dried blood spread about him. Gill's heart twisted with grief. He knelt next to his old friend and checked him over out of a forlorn hope, but the man's body was cold. He had been dead for hours. There was a hole in his chest where, from the look of it, someone had twisted a dagger. This was not an opportunistic wound. It was one intended to kill. There was no sign of the Cup.

The helpful stranger. François. It could only have been he who had taken the Cup. How had he known what it was? It didn't look valuable, and Gill was certain he hadn't talked about it. But Cabham had. If he was willing to die in the attempt to get it, François must have thought it was worth having. Gill swore. If the man had taken it and killed Barnot, he was likely hours away by now.

It took a moment for the full ramifications of that to hit Gill. There was still a dragon out there, and to have any chance of killing it, he needed the Cup. He hadn't just let himself down when he'd accepted that first drink. He had let down every single person who would lose their life to the beast. He vomited more water, then dry-retched until he thought his insides were going to come out. It was Villerauvais all over again. Could he not even learn his lessons the hard way?

He went back to the horse trough, plunged his head in, and held it there, his head upside down, bubbles coming out of his nose and tickling his chin. He contemplated staying there until he had rid the world of his failings, but knew that wasn't the answer. He allowed himself to topple backwards until he was sitting on his behind, water running from his face and hair and soaking his clothes.

"Refreshing?"

He looked up and saw Edine standing in the sunlight.

"Someone murdered my friend last night," he said.

Her eyes widened and her mouth dropped open.

"I think I know who it was," Gill said, "but he'll be long gone by now."

"I'm sorry. No one's ever been murdered here before. I don't know what to say."

Gill shrugged. "It was a bad night for the village, then. Three men came at us in the tavern last night. We killed them."

"I heard. Gaufre isn't pleased."

"I'll pay for the damage and clean-up."

"Do you think that had anything to do with your friend?"

"No. That was Cabham. We took care of him and the men he had with him. The murderer was someone else. He helped us against Cabham. He's long gone by now."

"I'll talk to the vicar and have your friend taken care of."

"I'd appreciate that."

She hesitated before speaking again. "I can understand the need to let loose a little when you're doing such dangerous work. All the more so when your success has come at a heavy price. The people are frightened. All their hope rests on you. It won't do them any good to see you like this."

"I'm sorry," Gill said. "I'll get inside and clean myself up."

CHAPTER

31

Solène rose early to head for the archive. She had spent only a little time with dal Drezony, feeling that they were repeating the same exercises over and over. She was glad to be getting away from the Priory—the character of the place had changed so quickly. Gone was the fraternal atmosphere of morning exercise and afternoon study. It felt more like a military camp in preparation for war. Dal Drezony didn't seem to like it either, but Solène couldn't see what might be done to stop it.

In her work in the archive, she was doing little more than paying lip service to the Prince Bishop's orders; she was sure that if there was something relating to the enlightened and their temple in the archive, she would have found it by now. Being there was simply a good excuse to get some time alone, and away from the braying, spittle-spraying Vachon, as he laid down his authority on everyone within shouting range.

A loud crack split the air, jolting her from her thoughts. There was a second crack, which was almost as much of a surprise as the first one. So uncharacteristic a noise bore further investigation.

She walked through the main garden courtyard, past the refectory building, and into a smaller, cobbled square that was surrounded by the stables. A group of people were gathered around an unladen cart. She could just make out the back of a shirtless male figure, tied with his arms outstretched, to one of the wagon's huge wheels. The Order's new commander, Vachon, was standing, arms akimbo, to one side. There was another ear-piercing crack as she drew close enough to see three angry red lines on the man's back. Her eyes widened with horror. One of the gathered men held a long, wicked-looking black whip.

There was a fourth crack, and then a loud cry—the first one the unfortunate tied to the wheel had uttered.

"What in hells is going on here?" Dal Drezony strode into the square, her expression a picture of fury.

Vachon turned to face her. "Matters of military discipline, Seneschal. Nothing to bother yourself with."

"Damn your eyes," dal Drezony said. "We don't flog people here."

"This is a military order, is it not?" Vachon said.

Dal Drezony's face twisted with indignation. "After a fashion," she admitted.

"Military discipline for a military order," Vachon said, turning back to the flogging. "Continue."

There was another loud snap and another cry of pain.

"Stop this now!" dal Drezony said, her face grey with anger.

"I don't give you orders in matters of sorcery," Vachon said, still not deigning to turn and face dal Drezony. "I'd thank you to show me the same respect in matters military."

Solène's skin prickled at the use of the word "sorcery." It was laden with all the connotations that caused people to fear magic so much.

"We don't practise sorcery here, and we certainly don't flog people. I strongly recommend you stop right now." Dal Drezony's voice came out like a growl.

Vachon finally turned to look at her again. He met her volcanic glare and gave her a thin smile. "We're done here anyway." He turned back to his men. "Untie him and take him to the infirmary. I'm sure the healers will have him back on his feet in no time. Magic does have some uses, I suppose."

"I do not want to see this happening here ever again," dal Drezony said.

"I suggest you shut your eyes when you hear the whip's report," Vachon said.

"I'll be taking this up with the Prince Bishop at the earliest opportunity."

"Please, do," Vachon said with another thin smile.

Dal Drezony walked away, glancing at Solène. It wasn't anger on her face that Solène saw, but fear.

▲▲▲▲▲▲

Solène paced up and down the archive's aisles, her mind clouded by what she had witnessed at the Priory that morning. She still couldn't quite believe it had happened. If this was the new direction the Prince Bishop intended for the Order, she wanted nothing to do with it. Perhaps he would take dal Drezony's complaint seriously. Living in fear of a flogging was no way to develop a controlled and focussed mind and increase one's magical skill. That thought brought her back to what she was supposed to be doing.

She had been trying to think of different words she might use to draw out the information she was looking for. She had tested dozens now, but had turned nothing up. She had begun to wonder how much value this temple could have after being lost and forgotten for so long. The Imperial mages had not been able to find a trace of it, but that didn't hinder them in developing enormous magical power that allowed the Empire to conquer half the world. Between her, the Cup, and the Priory's resources, surely the Prince Bishop and the Order would have all they needed.

It occurred to her that to use the Cup for a specific purpose, she had needed instructions. To do other specific magics with it might require similar, and the temple might provide guidance on how to shape an unimaginable amount of different magics. Recently the Prince Bishop had seemed to Solène like a puppy running on a frozen pond—its legs a furious blur of motion though it was getting nowhere. Her conclusion reminded her how clever and dangerous he was. Perhaps he knew more than he was letting on and his aims were far more focussed than she had recently assumed.

It was amazing how quickly contempt could creep in when you didn't like someone. She resolved to consider him more carefully in future, as she initially had. She could see his plan now. It had taken the Imperial mages centuries to perfect their art, learning new magics through trial and error, slowly advancing their skill and power over generations, while expanding their numbers to the force that became feared throughout the Empire. The Prince Bishop didn't have the patience for that. He wanted all that power within his lifetime. The Cup alone hadn't done that for the

Imperial mages, and it wouldn't do that for him, either. He would have power, and with time, he might have control, but he would not have a particularly large knowledge base of magic to draw on. That was what he was searching for—what he had Solène searching for.

It was a dangerous appetite to have. Solène had learned the danger of too much power the hard way, very nearly with fatal consequences. It took a long time to learn to properly control magic, she was discovering. Even now, Solène very much feared she'd never be able to acquire the mental discipline required to completely handle the raw power she could wield. She feared that she was a danger not only to herself, but to others. What would similar power mean for the Prince Bishop? It was a concerning thought, particularly if her efforts brought him closer to realising his goal.

Perhaps it would be better to not find anything about this temple. She knew failure would draw the Prince Bishop's ire, but better that than burning down half the city by trying to shape magics he had no business meddling with. Then again, perhaps locating the temple would give all mages the key to controlling their magic, her included. If they were going to be delving into the long-forgotten magical arts, the secrets contained in this temple might save a great deal of heartache. If she found anything, she could choose whether or not to share it with the Prince Bishop. What would the consequences be?

A dark thought occurred to her. She had the power, and possibly even the control, to stop the Prince Bishop right now. Feeling sick, Solène pushed the idea from her head. She had resolved that once all the tumult was behind her, she would learn to become a magical healer and devote herself to becoming the best. She could not begin that by killing. Or, rather, by killing again.

That brought her back to her initial problem. How could she find the temple if the Imperial mages couldn't? The information in the archive was merely a small part of their knowledge. Perhaps it had been nothing more than a legend even then, not worth searching for, and the Prince Bishop had become convinced of its existence from a fanciful mention. Perhaps by the time they were large and powerful enough to look for it, they no longer needed what it contained?

As she paced the aisles, she let her mind work its way back to where all of this started, with the Fount, the great magical energy of life that filled and surrounded all things. If she were to build a magical temple, where would she place it? Surely somewhere the Fount was particularly strong.

The Fount was a strange force, and the Order's understanding of it was limited to say the least. Beyond it existing, powering magic, and being both created and required by life, they knew little. They didn't know why it behaved the way it did—for instance, solid stone and water prevented its flow, which was why it was so weak in the archive, which was deep under stone, and why she always tapped more heavily into her internal reservoir when she used magic down there.

Living things created it within them and used only a little of it, so it was found in stronger concentrations where there was a large amount of healthy life. There were deeper pools of it in cities—the larger the population, the stronger the Fount was. Vellin-Ilora, the long-deserted Imperial capital, had been the most populous city ever known. The Fount produced there had fuelled the College of Mages and allowed them to create incredible magics. It had also allowed them to unleash enormous destructive force when the wars tore the Empire apart.

Knowing this was all well and good, but in a time of sparse population, when Mirabaya was inhabited only by barbarian tribes—and, it seemed, these enlightened, whoever they were—where would the Fount have accumulated? Solène shut her eyes and reached mentally for documents dominated by discussion of the Fount. She had refined her skill a little and no longer pulled ancient books and scrolls from their resting places, dumping them on the floor. Now she simply drew them far enough out of position that she would be able to see them when she walked past. She held the thought a moment longer, then took the small wheeled book trolley the Prince Bishop had appropriated from the university's library, and went to gather her haul.

The archive was large, and it took a little while to check every aisle, but she eventually turned up a half-dozen old, leather-bound tomes that would keep her busy for the next day or two. She didn't know if this progress would make the Prince Bishop happy, and she didn't care all that much. So long as she was seen to be making a genuine effort, he couldn't be too critical.

As she prepared to dig into the first book, she realised that even if her theory that the temple was located where there was a strong accumulation of the Fount was correct, the Imperial mages would almost certainly have come up with the same idea. Either she was wrong or it hadn't helped them find the temple—if it even actually existed. She thought it over, and decided that her logic was sound.

Perhaps the Prince Bishop was incorrect in stating that the Empire never found this temple. Just because there was nothing to say so in the archive didn't mean it hadn't happened. Likewise, a single text saying that the temple hadn't been located couldn't necessarily be relied upon either. The writer might have been working on misinformation, or might simply not have known.

Leaning forward, she let her forehead bang lightly on the table. The impact didn't do much to ease her frustration. It felt as though she was stumbling around in the dark, looking for something that might not actually be there. When did you give in to good sense and stop? She supposed that was the Prince Bishop's decision to make, but until then she had little more than rumour, theory, and second-guessing to guide her.

Pride took hold—she couldn't bear the idea of not doing a good job. With that in mind, she sat up, took a deep breath, and opened the first book.

It was a treatise on the Fount, much as she had expected. She looked for any indication of when it was written, reckoning something written later in the Empire would represent a more developed understanding of the subject. This book was from the thirteenth emperor's reign. Writers of the time conveniently seemed to always dedicate their work to the emperor of the day, making dating one of the few easy aspects of her research. She checked a few other books, found one written in the days of the penultimate emperor, and started there.

The early pages dealt with the basic things that she already knew, and she turned them quickly. When she got to a chapter on the theories of the origin of the Fount, she started to pay more attention. The Imperial mages had viewed magic as a science to be studied and tamed. In many respects, they had been right. However, it didn't take long for Solène to realise that they didn't know a whole lot more about the Fount than she did. Everything she read was theory and speculation. Considering the

Fount was a magical power that gave effect to the user's focussed desire, it was a very tricky thing to study—under experimentation, it would give you whatever results you desired, making empirical evaluation impossible. It made Solène laugh, thinking of those old mages, trying to work out a way to focus their mind on an experiment with no thought as to the result. She thought she was frustrated, but that must have driven them to insanity.

She read and read, scanning page after page as quickly as her mind could translate the old writing, and finally stopped at the sight of two words. *Fount Stones.* That caught her interest. Before the Empire, magic had been used by humans in a limited, almost religious way. Druids had been priests, healers, and mages. Their power was derived from these Fount Stones. It seemed the Empire had discovered a number of them during its expansion, and, showing great respect for cultures other than their own, destroyed every single one. The Imperial mages didn't need the stones, being able to draw on the Fount wherever it was. The druids, on the other hand, seemed to need access to these stones—or nodes as the writer called them—to carry out greater works of magic. Without the nodes, the druids posed no threat and the Imperial armies were able to advance unimpeded.

What if the enlightened had been a group of druids? It seemed likely. If they needed access to these nodes, then they would certainly have built their temple next to one. Solène sat back for a moment and rested her eyes, satisfied that she was getting somewhere. She certainly had something to report to the Prince Bishop, which was the important thing.

If the Empire had destroyed all the nodes they found, wouldn't they have done that when they had come to Mirabensis? If so, might they have destroyed this ancient temple without realising it? She had heard stories of how victorious soldiers behaved when given free rein in villages—picking them clean of anything of value, including whatever they found in churches. She doubted they were ever much different, and couldn't see an Imperial army treating an enemy temple with any great reverence. It had probably been stripped bare and burned to the ground.

Then it occurred to her—perhaps destroying it to keep it from the Prince Bishop was not the worst idea. . . .

CHAPTER
32

Pharadon wondered, as he watched the young golden dragon from a distance, if not killing the slayer had been a bad idea. When the time had come, Pharadon hadn't been able to bring himself to commit murder, for that was what it would have been. The man carried great pain, and was trying to extinguish it by protecting innocents from the actions of base dragons. Pharadon could not condemn him for that.

Pharadon was careful to remain downwind of the goldscale, not wanting it to catch his scent. To say he was surprised to see a goldscale was an understatement, as was his relief that it seemed far smaller, and less mature, than the others. A female, she must have hatched after the males, or fed less voraciously.

A brood always produced dragons of different colours, with no two of the same shade in a single clutch. Black, green, red, yellow, brown, and blue were the most common. Silver was unusual, bronze slightly less so, but goldscales? They were rare. Special. So rare and special that Pharadon, despite his long life, had never seen one before. His great old heart beat faster than normal at the sight.

That she was still of modest size meant he had a little more time than he had feared. Even so, Pharadon knew he needed to be as careful as possible. A great shock could be enough to cause her to mature, and then all would be lost. It was said that under the right conditions, a goldscale could reach enlightenment all by themselves. That was something Pharadon couldn't take the chance on, though. In another time, this juvenile would have become a queen amongst dragons. In this time, she might not even know the joy of enlightenment.

His trip to the village had apprised him of another danger—adventurers seeking to slay dragons. As individuals, none represented the threat the slayer did, but combined they were a problem he would have to stay alert to. There was also still the slayer. Pharadon hoped he would be able to avoid another encounter, but if they met again, it would be in honourable battle. Pharadon hoped there would be no need for killing, but he would not allow anything to stand in his way—the goldscale was too important. She had to be enlightened.

Alone, he would not be able to complete the task. Traditionally, enlightenment would be marked by a gathering, where the combined magical power of several dragons would provide the spark to complete the juvenile's journey to enlightenment. He believed it could be accomplished by two dragons, but it might as well have been a million—it seemed he was the last of his kind. All was not lost, however. There was another way. Dragonkind's priesthood had created vessels of intense magical power and stored them at their temple. He could use one of these.

He hovered in the air a while longer, watching, and debating the best way to go about it. He considered going to retrieve one of the vessels, but realised there was too great a danger leaving the goldscale here alone. Her siblings had been killed and he had no doubt she would be too. He would have to convince her to follow him, and start her on the path to enlightenment on their way to the temple.

He was fascinated by the young dragon's perfect golden scales, each one gleaming like the most perfect coin in a hoard. There was an innocence and naivety that was endearing about the juvenile, and Pharadon wondered for a moment if she was not better off as she was. A beast of instinct, she would feed, sleep, and exist in the most natural of ways, not questioning any of the things she did. No complications of life would weigh on her mind, and it seemed likely to Pharadon that she enjoyed far more peaceful sleep than he did. Part of Pharadon yearned for a similar simplicity of existence, and it occurred to him that perhaps enlightenment was as much a curse as a gift. It gave a great deal, but so too it took, and there was tragedy in that which made his heart heavy.

There was danger, too. Even a juvenile dragon could pose a threat to an elder, like Pharadon. All the more so a goldscale, whose affinity with the Fount was already likely as strong as his own. Tackling enlightenment alone was a danger, one that could see him killed if the goldscale reacted violently at the wrong moment. Still, it was a risk he was willing to take. What choice did he have?

Decision made, he headed for the temple, but had given only two beats of his great wings when he spotted a group of horsemen riding quickly in the juvenile's direction. There were a lot of them—at least twenty at a quick count. The adventurers. Pharadon grimaced in disappointment. It seemed they had her scent, and so there would be more killing after all.

Pharadon circled in a wide arc to bring himself behind the horsemen. He wondered if the slayer was with them, but could detect no magic. He was both disappointed and relieved. His flame would have no effect on the slayer, something Pharadon had learned the hard way, centuries earlier. These men, however, appeared to have no such protection.

He allowed himself to fall into a silent downward glide and started to prime his flame glands. This wasn't to be an honourable battle—he sought only to eliminate the threat to the goldscale. The first they knew of his presence was the heat of his flame. Those at the front of the group had the time to hear the screams of their comrades at the back, and some even had time to cast a backwards glance at the source of their impending death.

It was all over in the blink of an eye. The horsemen were nothing more than charred flesh and burned steel. Pharadon took no pleasure in it, and didn't dwell on his victory; he simply continued his flight in the direction of the temple.

⁂

Dorant sat in the corner of a tavern overlooking Place Royale Square on the Isle. The tavern had been long known as "the Little Palace," although that was not its original name. It was a play on its proximity to the old palace, in the shadow of which it sat—and also acknowledged that as much political change had been effected within its walls as in its larger, regal neighbour.

He glanced out the window and across at the cathedral, which dominated the far side of the square, at the courts of justice on the northern side, to his left. Coffeehouses, inns, and shops stood to his right. The Little Palace was often the focal point for citizen protests, which were common in Mirabay—taxes too high, food too expensive, the Watch being too heavy-handed. The people of Mirabay might fear dragons, and magic, but they were not afraid of protesting in the face of perceived infringement of their liberties. Things had been unusually quiet since the new king had taken the throne, but Dorant had known that wouldn't last forever. Dorant had long thought protest a necessary evil in such a large city. It was like a sealed pot on the fire—every so often one had to lift the lid to release some of the steam.

The citizenry's propensity for protest was what Dorant was now relying on. He was dressed in civilian clothes, and appeared to all intents and purposes no different from any other tavern patron. Two of his men were at the bar, likewise dressed in civilian attire. There were others in selected taverns across the city, but this was the most important one, where hotheads, students, intelligentsia, and agitators came to find receptive ears. He had frequented the place himself when he was a youth at the Academy. He had known early on that he wanted his career to have meaning; he didn't want to just slog through mud on the battlefield or act as hired muscle for a man of wealth and means. Joining the Intelligenciers allowed him to sate his desire to affect the sphere of politics.

His men were discussing the Prince Bishop's announcement. In a place like the Little Palace, they had to be very careful with their words, so Dorant had chosen his two best men and had decided to oversee them himself. The tavern's patrons were seasoned commentators and agitators. They would be quick to sniff out a plant, but Dorant hoped that even if they did, all his men were doing was starting a conversation that was on everyone's mind. The city was like a pile of dry tinder—it would likely ignite all by itself, but Dorant wasn't willing to wait. The abominable course the country was being steered on had to be changed immediately.

The operatives' conversation had been carefully crafted, but the key was that it had to be overheard and others had to join in. Dorant had to capitalise on the simmering discontent he could feel on the streets as he walked through them.

His men were experts at this clandestine type of work. Over the years, and always dressed as civilians, they had called in to the tavern every now and then, sometimes engaging in what was being discussed, sometimes not. That way, they had become known to the Little Palace's regulars, who did not know they were Intelligenciers. Disseminating and gathering information was best done by familiar, but not overly familiar, faces.

Neither of them had been involved in anything that had led to an agitator disappearing—the Intelligenciers' preferred method of dealing with those who had rattled the cage one too many times. Dorant was confident his men had good cover and were practised enough to know when the momentum had built enough for their participation to no longer be required. However, it was always a nervous time. Intellectual argument could turn to violence quickly in places like that—a quality that Dorant was relying upon—and he would rather the discontent was not vented at him and his men.

Gradually his men drew others into their conversation; Dorant didn't hear a single voice of dissent. People were nervous, feeling betrayed. The king who was supposed to protect them had unleashed something very dangerous. The dragons remained a distant threat, so remote that they were only one step up the ladder from the myth they had been just a few weeks earlier. When dealing with a large population, it was all about managing the hierarchy of fear. Last week it was the dragon, now it was magic. Would the latter be felt acceptable to banish the former? For Dorant, the answer was a definitive no. That didn't mean to say the public would agree with him, though.

The Prince Bishop had handled it skilfully, chosen his moment and his reasoning perfectly, making Dorant feel a little less ashamed of having missed the development of a cabal of mages under his nose. He wondered how it had gotten past him, and the only conclusion he could come to, disappointingly, was that the Prince Bishop was a smarter man than he. That didn't mean the Prince Bishop would win, however. It wasn't just about being smarter; what mattered was what you did with your smarts. The Prince Bishop was venturing into dangerous territory, most likely led by a healthy dose of hubris. That was not a weakness Dorant was prone to, and that was his advantage. He might have had the wool pulled over his eyes for too long, but he would not allow the aberration of sorcery to continue, not for so long as he drew breath.

The evening crowd was starting to build, and the conversation Dorant had seeded had grown to fill the tavern. He finished his ale and left, the cue to his men that their task was complete and that it was time to extract themselves. The air was crisp outside, carrying none of summer's unpleasant odours. At that time of year, with the leaves turning, he couldn't imagine a better place than Mirabay to live. He looked at the cathedral—a work of art—and at the slate-capped, limestone buildings that filled the Isle, buoyed by the sense that he was facing the great test of his career and not faltering. The hilt hit his ribs before he realised he had been stabbed. He turned his head, trying to see who had done it, only glimpsing a cloaked figure disappearing into an alleyway.

He tried to reach the wound, but couldn't. He could tell by the odd sensation on his back where the blade had gone in, and from that, what had been punctured. Perhaps he was guilty of hubris after all. There could be no question of the perpetrator, nor of the fact that he was indeed smarter than Dorant. Faster too. He could hear the debate in the Little Palace reach a crescendo as he crumpled to the ground. His last hope was that he was hearing the resistance forming, that his actions had been enough to start the tale of the Prince Bishop's end. And the end of sorcery. He watched the blood pool beneath him until he saw no more.

33

I t was a fine thing to stand on a balcony beside the king and watch the Order of the Golden Spur march out of the city in full battle array. They looked magnificent—the brilliant cream of their robes, the fluttering of colourful battle standards to which honours would be attached by the time they returned home. The Chevaliers' armour glittered, the mages' embroidered battle robes gleamed in the sunlight. At the head, the royal standard flew in pride of place. As in everything he did, Amaury made sure that the king got the credit. There was nothing worthwhile to be gained in taking any of it for himself.

Above all, if his efforts failed, he could be a long way away before the finger of blame was pointed at him. Not that it would be. He was almost certain of success now. Too many obstacles had been pushed aside. Anything that raised its head had been decapitated before it became a problem. Something that the commander of the Intelligenciers, and a number of his men, had discovered to their detriment.

Amaury had never expected that the dragon-slaying expedition would be greeted with cheers and garlands of flowers, and that proved to be the case—they were observed with ambivalent silence. Simply being accepted was more than enough for now; the important message was that these brave men and women were going out to risk their lives to protect the citizens of Mirabaya. Soon, he would set up medical clinics about the city to further highlight the benefits the Order could bring. Food would be preserved magically, ensuring there was no risk of people going hungry, water purified to make sure no one got ill. One step at a time, he would win the people's hearts and minds over to the Order. They might not be cheering now, but Amaury was confident that they would one day.

It was difficult not to become elated at the prospect that his long-laid plans were finally coming to fruition. Even had sight of the Order taking on the role he had always envisaged for them not been enough to bolster his spirits, the knowledge that the Cup was only a few hours from his grasp would have made this a great day even if the Spurriers were marching out under a barrage of abuse and rotten fruit. The former addict had pulled it off, which meant Luther was due a bonus for coming up with the scheme. A man like him was far too useful to neglect. Indeed, there might be a higher office in store for him.

However, the timing was far tighter than he would have liked. It had been his intention to first use the Cup on himself, and then, in the lesser way of the Silver Circle, on key members of the expedition. Commander Dorant had forced his hand by trying to stir up trouble, and Amaury's quick reaction hadn't come soon enough to stop the city's tension from tipping over the edge.

Trouble had flared up in a couple of the usual hotspots. Nothing that couldn't be contained for now.

The public needed to see action, to see the Order they feared marching off to defend them. The plan was for Vachon to find somewhere secluded to camp a day or so south, and wait for Amaury to bring him further information on the dragons' location. In truth, he would meet them to administer the Cup's bounty. When they returned, bearing the dragons' heads as trophies, then, perhaps, the city would greet them with joy and flower garlands.

Amaury smiled broadly as the expedition disappeared from sight, passing over the bridge from the Isle to the right bank, toward the gate that would take them out of the city to the south. Beside him stood the king, whose smile was so obviously forced, he might as well have been scowling. Every so often he would wave stiffly to the crowd. He might not have been happy with the way Amaury had brought the Order out into the open, but when he saw how well things turned out, he would be grateful. He would realise the great service that the Prince Bishop had done for the kingdom. One by one, the pieces were falling from the board into Amaury's pocket, proof indeed that hard work and perseverance eventually bore fruit.

▲▲▲▲▲▲

Within an hour of the discovery of Commander Dorant's body, the Intelligenciers of Mirabay had ceased to exist. Black robes and accoutrements adorned with the staff, skull, and sword insignia were cast aside in favour of the aprons of grocers, the jackets of bakers, the smart tunics of merchants pretending to be more successful than they actually were. Dorant's remaining men—for more than he had met their ends that night—did what they were trained to do, melting into the population.

Their mission remained the same, emergency protocols having long since been created in the event of a successful, concerted attack on their command structure. No one would have known that the man leaning on a wall next to a grocer's stall in one of the small market squares on the left bank of the river had worn Intelligencier black up until that morning. He chatted and joked like other men who had nothing better to do with their days. Every so often, he would pass comment on their new magical saviours, the tone of his voice conveying far more than mere words alone ever could. The people of Mirabay were well attuned to such rhetoric, priding themselves on sharp minds and even sharper tongues.

Traders and customers laughed and joked with him, voicing their concerns along with his. By late morning a crowd had gathered and the discussion had grown more serious. Two cream-robed individuals walked through the square shortly after the cathedral's bells had rung the midday chimes. The square was bisected by a street that linked the Order's headquarters to the Isle. The Intelligencier had chosen his spot with care: it was only a matter of time before members of the Order passed through.

It was unclear who threw the first rotting vegetable, or what type of vegetable that was. That first object was followed by a deluge, including a chunk of something more solid—a piece of a packaging crate or a market stall. When it struck its target, the mob cheered and surged forward. There was pushing and shoving, and someone let out a raucous cheer before holding a swath of torn cream cloth high overhead, the first trophy.

The Intelligencier didn't see steel being drawn, but he did hear the scream that followed. The second scream tore the mob apart in panic, revealing two bodies on the ground. Standing in the gap were a cream-robed man and woman, with drawn blades and fearful looks on their faces. It was disappointing that they hadn't used magic, but the Intelligencier was given to understand that not everyone in the Order was able to, at least not in any worthwhile way. Not yet.

His work done, he melted away with the fleeing crowd. The Order had murdered two citizens on the streets of Mirabay, in front of dozens of witnesses. Before the cathedral's bells rang again that day, the news would have reached every corner of the city. Commander Dorant's fire had been lit.

▲▲▲▲▲▲

Amaury's skin tingled as soon as Ysabeau walked into his office. Without a word, she offered him a leather pouch. He stood, reached across his desk, and took it reverently. Opening the pouch, he took out the Cup and cradled it in both hands, studying the swirling blue-and-grey patterns in the steel.

"Well done," he said.

"There wasn't much to it," Ysabeau said. "Just a hard ride with a special touch to speed it along. The other fellow did the hard work."

"You dealt with him?"

She nodded.

"Excellent," Amaury said, transfixed by the Cup. "Where did you find him?"

"Venne," she said. "Where the dragons are. Was hoping I might see one, but no luck."

"Venne . . ." Amaury said. *So that's where Gill has gotten to.* He wondered if he should have tasked Ysabeau with killing him also, but now that he had his main objective clutched firmly in his hands, it was easy to regret the opportunities not taken. Ysabeau might have ended up dead, and the Cup would still be in Gill's pocket. "You must be exhausted. I've had your room readied. Gaston will see that you have everything you need. Rest awhile. We can talk again later."

She moved to the door, and Amaury had the sensation that he had forgotten something.

"Ysabeau," he said. "Thank you. I couldn't have done this without you."

She turned and smiled. "You're welcome. Dad."

"All this effort will be worth it, I promise."

She shut the door behind her, leaving him with the object of his dreams. He set the Cup on his desk and sat, content for a moment to study its plain beauty. He had desired it for so long. For much of that time he had thought it might be nothing more than a myth, but here it was. To think that Amatus himself had held this little bowl in his hands, had drunk from it, received his great powers from it . . . the idea was intoxicating. It was such a simple little thing; it was difficult to fathom how much power it contained.

He had sent for a pitcher of water as soon as he was notified that Ysabeau had arrived at the city gates. As he reached for it, he realised his hands were shaking. He had to take five long, slow breaths to steady them. He poured in only enough to cover the bottom—perhaps one mouthful—and set the pitcher to one side. He was tempted to put in more, but he knew how dangerous this might be. Better to err on the side of caution. He could always drink more if needed.

He waited a moment longer, trying to fully appreciate what a monumental thing he was about to do. The world was about to change. He picked up the Cup in both hands, and after a brief hesitation, brought it to his lips.

The water was cool and fresh. Considering what other benefits it brought, he thought he would never again taste so wonderful a draught. He set the Cup down on his desk with as much reverence as he could, and waited. He had no idea how long it would take—he had found so little information on the Cup. He supposed that so monumental a change might take hours, or even days.

His initial impulse was to cure his hip, once and for all, but he knew that wasn't how it worked—that needed not just potent magic, but a knowledge of anatomy. That would have to wait until he had time to make sure he could do it right.

He felt no different. How could he tell if it had worked? A test. That was what was needed. Just because he didn't feel any different didn't mean that it hadn't worked. He focussed on creating a floating flame, a particularly good test of a mage's ability. Strength was obvious both in the flame's brightness, and in how long the light could be maintained. The room flashed with bright light. It faded quickly as Amaury's concentration dissolved into giddy laughter. The flash had been larger and brighter than he had ever managed before by so many degrees of magnitude, the two results were barely comparable.

He tried again, to make sure it wasn't just a fluke. Once more the room was filled with intense light. He held it for a little longer this time, but it was impossible to concentrate with the levels of elation he was feeling. The light faded and disappeared along with his focus.

Amaury slumped back in his chair, still chuckling. Usually his pathetic efforts exhausted him, but after this far more powerful demonstration, he felt no fatigue at all. There was another knock on his door. He considered telling whoever it was to go away, but he had requested regular updates on the sentiment in the city, which he could not afford to ignore.

"Come!" he said.

His secretary entered, bearing the expression he always did when the news was bad. "There's been trouble in the city," he said. "A mob attacked some of the Order on the street. Two people were killed."

Amaury felt his light mood drain away. He cleared his throat. "Brethren or citizens."

"Citizens, your Grace."

Amaury nodded. "How has the news been greeted?"

"It's still spreading, your Grace, but there are already some angry protests."

"The brethren. Did they use magic?"

"No, your Grace. Steel."

He nodded again. "Very well. Leave me be a moment. I'll have instructions for you shortly."

Amaury waited until his secretary was gone before letting out a sigh. Could he not have one day where everything went his way? He took a breath and tried to focus his mind, wanting to see his light show again. A kernel of light formed in the air in the centre of his office, but it grew no larger. He frowned and tried harder to focus, but nothing happened. He felt a flash of panic. What had gone wrong? He furrowed his brow and willed the tiny mote of light to get larger and brighter. Nothing happened. He slumped in his chair, exhausted now.

Grasping the flagon of water, he refilled the Cup, a little deeper this time. He poured it down his throat, ignoring the voice of concern that said he was being foolhardy. After a moment, he tried again, with all the concentrated determination he could muster. The room filled with a light so bright he had to shield his eyes. He let it go out, then allowed himself to relax. It still worked—it was simply that the effect hadn't lasted very long. That didn't tally with what the books had said. Amatus drank from the Cup, then had lifelong powers. Amaury had read nothing about him having to drink from it constantly. He must be using it wrong. But how? He had used the purest water, had drunk deeply. What more was needed?

He remembered the bad news his secretary had brought and chewed his lip for a moment. There was opportunity in everything, he thought. If there were attacks on members of the Order in the city, it might prove the perfect chance to rid himself of an increasingly nagging headache.

34

Gill had spent the remainder of the previous day in bed. His encounter with Edine had shamed him, and he couldn't bear it if anyone else were to see him in that state. He awoke that morning feeling better, but still burdened by what had happened. Had the remaining dragon wreaked more havoc while he was asleep? Still, what use would he have been? Hungover. No Cup. He wouldn't have been able to stop an angry dormouse.

He sat on the corner of his pallet bed, wondering what to do. The Cup was gone, and with it any hope of being able to kill the last dragon. His old friend had been murdered. There was no rambling house in Villerauvais for him to hide in now, nor any fields of vines to keep him supplied with wine and brandy. A gutter in Mirabay was the best he could hope for if he turned his back on Venne, and it was more than he deserved. No, he thought, he had to continue.

Might there be enough of a leftover effect from his last dose from the Cup to get him through the last slaying? He had used it a number of times in a short period of time—perhaps the effect was cumulative? It wasn't a risk he could take with Val, however. Telling the boy to leave wasn't the solution. Thus far the lad had been painstakingly loyal and attentive, and there was no way Gill wanted to meet his end knowing he had dragged Val to the same fate.

Then he had it. Use Val's loyalty to save him. Gill rustled up a pen and some parchment from his travelling bags, and started to write a note. The master at the Academy in Mirabay was an old friend of Gill's. At least, they had been friends in the past, before Gill had been cast from society in disgrace. He still owed Gill a favour or two, and Gill hoped that, being an honourable man, he would honour them.

As a Banneret of the White, the highest level of graduate the Academy produced, Gill had the right to nominate a person for Academy admission each year. Getting Val in was the easy part, however. Meeting the standards required to stay was far harder. Val would need a year of good instruction and hard training before he would stand a chance. Most who went to the Academy had been training for years. Val was nearly too old to enjoy that luxury. If he wasn't ready for admission in a year, perhaps a year and a half, his opportunity would pass.

Gill reckoned there was enough left in his family accounts at Laucelin's bank in Mirabay to pay for a year's upkeep, training, and other necessaries, as well as cover the boy's fees for the duration of his time at the Academy. His letter outlined what he wanted for the lad, and how he thought it was best handled. He added a line of thanks, then folded, sealed, and addressed the note before going in search of Val.

▲▲▲▲▲▲

Guillot watched Val ride away until he disappeared into the distance. He had told the lad he was giving him an important message to be delivered back to Mirabay, and that he was to follow whatever instructions the recipient of the letter gave him. As was ever his character, Val took on the task with enthusiasm, and was on his way a short while later. Gill felt bad for lying to him, but being killed by a dragon when he was still in his teens would be a waste.

He began his own preparations a short while later. There seemed to still be a slight trace of the Cup's effect in him, as he could feel a gentle tug coming from the west and reckoned that it indicated the presence of a dragon.

Assuming he survived the encounter with the dragon—a big if, even with what remained of the Cup's boon—there were other things he wanted to do. Catching up with the fellow who had murdered Barnot was top of the list. Then there was the mastermind of the whole mess, Amaury. He would still very much like to run a blade through Amaury's chest.

Some men got it all wrong, then carried a grudge with them for life. Amaury had stepped into Gill's blade that fateful day in Mirabay's arena. What he had been trying to do at the time wasn't at all the type of thing friends did to one another, but Gill had always known that their friendship had only been one of convenience.

Kicking dust into your opponent's face might be acceptable on the battlefield or in a fight to the death, but it wasn't done by gentlemen bannerets in the arena. The gods had shown Amaury the error of that effort—his leg had swung into the dulled tip of Gill's rapier, and the combined force of the kick and the thrust had driven the blade far into his hip. He had brought the injury on himself, but he'd never forgiven Gill nonetheless. If Gill lived past his dragon-slaying career, Amaury would surely send more men to try to kill him. He wouldn't allow Gill to redeem himself with the fame of slaying the dragons. That was an insult too far.

He thought of Auroré as he tightened the strap on his saddle, checking it once and then again, to ensure it would hold him when the time came. She would have been disappointed with what he had allowed himself to become, and he could only hope that if she watched from wherever the gods lived, she might understand that he was trying his hardest to be the best man he could be.

⁂

The pull was strong enough to guide Gill out of Venne and to the west. Just as a forest came into view, he felt a sharp, abrupt tug on his being. A great golden dragon emerged from the tree line. It was still some distance away, but even from afar, it was magnificent.

It stretched its wings lazily, looking at Guillot. There was nothing threatening in the act, and, if anything, Gill thought it looked carefree and not at all interested in him. Nothing about this creature seemed fierce or aggressive, qualities that had been all too obvious in the others he had encountered. The most likely reason for its behaviour was that it had recently fed, and hadn't previously encountered any humans who could pose a threat to it.

In all the time that Gill had known about dragons being back in the world, he hadn't had much time to observe them going about their day. Every one he had met was either trying to kill him or someone else. That dragons were magnificent creatures was beyond question, but this one was special even compared to the others he had seen. Its scales had the colour and lustre of pure gold, while the look in its blue eyes spoke of a curious intelligence that Gill had never seen in an animal. It was fascinating to watch the creature and feel that he was in relative safety. He would be the one bringing violence to that moment.

As peaceful as it seemed, Gill could not let it live. He watched it a while longer, enjoying the experience, much as he had the ride until now. The world was full of simple pleasures and you didn't need a bottle, a card table, or the adulation of your peers to find happiness. He only wished someone had told him that when he was younger. There was nothing to be gained by tarrying any longer, so he checked over his armour, and readied his lance. If the beast continued to behave in such a docile way, then Gill's job might not be so difficult after all. He might not have to pay for losing the Cup quite as heavily as he expected.

The dragon was ambling along by the tree line, minding its own business. Something felt wrong about what he was going to do, but he knew that like any wild creature, just because it seemed peaceful one moment didn't mean it wasn't capable of killing, of creating devastation. He urged his horse forward at a trot. It wasn't keen to approach another dragon, and it took some encouragement, but eventually it relented and they started to advance toward their quarry.

C losing the visor on his helm and lowering his lance, Gill urged his horse to a gallop. His world closed down to the narrow field of vision allowed by the slits in the visor. He leaned forward, bracing the lance, trying to keep its bobbing tip aimed at the spot where the dragon's neck joined its body. A good strike there would leave it ripe for a killing stroke with his sword. He watched the dragon fill what little space he could see, its beautiful golden scales becoming individually distinguishable.

Gill's vision was abruptly filled with red. His lance hit, bent, and shattered with a great crack, the impact launching him from his saddle. He could hear his horse whicker in terror as he sailed through the air; he landed with an all too familiar crunch of metal. He struggled to his feet as he tried to catch his breath. He flipped up his visor, then drew his sword. It had all happened so quickly, he didn't know what was going on. The only signal his brain could process was "danger."

He lifted his visor and looked around. A hulking mass of red flesh and scales occupied the space between Gill and the golden dragon. The beast was as big as the first one he had killed, and its face bore none of the docility of the golden one Gill had come to slay. He hadn't felt any trace of this dragon, and as surprises went, this was one he would rather have done without. He had already lost the initiative, but he wasn't willing to stand around waiting for death. As soon as he was steady on his feet again, he charged. There was no one to help him, no one to distract it. The big red swatted at him with one of its talons, but Gill managed to duck out of the way in time. As he made for the briefly visible clear path to the beast's underbelly, the dragon caught him with its snout and knocked him to the side again. Gill rolled away, coming to his feet with his sword at the ready; his head was spinning inside his helmet and he couldn't focus on what was in front of him.

A jet of flame arced toward him and he braced himself for the rush of hot air. He roared in pain as he felt the plates of his armour heat and start to broil his flesh through the quilted jacket he wore underneath. The Cup's boon wasn't working anymore. He dived out of the way, into another roll. This time he wasn't able to get back to his feet. He was still on his hands and knees when the clawed talons slammed onto his back and pressed him down, into the dirt.

The structure of his armour bore most of the weight, but he could feel the shaped plates of his cuirass start to flex, putting intolerable pressure on his chest. He fought to draw breath and tried to struggle free, but the weight on his back only increased. He flailed behind him with his sword, hoping to connect with dragon flesh, but found nothing but air. He was slowly getting pressed into the ground; soon the only give left would be from his squishy body. He roared at the increasing pain, feeling his eyeballs start to bulge. It wouldn't be long before his head popped like an overripe berry. He kept slashing back behind him as best he could, to no avail. He could feel the sinews in his shoulder strain to the breaking point as he cut and cut and cut at the awkward angle. Then the dragon withdrew its paw.

Every instinct in Gill screamed for him to take advantage of the momentary reprieve, but he was so embedded in the ground that he was stuck. He had to use nearly all of what little energy he had left to push himself out of the man print the dragon had created. When the ground finally released him, Gill scrambled away, then turned to face his foe. The big red beast stood looking at him intently. For an insane moment, Gill thought it looked familiar. He narrowed his eyes as he searched for recognition, but it was too bizarre a notion, no matter how uncanny it seemed. He got to his feet and readied himself for the next exchange.

"Put down your blade, Guillot."

It took everything that Gill had to not drop his sword in shock. His brains felt scrambled from all the tumbling about—had he imagined the voice?

"Put it down."

No, he hadn't. He held the sword out before him, and shook his head resolutely. He couldn't believe he was considering answering this creature.

"Enough of your kind have died," the dragon said. "Enough of mine too. Put down your sword and we can settle this without violence."

Gill's immediate reaction was indignation. This creature was no different than the one that had destroyed Villerauvais. No different than the one that had killed Beausoleil. Or was it? He remembered how peaceful the golden dragon had looked when he'd first spotted it, knew this one could have killed him with ease had it chosen to. Instead, it had released him. Why? He wanted to find out. He lowered his sword.

"On the ground," the dragon said. "Over there."

The Cup's effects had worn off. This beast could kill him easily, sword in hand or not. Gill shrugged and tossed it to the side.

"Good," the dragon said. "A moment, if you would?"

Gill nodded, and the dragon started getting smaller. At first Gill thought he might have been right about the head injury. Then he realised it was not just getting smaller—it was changing shape. Soon it started to resemble a human. A human that Gill recognised.

"François?" he said. He felt a flash of anger. This man had killed Barnot and stolen the Cup. Gill's eyes flicked to his sword and he wondered if he could get to it, and then to the beast, before it was able to revert to its dragon form. If it had wanted him to drop his sword, that meant it was vulnerable in this state.

"I apologise for my deception," the dragon said. "My name is Pharadon."

"You murdered my friend, Pharadon," Gill said.

Pharadon's brow furrowed. Gill found it hard to believe that only moments before he had been an enormous red dragon.

"I did no harm to anyone," Pharadon said. "Which of your friends was killed?"

"Barnot. The bald one." It occurred to Gill that Pharadon was naked. He did his best to avert his gaze.

Pharadon shook his head. "Both of your friends were still in the tavern when I departed. Both alive."

"You expect me to believe you?"

"Yes. You still live, do you not? Do you think it would be difficult for me to end you if I so chose?"

It was reasonable logic, but Gill was confused. Pharadon might have killed Barnot in self-defence after he was caught stealing the Cup.

"The Cup," Gill said. "Why did you take it?"

Pharadon shook his head. "It seems you have suffered some misfortunes recently, but you are very much mistaken in attributing them to me. I met with you because I wanted to understand you before I decided what to do. I chose not to kill you."

"That's very generous of you," Gill said. "But those of your kind that I've met haven't fared so well."

Pharadon laughed. "Dragonkind are not so different to humans. You can meet all sorts. Some better than others. Things were not looking so good for you only moments ago. That should inform you on where I lie on that scale."

"What's this all about?" Gill said.

"You're a dragonslayer. What your people call a 'Chevalier.' As best I can tell you're the only one, and thus the only one who poses a real threat to my kind. I want you to stop."

"Why not just kill me?"

"I had intended to, until we spoke, and I learned of your loss and your motivation. More killing won't make things better for either of us."

"Your kind have been doing most of the killing," Gill said.

"Indeed. As with your race, there are good and bad amongst mine. This goldscale has the potential to be good. I like to think that I do also. Leave us be, and we will do the same for you."

"If I disagree?"

"I'll kill you where you stand. I can smell that you have lost your magic. I suspect you know what that means as well as I do. If you choose to fight me, you will die."

As a younger man, Gill would have laughed in Pharadon's face, a display of defiance and bravado that would show how unimpressed he was. However, there was neither boast nor threat in what Pharadon had said. It was merely a statement of what would come to pass.

"What now, then?" Gill said.

"I'll take this goldscale deep into the mountains and we will never be seen again."

"What if there are more dragons?"

"A possibility," Pharadon said. "I will make it my duty to shepherd them into the mountains, far from where any humans dwell. There are many places on this world that are unknown to your kind. There is space for all and no need for conflict."

"And if you miss one?"

Pharadon shrugged. The gesture looked awkward—a movement copied from observation, not generated by emotion. "I don't have all the answers. If there are more dragons, some conflict might occur, but on this day, that is not necessary."

Gill felt there was more he should be saying. He had never been party to the negotiations that had ended any of the wars he had fought in; he now wondered if this was what it had felt like for the people on the weaker side of the table. Should he ask for something in return for agreeing? He couldn't think of anything.

"How is it that you can speak?" he said. None of the other dragons he had fought had shown any sign of being able to. He found it incredibly unsettling. A terrifying beast was bad enough. One that could speak and think was so much worse.

Pharadon laughed. "How is it that *you* can speak? Dragonkind were already old when your kind had their first reasoned thought. There were creatures and races before us capable of the same, and I'm sure there will be more after we have all passed from the world. None of us are unique, it is only our experience of life that is special, and that is what I wish to preserve."

A point of view like that was hard to argue against. What more was there for Gill to say?

"You won't be seen again?"

The dragon shook his head. Again, the movement looked somehow unnatural, unnerving. Gill wondered if it would look more normal in dragon form. "Any travel we need to undertake in the realm of humans, we will do at night. We won't be seen, and soon enough, we'll be far from here."

"Then I . . . I agree to your terms."

Pharadon smiled and nodded. The gesture was short, led by his chin, and seemed as artificial as all the others.

"I wish you well," Pharadon said.

"I'll be on my way then," Gill said.

Pharadon nodded again, still smiling. It was an awkward moment. Gill hadn't had the chance to look around for his horse, but chasing after it like an idiot while an ancient dragon disguised as a naked man watched was not an activity he could muster any enthusiasm for. He looked about and whistled. The horse owed him no great loyalty, and with the golden dragon still ambling about near the trees, Gill didn't expect it to respond. It did, however. Feeling relieved, Gill collected his sword and mounted. With no idea of what more to say, he gave Pharadon a salute and rode for Venne.

CHAPTER
36

Did you have any trouble getting here?" the Prince Bishop asked.

"I came in disguise. Took back streets. Things are tense. There's trouble in places, but so long as you're clever, it can be avoided."

"You bring good news, I presume, since you chose to run that gauntlet?"

"I think so, yes."

"Interesting," the Prince Bishop said. He walked to his office window and stood in silence, looking down into the garden.

Solène did her best not to let the awkwardness of the moment get to her. She had seen him do this a number of times now, and had come to realise it was a ploy he used to assert himself. He was free to move about, he had the power to take time to think, he could leave his visitors squirming in silence for as long as he chose.

"So, tell me what you've been able to find?" he said, without looking at her.

She had searched late into the night, finally falling asleep at her desk. Her first act on waking was to call on him to make her report. "I've searched with all my ability, and I can't find anything about the temple. I did find mention of nodes, though, where magical energy gathered naturally. The nodes are the only thing I have to go on. There weren't many of them, and it stands to reason that the temple would have been built on one."

"A reasonable theory," Amaury said, turning back to face her. "And you think these *nodes* will lead us to the temple?"

Lead *me,* she thought. She had decided she would use his help to find the place, then make sure he could never use it. "It's a guess, but it's the best I have to go on."

"And you can find these nodes?"

"In theory, yes," Solène said. "There are a lot of variables, not least the fact that no one's seen or interacted with one in a very long time. If they still exist, I should be able to trace them. That still leaves the problem of finding which one marked the location of the temple, and if there's anything left of it."

"A place of such powerful magic couldn't be completely destroyed," he said.

The certainty in his voice gave Solène pause for thought. She needed to help him enough to stop the dragons, but not enough to grant him all the power he sought. He was a clever foe, and dangerous. Either he knew more than he was letting on, or the pressure was starting to get to him. She wasn't sure which worried her more.

"That may well be the case," she said. "But it will take time to find them."

"Are you ready to move forward with this plan?"

"Yes," Solène said.

"I need you for one task before you start. After that, you'll have every asset you need in your search for this temple, including one of the new bannerets I've recruited to do any heavy lifting for you. He won't have any magic, but he'll be good with a blade. I don't want anything happening to you, and even you need to sleep sometimes. It's just like the old days—a mage with bannermen as bodyguards. I'm coming around to realising that it wasn't so bad an arrangement after all."

She opened her mouth to object, then closed it, realising that she didn't have any say in the matter. She was a Sister of the Order and he was her commander. That was how it worked. She could only hope that she had learned enough to keep her power under control.

"I'll need a little time to prepare. The rest of the day at least."

"Fine," he said. "Be ready to depart in the morning."

Ysabeau greeted Amaury with a smile when he walked into the salon of his townhouse.

"Has Gaston seen to everything you need?" Amaury said.

"Everything," Ysabeau said. "I hear there's trouble in the city?"

"It was to be expected. It will pass as soon as the Order do what I've ordered them to."

"You're sure this was the right moment?"

"I doubt there'll be a better one. Which brings me to why I've come home early. The trouble has brought us an opportunity. There's something I need you to do."

Her smile faded a little, and he wondered why, but was too busy to worry about it.

"Seneschal dal Drezony has become a thorn in my side. She's become an obstacle to the Order's future. Now is a good time to remove her. We can do it under the cover of the growing trouble on the streets."

"That stuck-up bitch?" Ysabeau said, her smile widening. "It's about time she had a fall."

"I remember your difficulties with her when you were still in the Order. I thought you might enjoy this job." He paused. "I have other people who can handle it, if you prefer?"

"No," Ysabeau said. "This is one I want for myself."

"Excellent. I need to visit the Priory. I'll send her on an errand, which should give you ample opportunity to deal with her. Make it look like a random attack, like mob justice."

"That won't be a problem."

"Come back here as soon as you're done. There's something else I need you to do, someone I'd like you to keep an eye on."

▲▲▲▲▲

Amaury sent word for both Solène and dal Drezony the moment he arrived at the Priory, then went straight to the office that was reserved for his use. He had set out his things by the time dal Drezony arrived. She wore the sullen expression that she seemed to keep at the ready for him these days, and said nothing as she waited to hear what he wanted. He placed his purple leather document case on the desk in front of her.

"The king would like some updates on the Order's status from you, in person."

"No longer trusts your word?" she said.

"Quite the contrary. I'm simply busy with other things. I've put together some reports that I've received from Vachon and others, that you might not have seen yet. Have a read through them before meeting with the king, and please make sure to return them to me at the palace after your meeting. I haven't had time to have copies made yet."

"Perish the thought that your records would not be up to date," dal Drezony said.

Amaury gave her a thin smile. "Indeed." He hoped Ysabeau made it hurt.

"The king requires your presence at three bells, sharp."

"The streets aren't exactly safe for us right now," she said.

"You have other clothes? Things that aren't in the Order's colours?"

She nodded. "I should be able to find something."

"Then I suggest you wear them. Things will settle down in a few days, but until then, I agree that staying within the Priory's walls is the best course for the most part, and going out in normal attire is advisable when trips outside the walls like this are necessary. I've assigned two platoons of the King's Guard to bolster the Priory's defences. They should be here and manning the walls before nightfall."

"I appreciate your concern."

"You're welcome," Amaury said. "You may go, but before you do, one more word of advice. I'd adopt a more respectful tone when talking to the king, if I were you."

She took the document case and left. He basked in the knowledge that yet another thorn in his side was about to be removed. He was full of excited energy.

For the first time in so many years, it felt as though anything was possible. His plans were coming to fruition, his dreams were about to be realised, and although he knew there would be more obstacles to overcome, he would be doing so with near limitless power—as soon as he worked out how to make the Cup's effect permanent. The people would come to accept what he had brought them as the great gift that it was, and would share in Mirabaya's glory when she took her place as the greatest power in the world.

"You wished to see me, your Grace?" Solène said, joining him a few minutes later.

"You recall the Cup we spoke about before?"

He watched her carefully, knowing that he was becoming a little paranoid. When had he come to think that everyone might be lying to him?

"I, yes, I remember it. The ceremony involved drinking from something they called the Amatus Cup."

"Precisely," Amaury said. He paused for a moment, wondering how best to proceed. How much did he want to tell her? How much could he trust her with? It could take him a lifetime to unlock the Cup's secrets. It might take her only an afternoon.

"My agents have located the Cup and delivered it to me," he said.

Solène looked shocked. The colour in her face drained away, and she seemed to wobble on her feet.

"Are you all right, Solène?" he said.

"Yes, yes, I'm fine," she said. "I'm just stunned that you were able to find something that's been missing for so long."

Amaury beamed with pride, then frowned. "How did you know it was lost?"

"Well, it must have been, or you wouldn't have had to send agents out to find it. The only mention of it that I found is from centuries ago."

He relaxed a little. He was becoming too suspicious. "True," he said. "Before I send you off to look for the temple, I need you to help me with the Cup. I believe it can confer advantages to our fighting men and women. With the arrival of these new dragons, we have to assume there are more still to come, that they are a new terror that we have to deal with on an ongoing basis. To successfully do that, we need to work out how to use the Cup to create a new generation of men and women who can deal with these creatures."

"I, I'll have to focus my study on that," she said.

Amaury studied her for a moment, then decided to change his approach. He needed her to help willingly, not under protest like dal Drezony. He would never get the best out of her otherwise, and would end up having to deal with her when she finally refused one of his commands.

"It's very important," Amaury said. "We now have the tool to defend ourselves, but not the knowledge to use it. Enough brothers and sisters of the Order have died trying to slay these beasts. I owe it to each and every one of you I send out to give you the best possible chance." He pursed his lips and collected his thoughts. "When I created the Order, it was with the betterment of all the people of Mirabaya in mind. Think of all the things that magic can do to make people's lives easier. Think of the safe haven it provides for young people like you, who would likely face the pyre if others learn they are mages.

"This is the most dangerous moment in the Order's existence. It could founder at any moment. Or it can become strong, vibrant, and integral to Mirabayan society. If we can slay these dragons, we can show the people that we are their saviours and they'll love us. Right now, a thousand years of that hatred and fear is threatening to boil over. Not only do we need this victory, we need it quickly."

She nodded slowly, as though digesting what he had said.

"I know I've been asking a lot of you, but with a little luck, that will all pay off soon, and you'll be able to take a well-deserved rest. Spend the evening searching for anything you can find. Learn whatever you can about the Cup. We have to leave in the morning, to do the best we can for our brothers and sisters."

"I'll do my best to find something."

"That's all I ask."

Solène trudged back to the Priory that night, no closer to finding an answer to her predicament. The city was still busy even at that hour, with animated groups moving about the place with menacing countenances. They had lit fires on street corners to stay warm. It was obvious that some people were looking for trouble, and she could only hope that they wouldn't choose her to find it. She had long since adapted to living under threat, so her fear now almost felt like slipping back into a comfortable old pair of shoes—bearing a secret that could get her killed, but going about her life as she needed to regardless.

When she got back to the Priory, the place was abuzz. She had no idea what was causing the flurry of activity, but she didn't really care. There was too much on her mind. The people around her seemed full of fearful energy. She barely recognised anyone. Most of those who had been there when she had first arrived, weeks earlier, had been sent on the dragon-hunting expedition, leaving only those too junior and the new hires who'd been left behind to protect the Priory. Some of the younger ones, who had been brought into the Order shortly after their talent for magic had manifested itself, had never known what it was like to live with the terror that she and the other older members had known. She couldn't help but feel a measure of contempt for them, wondering how they would have coped with her life if this was the effect of a day or two of danger.

Then she heard dal Drezony's name and stopped dead in her tracks. Spotting a young woman she recognised from the refectory, Solène approached her and said, "I heard people talking about Seneschal dal Drezony. Is something wrong?"

The young woman, a novice mage, gave a grim smile. "She was identified while out in the city. They murdered her."

Without a word, Solène stumbled away in utter shock, retreating to her room without conscious thought. She sat on the edge of her bed and burst into tears. Dal Drezony was the best the Order had to offer. She was its voice of conscience, its moral compass. Without her, the Order would be dominated by men like Vachon. These were not the type of men who staffed hospitals or cared for the poor. They conquered and destroyed. Who was left to guide the Order in the right direction?

Only Solène. She had something the Prince Bishop wanted and she possessed enough power that he had to take her seriously. She might not agree with the Prince Bishop, might not like the direction the Order was being taken in, but that didn't mean she had to stand by while it all fell apart. If he wanted her continued cooperation, the Prince Bishop would have to listen to her opinions. If he wanted her help, then she was going to need something in return. Her tears stopped and her resolve strengthened. She would see that the Order became what dal Drezony had intended—a force for good, something loved by the people rather than feared or hated. If not, the Prince Bishop could spend the rest of his days scrabbling in the dirt looking for his temple and trying to make the Cup work.

⁘⁘⁘⁘

Decision made, Solène slipped out of the Priory and walked quickly toward the palace, determination outweighing fear. Within a few streets of the Priory, she relaxed a little, knowing that she could blend into the crowd. No one would realise where she had come from. That didn't change the fact that she would have preferred to be pretty much anywhere else, doing pretty much anything else. The tension on the streets was so great now that it was not just the members of the Order who had to worry. She had heard that the City Watch had come under attack, as had some royal officials. Soon enough, she feared, disagreements between ordinary citizens would turn to violence.

Knowing there would be people gathered at the central square in front of the cathedral on the Isle, she took the longer route, around the back of the cathedral to the right bank at the eastern end of the city. She would have to walk the length of Mirabay to reach the palace on the western hill, but she reckoned she would have a safer journey through the less-populated southern section.

She was not surprised to see far more soldiers on duty at the palace than during her previous visits. They were far more alert, as well, and she was subjected to a barrage of questions before they sent for someone from the Prince Bishop's office to confirm her identity.

When she finally got to his office, she was shown straight in. The Prince Bishop looked at her with tired but hopeful eyes.

"Have you got anything for me?"

"I believe I do."

▲▲▲▲▲▲

The goldscale had wandered off into the foothills toward the end of Pharadon's encounter with the slayer—with Gill. Pharadon had needed to rest for hours after changing form—it still wasn't coming easily to him—and in that time, he had seen the goldscale following her curiosity, exhibiting all the encouraging signs of being perfectly suited for enlightenment. It was always thrilling to bring a mind from the darkness into light, no matter how many times Pharadon had done it. In this instance, it was both terrifying and exciting.

Pharadon could tell that the power this young dragon would enjoy after only a few years of maturity would make his own pale by comparison. It was an incredible thing to consider. Intimidating. Tragic that the goldscale would never have the chance to reside at the highest levels of dragon society.

Only hours remained before the goldscale would be too mature to be brought to enlightenment, so he knew he had to act soon if he hoped to get her to the temple in time. Once he had her subdued—in a kind of magical half sleep—he would have more time to prepare and carry out the ceremony, which he would do at the temple. So long as he was careful, he could keep the goldscale in half sleep for as long as a couple of weeks, though not much longer. While this semi-hibernation would prevent the juvenile from doing anything that would hasten maturity, such as excessive eating, it would not halt the slower, longer natural maturation process. So he would have time to prepare the temple and remind himself how the alternative process of enlightenment was carried out, but he would need to be mindful of the goldscale's development so that he did not miss his opportunity.

The human had asked him if he had taken his cup—what was he talking about? Pieces moved around inside Pharadon's mind until a connection was made. Might Gill's "cup" be a vessel of enlightenment? He had not encountered any human mages since waking, which struck him as odd. When he had exiled himself into the mountains, there had been many of them, with some capable of shaping magics as powerful as any dragon. The Chevalier had no detectable affinity to the Fount, yet he had the remnants of magical protections, which could have been bestowed only by a mage. Or by a vessel of enlightenment. Such vessels were imbued with the power to bring a single creature to enlightenment; afterward, they contained enough residual magic to confer abilities of respectable strength, albeit fleeting in terms of longevity. The Godsteel they were forged from had innate magical qualities, including an affinity to the Fount that allowed it to draw power to itself and store it.

He focussed on the goldscale again. The first goldscale had come to enlightenment all by itself. Watching the juvenile, Pharadon wondered if this had been the way: curiosity and exploration stressing its mind until it opened up and began to understand the things around it.

Back in dragon form now, he hovered over the goldscale, downwind and high enough that she would not be able to detect him with her normal senses. He added a little magic to mask his presence and set to drawing enough of the Fount to himself to shape the magic he needed to use. As tendrils of the Fount swirled up toward him and enveloped him, he purged his mind of all but the desire he wished to fulfill, refining the thought into a concept so precise that it seemed like it could exist on its own.

The goldscale started with surprise and looked about herself for a threat. She couldn't sense him, and she certainly couldn't smell him, so unless she looked directly at him, she would be unlikely to detect Pharadon. She moved about in agitation—she did not need to be enlightened to know that something was going on. Pharadon maintained his focus, forcing as much of the Fount's energy as he could toward his desired outcome. Gradually, the goldscale's movements began to slow, although they became more agitated. She looked as though she was struggling against invisible bonds, which was exactly what she was doing. At the same time, Pharadon's magic was trying to soothe her mind, which was proving far more challenging.

Eventually he could sense the quieting take effect, the fear and resistance born of the goldscale's instinct for survival giving way to the weight of the magic Pharadon pressed upon her. Eventually, she sat and grew still. Now for the hard part, Pharadon thought. No creature could be brought to enlightenment unwillingly. Even in its base state, a dragon's mind contained a kernel of wisdom and insight. The savage parts of its being prevailed most of the time, but base dragons could, in moments, be capable of behaviour as refined and insightful as any of their enlightened brethren.

Enlightenment allowed wisdom and insight to take charge, but even afterward, the savage part remained, lurking deep within, waiting for any opportunity to reassert itself. Having heard Gill's story in the small village tavern, Pharadon knew the tragedy in Alpheratz's life had caused the balance to shift, allowing his more savage instincts to control him. That sort of tragic descent was feared by all enlightened; thankfully, few ever had to contend with it.

When he was certain the goldscale was not going to attack him, Pharadon landed and approached in as unthreatening a way as he could. Memories of his long-ago enlightenment let him recall how powerless he had felt at the time. Though still young, he had seen dragons fight and kill one another, and had been afraid he was about to meet his end. However, the old dragon who was going to enlighten him had sat next to him and started to tell a tale. At the start of their path to enlightenment, each dragon was told a similar tale, one that had taken on features added by each teller. Whole clans and even individual generations could be identified by how their story differed from others'.

"Araxion was the first of our kind to call himself enlightened,"

Pharadon said now. The juvenile goldscale looked up at him with wild eyes in which he could see a glimmer of awareness. "Like you, he was a goldscale, as rare a thing then when the sky over these mountains was filled with our kind as it is now. You are fortunate to be blessed so, and I hope that you can come to understand that.

"Araxion's time was a savage one, a time without reason, but Araxion was different. Araxion asked questions of the world around him, as I have seen you do. He wanted to know, to understand, but his mind was still in the dark and could not make sense of what he experienced, nor give voice to the questions he was trying to ask. He struggled with this for days. For weeks. For months. Then, one day, he understood the question he had fought to find within himself. It was the first question of all things: Why?

"Why does the sun shine? Why does the wind blow? Why do the tides ebb and flow? Why am I?

"The question showed Araxion that a path existed, a path that he had yet to venture down. Ask yourself, of all the wonder you have witnessed during your short life, who are you, and where do you fit in it all?"

The goldscale's eyes narrowed for a moment. Pharadon felt encouraged.

"Once he understood that there were questions, he was compelled to seek out answers. He flew long and wide, visiting places where no dragon had ever been. The world was young then, but the lands were filled with beasts, and the seas with fish. Araxion was the first to give voice to the question, and he realised there was no one but himself to answer it. Araxion had grown old by the time he understood.

"The answers were to be found in only one place. The place where it had all started, where the question had fought its way from the darkness to be expressed. His mind.

"He looked within himself once more, struggling to find that answer in much the same way he struggled to find the question. He could tell it was there, somewhere, like a scent on a summer breeze, but he could not grasp it. He raged within himself, and at moments was tempted to abandon his quest. His lifespan might be great, but he had sacrificed much of it to the question, while his kin revelled in simplicity. They fed, they flew, they fought, they revelled, they mated . . . but Araxion could not allow himself to let go of the glimmer of light that led him along this seemingly endless path.

"Then he did something that no dragon before him had done. He opened his eyes and he saw, truly saw. The world was bathed in a dancing blue light, coruscating across every surface, making it look like a great sapphire that had caught a flame. He saw the Fount, the energy of life, of the world, and of all things in it. He saw the sun rise above the horizon, and he understood. He saw the rain fall from the clouds, and he understood. He saw himself reflected on the surface of a still lake, and he understood. He asked himself who he was, what he would be, why he was, and he understood. And he rejoiced."

The goldscale's eyes narrowed again. The glimmer of awareness was still there, and Pharadon had hope.

"I ask you the questions he asked of himself, that were asked of me and of all the others of our kind who know the joy of enlightenment." He raised his voice to a crescendo until it boomed like thunder. "Who are you?"

The goldscale stared at him blankly, but Pharadon could see the light within her burning steadily. No dragon ever responded to the first demand.

"What will you be?" he continued.

The goldscale's eyes narrowed again. Its brow furrowed.

"Why are you?"

The goldscale's eyes flashed bright and then settled to a faint blue glow. Pharadon felt a shiver of relief and joy run through him as he realised that he was not to be alone, that he was not to be the last of his kind. The young dragon's mind had opened itself to enlightenment. In that moment, to Pharadon's eyes, the world was bathed in the glory of the Fount, that beautiful blue light, and he knew the joy of wonderment as freshly as he had first experienced it during his own ascent to enlightenment.

Pharadon could tell that the goldscale had seen the Fount too from the way she looked about herself. The hard part had been successfully completed. The parts of the goldscale's mind that had lain dormant up to that moment were now filled with energy, creating the impossible from nothing more than thought. But unless the goldscale drank from a vessel of enlightenment, that energy would ebb away like a dying light, leaving only darkness in its wake. Pharadon had won more time for his task, but it was not limitless.

"Come with me, if you desire it," Pharadon said, "and I will show you where the answers lie."

It was not unknown for a dragon to refuse such an invitation. Pharadon could remember how terrifying that was—to be on the verge of understanding something so enormous that it threatened to cleave your mind in two. Some dragons were too afraid. Some were too close to their descent and could not be pulled from the precipice. Some were too haughty to think they could be any better than they already were. Such refusals were sad for all involved—any dragon that would not accept enlightenment would be put to death.

The goldscale nodded her head; she was uncertain at first, but as she looked about herself, realising the great power that made the world work, the nodding became ever more vigorous.

CHAPTER
38

Since Gill's encounter with the dragons had ended in the mid-afternoon, he knew it would be after dark by the time he got back to Venne. That in itself was no great problem, but he couldn't face going back there, so took the excuse to camp out for the night and give himself some time to think. He hadn't come up with any answers to his worries by morning, however, and was still confused when he rode back to Venne. It seemed he had laid the threat of dragons to rest, but he hadn't slain them. How did he explain that to the villagers? He doubted very much if any of them would believe the conversation he had had with Pharadon. He doubted any of them would believe that dragons could talk, much less take on human form. He wasn't sure he believed it himself, though he had seen and heard it.

Could he trust Pharadon? Although the dragon's behaviour suggested he was being earnest, it was unsettling to know the two dragons were still out there. They could have killed Gill easily if they had chosen, yet they had not. Having witnessed the beasts cause so much death and destruction, Guillot found it difficult to think of them as intelligent and reasoning. Yet he recalled the expressive face of the first dragon he had killed, remembered wondering what it was thinking.

There was no way he could tell the villagers what had actually happened, which meant he needed to come up with something else, and come up with it quickly. The previous day, everyone had known that he was riding out to go after the last of the dragons, and when he returned, they would want to know what had happened. He believed he had two options. Either he said he couldn't find it, that it seemed to have moved on, or he said he had killed it.

If he told them he had killed the gold one, and someone then saw it in flight, would the whole cycle of panic and terror begin again? That wasn't the answer. Perhaps a truth that omitted some of the facts, allowing the villagers to come to their own conclusion? It felt a little devious, but it seemed like the best solution that was available to him.

What to say? That the dragon was gone? That was too nebulous, and invited further questioning. He needed something better. Only when he was within sight of the village did something better occur to him—and just in time. As soon as he was spotted, a small crowd gathered near the remains of the tent village that had been set up by the adventurers.

"Did you kill it?" someone shouted, once Gill was within earshot.

He did his best to give them a broad smile. "It won't be bothering you again."

There was a cheer, and he felt like a fraud, but only for a moment. After all, he had killed the other two, not to mention the big one that started it all. So long as Pharadon kept to his word and stayed out of sight while he took the gold one deep into the mountains, no one ever needed to know the truth. Gill did his best to wave and respond to the adulation, as uncomfortable as it made him. He couldn't get back to the tavern quickly enough, though even there, there were eager villagers to help him down and take his horse away for grooming and feeding. Celebrity did have its perks.

Inside the inn, at the sight of Gill, Gaufre reached for a bottle of the wine he kept on his top shelf. Gill's stomach turned at the thought and he shook his head.

"Just some water." He sat near the bar, knowing he wasn't going to get any peace for a few hours yet, until the news that the danger was ended had reached everyone, and they had all come to see their conquering hero. The dread he felt at this thought was something of a comfort to him—he would have been far less impressed with himself had he been looking forward to the adulation, as would once have been the case.

Edine entered the taproom and walked over as soon as she spotted him.

"It's over?" she said.

He nodded. A question he reckoned he could answer honestly. "It is."

It looked as though a weight had been lifted off her.

"I'd say 'thank the gods,' but I suppose it wasn't them who did it," Edine said. "I can't begin to tell you how grateful I am. How grateful we all are."

Gill nodded and smiled. What was there to say?

"What next?" she said.

"Some sleep would be a good place to start. After that?" He shrugged. "The first dragon destroyed my seigneury, so there's no reason to go back there. I'm sure I'll come up with something."

"There's plenty to be done here over the next few months," she said. "We could always use a hand, particularly since we don't have a seigneur anymore."

"I appreciate the offer," Gill said, "but I'm not sure I'm ready to take on such responsibility again so soon."

"Well, give it some thought," she said, before leaving him.

⁙

Gill sat by the tavern's bar the next morning, nursing a mug of poor coffee, having kept to his room for as much of the previous day as possible, anxious that at any moment he'd be discovered as a fraud. He claimed to need rest, an excuse that was readily accepted. He would have left Venne already, were it not for the fact that he had nowhere to go. His incipient career as a dragonslayer seemed to have come to an end, although he couldn't say he was sorry about that.

He wondered what Solène was doing. He hoped things in the city were working out for her the way she wanted. He hoped Val was safely on his way to Mirabay. He thought of Beausoleil, whom he had underestimated, and Cabham, whom he had overestimated, and of Barnot and the loss of the Cup. Tracking down the killer and the thief might be a worthwhile way to spend his days, but without the threat of dragons, there didn't seem to be any need for the Cup. For the killer, he had no idea of where to start.

Even at his lowest ebb, Villerauvais had always been in the background, like a safety net. No more. A return to his former life of soldiering didn't appeal. He'd seen enough destruction for one life.

Slaying the dragons, and preventing them from harming anyone else, was, on reflection, the only positive use he had ever put his sword to.

Finished with his coffee, Gill walked outside. The destruction the dragons had left behind was evident. The air was damp and still held the smell of smoke. The village had lost a number of inhabitants that night. It would take the survivors some time to rebuild, and without a seigneur to oversee matters, Edine would have to shoulder much of the burden of the work. He'd never been good with his hands, unless one of them had a sword in it, so he couldn't even help rebuild.

He started to explore the village, walking the few narrow streets that led away from the square. He could make out what some of the buildings had been before the attack—a bakery, a smithy, a mill— while others were so completely destroyed, it was impossible to tell. The villagers had started clearing, but they had a long journey ahead to erase the devastation of what had been only a few moments of de-struction. It would take money to rebuild, but with two dragon car-casses to plunder, Venne would have plenty of that soon enough. He wondered what had become of his own trophy, left with the taxider-mist in Trelain. He didn't feel quite so enthusiastic about it anymore.

A worry lurked within him. What else could he have done? He would have been burned to a crisp if he had tried to fight, and it hadn't seemed that fighting was necessary. Had he made the right choice? Would the people care that it was the right one, if they found out?

CHAPTER

39

Solène and the Prince Bishop travelled out of the city in an unmarked carriage before dawn. The driver had been given clear instructions to waste no time, and as the carriage bounced about on the muddy city streets, she hoped that the whole journey was not going to be as uncomfortable as its beginning.

The Prince Bishop watched the streets nervously through a crack in the cabin's window blind until the city walls were well behind him. Only then did he sit back and force a smile. A plain wooden box with a brass lock plate sat on his lap.

"How did you find it?" he said.

She shrugged. "I pieced information together from a number of documents."

His face darkened. "You're sure it will work?"

"Absolutely certain."

"What does it do?"

"I'm not sure of everything, but it seems to protect the beneficiary from fire. It might bring some other benefits, but that's the main one, as best I could find out."

"I can see how that would help. Coupled with their military skill, Vachon's people should be able to manage killing the dragon."

"Where are we going?" Solène said.

"The Order's expedition is waiting for us at Gardonne. We'll administer the Cup's . . . What are they called?"

She shrugged. "Its gifts."

"That fits. We'll administer its gifts and the Spurriers will continue their journey to the region that's currently afflicted. I only hope they have time to deal with the matter and return to the city before the next incident occurs."

"You think there'll be more?" Solène said.

"We have to be prepared for the eventuality. That's why it was so important to learn how to make more fighters like the old Chevaliers of the Silver Circle."

"What then? Do you think that will be enough to make the people accept the Order?"

"No, but it will be a step in the right direction. This will show them that the Order will protect them. Next, we'll show that we can also help them. Restore and maintain order. Heal. That sort of thing."

She wondered how he intended to maintain order, and felt the sickness of worry return to her stomach.

"With Seneschal dal Drezony gone," Solène said, "I'd like to take a more active role in the Order."

The Prince Bishop smiled indulgently. "That's exactly what I intended for you. As soon as we find this temple, and learn what more the Cup can do."

"You think the Cup is capable of more?" she said.

"Of course," Amaury said, then paused. Solène could see from his expression he thought he had said too much. "Perhaps, perhaps not, but it's best to know one way or the other, don't you think? It would be a great crime to have the key to unlock so much potential and not explore it fully."

"I suppose so," Solène said. She would have preferred that he not suspect, but he was too intelligent to not have come up with the question. "Sometimes I worry, though."

He frowned, leaned forward, and raised a questioning eyebrow. "Really? Why?"

She shrugged. "It took the Imperial mages generations to learn how to exploit and control magic. Might we be foolhardy, rushing in and looking for shortcuts?"

"But you already have their level of power, Solène. And if you do, I'm sure others do as well. I'm seeking a way to help you. The sooner we learn to tame this great power of yours, the sooner you and others like you will be safe to explore your potential to its fullest."

She had to admit he had great skill in identifying what someone wanted to hear and saying it in a way the person might actually believe.

He leaned back and grimaced at the uncomfortable ride. "I wish we could have taken my personal carriage," he said. "But all things considered, I thought an unmarked one was a better choice.

"I think the temple is the key to everything. The archive has too many holes to be fully relied upon. The Cup and the temple are connected, and it is there that we will learn what the vessel is fully capable of."

Solène forced a smile and nodded. She had no difficulty giving the Prince Bishop the means to defend the realm from dragons. Handing him unlimited power was an entirely different problem.

"I'm going to sleep awhile if I can," he said. "I haven't had much opportunity for it over the past few days. Wake me when we arrive."

He shut his eyes and was snoring gently a few moments later. Solène watched him, wondering if he was really asleep or using a ruse to put her off guard. She wondered if a man with as many schemes as he ever truly slept.

It was the middle of the night when they arrived at the camp, though Solène suspected dawn could not be very far away. Everything about the place said military, from the orderly grid layout to the presence of a large command tent at the centre. Lit with campfires and flickering torches at regular intervals, it was exactly what she imagined an army camp to look like, though she assumed this was much smaller than one of those. Something about it made her feel ill at ease when she thought of the Order and its aims, and there was no longer the comforting knowledge that dal Drezony was working behind the scenes.

The Prince Bishop woke as soon as the carriage lurched to a halt, adding support to her suspicion that he had not been asleep at all. When he and Solène got out, they were greeted by Vachon, who looked as though he had only just hauled himself out of his camp bed.

"Your Grace," he said. "Good news, I hope?"

"Indeed," the Prince Bishop said. "Sister Solène here will administer a magical rite that will aid you in your fight against the dragons."

"About that," Vachon said. "Word passed through the local village that one of the dragons has already been killed."

This was a surprise to Solène, but if the Prince Bishop wasn't expecting the news, then he certainly didn't show it.

"Was there anything else?"

Vachon shook his head. "No. Only that every unemployed banneret and his dog has turned up at the closest village, Venne, looking to kill a dragon. Sounds like one of them managed to pull it off."

"All the more reason to move quickly, then," the Prince Bishop said.

"We'll be ready to ride hard once you've done what you have to do. I'll take a flying column with me and leave some people to break camp and follow us. The village is less than a day from here. With a bit of effort and some help from your sorcerers, we can be there in time for supper."

"Very good. Have your people ready themselves. This won't take long."

Vachon barked out commands, and a dozen men and women in the Order's cream robes grudgingly emerged from their tents and assembled in front of them. The Prince Bishop presented the box to Solène, who opened it. Inside, the Cup sat nestled in wine-coloured velvet like a religious artefact. Trying to give the impression that she had never seen the thing before, she took the Cup from the box, showing as much reverence as she could. The Prince Bishop smiled genially, with the arrogance of one who thinks he has the solution to everyone's problems.

"We'll need water," she said. "Not much. Just a drop for everyone here."

Vachon issued another command in his usual abrasive tone, and a full water skin was presented. Solène filled the Cup halfway, then took the slender dagger from her belt and dipped the tip into the water.

"Who's first?" she said.

She expected Vachon to volunteer, but he hesitated. Even one so blustery as him feared magic, it seemed. Eventually his will overcame his misgivings and he stepped forward. "It's safe?" he said.

"Perfectly," the Prince Bishop said.

"Open wide," she said, enjoying the experience of being able to command Vachon to do something he was clearly afraid of. Her mind flashed back to the impassive way he had watched the man being flogged at the Priory; she wondered if there was any way she could add a dose of vomiting and diarrhoea to the Cup's gifts, but reckoned this wasn't the time to start improvising. She lifted the dagger from the water and began reciting the charm in old Imperial—she wanted to make it as difficult as she could for anyone to replace her—as she waited for a droplet to form at the tip of the blade. She lifted the dagger, allowing the drop to fall from a height into Vachon's mouth, trying to give the Prince Bishop and everyone else a bit of a show.

Vachon winced as the cold liquid hit his tongue, then smacked his lips and looked at Solène. "Is that it?"

She ignored him and finished the recitation, only then looking him in the eye. "Yes. Next."

"I don't feel any different."

"You won't until it matters. Next."

She repeated the process for all the members of the Order. The Prince Bishop watched in silence. When she finished and stepped back from the row of people, he asked, "You're certain that's all that's required?"

"As certain as I can be."

"How long will it last?"

"I don't know for sure," she said.

"You heard her, Commander. We don't know how long the effects will last, so you best get it done quickly."

"Can't we bring her and the Cup with us?"

"Not possible," the Prince Bishop said smoothly, "though I wish it were."

Vachon furrowed his brow in thought. "I need some idea of the duration."

Solène furrowed her brow also, trying to recall how long after the ceremony Gill had killed the first dragon. She had a rough sense of the rate at which her own magic decayed. In theory, the Cup's power should be stronger than hers, and the old Chevaliers were not allowed to take the vessel with them, so it stood to reason the effect would last long enough to get the job done. She took a guess. "After two days, you should expect the effects to have dissipated below a worthwhile level. The magic might last longer, but it would be a serious risk to try to find out."

"That'll be long enough," Vachon said, as firmly as though he had hunted enough dragons to know exactly how long it would take.

"Prepare your people for the march, Commander Vachon," the Prince Bishop said, and added, "A word in private with you before you go."

▲▲▲▲▲▲

"There's a man I believe to be at large in the region you'll be travelling to, Commander," Amaury said once he and Vachon were a distance from Solène.

"At large?" the Order's new commander asked.

"He's a fugitive from the king's justice. He did some work for the Crown in the recent past, but has been actively obstructing us at every opportunity since."

"Want me to kill him?"

"I'd prefer not. I'd like him arrested and brought to me in Mirabay. He's a tricky character, but if the Cup has given you the abilities to deal with dragons, then I expect you and your people will be able to deal with him too, so long as you exercise due caution and skill."

Vachon nodded. "Who is it?"

"Guillot dal Villerauvais."

Vachon laughed broadly, then stopped when he saw that Amaury was serious. "Villerauvais? Didn't he kill the first dragon? People talk about him like the sun shines out of his arse. Seem to remember them saying something similar a few years back."

"Do you know him?"

"Met him once, years back. We were both in the Royal Army then, fighting in the north."

"Well, he slew the dragon with the help of your comrades-in-arms, who were sadly killed in the process. Since then—"

"I don't need a reason or an explanation, your Grace," Vachon said. "In fact, I prefer not to have them. Just give the order, and I'll carry it out. Life's simpler that way."

Amaury smiled. This was exactly the type of man he liked working with.

"He was last seen in Venne. Chasing these new dragons, I expect."

Vachon nodded. "What am I arresting him for?"

"Murder. Treason. Does it matter?"

Vachon smirked. "What if I can't take him alive?"

"Kill him if you have to, but only if you have to. I don't care if you have to knock him about a bit first. In fact, I'm happy for you to put some manners on him. It'll be a taste of what's to come."

Vachon sighed. "Sad to see one of the greats fall like that. Some people just can't seem to stay ahead, can they."

Amaury raised an eyebrow. "I didn't take you for the sympathetic type, Commander."

"Not sympathy," Vachon said. "Just a little theory of mine about fame, and those who're hungry for it. Nothing good ever comes from it. Mark my words."

Amaury smiled. "Indeed. That brings me to the other thing. I need to borrow one of your people. Someone handy with a blade who can work as a bodyguard."

Vachon thought for a moment. "I have someone well suited to such work."

"Marvellous," Amaury said. "I wish you well and look forward to hearing of your success."

He left Vachon, returning to Solène, who was waiting for him at the carriage.

"Do you have everything you need to start searching for these nodes you spoke of?"

Solène nodded. "I think so."

"Good. Vachon has delegated one of his men to accompany you." He took a purse from his belt. "This should cover whatever expenses you might incur. I think it best if you start your search now, rather than return to the city with me. Things might get difficult there in coming days, so it's best if you are away and working, rather than cooped up at the Priory."

CHAPTER

40

"Banneret Olivier, at your service."

Solène looked him over. He was every bit the type of man who had come into the Order in the past few weeks—a military figure rather than one of the more eclectic types that had previously filled the ranks.

"You'll do what I say, when I say it," she said. "We'll go where I say. Understand?"

"Those were my orders, Sister. I intend to follow them."

"Good," Solène said, somewhat surprised at his attitude.

"Might I ask where we're going?"

Solène shrugged. "I'm not entirely sure yet. I know the direction and have an idea of what I'm looking for, but I'm not sure how far we'll need to go and I'm not sure if we'll ever find it." She was lying, but felt no need to be honest.

"We certainly won't find whatever it is by just standing here."

"Very true," Solène said. "Are you ready to leave?"

"I'll get my horse."

Solène watched him go and wondered where his loyalties lay, then wondered why she was even asking the question. She lived in a nest of vipers now, and assuming everyone was about to bite her would rarely see her wrong.

Being far from others would be the perfect opportunity to experiment with more powerful magic. So long as she didn't overdo it and endanger herself, there would be no one else to harm. Other than Olivier, of course. She had to get rid of him. The question was, how?

A horse had been brought for her; she considered jumping onto it and galloping for the horizon, but couldn't see that working out well. There were too many people around who were sure to stop her. She'd just given them a range of protections that she couldn't claim to fully understand. It was possible that she had given them defences against all forms of magic, not just the dragon variety.

Olivier returned, a chivalrous smile on his face. "I'm ready, Sister," he said.

"Perfect." Without another word she mounted and urged her horse into a canter. They rode south, because that was the direction the animal was already facing. The nodes were said to be in remote places, so why not start with the mountain regions? When she reached the foothills, she would skirt along them until she detected something, or until it became clear they were wasting their time.

"A fine day, don't you think?" Olivier said, after they had ridden a short distance, and the sun had broken the horizon. "I always love this time of ye—"

"I need to concentrate," Solène said. Days of magically provided rest rather than proper sleep had her feeling strained and irritable. "Spells, and whatnot. Wouldn't want them going wrong."

He blanched at the mention of magic, then shut his mouth and kept it shut, much to Solène's satisfaction. She wasn't being entirely churlish and untruthful, either—she needed to work out how she was going to find the temple and what she was going to do when she did. She was growing ever more uncomfortable with the extent of the Prince Bishop's ambition. This was her chance to get to the temple first and make sure the Prince Bishop never got his hands on the knowledge it might contain.

It occurred to her, as they rode, that perhaps the old Imperial mages hadn't really needed any of what the temple offered. They already had all the power anyone could have wanted. Perhaps the temple was nothing more than a historical curiosity to them and they hadn't been all that committed to finding it.

For her and others at this time, circumstances were rather different. If the temple held the key to instant power or to unlocking more from the Cup, as the Prince Bishop seemed to suspect, she definitely wanted to get there first. For some time now she had lived with the fact that she could easily kill not only a great many other people, but also herself. That had taught her both fear and respect. The Prince Bishop had learned neither of those lessons, and she suspected he didn't have any difficulty with the idea of blowing up a number of unfortunate bystanders as he played with his new power.

The alternate scenario, in which he learned how to control that power and bend it to his will, was even more terrifying. If she got there first, she could ensure that neither eventuality came to pass.

She was all for people learning to use magic again, and felt the Order was as good a vehicle for that as any, provided the magics were used in an altruistic way. However, she felt magic should be learned slowly, with lots of trial and error at low levels of power that wouldn't lead to catastrophic results.

Amatus had had the enlightened to guide his way. He was able to pass his learning on to others. Despite what Solène assumed were good intentions at the start, eventually power had completely corrupted the Imperial mages. Magic had ended up limited to an elite body of people, to the exclusion of all others. It was easy to see how that had led to the horrors of sorcery that were still whispered about to this day. Might the Order be able to avoid that same fate? It was a question she couldn't answer. Regardless, magic was in the world, and past mistakes couldn't change that, nor stop its return.

She turned her attention back to her task, revelling in how much clearer her senses felt now that she had greater mastery of her mind. She recalled how Leverre had described the Cup to her, and how it had felt the first time she had sensed it, like a knot of threads in a sheet of cloth. By all accounts, the nodes were possessed of energy on an entirely different scale. If they still existed, surely they would be easy to find. She took advantage of Olivier's silence, and let her mind drift out, not actively seeking the Fount, but accepting that it was there, like the ground beneath her feet. She could feel it with her mind's eye, sensing its ripples and creases, the places where it pooled like drifting snow in winter and the barren patches that the wind stripped bare.

In moments like that, she could empathise with the Prince Bishop's desire to know it all, and know it now. The uncertainty of not knowing was the most frustrating thing she had ever encountered. To think that answers to all her questions might exist, might be waiting to be found, was tantalising.

She felt nothing out of the ordinary, but in reality, she didn't know what she was looking for. She glanced over at Olivier, who smiled earnestly, but maintained an obedient silence. She wondered if he had figured out that she had no idea where they were going.

"How long have you been in the Order?" she said.

"Only a few days," Olivier said. "A number of us were recruited out of the Academy. It's an exciting proposition that was hard to say no to."

She could agree with that, at least. "What attracted you?"

"It seems like the place to be. The new Chevaliers of the Silver Circle. With a man like the Prince Bishop backing it, the invitation to join seemed like the opportunity of a lifetime."

"The magic doesn't bother you?"

"It did a little, at first. But I heard they've already been using it over in Ostia. We can bury our heads and ignore it, or we can get on with it, no matter how distasteful we find it. I don't fancy the idea of being ruled by an emperor in Ostenheim. Do you?"

Solène shook her head.

He seemed earnest enough. She didn't know how much the Prince Bishop trusted her, but she had no reason to suspect Olivier wasn't there purely to keep an eye on her. The Academy created hard men to do the dangerous jobs the king needed done—she had seen that at first hand with Nicholas dal Sason. Olivier might wear a veneer of chivalry, but that didn't mean he was naive or full of youthful enthusiasm. If he was, all the better for her, but she would keep an eye on him and ditch him at the first opportunity.

▲▲▲▲▲▲

They travelled along a major road for much of the morning; to Solène's surprise, there was no traffic on it for as far as the eye could see, and she and Olivier hadn't passed anyone since leaving the Order's camp, either. Solène assumed that word of the new dragons had spread and that people were finally seeking safety indoors. It made her wonder what had become of Gill—if he had finally run out of luck, either at the claws of a dragon or at the hands of whoever the Prince Bishop had sent to take the Cup from him. It seemed unlikely he had survived if the Prince Bishop had the Cup. Good men and women didn't seem to last long these days. Leverre, dal Drezony, and now, it seemed, Gill also.

She allowed her mind to drift, hoping she would detect something unusual in the pattern of the Fount that would lead her to what they sought. She tried to imagine where the Fount would gather out in the countryside. Her only experience of it was in towns and cities; their dense concentration of people and animals generated an enormous amount of energy. In the past, when there were far fewer people, that wouldn't have been the case. Accumulations that occurred at that time had to be entirely natural. What might have caused them?

Solène began to concentrate on identifying anything unusual. It felt like casting a fishing line out into a great, never-ending lake, without knowing if there were actually any fish in it. She found it difficult to maintain the focus needed to hold on to that single thought as she tried to keep control of her horse and remain in the saddle. The beginning of a plan to rid herself of Banneret Olivier was also lurking in the back of her mind and intruding on her thoughts.

When her brain felt as though it was straining against the confines of her skull and needed a rest, she got the first sense of something odd. There was only one way to investigate the sensation, and she didn't want the Prince Bishop's spy there when she did. It was time for her and Banneret Olivier to part ways.

"I'm starving," she said. "Why don't we set down by that stand of trees and have something to eat?"

"Sounds good to me. Any luck on working out where we're headed?"

"Perhaps," she said. "I'm getting a bit of a sense for it. Some food and rest will help with that."

At the copse of trees, they dismounted. "No point unsaddling," she said. "We won't stay long. Why don't you make a fire? I could do with some hot coffee. I'll take care of the horses and get the provisions."

Olivier nodded, and set about gathering wood. She led the horses to a tree and tethered them on a long rein so they could get at the grass. When Olivier had his back to her, Solène undid the buckles on his saddle. He had a small fire going by the time she returned with bread, cheese, some cold meat, and the all-important coffee paraphernalia.

They set about making filled rolls, then started to eat. After a few bites, Solène began to focus on what she wanted to achieve, doing her best to exclude all other thoughts.

"You're not eating," Olivier said a moment later.

"Small appetite," she said, doing her best not to be distracted. In another moment, his face twisted in discomfort and he placed a hand on his stomach.

"I think that meat may have been off," he said, grimacing. "Better you don't eat any more."

Solène released her focus. "It certainly didn't taste quite right."

"Beginning to regret not having a small appetite myself," Olivier said in a strained voice.

His stomach gurgled loudly enough for Solène to hear it.

"Pardon me," he said.

She couldn't tell if his cheeks were flushed from embarrassment or from the chaos that was beginning to unfold in his guts.

"If you wouldn't mind excusing me a moment?" Olivier asked urgently.

"Of course not," she said.

He stood and hurried into the trees in a fashion that could only be called comical. Solène did her best not to laugh, knowing it was she who was responsible, not the food. Considering the colour of the Order's robes, she wondered if perhaps a bash on the head would have been kinder, but the die was cast now. Hopefully he would be fine in an hour or two; not having used that magic before, she couldn't be sure how long the discomfort would last, but she figured she hadn't invested enough energy in it to discommode him for more than the remainder of the evening. More than long enough for her to have put a decent distance between them.

Solène gathered up her provisions, pulled Olivier's saddle to the ground, untethered his horse and gave it enough of a slap on the rump to send it cantering off, then mounted her own, and galloped away in the intentionally wrong direction.

▲▲▲▲▲▲

Solène rode hard until darkness made it dangerous to continue. She had turned onto her proper course after a couple of hours, but the sensation she was tracking remained vague and indistinct. She was no longer confident it was guiding her to what she sought, or even guiding her anywhere at all. It was time to stop and rest; she chose a camping spot far from the road.

She had seen no sign of Olivier following her, not that she expected it. He would be pretty exhausted after his stomach trouble and it would take time before he was ready to jump in the saddle again. Even so, she didn't feel she could risk lighting a fire. She settled in for what she knew would be a cold night under a cloudless sky.

Exhausted, she lay back and felt her mind start to drift into the half place between being awake and asleep. Random thoughts flitted about, covered in the Fount's blue glow. She was too tired to force sense or order upon the jumble. Just as she made the final slide into sleep, the swirling objects, ideas, and scenes coalesced into a solid stream flowing clearly in the direction of the vague sensation, and ending in a tight ball of intense blue light that pulsed like a beating heart. Waves of energy washed over her. Her final thought before sleep took her was that she knew the location of a node.

CHAPTER
41

When Amaury arrived at the palace, he saw even more protestors gathered than there had been when he left the city, and their mood was anything but improved. They pelted Amaury's unmarked carriage with rotting castoffs from the local market. Adding to the Prince Bishop's displeasure was the fact that he had been summoned by the king—a message had been waiting for him when he returned to his house from the Order's former campsite. He was tired and cranky, and dealing with the king was the last thing he wanted to do, but he had no choice.

Before heeding his master's call, Amaury had sent word to Luther, asking to find him some mercenaries who could be suborned into the Order, at least on a temporary basis. Amaury was no longer willing to rely on royal troops—he needed his own people at the Priory.

He swept through the corridors of the palace to his office, ostensibly to collect some documents before attending on the king but actually to gather his thoughts. He realised he was nervous. He tried to excuse it as a symptom of fatigue, but the truth was that he had been stretched perilously thin since the first dragon had appeared. He knew he couldn't continue like that for much longer. *The Cup might help,* he thought.

Until news of Vachon's victory over the dragons arrived, he had no arguments to make in the Order's favour. He would just have to improvise. The sooner Solène found the temple—and the answers he sought—the better.

All the usual suspects were gathered in the king's private audience chamber, as Amaury had suspected they would be. Not one of them would miss the opportunity to take advantage of Amaury's difficulties.

"Highness," Amaury said with a curt bow when he entered.

"You've seen the crowds gathered outside the palace gates?" the king said.

So much for small talk, Amaury thought.

"I have, Highness. A little larger than I had expected, but this isn't really anything to be surprised about. As we speak, the Order is on its way to kill the dragons sighted near the seigneury of Venne."

"The moment has passed for a success to pull this back from the brink," Boudain said. "There have been flare-ups of violence throughout the city, directed not just against members of the Order, but also against the City Watch, royal officials, and other citizens." The king looked directly at Amaury. "There's an easy way to stop it all."

"Which is?" the Prince Bishop said, already knowing the answer.

"We disband the Order."

"Highness, I don't think that's a good idea."

"You mistake me, Prince Bishop. I'm not asking for your counsel. I'm giving you a command. The Order is to be disbanded immediately. I've had the relevant decrees drawn up, signed, and sealed." He slid some pages across the table.

Amaury blanched. "I . . . That's just not possible, Highness. Things have developed too far. You can't just shut it down now."

"I can, and I have," the king said.

Amaury scanned the faces of the others in the room, every one of them puffed up with self-importance and self-righteousness. He knew exactly what was going to happen. The Order would be destroyed and he'd be made a scapegoat. They'd throw him to the flames, and walk away blameless. He felt his temper flare.

"You can't," he said, more hotly than he intended. "You knew what you were getting into, and agreed to it. Wholeheartedly."

"I admit I agreed to your plans, but that was in the early days of my rule, when I was naive and overly reliant on my counsellors. I can't be blamed for failing to see bad advice at that point in my reign. I can only be blamed if I continue to act on it."

The king's words all but confirmed Amaury's fears. He had to be clever now, make it appear as though he remained a diligent, loyal servant of the Crown even as he moved to protect himself. Forcing a smile, he took the papers from the king's desk and placed them carefully into his purple leather folder.

"It is my privilege to serve, Highness. I will see to it your decrees are carried out."

"Excellent. There may be a time for your Order, Amaury, but that is clearly not now. I need the people's support more than I need sorcerers to help fight my wars. You can't defend a throne if you no longer sit on it."

"A wise outlook, Highness."

"If you feel the Order's members are likely to cause problems, I can have the City Watch ready to move and arrest them," Commander Canet said.

He was always one to try and stick his beak in for attention. Amaury didn't do him the dignity of addressing him directly.

"I don't think that will be necessary, Highness. As the matter is pressing, if I might be dismissed?"

The king waved his hand. Amaury refused to meet the gazes of his rivals as he left.

In the hall, with the door to the king's office closed firmly behind him, he took a moment to settle his thoughts. That he hadn't been arrested yet was a positive. It gave him time and freedom to do what he needed to do. The king probably thought it best to allow him to start the process of shutting down the Order, lulling him into a false sense of security before throwing him to the wolves. Amaury had already orchestrated the death of one king. Doing so again, particularly in an unsettled time like this, would be no trouble at all.

Hurrying to his office, he prepared several letters. Once he'd given them to his secretary to hand-deliver, he would retire to the Priory, where he could hole up until what needed to be done was done. The first message was to Luther—he needed those mercenaries, and more, as quickly as possible. They should be sent straight to the Priory, where they could be inducted and armed.

For the second letter he used a special ink that would be revealed only if heated carefully. He kept a supply of everyday missives written in ordinary ink—letters detailing the mundane, day-to-day matters of state. Selecting one, he wrote his message in invisible ink between the existing lines. There was likely some magical approach that would work better, but there hadn't been the time or resources to devote to such specific matters.

His hand shook—he was more nervous than he liked to admit, even to himself. In times of crisis, he had always been able to lurk in the shadows and take advantage of the fact that eyes were always directed elsewhere. Now, he was in danger of being dragged into the spotlight. He had no idea how to operate under such circumstances, and that frightened him.

There was no direct heir to place on the throne for a tidy replacement as there had been with the previous king. Boudain had half a dozen cousins with more or less equal claims, and that would mean civil war. He could choose the winner by putting the backing of the Order behind them. Once the people knew the Order had saved them from dragons, their opinions would change quickly. He and the Order could easily deliver the throne to the strongest contender—but what sense was there in starting over with an unknown royal? Was not he, himself, the best candidate?

He had previously dismissed the idea, but he had been down this road once already, and removing a king was too stressful an act to be repeated every few years. He already wielded much of the authority of state; he had his own private military force that was paid for out of the king's coffers. All he needed to do was remove the other advisors, which would be easy enough. The quick promotion of some senior nobles would make them happy without causing him to cede any real power. Several nobles were already in his pocket; he could count on their support if he pulled the coup off successfully.

He stopped and set down his pen. A coup. How had he come to such a momentous decision so quickly, and without thinking it over? He was panicking, and that was not good. Amaury stood and went to the window. The garden below was empty, and he allowed his gaze to drift as he considered what he was planning to do.

His people in the palace would be able to give access to his men and keep the king's guard at bay. He would need a visible presence on the street also. The fact that the people feared the Order would play in his favour for the time being. Or perhaps it was time to have the healers still at the Priory set up clinics—show the people what a help they could be.

The stick or the carrot? Which should he choose? He kneaded his temples with his knuckles and wanted to scream.

It had been a long time since he had contemplated thoughts that would get him beheaded. He had gotten away with it the last time, against a more experienced and stronger king. Why not again? Of course, the last time, he had not been planning on taking the throne for himself, merely replacing its occupant with someone he had thought would be easier to deal with.

This was a far different proposition, and he needed to consider the consequences in more detail. Not only did he have to get rid of Boudain the Tenth, he would have to seize and hold power for himself. That was a far more difficult thing to do. That would make him the target. He didn't like that idea.

What alternative did he have? The king was going to paint him as the villain who was dragging magic back to the fore. He could imagine the proclamation, portraying the young king as appalled by the practices of a powerful and established minister who had been deposed once his treachery became known.

Still, a coup?

This solution did not sit well with him. It was the act of a panicked man. Something similar had happened in Ostia, across the Middle Sea, only a decade or so before, and that man, Amero dal Moreno, was still known as the Usurper of Ostia, though he had been dead for many years. That was what Amaury would come to be known as. Usurper. Tyrant. Despot. Regicidal Megalomaniac. That was not how he wanted to be known. After all, he had the best interests of the kingdom at heart.

The King of Estranza was finally getting control of his realm, and the Humberlanders had just won a war against their northern neighbours, the Ventish. It was only a matter of time before their attention turned to Mirabay, or her trading posts on the Spice Isles.

A tyrant having recently seized the throne was more than enough reason for any self-respecting monarch to invade their neighbour. *No, Amaury thought, I can't take power for myself.* As the thought took hold, he realised that not only could he not safely take it, he didn't want it. He had everything he wanted where he was, and would soon have even more if the king's attempt to assert his authority didn't get in the way.

Who, then, could he place on the throne? *Things would be a lot easier if Boudain had managed to squire an heir,* Amaury thought. An infant or child on the throne was the ideal puppet through whom he could rule. Given the absence of an heir, Amaury had been named regent when Boudain took the throne, in case the king became incapacitated. None of the cousins presented themselves as particularly attractive, and they all shared the same burden: he would have to get one safely onto the throne and deal with the civil war the rest of them were certain to stir up. Civil war would leave them equally open to invasion.

When a solution finally occurred to him, a broad smile spread across his face.

He didn't need to overthrow the king. He also didn't need to find the leverage to make sure he was able to influence the king. What he needed to do was to make the king more malleable. A way to turn everything on him that he was planning to dump on Amaury. He could use the Cup to pacify the young king's mind, but what then? That only saved the Order from being disbanded. The Prince Bishop was inextricably linked to the Order, so there was no way he could pass the blame for it on to someone else. But then again, he would not need to. As soon as word got back to the city that they had killed the new dragons, that they were ready and willing to continue keeping the people safe from future attacks, they would be embraced. Then he would be able to guide the king in the way that made the most sense for the kingdom, while the Order would be able to continue developing its potential thanks to the Cup and the temple, once Solène found it.

He crumpled up the letters and held them over a candle flame until they took light. A coup was not the way forward. He threw the burning papers into the bronze bucket he used for this purpose, and watched until there was nothing left but ashes. That done, he turned his gaze to the Cup, sitting on his desk. Was there a way to use it that would give him the control over the king that he needed? It had given the Order the ability to fight dragons. It had allowed him to create a powerful light far beyond anything he had been capable of before. It seemed reasonable to presume there was a way to use it to bring the king around to his way of thinking.

He supposed there was only one way to find out.

CHAPTER

42

Gill lifted a fresh beam into place over the doorway into the bakery. It was hard work, and even in the cool autumn evening air, he was sweating. There was still much clearing and heavy lifting to be done in the village, the only labour to which Gill was suited. The masons and carpenters were already working on reconstruction, with some of the burned-out buildings starting to take new shape.

Despite the fact that his arms ached worse than after his first day at the Academy, Guillot felt good about himself for the first time he could remember. He had helped people before, but that had always meant killing or destroying something. This was the first time he was helping to build something that would be of use. He might only be carting away waste and hauling lumber, but the work was deeply satisfying, and it made him wonder why soldiers were lauded while builders largely went unnoticed.

As buoyant as the day's labour had made him feel, it also dragged him down. This was how things should have been in Villerauvais. How he should have been in Villerauvais. The realisation that it wouldn't have made any difference was equally saddening. At least the years leading up to that event would have been better. The church bell rang, signalling that the day was done and supper was ready.

With so many homes destroyed, meals were prepared and consumed communally. Rough tables were set up in the square, and the villagers ate and relaxed together after the day's efforts. They laughed, joked, and teased each other with the same camaraderie Gill had experienced at the Academy and in his old regiment. Their shared day of work for a common cause had created a bond between them the like of which few other things could. The contentment Gill felt made him anxious. He had taken happiness for granted before, and it had been taken from him.

Despite all that had happened to them, the people of Venne were putting a brave face on things; they were rebuilding. Tragedy or mistakes didn't mean your life was over. You picked yourself up, you rebuilt, you moved on.

A number of horsemen clattered into the square, breaking the contented hum of conversation and laughter. At first Gill thought the newcomers were one of the groups of bannerets returning after an unsuccessful dragon hunt, but a quick glance told him this was not the case. The riders were all wearing the Order's cream robes. Gill strained to see if Solène was with them, but didn't recognise anyone.

Edine stood from her seat at the top of the head table.

"Welcome to Venne," she said. "Is there something we can help you with?"

"We're here on behalf of the king to slay the dragons in this region," the lead rider replied.

He had a worn face with a twisted nose that had seen plenty of bad weather out-of-doors, and hair cropped so tightly it was impossible to tell what colour it was. Something about him seemed familiar, but Gill couldn't quite place him.

"We're grateful for your journey, but the problem's been dealt with. The dragons are dead."

The man nodded. "You're the head of this village?"

"I am," she said.

"Perhaps we could speak in private?"

She shrugged, then gestured to the mayor's house. "This way."

The man dismounted, casting a glance over the gathered crowd as he did. Gill couldn't be certain, but it seemed as though his eyes stopped on him for a moment. He followed Edine into the mayor's house and shut the door behind them.

"Bit late," someone said.

"King's always late," someone responded. "Unless it's for a party."

There was some laughter, and then everyone got back to their dinner. Gill wanted to do the same, but couldn't help feeling concerned.

These were the Prince Bishop's people, and in his experience, their appearance was rarely a good thing.

He had barely swallowed his first mouthful of food when Edine appeared in the doorway and called to him.

"Gill, would you mind joining us a moment?"

He nodded and got to his feet. Once he was inside the house, Edine turned to face him.

"Commander Vachon here says the dragons aren't all dead."

Gill looked at Vachon.

"How would he know?"

"We can tell when there are dragons near," Vachon said. "And I can tell there's one near."

Guillot looked at him carefully, trying to gauge whether he was telling the truth or not. If Vachon could detect the dragons, then he had undergone the ritual with the Cup. That meant that the Prince Bishop had the Cup, that he was the one responsible for the theft and for Barnot's murder. Gill cursed himself for not thinking of it sooner. Every time something in his life went wrong, Amaury was connected in some way.

"I said the dragon won't bother you again," Gill said, trying to explain the situation without revealing anything important. "And that's the truth."

"You mean you didn't kill the last one?" Edine said.

He hesitated for a moment, then shook his head. "I didn't need to. It fled into the mountains."

"What's to stop it coming back?"

"It won't. You have my word on that."

"We're supposed to believe that?" Vachon said. "It's a good thing the king isn't as cavalier when it comes to the safety of his subjects."

"I've killed three and chased a fourth off," Gill said. "Where were you while that was happening?"

"We were dispatched as soon as we were ready to properly deal with the threat," Vachon said.

As soon as the Prince Bishop got his hands on the Cup, Gill thought.

"There will be no more trouble with dragons here, or anywhere else," Gill said. "You can take my word for that or not. I really don't care. I've done more to protect this region than the king, the Prince Bishop, and all their men. You can come here and question my honour all you like. What I've done here will speak for itself."

The door opened and two more Spurriers walked in. Vachon gave them a nod, then turned back to Gill.

"I want more than to question your honour," Vachon said. "In the name of Boudain the Tenth, I arrest you for murder and high treason."

Gill did a double take. "Pardon me?"

"You heard," Vachon said. "Take him."

The other two Spurriers moved to seize Gill. His hand automatically dropped to his waist to draw his sword, but he wasn't wearing one—no need for a sword to cart timber. His sword was leaning against the end of the bed in his room at the inn. Each man grabbed him by one arm, leaving him little option but to go with them. Trying to get away now would earn him nothing but a beating. He'd have to bide his time and hope an opportunity presented itself.

"You needn't worry, ma'am," Vachon said, as Gill was bundled toward the door. "We'll take care of the dragon for you. And this rotten cur."

The last thing Gill saw as he was shoved out of the building was the disappointment in Edine's eyes.

***

"Where are we headed?" Gill asked. He was mounted on his own horse, with his hands bound and tied to the saddle's pommel. They had gathered his things from the inn, and loaded them onto the horse in front of Gill. He stared longingly at the hilt of one of his swords, sticking out tantalisingly, but so out of reach it might as well have been a world away.

"Shut your mouth," Vachon said.

"I've a bit of experience in this line of work. I might be able to help."

"If you don't shut your mouth, I'll shut it for you."

"Don't know where you're going, then?" Gill said, forcing a condescending chuckle.

Vachon backhanded him in the face. It was a respectable blow; Gill ran his tongue around the inside of his mouth to make sure all of his teeth were still where they were supposed to be.

"Don't blame yourself," Gill said. "Dragon hunting is a tricky business. I wouldn't worry too much, though. Getting killed by one is pretty easy, so you won't have to go home a failure."

Vachon hit Gill again.

"Bring him down the back," Vachon said to one of his men. "Keep a careful eye on him."

Gill feigned hurt. "Was it something I said? We were getting along so well."

The man came alongside Gill and took hold of his horse's reins, then took him to the back of the group.

"Your boss doesn't have a clue where we're going, you know," Gill said.

"Yes, he does. We all know. We can sense the creature."

Gill looked over his shoulder at the mountains, which were dropping away slowly into the distance. He reckoned they were heading east, which on the face of it didn't make much sense. If Pharadon was heading deeper into the mountains, then they should be chasing him west, or south. He wondered if Vachon had used the Cup correctly.

CHAPTER
43

Ysabeau had to admire the young woman's resolve not to light a fire. It was a cold night, and was only going to get colder before dawn broke. Ysabeau had been on Solène's trail for much of the afternoon and evening, riding hard and drawing on the Fount to keep her horse fresh, in the hope of catching up before Solène found anything.

Without a fire, Ysabeau had almost missed Solène's campsite in the dark. It was only by chance that Ysabeau had been drawing on the Fount while she was passing by, giving both her horse and herself a little freshen-up. Solène's magical energy gave her away, lighting her up as clearly as if it had been daylight. Wrapped in a warm blanket, Ysabeau was settling in for the night, having found a good vantage point from which to watch her quarry. The woman didn't seem like anything special, but if her father was to be believed, she was the most powerful mage alive, albeit not yet fully able to tap into her powers. The Prince Bishop had once hoped Ysabeau would be that powerful, that useful to his plans. Sadly, her abilities were modest at best; she just had a little more flair than most at using them. She hated this woman, Solène, though they had never met. She threatened to give the Prince Bishop—Ysabeau's father—what his daughter never could.

There was supposed to be a member of the Order with the woman, but there was no sign of him. Whatever Solène had done to him meant that he hadn't given chase, which made Ysabeau curious. Had this one developed a taste for killing? Ysabeau knew she needed to be careful, whether her guess was right or not.

She did her best to make herself comfortable, hidden by a tree, but in a position that gave her a clear view of where Solène had made camp. As she created some magical heat to keep warm, she wondered if Solène had done the same. It was tricky magic to create heat without also generating light. If everything Ysabeau had been told about the all-powerful Solène was true, she certainly had the potential, but Ysabeau had always thought that the people with the most potential were the least attracted to hard work.

A lifetime of shaping strong magic with mediocre power allowed Ysabeau to do far more than many who had a greater affinity to the Fount and far more raw material to play with. This had always frustrated her, and was why her tenure at the Order had been so short. Dal Drezony had pushed her out and the Prince Bishop had done little to stop her. It seemed he had more interest in the skills his daughter had picked up living on the streets of Mirabay, rather than her potential as a mage. Over time, she had made her peace with that, but where she came from, you didn't let a score go unsettled, and that's what the blade in dal Drezony's heart had done.

Still, Ysabeau's satisfaction at having killed the seneschal was tempered by a less enjoyable feeling. Guilt? Doubt? Whatever it was, she put it from her mind.

It was curious to think that both she and her quarry had nearly suffered the same fate. Pulled from the flames by different saviours, both had ended up, for a time at least, as protégées of the Prince Bishop.

She reckoned everyone was born with a certain amount of luck. You could only rely on it for so long before it ran out. Her magic had carried her a little farther than most, but she was under no illusion that one day, in the not so distant future, she would take the job that ended her. Completing this one meant she wouldn't need to take another.

▲▲▲▲▲▲

Solène woke with a start. She was stiff as a board from the cold, but otherwise refreshed and feeling positive. Just as she had before falling asleep, she reached out for the Fount, and there it was, like the ripples on a pond after a stone had been thrown in. She could see her way to the centre of the disturbance as though it was signposted. She packed her things as quickly as she could, then mounted her horse, grimacing in discomfort. She had never done much riding, and it was telling on her now. She urged the animal on, wincing as the movement made itself known to her tender backside and thighs.

Her excitement at the prospect of finding what she was looking for made the discomfort somewhat easier to bear. She had to remind herself that she might not have found the temple, but if what she sensed was a node, and her theory that the temple would have been built on one was correct, then it was a possibility. Even if she came up short it meant she was now able to sense nodes, and therefore would be able to find others.

Her excitement at this prospect drowned out the quandary of what to do when she did. The waves grew stronger as the day progressed and she kept guiding her horse into their centre, knowing that was the way to the node. At times she felt dizzy, and had to hang on to the saddle's pommel to keep herself on the horse. Even in the city she had never felt that much energy. It was terrifying and intoxicating at the same time.

Any magic she used now would be far more powerful than anything she had done before, and if the Fount continued to grow as she got closer to the node, then her potential would be virtually limitless. For the first time, she thought she understood how the Imperial mages had been able to do what they had done. If they had been able to tap into reservoirs as strong as this, the stories that she had heard of their feats were modest in the extreme.

Her excitement grew ever greater as she neared the centre of the ripple in the Fount. Her head swam in the raw energy, which felt as though it was trying to both pass through her and make her one with it. She was overcome with a terrifying sense of losing control. Part of her wanted to join with it and allow her mind to run free with virtually limitless power. Instinct told her to resist, that letting go of control would destroy her. Stopping her horse, she fought for control of her mind, to shut out the raging tempest of energy. This was what made magic so much more dangerous in the days before the mage wars drained the Fount to exhaustion. Mages would have had to be so much more careful to avoid killing someone or destroying everything around them. She could understand why it had taken Amatus and his time with the enlightened to bring people to the point where they could shape it safely.

Once her mind steadied, she continued riding, wondering why the Fount was drawn to this place—whether the nodes gave rise to the Fount or the Fount gave rise to the nodes. Considering what she knew, she decided it was likelier that the Fount was drawn to these places for some reason—one she was unlikely to ever understand.

When the intensity of the energy faded a little, and started to pulse again, Solène realised that she had passed through the node. She pulled her horse up and looked around. There was nothing out of the ordinary in the surrounding landscape, a plain grassland. A person with no affinity to the Fount could walk right through without ever knowing there was anything unusual about the place. There wasn't even a variation in the colour of the grass to mark the place.

She had entertained romantic notions of an ancient tree, or a stone plinth left behind by the enlightened, to signify the power that dwelled here. This landscape was so innocuous that she questioned whether she was imagining things—it had been a very cold night and she hadn't slept properly in some time. She shook her head. No, that was unlikely. She never got sick, something she realised now was likely one of the benefits of her natural affinity with the Fount.

She dismounted and led her horse back to the centre of the ripples. Now that she had disciplined her mind against the rush of energy, it didn't feel nearly so overwhelming. It was like the difference between standing outside in a furious storm, or being tucked up safely inside while it raged against the walls. Her disappointment grew as she wandered around the edge of the node, looking inward for any sign of something unusual. Could this really be all there was to it? Was the temple here, or did she need to look elsewhere? She wondered how many nodes there might be. Surely such an intense concentration of magical energy had to be a rare thing.

Her horse let out a whicker of surprise and surged against the reins. She struggled to bring the animal under control, speaking to it in a soothing voice and trying to calm it. Thanks to her limited experience with horses, she had no idea what the correct approach was. It occurred to her to try using magic to soothe it—she didn't want to be stuck out there with no horse—but thankfully, it settled quickly. When she looked for what had spooked it, she saw that one of its hooves had broken through the surface of the ground somehow. She walked over for a closer look.

Beneath a layer of grass and soil, Solène spotted what looked like wooden planking. It was old, blackened, and rotting, but she could see the hard edges that indicated that the wood had been worked at some point.

She got down on her knees, then started pulling away soil and grass until she'd cleared a panel of boards. Finding a gap, she tugged at one board until she was able to pull it free, snapping it in half as she did, the ages-old timber giving way. Panting from her efforts, Solène found herself staring down into a dark chamber. Just enough light got in to let her see the gloomy cut-stone edges of its walls. She had found it.

PART THREE

CHAPTER

44

Solène cast a globe of light into the centre of the room beneath her and watched in awe as illumination fell on surfaces that had been in darkness for countless years. She could barely believe she had found what she was looking for. Whilst there was probably some safe way to get down, she couldn't see it, and realised it might be buried under several hours of digging. The drop to the floor didn't look far enough to cause injury, but getting back up would be a problem. She wondered if she'd be able to magically float herself out, but since she'd never done it before, she wasn't sure she could. Simply desiring a certain result didn't guarantee it—at least not without the potential for unwanted side effects.

Aside from that, she was afraid to attempt using magic in the presence of so much energy. If she allowed it to channel through her body, it could burn her out in an instant. As it was, in normal circumstances she still struggled to draw only the amount of the Fount she needed for whatever it was she was attempting to do. With so much around her, to even consider trying something new was madness.

Her horse had thankfully remained close by. She went through the saddlebags the Order had packed for her, to see if there was anything useful. Fleetingly she wondered where Banneret Olivier might be. She hoped that his stomach troubles had settled and that the Prince Bishop didn't punish him too harshly when Olivier finally owned up to having lost her.

At last she found a length of rope in one of the bags. It looked long enough to reach the floor. The thought of the task before her made her wish she'd been more diligent in attending physical training at the Priory; she wasn't at all certain she'd be able to haul herself out. Maybe she could tie one end of the rope to the saddle and somehow encourage the horse to back away from the hole, pulling her out.

If she tried that, there would be risks: the horse might wander away, taking the rope with it; its weight might cause it to fall through the old wooden boards. It seemed like her only option, however. Hopefully there'd be something down there she could tie the line to until she was ready to use it.

She tied the line to the saddle, then backed up to the edge of the hole. The horse took a step forward as she lowered herself into the cavern. She dropped several feet before the line went taut and arrested her descent. Swinging in the darkness, clinging to the rope for dear life, she questioned the sense in her idea, before remembering that the drop to the floor wasn't the issue, it was the getting back out. She shimmied down the short distance and planted her feet firmly on the old flagstone floor. Her magical light was still burning away faithfully, showing no signs of dimming. She could still easily recall when maintaining the focus to create a light had been challenging. Now she could do it with barely a thought. It gave her hope that all of the other things that seemed to pose so great a challenge to her truly gaining control over her magical ability might also one day seem so easy.

When she looked around, her initial impression was one of disappointment. Once, generations ago, the space might have been something impressive, but now it was just a damp room of cut stone. She placed her hand on one of the walls; the stone was smooth, cold, and completely unmarked. There was no ornamentation visible anywhere, which struck her as odd for a temple—even for the remains of one. Where was the decoration? The inscription?

Before exploring any farther, Solène secured her line to an old root that dangled from the ceiling. Then she walked slowly along each wall, running her hand along it and trying to sense what might lie beyond—stone, soil, or perhaps other chambers, as had been the case when she and Guillot had explored the remains of the stronghold of the Chevaliers of the Silver Circle, under Gill's old home.

She wondered what this chamber looked like when it was still being used, and what might have gone on there. The stone flags beneath her had been worn smooth by the passage of countless feet. She could tell it was an ancient place, but perhaps not the one she was looking for. What if the Prince Bishop had other people searching for the temple? What if they found it before she did? In such a case, all that she could hope for was that there was nothing to find, or at least nothing he could understand.

She continued to walk and run her hand along the wall but stopped when she felt a draft at her fingertips. She could feel the air moving but couldn't see where it was coming from. Closing her eyes, Solène reached out for the Fount, but the energy was so strong that she couldn't see any distinct forms—it was like a brilliant, blinding light coming from all directions. Using her regular vision, she inspected the wall, but could see no obvious sign of a doorway. Nonetheless, air was coming from the other side of the wall. Surely there had to be a way through.

Finally, her fingers landed on a groove cut into the stone—perhaps the outline of a door. She shifted position to allow the magical light to fall on that section of wall, but still had to squint to make out a faint etching that must have been exposed to the elements for a long time before the room was covered over. When she looked closely, she could make out fully formed shapes that seemed to represent letters. This dashed her hope that she might have found the edges of a door, but it was the only marking she had found, so perhaps it was significant.

This time Solène opened her mind to the Fount carefully, focussing on the idea of opening a window only a crack to let in some fresh air. In her mind's eye, she could see the Fount raging on the other side of the window, a great, swirling tempest that would flatten all before it. The pressure on her was enormous, but she fought against it, allowing only a tiny amount to touch her. She could feel her skin tingle as it energised her, as she sought meaning in the words carved into the stone. They remained unintelligible.

She wanted to try again, but she was worried. It had taken a huge amount of strength to keep the Fount from smashing through her meagre resistance and flooding her body. Dal Drezony had thought such a torrent was likely to be fatal, and Solène wasn't sure of how many more times she could dip into the mass of energy without being overcome. She took a deep breath and visualised the window opening a little farther, then turned her thoughts to the meaning of the writing. The Fount raged and beat against her, but she stood firm. Having to split her mind between keeping it out and achieving the goal she had set strained her to the point of physical pain. When it became clear she was not going to succeed, she stopped, shutting the window and blocking out the surging power beyond. She wanted to scream with frustration.

Already the power she had used was far beyond what she had needed to decipher the texts in the Prince Bishop's archive. She considered trying again, but knew it was a waste of time. Whatever the writing was, it was old—too old to share enough common ground with her own language to enable her to effect a translation.

Perhaps she was worrying over nothing. This looked more like a hermit's cave than an important temple . . . but why would anyone bother putting up—and later, concealing—an unimportant building on such an important site?

She flopped back against the wall and allowed herself to slide down into a sitting position. A wave of fatigue swept over her. Trying to control the Fount had left her exhausted; all she wanted was to close her eyes. There was nothing to stop her doing exactly that. Olivier had no idea where she had gone, and an hour or two of rest wasn't going to hand the temple over to the Prince Bishop.

Her heavy eyelids slid shut and her mind drifted toward sleep. Her thoughts were manic, as they had been the previous night—jumbled and incessant. It was as though they had a will of their own. She supposed it was because she was so close to such an immensely powerful concentration of the Fount. Still, she drifted toward sleep.

Until a whispering voice jolted her awake.

"In this place, we are one," it said.

A chill raced over her skin. She looked about the small room, still illuminated by her magical light. There was no one else present. She pressed her ear against the wall through which the draft was coming, but heard nothing but the gentle movement of air.

Back in her home village of Bastelle, on the late-winter evenings, there were always ghost tales told. Even as a child, Solène had never believed them, but now? The thought of the voice sent a chill over her skin. There was nothing human about it.

She got to her feet and went to the rope. Just touching it—her escape route from that dark, damp, and seemingly haunted place—was comforting. She freed the line and took a firm grip of it. As she was about to whistle for the horse to move, she heard the whisper again.

"In this place, we are one."

"Who are you?" Solène said, turning around in the hope of seeing the speaker.

Silence. She was alone down there. Solène swore, tugged on the rope, and whistled for the horse. Nothing. Whatever her horse was doing was clearly more interesting to it than pulling her out of the hole. She started trying to pull herself up it, hoping that it would resist her and start moving away from the hole.

"In this place, we are one."

"Shut up!" Solène said. "Come on, stupid horse." She pulled at the rope again, but it wouldn't move. "Go back!" she shouted. No response. She felt the clench of fear on her gut, the like of which she had not experienced since she was nearly burned alive in Trelain. She had no idea where the voice had come from, nor what had uttered it. She inched up the rope, straining for all she was worth.

She had covered half the distance to the surface by the time her arms started to burn. She clung to the rope; she simply didn't have the strength to pull herself up any farther. She was tempted to try magic again, but knew she was too tired, both physically and mentally, to block the surge of energy or hone an untested and dangerous piece of self-directed magic. As though intentionally seeking to compound her problems, her unseen horse walked forward, dropping her back to the chamber's floor. *Perhaps using the horse like that wasn't such a good idea after all*, she thought.

"In this place, we are one."

Solène pressed her hands to her temples, realising that she hadn't heard the voice with her ears. It was inside, in her head. The pressure of the Fount all around her was doing something to her, feeding her crazy thoughts and images, and now she was hearing things too.

What in hells did it mean, anyway? *In this place we are one.* It was cryptic nonsense. Who or what was she one with?

Her hands were shaking. She was stuck down in a hole, terrified to try magic, and something very creepy was happening. That or she was going mad, a thought that was no more comforting. Try as she might, she couldn't see a solution to her problem. The only positive she could draw from it was that if she couldn't find anything down there, then the Prince Bishop wouldn't either.

There was only one way to get out, and that was with magic. She chastised herself for being foolish enough to go down there without a better plan in the first place. She looked up at the opening. It seemed so close, yet it was too far away. She considered giving the rope another try, but knew that would do nothing more than sap away some of the energy she still had.

She took a deep breath and started to focus her mind.

"In this place, we are one."

"Shut up!" she screamed, halting the process of opening her mind to the Fount before the distraction of the voice caused her to lose control of herself. She settled herself. If the voice was in her mind, then she simply needed to maintain a little more mental discipline. She started the process again, following the slow steps that dal Drezony had taught her to ensure she was relaxed, focussed, and immune to wayward thoughts or distractions. She started to open the mental window and imagined herself rising from the floor, toward the opening above her.

As though hit by a great gale, her mental window slammed open. Solène let out a cry of shock as the Fount rushed in. She tried to close her mind to it, but it was too late—the energy flooded over her. Into her. Through her. She struggled to breathe as the invisible force threatened to drown her. Her head was filled with thoughts and images that passed so quickly she couldn't make sense of them. Her skin tingled, then burned. Even with her eyes closed, she was blinded by the intense blue light that seemed greater even than the sun. The sound was deafening, roaring like waves thundering against a cliff. The whisper repeated over and over, growing in volume until it was a scream. She screamed herself, trying to block out the alien sound. She felt like her head was going to split asunder. Then everything went dark.

45

It was dark beyond the hole in the roof when Solène woke. It was dark where she was too, her magical light having faded to oblivion. She sat up, feeling hungover. Her body was tired, her mouth was dry, and her head throbbed, but she was alive, which was more than she was expecting. She didn't know much about Fount burnout, as it had been called at the Priory, beyond her own glancing brush with it during her early days there. She knew people had been killed by pulling too much of the Fount through them; the passage of so much energy not only drained their own internal reservoirs but consumed every fibre of their body as though they had been burned by an invisible flame. As punishing as what she had experienced was, it had clearly fallen short of that.

She might have lain there for hours or days. It was only the lack of a rumbling in her belly that made her think the former was more likely. The echo of what had happened still reverberated in her head. Remembering the ghostly whisper sent a shiver over her skin. She wiped her red hair, matted with sweat, from her brow. She stood hesitantly, wobbling on her feet. There was nothing near to hold on to to steady herself, and the lack of any focal point made it even worse.

She cast a fresh globe of light. Dizziness gone, she turned slowly, mouth agape. The walls, which had been bare stone on her last inspection, were now anything but. Richly decorated, with carved reliefs and intricate writing in a script that was entirely alien to her, this place was every bit what she had thought an ancient temple might look like, and far, far more. She wandered along the walls again, entranced by the carvings, which looked as fresh as though they had been done only days ago.

The first thing that struck her was how important dragons were to the enlightened. Almost every relief bore the carving of one of the great creatures. The thing that surprised her the most was that they seemed to be existing peacefully with humans.

Everywhere she looked, there was text. Knowledge that had been forgotten for centuries. As exciting a prospect as the Prince Bishop's archive had been, this was an entirely different proposition. These inscriptions had been carved by the first people to learn how to use magic properly. She wondered what their circumstances had been. People with a natural connection to the Fount, like her? It amazed her to think that she might share an experience with the ones who started it all. She wondered what their lives had been like—the trials, the tribulations, the dangers—when they discovered they were different.

The next surprise came only a moment later. Where she had felt the draft coming through the wall, there was now a massive opening, a gaping maw that ten people could have walked through shoulder-to-shoulder with plenty of room to spare. The opening—an archway—was surrounded by ornate carvings, mainly of dragons, but with some people and lettering also. The style was exotic and intriguing and unlike anything she had ever seen before.

A stone-flagged ramp led down to another level. Solène had to stop herself from rushing forward to investigate further. She was already stuck down here and, change of circumstances notwithstanding, she had yet to figure out a solution.

Still, with no easy way up, she decided she might as well continue on and see if there was another way out. She proceeded slowly, trying to take in the magnificence of the carvings while also considering what might have brought about the change. One moment she had been in a dark, dank room, little different from an old cellar, and the next she was in the ornately carved antechamber of what she presumed to be the Temple of the Enlightened. Were it not for the fact that the hole she had created was still there, she would have thought she had been transported to a different time or place. Something about her overwhelming interaction with the Fount must have done it, and she was both curious and afraid to find out what exactly had happened.

She peered through the arch, looking for any obvious danger. She was feeling fresher than she had before the Fount had bombarded her, and the hangover-like symptoms she had woken with were fading. Very slowly, and very carefully, she opened her mind to the Fount to see if she could spot anything untoward.

She braced herself for the expected flood of power, but what she felt couldn't have been more different from a storm, more like a perfect summer's day. Where before, the Fount had been like a raging torrent of primal energy, now it flowed around her evenly, with no terrifying confusion. It was peaceful. Calming, even. It felt as though her mind belonged there. She recalled the whispered words—*in this place, we are one.* Was this what it meant?

Her understanding of what an affinity with the Fount meant was too limited for her to be able to take any conjecture far. She had been born with it, as had some others she had met at the Priory, like dal Drezony. In Imperial times, children were trained to develop an affinity with the Fount, making them as potent as—if not more potent than—anyone born with one by the time they were adults. As the Prince Bishop had discovered to his chagrin, it was something that had to be cultivated from a young age—the older you got, the less bountiful an affinity you could develop. It was the reason he had wanted the Cup, and the reason he now wanted the temple.

The passage leading down was wide, and the roof was far higher than she expected. Large enough for a dragon, she thought. Everywhere she looked, dragons featured in the reliefs. She modified her light so that it would follow her, and started down. The reliefs along the passage were painted bright, vibrant hues. There were many different colours of dragon represented, and various shades of each. Their eyes were rendered with gemstones. To her inexpert eye, it looked as though there were rubies, sapphires, and emeralds, and there were others of various colours, the names of which she did not know. There was an unimaginable fortune on the walls. If she used her dagger to pry them from their sockets, she would have enough money to start a new life of luxury anywhere she chose. She didn't feel the least compulsion to do so, however. She would rather start again with nothing than destroy the beautiful, incredible works of art lining the walls.

Finally she reached the bottom of the ramp, where there was another great archway, just as ornate as the first. The illumination of her light didn't reach far beyond the arch, but even as she walked toward it, she realised that everything she had seen so far paled by comparison to what lay ahead.

▲▲▲▲▲▲

Ysabeau stroked the horse's muzzle with no affection. She had taken control of the animal as soon as she had realised what Solène was up to. She had considered hauling Solène up, but reckoned being stuck down there would motivate her to explore properly and find what Ysabeau's father needed. Instead, it seemed the woman had decided to take a nap, leaving Ysabeau with a long, cold wait. Once Solène woke up and disappeared deeper into whatever lay beneath the ground, Ysabeau decided it was time for her to follow. She had a rope in her packs, but Solène's was as good as any. She untied it from the horse's saddle and secured it to a spike she had placed in the ground. She would have no problems hauling herself out of the hole. The redhead might surpass Ysabeau in magical ability, but in terms of physical ability, Ysabeau was confident she held the upper hand.

She checked that the line was secure, then slid down it with practised ease. She dropped to the floor without making a sound, then looked around. She would have whistled through her teeth in appreciation for her surroundings were the need for silence not absolute. They were magnificent, and quite unlike anything she'd ever seen before—and she'd seen quite a bit, from the seraglios of the Shandahari Khagans and the court of the Sultan of Darvaros to the palaces of the Moguls of Jahar.

She drew her rapier—a Telastrian blade she had liberated from the Count of Somerham, moments after she had cut the Humberlander's throat. While she was aware of the value of blades like that, and how sought-after they were, her interest in it was entirely practical. Telastrian steel had an interesting relationship with magic. It was what had made these weapons so sought-after in Imperial times. The metal acted like a sponge, soaking up magical energy, rendering it, if not entirely harmless, then far less potent than it would have been otherwise. She hadn't had much call to use that power, but she had kept the rapier, thinking it might come in handy in future. She reckoned that day had come, although it would be better for everyone if she was able to avoid an encounter with Solène completely. She didn't see how that would work, but she was an eternal optimist.

She followed Solène's light, being careful to stay far enough back to remain hidden in the darkness.

CHAPTER
46

Amaury's hands were shaking as he approached the king's private offices. The Priory had done some experimentation on pacifying people—making a rioting protestor see reason—in an effort to find a humane way of dealing with the civil strife Mirabay was known for. He hoped it would work for his predicament. There wasn't time to test it now—he had no option but to trust that he had it down, and try it for the first time in anger.

Heart racing, he knocked on the door and waited for the king's private secretary to open the door. With a forced smile on his face, Amaury said, "I had hoped to give the king an update on matters we discussed earlier."

"Show him in," the king commanded from behind the secretary, who then ushered the Prince Bishop into the office.

"What progress, First Minister?"

"Might I sit, Highness?" Amaury said.

"Of course." The king gestured to a chair.

Amaury sat, took a moment to gather his thoughts, then sought to exercise the magical gifts he had tried to draw from the Cup, even as he spoke to the king.

"I've come to implore you to reconsider your command to disband the Order."

The king sat back in his chair. "I'd rather hoped that you were here to tell me that that was well under way."

"We've come too far, worked too hard, and achieved too much to turn back now, Highness. Every other ruler around the Middle Sea is, at this very moment, considering how to employ magic to strengthen their states. We are ahead of them all." His head throbbed as he tried to direct his mental energy to force the king to agree with him.

"You've seen the mobs outside?" the king said, his tone still even and calm. "You've heard the speakers inciting the people to stand up against what they are calling 'the abomination of magic'?"

"Of course," Amaury said.

"How long do you think it will be before mobs smash down the palace doors to claim the head of the man—the men—responsible?"

Amaury shrugged.

The king continued, "Chancellor Renaud says it might only be a matter of days. My grandfather was deposed, you know."

Amaury nodded. *Of course I bloody well know.*

"I'm told the sentiment in the city was not nearly so vitriolic then as it is now. This is a very serious crisis, Prince Bishop."

"I understand how serious it is," Amaury said, his anger and frustration growing at the lack of effect of his magical efforts. "Which is why we must appear strong. Resolute." He directed every ounce of thought he could at the king. *Give in to me. Give in.* The king showed no sign of weakening.

Perhaps he needed to drink more from the Cup to achieve his goal. He took the Cup and a flask from his robes.

"I apologise, Highness. I'm developing something of a sore throat. The physician told me to drink of this draught whenever I feel the ache coming on. Would you indulge me a moment?"

The king nodded and gave a flick of his hand to signal his consent. Amaury filled the Cup and raised it to his lips. His hand was shaking again, now out of anger. Who did this pup think he was? Amaury might have steered him down this path, but the boy had agreed to everything. He'd seen the potential in all that Amaury was working toward, had hungered for the benefits it would bring him—and now he was willing to cast all that to the wind, and Amaury with it. Amaury would crush him. Destroy him.

He had swallowed the last drop of water before he realised he had not actually focussed his mind on what he wanted to do, nor had he fully considered just what it was he wanted to do. He took a breath and wondered if the king would permit him a second drink.

Amaury focussed his gaze on the king's face. Boudain stared at him blankly. The left side of the young man's face looked as though it had drooped somehow, and Amaury could see dribble slide out of the left-hand corner of his mouth.

"Highness?" Amaury said.

The king let out a strained sound, as though he was trying to say something, but wasn't able to get the words out.

"Highness?"

The king let out the same strained sound and tried to move, without success. It seemed that more than just his face was paralysed.

Frozen, Amaury wondered, had *he* done this to the king? Had the anger and frustration he'd felt been visited upon the king by magical force? He had to stop himself from smiling. *This could work out far better than I had hoped,* he thought.

He stood, put the flask and Cup back into his robe, and went over to the king. He slapped the king's face gently. "Highness? Highness? Can you hear me?" Though it seemed Boudain could not move, he was glaring angrily at the Prince Bishop. He knew that Amaury had done something to him. He seemed more certain of it than Amaury himself was.

What to do now?

The Prince Bishop opened a drawer in the king's desk—a special drawer that contained only the document Amaury had insisted the king make out the day he was crowned. The document appointed Amaury, as First Minister of Mirabaya, regent until a new king or queen could be crowned, or chosen by the council of nobles, if there was no direct heir. If the king's condition continued as it was, and Amaury was most hopeful that it would, then no successor was needed. The king still lived, and long may he live. He did, however, need a regent while he was incapacitated.

The document was there. Amaury breathed a sigh of relief. From the fire to the cauldron. It was unfair of him to be disappointed in the Cup. Perhaps it would be enough after all, even if they never found the temple.

"A wise chancellor would have told you to tear this up the moment you decided to turn on me," Amaury said, "but I've always thought

Renaud to be something of a fool. So hard to get good help these days. You should consider yourself fortunate that you have me."

The king did his best to glare at Amaury. His chin glistened with drool, which was starting to drop onto his expensive doublet.

"Help!" Amaury shouted. "Help! The king's taken ill! Help!"

There was a commotion outside, then the door burst open. The king's secretary flew into the room, followed closely by the guards, two of the finest bannerets money could buy—Amaury knew that for a fact; they were both his men.

Amaury looked at the secretary with as much strain on his face as he could muster. "Send for the king's physician! Quickly!"

He made a show of loosening the king's collar and mopping his brow and chin with a handkerchief while the guards looked on. The royal physician was never far away—and capable of much less than one of the Order's more mediocre healers, but the king didn't have the confidence in them that Amaury did. That thought reminded the Prince Bishop that he should get some treatment for his hip—it had felt a little stiff on his way to the king's office. The sooner he could get someone capable of performing a lasting treatment, the better.

As Amaury continued his show of caring for the wounded King—whose eyes remained tight little balls of fury—the physician arrived.

"What's happened," asked the man, a self-important professor from the university's School of Medical Arts.

"I'm not sure," Amaury said. "We were discussing matters of state one moment, and the next, he began slurring his words, then slumped a little in his chair and seemed to lose the power of speech."

The physician pushed Amaury to one side and began inspecting the king. Every so often he would let out a "hmmm." He continued this for what struck Amaury as an unnecessarily long time. It seemed obvious that the king had suffered a malady of the brain. Such things were not entirely unusual in people under a great deal of stress, though on this occasion, the origin had been quite different.

Eventually the physician stood.

"It would appear His Highness has suffered an attack of apoplexy. How severe it is, I cannot say at this point. He's a young and healthy man, which makes apoplexy a little unusual, but all things considered, I expect he's under a great deal of stress. Once the initial trauma has subsided, I suspect he will recover almost completely, but until then, he must rest and be given around-the-clock care. My staff and his usual servants will be able to take care of that."

"Thank you for your prompt diagnosis, Royal Physician," Amaury said. "Please put into motion whatever measures you feel are necessary to speed His Highness to a complete recovery."

The royal physician nodded with a mix of magnanimity and benevolence, as though his influence would fix all. Such men were easy to manipulate, so Amaury loved dealing with them. A little flattery, the display of more respect than was warranted, and Amaury was confident he could get the man to dance a jig.

"Before any of you leave, I need to have your word that you will speak to no one about this," Amaury said. "The kingdom is in a state of high anxiety, and the news that the king has fallen ill will only exacerbate that. Royal Physician, consult and employ only your most trusted colleagues and tell them no more than they need to know. I will need them all to remain here until we've weathered this storm."

"You have my word," the physician said, nodding again, clearly impressed at being involved in such important matters.

Amaury turned to the king's secretary. "I need you to fetch my secretary immediately. After that, bring the chancellor, Commander Canet of the Watch, and General . . ." Forgetting the man's name, he snapped his fingers in an effort to bring it to mind.

"Marchant?" the secretary supplied.

"Yes, General Marchant. That should do for now." The man departed and Amaury turned to the guards. "No one is to come in here without my say-so. Understand?"

They both nodded.

"Good," Amaury said. "Back to duty." Once they were gone, he returned his attention to the physician. He'd forgotten this man's name as well, not that that was important when he seemed to prefer the use of his official title.

"Is His Highness's condition likely to deteriorate further?"

"I shouldn't think so," the physician said. "It's usually the initial attack of apoplexy that causes the injury. After that, it's simply a matter of care and rest to ensure the best recovery. I wouldn't expect another attack."

"That's encouraging news. I can keep watch over him while you ready your team. Once again, I must emphasise how important secrecy is."

"I completely understand. I'll get to work. Try to keep him calm and comfortable while I'm gone. I'll return as quickly as possible."

"Your dedication to His Highness is admirable," Amaury said.

The physician nodded and left Amaury alone with the king. Amaury looked at him, arms akimbo.

"Well, Boudain, I'll wager this isn't how you saw your evening going. I'm afraid I don't hold out the same hopes for your recovery that the royal physician does." He tipped Boudain out of his chair. The king thudded to the floor with a grunt. Amaury dragged him out from behind the desk, where he would be easily seen by the advisors when they arrived. As an afterthought, he placed a cushion under the king's head, and arranged his limbs in a way that made it look as though he had taken some care with the man. That done, Amaury seated himself in the king's chair. He placed the regency decree on the table before him and leaned back to wait for his secretary, who was no doubt at that moment making haste toward him.

Amaury had not intended any of what had happened over the last hour, but if he played his cards right, it could all work out very well for him. The gods, it seemed, continued to smile on him.

So much gold, Solène thought as she surveyed the main chamber. It was everywhere. All the reliefs were covered in gold leaf. The jewels were abundant, and anything not jewelled or covered in gold was painted in bright, vibrant colours.

Most art Solène had seen depicted violence of some sort—bannerets in field armour, battles, depictions of legendary fights against mythical beasts. There was none of that here. Dragons featured prominently on every wall, and she was coming to believe that the enlightened had worshipped them. She supposed that so powerful a creature might have seemed godlike to people long ago. She shuddered when she thought of the reality of them, all fangs and claws and flame.

She was standing in a vast space with a vaulted ceiling, the craftsmanship of which easily rivalled that of the cathedral in Mirabay. It was all the more impressive considering how old it was. In the centre of the room, the stone-flagged floor gave way to a circular opening that revealed the soil below. In the middle of this stood an oddly shaped chunk of rock. It was about Solène's height, rough and jagged, and very definitely the focal point of all the energy swirling about in the temple. This was the node. She walked closer, wondering if the rock was an ancient marker for a natural phenomenon, or if the boulder was, in itself, the node. Perhaps something about the stone caused the energy to accumulate here. Swirls of something in the rock reminded Solène of Telastrian steel. She knew the steel possessed magical properties, so perhaps that had something to do with it. She was tempted to touch the stone, but considering how much energy revolved around it, decided it was better not to. She reckoned she had used up her allowance of luck for one day.

She walked around, taking it all in. There was a huge amount of inscription mixed into the reliefs, but she could not understand it. The temptation to try to read the meaningless scrawl was growing, but she was still intimidated by the raw energy surrounding her. She had never been in a place before where the Fount was so strong she could feel it without having to open her mind to it. She stared at the reliefs, trying to imagine their meaning, and remembered the haunting whisper. She thought of the torrent of energy that had overwhelmed her, how it had felt as though it was consuming her. But it hadn't. She still lived, and now, a short time after waking up, she felt none the worse for the experience.

Quite the opposite, in fact. She felt light on her feet. Rested, well-fed, and ready for anything. What had happened to her? And what, for that matter, had happened to this place? The drab stone walls of the antechamber had been magically transformed while she slept. Her interaction with the Fount seemed to have caused it somehow, and it was both frightening and exciting to wonder if any similar change had taken place in her.

There were two more ramps leading down into this chamber, one on each side of the room, but the far wall was solid, and completely covered in decoration. Sitting just before it was what Solène took to be an altar. She did a double take when she saw what was on it. The Cup.

She knew it couldn't be the same one, but it looked identical in every respect. She walked over to it, and studied it closely, but didn't dare pick it up. In every respect, it seemed the same, but some instinctive sense within her said there was a subtle difference. She walked around the altar so as to view it from every angle. Small and pot-shaped, made from Telastrian steel—but steel that was dull, not shined up to the usual mirror sheen of the blades that were more usually made from it. Why was this one different from the Cup that Gill, and now the Prince Bishop, had? There was far more power in it than in the one Solène had used on Gill and the Order's dragon hunters. That wasn't to say Gill's didn't have power. It did. Plenty, but it wasn't on a scale to match this one.

This one was all raw energy. An incorrectly delivered spell that drew on this Cup would be catastrophic, and not just for the person on the receiving end. The uncontrolled energy could devastate a wide area around it, likely leaving only the Cup itself intact, sitting in the crater its use had created.

The altar was carved with depictions of Cups in use, much like the sculpture in the chamber beneath the ruins of Gill's house, although judging by how many dragons were depicted in the reliefs, she doubted these rituals were intended to facilitate dragon slaying. There were noticeable differences to the method Solène herself had used. Instead of taking a droplet from the Cup, the participants in this ceremony seemed to be drinking fully from it, draining it.

She circled the altar again, this time focussing on the carvings, and stopped in shock when she saw one depicting a human figure administering a draught from a Cup to a dragon. She stood, dumbfounded, staring at it. Had they been able to exert some kind of control over the dragons? If their magic was so strong, it seemed like a reasonable theory. If dragons were to continue being a problem, the frieze offered an exciting prospect for a more effective way to deal with them—one that wouldn't put lives at risk.

▲▲▲▲▲▲

Darkness meant they could continue their journey. Even now, Pharadon could sense the pathways in the young goldscale's mind opening up. It had taken longer than Pharadon had hoped to reach the temple—the goldscale was easily distracted, wanting to investigate every new sight, sound, and smell. Frustrating though it was, Pharadon had to indulge her as much as possible, guiding the goldscale gently rather than trying to force her. Amenable though she might be, Pharadon knew she could turn on him in an instant, and then all would be lost—perhaps even his life.

He circled the site when they reached it. His fear that its power had dissipated over the years was unfounded. If anything, there was more power coursing around the ancient standing stone than he had experienced before. More surprising was the fact that the temporary cover they had erected to hide the cavernous structure below—and then magically encouraged grass to grow over—was still intact. It looked as though one small portion had collapsed, but the area seemed to be deserted, so he wasn't too worried. There were, however, two horses nearby, and some other signs of disturbance, which meant humans. That was far from ideal, but at this stage, he would kill without hesitation, to make sure the goldscale's enlightenment proceeded.

He looked at the young dragon, whose joy was evident. It was the greatest concentration of the world's energy that the young dragon had ever experienced, and it was invigorating, even to an ancient like Pharadon. With only one way to get in, he swooped down, trying to remember where the edges of the covering were—if he landed on it, his great bulk would smash the barrier, and he was hoping for a tidier solution.

The covering was fitted with a handle that was intended to allow it to be lifted off and discarded. Pharadon searched through his memory for its location. There were no surface landmarks to gauge it by— trees had germinated, grown, died, and disappeared to be replaced by others in the time since he was last there. Instead, he used the focal point of the Fount, around which the temple was built, as his reference, and after some careful clawing around, he found the handle. Gripping it with his talons, he gave a great beat of his wings to pull the "lid" free of the ground. He'd raised it only a small way before it disintegrated into a mass of rotten wood, grass, and soil that crashed down, littering the antechamber below. If Pharadon had been able to shrug in dragon form, he would have. He'd have to create some new form of concealment before he and the goldscale left the area.

To his relief, the temple's magical protections seemed to be intact, and the familiar sight of the entryway stirred memories in the dustiest recesses of his mind. It was a pity he'd made such a mess, opening it up. Fights to the death had started for far less than fouling the Temple of the Enlightened and he remembered at least one or two dragons who would have taken offense at his inadvertent act. The goldscale, who didn't know any better, had watched the whole process with curiosity.

The way below was clear, but he saw light coming from within. Pharadon hoped the humans would not pose too much trouble.

▲▲▲▲▲▲

Ysabeau had always had a healthy sense of when danger was coming and when she needed to make herself scarce. She felt it came of having been born with a magical gift in a world where such people got burned at the stake. On this occasion, it was easy to tell that trouble was coming. It seemed like the world had crashed in behind her. She had been pelted with flying debris and didn't intend to hang around in the open long enough to find out what had caused it.

The temple's abundant decorations offered plenty of opportunities for concealment. She'd tucked herself behind one of the ornately carved pillars that held the roof up before the dust settled, and decided to use a little magic to make sure she went unseen. She opened her mind to the Fount—and shut it again almost as quickly. The energy had hit her like a hammer, knocking the wind from her. There was no safe way for her to use magic in that place. She could only risk using it if she absolutely had to.

The increase in light coming from behind her told Ysabeau that the antechamber had somehow been opened to the sky. When two large shadows blotted out the moonlight and starlight, Ysabeau suddenly felt very afraid. It was a primal, instinctive emotion that she could neither explain nor control. It angered her. She was not one to frighten easily, but all she wanted to do in that moment was find the deepest, darkest corner and squeeze herself into it. The shadows moved toward her, and Ysabeau had to stifle a gasp when she saw them: two dragons, one large, one small.

As curious and awestruck as she was, she had to be careful to remain unseen by these dangerous creatures of myth. She had no desire to be burned to death or eaten by one of the beasts. She held her breath as they passed, seemingly oblivious of her presence. Only when they had disappeared from view into the next chamber did she breathe a sigh of relief.

CHAPTER

48

"I t wears off, you know," Gill said. The Spurrier ignored him, but he was too bored to stay silent. "The magical protection. It wears off. By now you might be completely vulnerable to the dragon. We both know how things went for the last Spurriers that tried to kill one unprepared."

"We're close!" Vachon shouted from the head of their small column, pointing to an area of grassland lit with ghostly pale moonlight.

Even so many days after having last used the Cup himself, Gill could feel a gentle pulling sensation in that direction and wondered if he was benefitting from a cumulative effect, having drunk from the Cup a number of times. He knew that the protections had faded long ago, but that might have had something to do with the skill of his application. A proper mage might have been able to make it last longer. Either way, he was glad the Spurriers were the ones who were going to bluster in and find out the hard way if the Cup's boon was still active.

They had barely paused since leaving Venne, so Gill was confident his teasing had had some effect on Vachon. He hadn't wasted a moment in getting to the dragons, and now that they were close, the tension in the group had ratcheted up noticeably. None of these men or women had ever seen a dragon before and now they were preparing to fight one. He didn't envy them, but could at least appreciate that they were going about it in a professional way. There hadn't been much chatter among them to begin with, but now there was complete silence. They were riding fast—a particularly uncomfortable thing for Gill since his hands were bound, but he managed to hang on.

Vachon held up his hand, a great slab of a thing, gnarled like an old tree trunk, bearing the scars and swellings of a lifetime of fighting, and his followers stopped immediately. Gill had to strain around the Spurrier guarding him to see what had caused their abrupt halt. Before Vachon was a huge, almost perfectly square, hole in the ground. Clearly it wasn't a natural feature; it seemed Pharadon had made a stop before heading deep into the mountains as agreed.

Orders were given by hand gesture in silence. The Spurriers dismounted and started to attend to their kit. Gill's guard unceremoniously pulled him to the ground and left him in a heap. Despite his bound hands, he managed to manoeuvre himself into a cross-legged sitting position and watched as the Spurriers donned their armour and checked their weapons. He cast a wishful eye at his own, still secured to the back of a packhorse. Gill wondered if they were going to leave him aboveground. He doubted Vachon would want to face the dragon a person down, but Gill could cause merry havoc if left unattended. It would be a long walk home without horses, if any of them survived.

As Gill watched, he realised the Spurriers were quality. Although one or two had paled considerably when faced with what they had to do, they went about their preparations silently, precisely, and without hesitation. Vachon, now fully armoured and looking every part the warlord, approached Gill.

"Anything you want to tell me before we go down there?" he said. "One old soldier to another."

Gill finally realised why he found the man's face familiar. "We've met before, haven't we?"

"Aye, we have," Vachon said.

"Rencarneau? Was it?"

Vachon nodded. "Your memory's better than I gave you credit for. I was with Endraville's Heavy Foot."

"Ah," Gill said. He recalled Endraville's Heavy Foot leading the advance on the left flank, where he'd also been stationed, with the Royal Guard. Vachon's fellows had been massacred by lunchtime, with no more than a dozen survivors. "A bad day."

Vachon shrugged. "It wasn't the only one in that campaign. The Royal Guard gave a good account of themselves that day. Until Rencarneau, I always thought your lot were a bunch of ponces. Feathered hats, fine swords, jelly for spines."

Gill laughed. "You aren't the only one."

"As few of us as made it off the field that day, there'd have been none if the Guard hadn't advanced when they did."

"What else could we have done?" Gill said, feeling a pang of sadness that they were enemies now.

"I'm asking you for the same today. Anything that'll help me bring all these folk home, still breathing."

"The Cup's already given you more than I can. The rest is a combination of luck and effort."

Looking unconvinced, Vachon nodded slowly. "We'll be taking you down there with us."

"With my hands tied and no armour?" Vachon shrugged. Guillot continued, "That's mighty generous of you."

"It's in your interest to make sure we can do what we came to do, or you're as dead as the rest of us."

"Well," Gill said. "When you put it like that. This one's a boy dragon, and he particularly likes it when you tickle his—"

Vachon's fist smashed into Gill's face. Guillot flopped back on the ground, head ringing. He checked over his teeth, which were all present, and was surprised by how resilient they were proving to be. He struggled back up to a sitting position.

"I'd save your strength," he said. "You're going to need it." He flashed Vachon a toothy smile, realising it might be the last one he ever gave. His teeth could hold out for only so long.

Vachon turned back to his people and started giving more orders, in a whisper. Gill suddenly got the sickening feeling that he might be used as bait. He wondered if he'd be able to talk the dragon out of eating him a second time. His guard returned, fully armoured now like the rest of his fellows, and hauled Gill to his feet. Making no effort to assist, Guillot forced the man to haul his dead weight up. Once he was standing, the Spurrier shoved him toward the hole.

As Gill got closer, he could see an array of fine carvings below. Even from above, the big space was impressive. Amazing to think it had lain here, entirely unknown, for who only knew how long, like the hidden, long-forgotten chamber underneath his old family home. He wondered how long ago this place had been covered up, and by whom.

The Spurriers had moved out around the hole and were doing their best to get an idea of what awaited them down there. Satisfied that there was no immediate danger, Vachon ordered that lines be thrown down, and one after another, they started to drop into the hole. Gill was shoved forward and handed a rope. Although he went to great pains to show how awkward it would be to climb down with his hands bound, when he started, he found it wasn't all that difficult, and he was soon at the bottom. The stone flags below his feet were covered with a mixture of soil, grass, and old splinters of wood—the remains of whatever had covered it, Gill reckoned.

Once they had all assembled on the stone floor, the Spurriers drew their swords and looked around. Gill had already spotted the large opening leading down and the hint of light at the far end. He wondered how long it would be before Vachon saw it. Like everyone else, the Spurriers' leader seemed transfixed by the intricate carvings covering the walls.

▲▲▲▲▲▲

Solène jumped at the thunderous commotion from the antechamber. She took cover behind the altar, and peered out to see what was going on. *It couldn't be Olivier, could it?* Her ability to conceal herself was negated by the fact that she had created the large globe of light that hovered in the centre of the room. She thought about trying to dismiss it, but reckoned it was already too late for that. If someone was coming after her, they already knew she was here.

She didn't know what to do. There were two other exits from the chamber, but she had no idea where either led or if the passages were clear or had become filled in over the years. She was tempted to run but remembered her responsibilities, that there might be secrets in that place which the Prince Bishop could use to further his aims. She couldn't stand by and allow that to happen, but was this the right time and place to fight that battle?

Solène froze at the sight of an enormous red dragon lumbering down the ramp she had used, followed by a golden one. Her shock subsided quickly, but before she could move, she saw its great orbs of eyes fix on her. It halted, crouched, and snarled at her. Solène wasn't sure what to do. She dropped into the low, balanced position the fencing master at the Priory had taught her, but felt ridiculous—she wasn't holding a sword.

Though the idea of doing it still frightened her, she opened her mind to the Fount anyway—*better to be killed by it, than eaten by a dragon,* she thought.

The dragon blinked. It was an alarmingly human gesture; Solène paused before trying to unleash every bit of magical power she could in the dragon's direction.

"What brings you to the temple?" it said.

Solène's jaw dropped. It took her a moment to gather her thoughts enough to respond. "You can talk?" She frowned, realising she should have spent a little longer gathering.

"That would appear self-evident," the dragon said. "What are you doing here?"

"I . . . I'm looking for something."

The dragon nodded and seemed to relax a little as it looked around the temple. The golden one shuffled out from behind it but remained silent.

"Have you found it?" the red one said.

"I don't know."

"Be at ease," the dragon said. "I can see no reason for us to fight, unless that is what you wish."

"No," Solène said, standing straight. "I'd prefer not to."

"Excellent," the dragon said. "Then I suggest you leave." Before she could move, its pupils narrowed to slits. It cocked its head and gave a long sniff.

"Wait," it said. It edged toward her and gave another long sniff. "Well, you *are* different, aren't you?"

"I don't know what you mean."

"Most of your kind have to be led to magic, but some are born to it. You are one of those, aren't you?"

"I . . ."

"There's no need to dissemble. I can smell it on you, and I know that is why you are here. Fortuitous timing, I think, as you would not have found what you seek were I not here to show you."

"What do you mean?"

"Some of your kind have become enlightened. You wouldn't be the first. Even without the ritual, you are close to enlightenment. Somewhat like this goldscale here," it added, tilting its head to indicate the smaller dragon.

"I don't understand."

"In this place, we are one," the dragon said.

Solène's eyes widened. The dragon appeared to smile.

"Ah, so you *have* heard the Fount call to you." It moved a little farther into the chamber, the smaller gold dragon shuffling behind it like a duckling following its parent. "So, what to do?"

Did it see her as a threat that needed to be destroyed?

"I apologise. I am Pharadon, Drake of the Crooked Mountain. You are?"

"I . . . I'm Solène." She was still struggling to absorb the fact that she was having a conversation with a dragon. That they existed at all was something she was only beginning to be accustomed to; this was almost too much for her.

"I have encountered two others of your kind who were like you. They came here for enlightenment. Is that what brought you?"

"In a manner of speaking. Well, perhaps. I don't know what 'enlightenment' is."

"It's the higher state. It's being a creature of reason, a creature at one with the Fount, where shaping it is as easy as drawing a breath of air. For your kind, it is more." Pharadon paused, and adopted a thoughtful expression. "I apologise if this startles you, but please bear with me a moment."

Solène's eyes nearly popped out of her head as the dragon began to shrink and take on the shape of a human man. A naked human man. Solène turned her gaze away; when the dragon cleared his throat, she looked back and saw that he was fully clothed in tunic and britches of contemporary style. She could have walked past him on a street and not suspected there was anything unusual about him. He stretched his neck and walked toward the altar.

"I'm not as accustomed to human form as I once was," Pharadon said. "It takes a little practice. The clothing in particular, but I'm getting the hang of it again. I've brought this goldscale here to be enlightened. All dragonkind are capable of it, but most require the ceremony to reach that state."

"Are you a dragon or a person?" Solène said.

Pharadon smiled, an awkward-looking expression at first, which softened a little as he looked at her. "Does it matter? I am what I choose to be, when I choose to be it. That is one of enlightenment's great gifts. The physical body is secondary to the mind. Its servant, if you will. We find the greatest comfort in the form we are born to, however, and are restricted in what we are capable of when in a different one. The Fount brings great power to an individual, as I'm sure you have realised, but it is limited by what our minds and bodies are capable of channelling. Enlightenment extends that limit, and it is a life well lived to search out and explore the boundaries of what we can achieve."

"Why are you telling me this?" Solène said.

"Because you are one short step away from enlightenment. When I look, I can see your presence in the Fount. It's the responsibility of all enlightened to offer the opportunity to others capable of it."

"Not all are capable?" Solène said, grasping onto the hope that no matter what he did, the Prince Bishop would never be able to acquire the magical power he sought for himself.

Pharadon shook his head. "All beings of higher thought may be enlightened. That is not to say they are capable of *being* enlightened. There is a distinction. Having the power enlightenment brings, and being enlightened are not necessarily the same thing. The former can be taken by anyone, while only a few have the potential for the latter."

"Why do you think I do?"

Pharadon shrugged. "I just do."

Solène felt her heart sink. Should she take this step purely so she could prevent the Prince Bishop?

"All you need to do is open your mind to the idea and drink from an untouched vessel of enlightenment." He gestured to the altar and the cup that sat on it. "The Cup can give magical blessings to many, but can only enlighten one. This one is yours if you wish it."

Solène hesitated. "Don't you need one for your . . . friend?"

"There are others here."

"What will . . . happen . . . to me?"

"Nothing. You will simply become one of the enlightened. A being in harmony with the Fount. One of us."

Solène frowned, not sure if she had taken the correct meaning. "One of you? Do you mean a dragon?"

Pharadon began to answer, but was drowned out by shouts. Vachon and a dozen Spurriers entered the chamber. Behind them, with his hands bound, was Gill.

CHAPTER
49

ods alive," Vachon said.

There was only one dragon—the gold one—in the chamber when Gill and the Spurriers got there. To Guillot's complete surprise, Solène was there, standing next to something that looked like an altar. He had blinked and looked again, but still couldn't believe it was her. Pharadon, in human form, was standing next to her. Confusion swirled through his mind.

"Gill?" Solène said.

He shrugged, lifting his hands high enough that she could see they were tied.

Pharadon had broken their agreement, and dislike Vachon though Guillot did, perhaps the beasts did indeed need to be eradicated. Seeing Solène in proximity to the deceitful creature worried him, and he was tempted to take up a sword and help the Spurriers in whatever way he could.

Vachon was in front of his fighters, sword drawn, but clearly had no idea what to do next. Who did, the first time they encountered a dragon? Vachon's gaze was locked on the gold dragon, which didn't seem particularly interested in anything that was going on. It was looking curiously at the reliefs as though struggling to understand them.

Finally Vachon acted. He moved quickly, attacking the gold dragon. His blade snapped on impact against the armour-like scales, which was exactly what Gill expected would happen. The goldscale let out a hiss. Out of the corner of his eye, Guillot saw Pharadon move. In the next instant, Vachon flew through the air and was pinned against the wall, held in place by some great unseen force that was causing him visible discomfort.

"Put down your weapons," Pharadon said. "There is no need for violence."

Gill could see that the Spurriers were twitchy and unclear what to do. Their instinct was to attack, but it didn't seem like there was a clear enough chain of command for someone to take over from Vachon. Gill glanced at Solène, who didn't seem to be in any way threatened by Pharadon. Noticing Gill's look, she shook her head subtly.

What's that supposed to mean? he wondered. She indicated Vachon with her eyes, telling Guillot that the Spurriers—her comrades, he assumed—were the ones she was worried about.

"I'd do what he says," Gill said to the fighters. "He can turn your boss into raspberry jam if he chooses. Nothing to lose in hearing what he has to say." Despite his words, he wasn't confident that was the case, and wasn't altogether against the idea of Vachon meeting an untimely end.

The Spurriers relaxed a little, but there was still enough tension in the chamber that Gill could feel its weight bearing down on him. Pharadon didn't release Vachon, who seemed to have been robbed of the power of speech.

"What are you doing here, Pharadon?" Guillot said, taking advantage of the momentary equilibrium in the room.

When Pharadon looked at Gill, his concentration must have slipped, for Vachon gave a strangled shout of "Shut him up!"

One of the Spurriers made to strike Gill with his free hand; Gill dodged to the side and kicked. The Spurrier turned as he dodged, swinging his sword arm toward Gill. With a quick move of his still-bound hands, Gill disarmed the Spurrier and made the sword his own. Backing away quickly, he allowed himself a smile at the move he had just pulled—he hadn't managed anything that fluid in quite some time.

He shifted position to trap the hilt of the sword between his thighs and sliced his bonds off. The sword was in his hand in an instant—a regular steel blade that he knew would be of use only against the Spurriers. He still wasn't entirely sure who he was going to be fighting.

"Solène, would you mind coming over here and telling me what's going on?"

"Sister, what are you doing?" one of the Spurriers asked as she gave Pharadon a parting look and stepped toward Guillot.

"Trying to make sure no one dies," she said as she crossed the chamber.

"What are you doing here?" he whispered once she was in earshot.

"Looking for this temple. The Prince Bishop thinks it's important, and he's right. It could give him all the magical power he's been after."

"And you're not in favour of that?"

"No, of course not."

"But the Order. These are your comrades, aren't they?"

"Not anymore. The Order has changed. I don't want to see them hurt, though."

"So *they're* the bad guys?" Gill said, trying to pull sense out of it all.

"Not all of them. Maybe none of them. They're just following orders."

"I've heard that before," Gill said. He raised his voice slightly. "Pharadon, what are you doing here? You said you were headed for the mountains."

"I am," Pharadon said. "As soon as I've done what I came here to do."

One of the Spurriers finally took some initiative. A dagger whistled through the air and struck Pharadon in the shoulder. Letting out a grunt that sounded half animal and half human, he stumbled backwards. Vachon dropped to the floor from his position halfway up the wall and quickly got to his feet. He and some of his comrades went after the goldscale, who was finally starting to pay serious attention to the humans.

Gill swore. Who was he supposed to side with—a thug like Vachon, who was at least human, or a pair of dragons? The gold dragon belched out a jet of flame—not nearly so great as some of the ones Gill had experienced, but in a confined space, it was more than enough. Or it would have been, if the Spurriers hadn't been given the Cup's boon, which was obviously still working, as none of them were even singed. The dragon seemed surprised that its weapon had no effect, but was quick to lash out with fangs and claws.

Two Spurriers came for Gill, who made his mind up as to what side he was on, at least for the moment. "Sorry, Solène," he said. The Spurriers slashed at him from each side, one high, one low. Gill parried the first and carried the momentum from the strike down to divert the second. He fired in a quick thrust that cut only cloth, but smiled at how loose his body seemed to be. Joints that had complained with every movement for years were smooth and pain free. His muscles were responding faster than he could recall, and he had thrust twice more before he had even finished the thought.

The second thrust caught the targeted Spurrier below the collar bone. He cried out in pain and his sword arm went limp. Gill stamped forward, cutting low, then kicking the wounded man to the floor as he straightened. Another Spurrier joined the melee. Behind them, Gill could see the others, led by Vachon, herding the gold dragon into a corner. Solène had gone to Pharadon's side. He didn't have time to consider her choice to avoid the conflict, or curse her for not helping.

Guillot parried a thrust that was headed straight for his heart, then stepped forward and to the side, skewering his attacker through the midsection. He pulled the blade free and slashed at the final Spurrier confronting him, to buy a little time to catch his balance. With his weight back where he needed it to be, he launched into a rapid sequence of thrusts. The Spurrier batted them away, steel clashing and echoing about the chamber, his face a picture of concentration. He was good, had a fast blade.

The dragon roared. Gill's enemy's concentration faltered. His blade was a fraction too slow. A tidy thrust through the chest to finish him, and Gill was able to take a breath.

The gold dragon was cornered but the Spurriers seemed reluctant to get too close. They goaded it with their swords but none seemed brave enough to step within range of teeth or claws. Gill could see the expression of terror on the dragon's face. It was bizarre to see the creature of so many people's nightmares fighting for its life, afraid.

"Leave it alone," Gill shouted, then winced—was he really telling humans to stop trying to kill a dragon?

Stepping out of the group, Vachon turned to face him. "You'd betray your own kind to protect this monster?"

Gill shrugged. "I'm not sure we *are* the same kind."

Vachon smiled, the type of smile a bastard makes when he's about to kick a puppy. Gill took his guard, and Vachon did the same. Vachon came at him like a bull, blade cutting like a butcher's cleaver. Gill countered his blows, but his hand stung from the force of each deflected strike. A competent banneret who had spent years soldiering, Vachon clearly knew a sword wasn't the only thing you used when you were trying to kill someone. Gill continued to parry, finding a smooth, flowing rhythm that reminded him of his youth, but he didn't have the speed to get out of the way of a shoulder charge. Vachon knocked him to the ground and left him breathless. Guillot had grown used to dealing with that in recent days, so with barely a pause, he rolled to his feet as he fought to draw air into his lungs.

His opponent slashed at Gill with wicked cuts in rapid succession. Gill danced back on the balls of his feet, revelling in the sensation of ease, one he hadn't enjoyed in years. It was this feeling that had made him want to become a swordsman. There was joy in it. Gill thrust; Vachon parried and riposted. Gill met the blade with his, but the strike was too wide. His body might be back in form, but the speed of his thoughts had yet to catch up.

Vachon barrelled into him, slamming him into the wall. Gill smashed down with the pommel of his sword, missing Vachon's head and catching him on the shoulder instead. Wincing, Vachon stepped back and grabbed Gill by the front of his shirt. Vachon's other fist followed, the guard of his sword threatening to rearrange Gill's face.

Guillot managed to twist enough to dodge the worst of the blow, but it caught his left cheek and rattled his brain. Strong as an ox, Vachon pinned Gill to the wall with one arm, and pressed his fist into Gill's throat. Choking, Guillot kicked at Vachon, who seemed oblivious. His eyes burned with rage; it was easy to see that he took joy in killing.

Gill tried to bring his blade to bear, but the best he could do was slide the edge along Vachon's thigh. The sword's previous owner had kept a keen edge on it, and Gill could see a flicker of pain on Vachon's face. Gill kept sawing until Vachon roared and leaped back, hurling Gill to the side. Fighting to breathe, Guillot massaged his throat as he stumbled to his feet. He turned just in time to see Vachon coming for him again. Was there no stopping this beast of a man?

Limping now, Vachon was not nearly so fast as he had been. Gill lunged with everything he had and felt his blade connect. Then Vachon was on him, pummelling him with fists the size of small hams, batting Gill's head from side to side. His vision narrowed and his mind grew distant. Instinct told him to twist the blade, which he did, before everything went dark.

▲▲▲▲▲▲

Gill woke with a start to see Solène's face hovering over him. His last memory was getting a face full of Vachon's spittle as the man vented all his fury on Gill's head. Sitting up, Guillot looked at the half-dozen bloodied and charred corpses scattered around the goldscale, which looked remarkably placid, considering what it had done. Revulsion swept over him—they had utterly failed to prevent any killing, as Solène had wished.

"What happened?"

"You killed Vachon," Solène said. "He managed to knock you out before he dropped. The goldscale . . ." She shook her head. "Well, you can see for yourself. Pharadon was able to subdue it once I'd taken the dagger out of his shoulder. It was Telastrian steel. They all had one."

Gill grimaced. "I'm sorry for the loss of your comrades. I know only too well what that's like."

"I barely knew them, to be honest. Most are—were—mercenaries the Prince Bishop hired recently. So much death, though . . ."

He let her help him to his feet. Considering the fight he'd been in and the beating he'd taken, he didn't feel all that bad. He suspected he had Solène to thank for that.

The Spurriers might have been dealt with, but there was still the question of the dragons, however benevolent Pharadon might seem. Gill was under no illusion that he would be able to slay the two beasts, but he at least wanted some answers.

"I want to know what you're doing here," Gill said to Pharadon, staring at the man who was also a dragon.

"I have to bring this goldscale to enlightenment before we can leave

the area. Once I have, we will leave the lands of humankind forever."
Pharadon paused. "I saw no reason to tell you this before. You would
not have understood."

"The Cup!" Solène said. "It's gone!"

Pharadon turned. "It must be here somewhere."

A badly wounded Spurrier had propped himself up against the
wall. Now he let out a raspy chuckle.

"You didn't even notice her," he said. "She walked right in, took it,
and walked out again."

"Who?" Solène said, walking over to him.

"Heal me and I'll tell you."

Looking furious, Solène clenched her fist, then took a breath and relaxed. Gill wondered if she was still thinking of the day she had told him
about, when she had needed to kill to save her life. He had thought she
would get over it and realise that sometimes you have to do things you
don't like, but it seemed she hadn't.

Gill had no similar compunctions. He picked up a dagger from the
floor and strode over to the Spurrier who had spoken. Pressing the tip
against the soft part under the man's chin, he applied a little pressure.

"Talk fast. She does nothing until you tell us all you know," he said.

For a man who had just seen Gill kill three of his comrades, including his commander, and probably still expected to be eaten by a
dragon, the Spurrier held out for a remarkably long time. There was
blood trickling down the dagger's blade and pooling on Gill's hand
when he finally made to speak.

"I don't know who she was. Dark cloak with a hood. I barely noticed her myself. Moved like a cat. Knew what she was here for. No
hesitation. Took the cup from the altar and was gone."

Gill looked at Solène, who shrugged. He reckoned from the man's
expression that he had said all he knew. Tossing the dagger to one
side, Gill stood and moved away. Solène knelt beside the wounded
man. From the look on her face, it didn't seem that she'd had time to
increase her knowledge of healing.

Her eyes were squeezed shut and her face was a picture of concentration, but Gill had seen enough wounds to know it would take

a miracle, rather than magic, to save this man. Indeed, between one breath and the next, he expired.

"He's gone," Gill said. "I'm sorry, Solène, but no amount of magic could have saved him."

She nodded grimly, and looked at him with such pain in her eyes that he felt ashamed at what he had done. Still, he had found out what they needed to know, and he was certain the man had been on borrowed time.

"We have to catch her, Gill," Solène said. "We can't let the Prince Bishop get that Cup."

"No, it can't be," Pharadon said.

Gill turned to see that a cylindrical stone plinth lined with shelves had risen from the floor. More magic, he supposed, since it had moved silently and without vibration.

"There should be more cups here," Pharadon said. He looked at the goldscale with an expression of panic on his human face. "Unless one of my brethren took them into the mountains to hide them from your kind . . ." He stared into the distance for a moment before speaking again. "They could be anywhere. It could take years to find them. It will be too late."

"Too late?" Gill said.

"She can only be brought to enlightenment while she's a juvenile. She's not far from maturity now."

"What can we do to help?" Solène said.

He furrowed his brow in thought. "I can quiet her—put her into a sleep that will slow the process a little. I might gain a few more days, perhaps. But I still need that cup. It's the only way I can be sure of enlightening her."

His face, which had been pale and drawn with worry, sharpened.

"Gold," Pharadon said. "Do you have any?"

"Pardon me?" Gill said.

"I need some gold. A coin or two will do, but the more the better."

Gill reached for his purse and tipped out a few coins. Only one was a gold crown. He tossed it to Pharadon, who caught it without having to look. He placed it on the ground in front of the young dragon, and started to speak in a hushed tone. The dragon lay down and placed its head on the coin. Its blinks grew slower as Pharadon continued to speak, until its eyelids remained shut. When Pharadon saw their curious stares, he shrugged.

"Dragons like gold," he said. "Now, we're ready to leave."

"We?" Gill said.

"You have to stop the vessel of enlightenment falling into the wrong hands, and I need to use it. I'm going to help you."

CHAPTER

50

Ysabeau rode as hard as she could, away from that strange, ancient place. She could feel the Cup she had taken pressing against her hip. It was uncomfortable, but she liked to know it was there. She could feel the power in it; far more than was in the Prince Bishop's. Recalling what the dragon had said about a Cup being able to enlighten only one person, she wondered if her father's had already been used. If so, the one she was bringing him would more than make up for the fact that she had found out little on how to use it.

Her horse was starting to tire, even with magical help, but so long as it got her to the next town, she didn't care. She could find a new mount there, and send word that her mission was a success. She had found the temple and what her father needed—a Cup that still had all its power.

She continued to use her magical veil to conceal herself, though now that she was drawing away from the ancient temple, it was becoming more taxing to maintain. Nonetheless, she persisted. She had stolen something she was certain was a relic of some ancient dragon culture, and done so in front of two dragons. That they could transform themselves into humans left her with a lingering sense of terror, but her greatest fear at that moment was to look over her shoulder and see one sweeping down behind her, a great jet of flame erupting from its mouth.

She couldn't wait to see the look on her father's face when she brought him the Cup.

▲▲▲▲▲

Amaury sat at the king's desk as the three royal advisors were shown into the room. When they had heard the news, they had all demanded to be allowed to call on the king, who was now in his bedchamber, attended by the royal physician and his staff. Amaury had been content to allow the visit. Seeing the king as he was would soften their resolve, and Amaury wasn't in the mood for a hard fight.

Filing into the king's office, they all looked less full of bluster than usual, as they took their seats without waiting for Amaury's permission. That didn't bother him. No amount of disrespect would lessen the enjoyment of what he was about to do.

A dozen armed members of the Order were waiting in concealment. He could have used the Royal Guard for the job, but reckoned it was time that everyone realised there would be a new way of doing things in the Kingdom of Mirabaya.

"I'm glad you could join me, gentlemen, at this most distressing time."

"What did you do to him?" General Marchant said. The soldier, rather than the politicians, was always the one to give him the most direct trouble, and Amaury was prepared.

"I ensured he got immediate medical attention. Were it not for my haste in acting, he might have died. As it is, hope remains that he will recover. I have here a document, signed and sealed by the king, appointing me as his regent in the event of his incapacity or demise before his legitimate successor has reached majority."

"I'll never agree to that," Chancellor Renaud said.

Amaury laughed. "You don't need to. Everything required by law for me to take up the regency is contained in this document. I didn't bring you gentlemen here to approve of these arrangements. I brought you here—" He reached forward and rang the king's desk bell. "I brought you here to have you all arrested for treason."

On cue, the two doors into the room opened and several Spurriers stepped in. They were new appointments all, found for Amaury by Luther; some of them looked as though they had spent the previous day hopping from bar brawl to bar brawl on the docks.

"You can't do this," Canet of the City Watch said.

"Can and have. Your counsel to the king of late has clearly been

contrary to the best interests of the kingdom. The appropriate paperwork has been completed and signed by the Lord Chief Justice"—a
man long under Amaury's thumb.

"All that remains is for you to take up your new accommodations
downstairs. Take them out."

There was a volley of protests that had reached begging on the part
of Renaud by the time he was being muscled out the door. Amaury
considered having them fed poison—an untraceable one created at
the Priory. Men and women sent down to the dungeons were rarely
seen again, so it was unlikely questions would be asked. If anything,
the poison was more than was necessary, but Amaury knew there was
no hurry to decide. The last thing he needed were figureheads around
which opposition could be mounted.

When peace and quiet reigned in the office once more, he sat back
to think. Three letters lay on the desk, notifying the new appointees of
their roles as counsellors to the king. They were all senior noblemen
of rank, befitting the honour.

The first was an inveterate gambler whose notes Amaury held,
making him bought and paid for. The second was fond of dream seed,
so as soon as the Prince Bishop trained someone in the Order to do
what dal Drezony had done with Barnot, the man would be little
more than a puppet on a string. The third, well, despite himself, Amaury had always gotten on with him, and it would be useful to have
one advisor who didn't tell him only what he wanted to hear.

The king was still the king, but Amaury was now very much in
control. There would be no more obstacles to his plans; he could bring
about his intended future. All the same, there was a sickening twist
of fear in his gut. Everyone would know he was the one making the
decisions now. He was the one whom the assassins or the angry mobs
would come for. If he didn't find a way to make the Cup work the way
he believed it could, everything he had worked for might all still come
tumbling down around him.

▴▴▴▴▴▴

Pharadon landed at the edge of the opening to the temple, where Gill
and Solène were waiting for him. Gill shielded his eyes from the cloud

of dust and grit raised by the dragon's flight, then looked hopefully to see if the dragon had returned with the stolen Cup.

"I couldn't find her," he said. "There is no one for miles around, and I covered far more ground than she could have."

"She can't simply have disappeared," Gill said.

"Yes she can," Solène said. "If she can use a little magic, she could make herself all but invisible. Particularly at night. No one saw her in the temple save for that one Spurrier, and he said she was hard to see, even when he was looking right at her. If she's one of the Prince Bishop's agents, there's a good chance she can use magic. If she was given a task this important, she's probably pretty good."

"Did you meet anyone of her description in the Order?" Gill said, hoping that they might at least know what she looked like.

Solène shook her head. "I don't think so."

Gill let out a sigh, and looked out toward the moonlit horizon. "We have to go after her. At least we know where she's headed. . . ."